Also by Laramie Dunaway

BORROWED LIVES
HUNGRY WOMEN

LESSONS IN SURVIVAL

LARAMIE DUNAWAY

WARNER BOOKS

A Time Warner Company

Warner Books, Inc., 1271 Avenue of the Americas, New York, NY 10020

W A Time Warner Company

Printed in the United States of America
First Printing: February 1994
10 9 8 7 6 5 4 3 2 1

Library of Congress Cataloging-in-Publication Data

Dunaway, Laramie.
    Lessons in survival / Laramie Dunaway.
        p.   cm.
    ISBN 0-446-51700-3
        1. Divorced women—California—Family relationships—Fiction.
    2. Children of prisoners—California—Fiction.   3. Bank robberies—
    California—Fiction.   I. Title.
    PS3554.U4632L47   1994
    813'.54—dc20   92-51022
                                                             CIP

Book design by L. McRee

To L, whose wisdom rivals the ancient sages: "Just live already."
And whose patience rivals the saints: "*Oprah* again?"

Lesson #1

Do not shake.
Contents under pressure.

· 1 ·

I drove home still thinking about that dead grasshopper I'd just dissected for my class, its thorax as hard to crack as a tin thimble. Watching me struggle over it, my students had become restless and giddy, so I'd made some offhand joke about the grasshopper being a typical male, afraid to open up to a woman. They'd laughed and groaned, as usual. But then when I'd finally dragged the scalpel across the grasshopper, splitting open his tough skin and exposing his tiny organs, one student in the back, an anorexic seventeen-year-old named Lisa Drought, jumped up and screamed, "That's what they did to Jesus!" The class turned and stared at her, then turned and stared at me, waiting for a response, a voice of reason. Stunned, I didn't know what to say except that Jesus didn't have an exoskeleton.

That's what was on my mind when I turned my car onto the street where I lived. I was wondering if tonight, after sticking her finger down her throat and vomiting up her mother's pot roast dinner, Lisa would doze off in a delirious dream of crucified grasshoppers and satanic blond biology teachers. I'd sent a note to the school psychologist, but these things were tricky. Lisa's name would be passed along to all the appropriate people, but no one would actually do anything, including me. Driving home now, I remembered her huge eyes bulging from her pale skeletal face, the only discernible color coming from her bright red lipstick. I couldn't shake that image.

That's why it took me by surprise when my car was ambushed on my own street by a pack of yapping reporters.

There were six or seven of them, maybe more. I couldn't be sure of details because it was so dark and foggy outside and a couple of them were shining minicam lights in my face, burning my retinas. I shielded my eyes with one hand while squinting through the windshield, tapping the gas pedal just enough to keep the car rolling forward but trying not to run anyone over. I didn't try too hard, though. I could have lived with the guilt of a crushed toe or two.

At first, the reporters just trotted alongside the car, like Secret Service agents in a presidential motorcade. They kept waving their hands and shouting my name over and over. "Ms. Erhart! Ms. Erhart! Ms. Erhart!" they hollered. Sometimes when they were all shouting like that, a couple of them would accidentally harmonize my name. It sounded cheerfully melodic, like a gospel song or a Broadway show tune.

My headlights reflected oddly off their bodies, fusing their jouncing torsos into one gray clump of a beast, something grotesque out of Greek mythology with many yammering heads and flailing arms. Something that usually needed killing.

I was worried. They had never been this aggressive before. For the past couple days, they'd been content with merely shouting at me from the sidewalk. Now they were everywhere, pelting me with their intimate questions about my family, my past, my sex life. I kept the car moving slowly through them, my bumper nudging them aside.

Suddenly, they started grabbing. Their hands clamped onto the fenders, the roof, the radio antenna, the windshield wipers. They tried to wrestle the car to a stop right there in the middle of the street. Their bodies thumped against my doors like bumper cars. Now I was scared. I felt as if I was trapped inside a car-wash tunnel with giant floppy rollers banging on all sides. Thank God I'd remembered to lock my doors, because someone kept yanking on the handle, trying to get in.

A metallic clunk against my window startled me and I spun around, to see a fist-sized microphone knocking against the glass. A chubby woman with fried blond hair jogged alongside the car. Her giant microphone clattered against my window. She huffed and wheezed: "Will you be . . . at the prison . . . on Saturday . . . Ms. Erhart? Is there going . . . to be . . . a family reunion?"

I pushed my middle finger against the window, where it aligned perfectly with her nose flattened against the glass. She pulled back as if I'd laid a hot poker against her skin. I turned away. A tiny pulsing pain started behind my left eye and spread through my entire skull. Even my hair hurt. I knew these had to be phantom pains, since I had amputated most of my long hair two days ago in a half-assed attempt to disguise myself. Now, instead of the long, shiny ponytail familiar on TV news, I had a short, stubby ponytail that looked like a brussels sprout growing out the back of my head.

"Over here! Over here!" a young Latina shouted through the passenger window. Her lips brushed the glass, leaving a smear of hideous pink lipstick. She ran awkwardly on high heels beside the car, one hand holding my side mirror for support. I was mesmerized by her hair with its huge billowing front bang like the mainsail of a whaling ship. "Ms. Erhart, have you spoken to them at the prison yet?" she mewed with fake sympathy. "Is all forgiven, dear?"

I reached over and cranked up the radio as high as it would go. The serrated chords of "Jingle Bell Rock" blasted out of the speakers. The windows rattled and my fillings ached. I'd read somewhere that farmers in Iowa were piping rock music through underground speakers in their fields to chase away gophers. Apparently, reporters were a tougher breed. The music only seemed to stimulate them, as if until now they'd all been dancing in the street to silence and finally had something to justify their frenetic movements. I'd given them a sound track.

"Miss Erhart! Hey, lady! Blue, right here!" A small man in a denim jacket with a laminated press pass clipped to his pocket hopped butt-first onto the hood of my car. The metal dented under his weight. I couldn't make out his features because the cracked glass around the bullet hole in my windshield eclipsed his face.

"Hey, Blue, I hear you don't shave your underarms. Is that some kind of New Age fad or a butch feminist statement or what? You some kind of a dyke?"

A couple of the reporters laughed. I stomped the gas pedal and they all jumped back. The man in denim rolled off the car and crashed into the chubby blond woman. They both fell to the ground. "Did you get that?" he demanded of one of the minicam operators as he jumped up. He stepped over the flattened blond woman and grabbed the cameraman's arm. "Did you fucking get that!"

Having broken free of the crowd, I shifted, grinding the gears before finally finding third. In the rearview mirror, I saw them all running after me, cameras flashing, minicams whirring. Running through the foggy dark, they looked like outraged villagers come to drive a wooden stake through my heart. I'm not fucking Vampira, I wanted to shout, I'm just a high school biology teacher. Not worthy of all this attention. My students had been almost as bad: While I was slicing through the grasshopper's abdomen, laying bare the wonders of his testes and mushroom gland, they were badgering me about when I was going on "Oprah."

The house I shared with Mitzi Rosen and her daughter was only fifty yards away, at the end of the cul-de-sac—a cul-de-sac where everyone was overinsured and no one had ever seen a real bullet hole before. The lawns were as coddled as putting greens. On weekends, all garage doors remained open and men in flip-flops and gaudy shorts the color of patio furniture stood in them exchanging tools. The women, most of whom also had jobs in order to afford the heavy mortgages, bicycled maniacally with their kids to make up for a week's worth of guilt over day care and microwaved dinners. The kind of place hip comedians enjoyed ridiculing. But I liked living here. It was very clean and people always said hello and remembered your name. It was like living in a doctor's waiting room.

The reporters were gaining fast. I swerved into our driveway, reached up and punched the button on the remote garage-door opener clipped to the visor. The heavy wooden double door slowly yawned open. In the mirror, I watched the reporters rushing closer. Now they were on the lawn, trampling Mitzi's cactus garden. The man in the denim jacket led the pack, his minirecorder thrust forward like a Geiger counter.

The garage door groaned upward, not yet high enough for my car to duck under.

"*C'mon c'mon c'mon,*" I chanted.

"Ms. Erhart!" the chubby blond woman hollered as she chugged along with a limp now. Her voice was high and strained from exertion. "Ms. Erhart, do you own a gun?"

I raced the engine and popped the clutch. The car jumped forward and scuttled into the garage, the radio antenna twanging against the bottom of the still-opening door. Once inside, I double-jabbed the remote and the door began to close.

I climbed out of the car in time to watch the reporters gather outside the garage in a ragged line like poorly trained recruits. Their heads were cut off from view by the descending garage door. One of the minicam operators squatted lower and lower with the dropping door, still filming my legs. He leaned the camera sideways, his cheek almost touching the pavement.

"Knock it off, Chomsky," the man in denim said, lightly kicking Chomsky's leg. "We already know what her fucking garage looks like."

"Right," Chomsky said, still filming. He grinned lewdly at my legs and winked at me with his free eye.

The garage door thudded against the cement. I could hear the reporters muttering outside as they dispersed. I heard the word *bitch* at least twice.

My stomach felt twisted and knotty. I pressed my fist against my diaphragm and breathed in deeply, just the way I'd read about in those stress articles. I sucked in a lungful of dank garage air and forced it down . . . down . . . down. Deep into my abdomen. Holding it there a few seconds like a captured bird. Then I exhaled, freeing the bird on my ill wind. But slowly. Like in the articles. Pushing firmly toward my spine with my diaphragm, mouth slightly agape. I emitted a low rattling growl like a clogged vacuum cleaner. Very attractive, Blue, I thought, snapping my mouth shut.

It hadn't helped, anyway. Nothing helped. Ever since the prison officials made their surprise announcement to the press a few days ago—that the release of my parents was going to come *a year early*—my life had been kicked into emotional turbocharge. I had constant headaches, earaches, diarrhea. Everyone I knew had been offering me advice on how to relax: breathing techniques, visualization methods, stretching exercises, biofeedback machines, sexual appliances. Some just handed me medication: a fistful of Valium, some capsules of Nembutol. Someone—one of my students probably—slipped a marijuana joint the size of a bratwurst into my purse. I immediately flushed it down the faculty toilet along with the tranquilizers. I appreciated the gesture, though.

I leaned over the hood of the car and ran my hand over the windshield, lightly touching the bullet hole that had mysteriously appeared two days ago while my car was parked in the faculty parking lot. The police found the slug embedded in the driver's seat. *Just a .22, probably a kid*, the investigating officer had speculated. *You gotta expect this kind of thing . . . considering who you are and what your parents did. Goes with the territory. People go nuts over stuff like this.*

I traced the edges of the hole with my fingertips. No larger than a wren's eye. The glass around the hole was cracked like peanut brittle. The thought made me hungry. I opened the glove compartment and reached into my candy stash, digging past a Snickers and Payday for a 3 Musketeers. I tried never to eat sweets in public, because inevitably someone would ask me how I managed to eat so much candy and stay so thin. Heritage, I would answer apologetically, luck of the genetic draw. That only seemed to enrage people, as if I was deliberately keeping my special diet secrets from them. Truth is, I eat like a horse, exercise sporadically, and never gain a pound. To some, that makes me more of an outlaw than my parents.

I grabbed my briefcase from the car and knocked loudly on the door that led into the house. I heard footsteps bouncing down the stairs.

"Who goes there?" intoned the voice on the other side.

"Me," I said.

"Is it a friendly spirit, Bullwinkle?"

"Don't make me kill you," I said.

"Ah, the spirit of Christmas present. Enter and spread joy and goodwill to all." The door opened and Kyra, Mitzi's thirteen-year-old megagenius daughter stood in the laundry room, grinning. She thought this was all very amusing. "I see you've made it through the gauntlet of fame again. You know, of course, you're thwarting the public's right to know. That's on your conscience, Blue."

I closed the door behind me, then locked and dead-bolted it. "How much time do I have?" I asked.

She held out her hand. "Gimme."

I broke off a piece of candy bar and dropped it in her palm. She popped it into her mouth. "Mom called a few minutes ago. She thought you'd already be here, dressed and ready to go."

"I had to dodge a couple reporters at the school. Principal Coltrane finally sneaked me out through the cafeteria kitchen. By the way, I saw tomorrow's lunch. It's clam cakes. Consider yourself warned."

She made a gagging noise.

I hoisted my overstuffed briefcase onto the washing machine. "How much time do I have?"

"Mom said she'd be home by seven with the new plan. You're supposed to be ready by then. 'Ready to rock 'n' roll.' Those were her exact words, I swear."

I stiffened. "*New* plan? What new plan?"

"She didn't say."

"Why do we need a new plan? I knew the old plan. What the hell was the matter with the old plan?"

"She didn't say."

"Damn it, sometimes your mother is . . ." I took another deep breath. Pushed it down. Released the goddamned captured bird. "What time is it now?"

Kyra reached into the bib pocket of her black overalls and pulled out an old brass pocket watch. "Quarter to seven."

"Fifteen minutes? Fuck!" I brushed past Kyra, ran through the kitchen, up the stairs, down the hall, and into my bedroom, kicking off my shoes and pulling off my blouse along the way. Kyra ran behind me, gathering up my discarded clothing. "Forget I just said that, Kyra."

"Said what?"

I made a face at her. "Don't be cute. The *f* word."

"Oh, that."

"It kinda slipped out. For your mother's sake, pretend I said *fudge*, okay?"

"Fudge?" She shook her head. "Try Fudd. Like Elmer Fudd. Fudd you and the horse you rode in on, motherfudder. Go ahead. Try it."

I stepped out of my skirt and kicked it at Kyra. "Don't make me kill you."

The skirt floated to Kyra like an angel. She snagged it out of the air and folded it neatly and placed it on top of my folded blouse. She set the flats beside the pile. She hated mess. "You need new heels, Blue," she said. "And a shine wouldn't kill you."

"I'm thinking maybe a pillow over your face while you sleep," I said. "I just kind of lean against it for a few minutes until the squirming stops. I claim you swallowed your tongue. Autopsy reveals death by suffocation. I'm in the clear. What do you think?"

"The autopsy would reveal microscopic bits of fabric from the pillowcase lodged in my nostril. And there would probably be trauma to the facial area, bruised lips, nose, and so forth. Keep trying." Kyra pulled a flashlight the size of a thermos bottle out of the hip pocket of her overalls and walked over to the window. Black overalls and red high-top Keds were all Kyra ever wore, all she had worn every day for the past two years, since she'd dropped out of QED, the university's child-genius program. Her red hair was pulled up into a tight samurai knot on top of her head, her only hairstyle since then. The symbolic meaning behind her clothes and hairstyle was her secret.

Kyra wedged the enormous flashlight between the slats of the closed blinds and clicked on the beam. "That jerk from *People* magazine just pulled up in a fancy-ass Jeep."

"Which one's he?"

"You know, the skinny bald guy with the pink scalp. Looks like a nipple with a camera."

I laughed. "How many are out there? Counting the nipple."

"Eight or ten, I think. They're just standing around the yard like mall zombies waiting for the stores to open." Kyra made a machine-gun noise with her mouth as she swiveled the flashlight back and forth. "Eat lead, Nazi scum."

I sat down on the edge of my bed. My headache had spread to my sinuses; my eyes watered. I dug out a couple Advil from my bedside drawer and dry-swallowed them. I chased them down with a Reese's Pieces. Someone was doing some hot soldering behind my eye again. My missing hair was screaming in agony. I turned on the clock radio next to my bed and spun through the stations, hoping for some Jimi Hendrix–type buzz-saw guitar solo to lobotomize my anxiety. But it was eight days until Christmas and "Jingle Bell Rock," "Rockin' Around the Christmas Tree," and Alvin and the Chipmunks singing "Please Christmas Don't Be Late" seemed to be on every station. I finally settled for the tail end of some perky Christmas bells song chirped by a squeaky boys choir that sounded like Munchkins having a group enema.

I stripped down to only my bra and panties and began recklessly ripping through my drawers in search of the Holy Grail of lingerie: an unfrayed bra. I had only one left, if I could find it. Then I remembered it was down in the washing machine, damp and smelly and stuck to the side of the drum because I'd forgotten to dry that load after washing it yesterday morning. I looked into the mirror over my dresser, examining the bra I had on. Except for the blue ink stain at the cleavage, it looked okay. What did it matter, anyway? No way was anybody going to see my bra tonight, no matter how terrific the evening went. Things were not going to get out of hand. That was one area of my life right now I *could* control. No sex.

I glanced at the ink stain again. That stain was part of the reason I was rushing around like a fool. A couple of weeks ago, I'd nodded asleep in bed while grading student essays on the digestive system and my pen had slid out of my hand, down my chest, and wedged itself between my breasts like a beached submarine. The ink had soaked into the bra, forming a mini-Rorschach blot that looked like a squashed roadkill. The ink had also seeped through to my skin, leaving a matching tattoo on my left breast that took days to scrub off completely. Which led to my boyfriend, Dale, accusing me of having a hickey. I had laughed at first, thinking he was joking. *Jesus, Dale, a hickey on my boob? I'm thirty-one, for Christ's sake.* He'd given me his morose stare, the one he probably used on students he caught smoking in the rest room. "You know, Blue," he'd said, "sometimes you can be so insecure." He had me there. Dale was a drab but dedicated social science teacher who still thought Nixon got a raw deal. But I was at a time in my life when I needed drab, I guess. Drab was good. Drab was predictable. Plus, I was pretty drab myself. But after the ink-stain incident, when he started sulking around his apartment, grading exams and giving me the silent treatment, I got dressed and left for good. I decided that was the last time Dale, or anyone for a while, would see my breasts. My breasts were going underground, like an informant in the Witness Protection Program.

Yet here I was, two weeks later, getting ready for a blind date.

I shook my head in disappointment at myself as if I were my own mother disapproving of what had become of me. I had done a lousy job raising me.

The song on the radio ended and, after a brief freeway-traffic update, the Eagles started singing "Hotel California."

Kyra spun around and lunged for the radio. "Eagles alert! Eagles alert!" She grabbed the tuner and twisted to a different station. "Whew! Close call."

"Thanks," I said.

She gave me a thumbs-up and returned to the window, clicking on her flashlight. Kyra was just being protective. She knew that the Eagles reminded me of my ex-husband, Lewis, who looked just like Don Henley and whose favorite pickup line before we got married had been, "There's gonna be a heartache tonight, I know." Then he'd make a goofy face, brush his wavy bangs out of his eyes with his thumb, and laugh at himself. It was that damn laugh, that shrugging "aren't I full of shit" laugh that always got the girls. Anyway, hard to believe now, it had even gotten me.

How low had I sunk since divorcing Lewis a year ago? It had taken me six months to feel good enough about myself even to go out on my first date, and that was with pleasantly dull Dale. He was the only man I'd dated since the divorce. Thing was, though, I didn't miss Dale. Not his good-natured charm. Not the comfort of knowing he would be waiting home for my call. Not even his skinny but enthusiastic body. Nothing. That depressed me more than anything else, that I could date a man for five months and not feel any loss when he was gone.

My life was not supposed to have turned out like this.

Mitzi, who had set up tonight's blind date, had tried to reassure me: "Dating Dale was like wearing a training bra. Now you're ready for the real thing." I'd reminded Mitzi that a blind date was not the "real thing." Mitzi had snorted. "These days it is, babe. Dating today is like trying to buy shoes in Russia. You take what's available and if it doesn't fit just right, your feet will swell or chafe a little. But they'll adjust."

That was the motto for love in the nineties, I thought. Adjust.

I whistled at Kyra. "Countdown?"

Kyra pulled out her watch again. "T minus nine minutes and counting. You're not going to make it."

"Like I care," I said. But I picked up the pace. I slid open the mirrored closet door. My few drab clothes stared back like an unsympathetic jury.

Are you going to keep teaching here, Ms. Erhart? Now that you're a celebrity and all. One of my students had asked that today. *Of course I will,* I'd answered, surprised. *Why wouldn't I?* But the other students had laughed incredulously; they didn't see why anyone would want to keep on working once they'd become famous. To them, the goal of every act, every job, every breath was celebrity. Get famous, now! They saw no distinction between fame and notoriety.

Not that I had ever asked for any of this fuss. I'd been perfectly happy all these years hiding out amidst the dust bunnies of obscurity. Dissecting my grasshoppers, swabbing microscope eyepieces with alcohol because ignorant parents thought their kids might catch AIDS from them, scrubbing the smell of formaldehyde out of my hair every night. Then one day, the governor decided my life wasn't complicated enough and so he signed a piece of paper that resulted in a prison press release about my parents' early release. And the media suddenly swept under their bed and found me. Now I was determined not to allow them to make me a prisoner, too. Which was hard to do, since they were routinely rooting through my garbage to steal discarded letters and wadded panty hose.

God, I had to do something to reestablish some normalcy in my life, some sense of order and control. Even if it meant going out on the first blind date of my life. Even if it meant sucking in my gut and sticking out my chest and making inane small talk until we were both comatose over our clam chowder. Even if I was convinced he would be so repulsive and gross that I would weep at the sight of him and beg him to marry me because that's exactly what I deserved out of life.

"You'd better hurry," Kyra said from the window. "Your future awaits you, dahling."

I wandered over to the window and stood beside Kyra. The reporters down below were scattered across the lawn, talking to each other. Some leaned against their cars; some sat inside their cars sipping coffee. A white Lexus drove down the street, spotlighting everyone with its headlights. The reporters' heads turned in unison, their bodies tensing as they evaluated the intruder for newsworthiness. The white Lexus swung into the driveway across the street, drove into the garage. But the reporters had already turned away, dismissed the Lexus, the driver, and his life as insignificant.

"Hey, Blue," a reporter shouted up at me. I squinted through the blinds. Kyra shined her flashlight on him. The nipple with the camera, the guy from *People*. "Blue. Your folks have been in prison for twenty years. Once they were the most-wanted couple in America, on the covers of *Time*, *Newsweek*, and *Life*. You used to visit them every week. Yet our recent investigation reveals that you haven't spoken to them in almost ten years. What was that all about? What happened between you?"

I didn't say anything. I just stared at him. Kyra clicked off the flashlight beam and he disappeared into darkness.

Someone else, a woman, shouted, "Blue, what's the first thing you're going to do when you see your parents? Hug them? Cry? Who will ask forgiveness first, you or them?"

I closed the blinds and sighed. "Don't make me kill you," I said.

· 2 ·

"T minus five and a half minutes," Kyra announced. "Your love connection is on his way. He could be the wind beneath your wings." She laughed.

I searched through the closet for something appropriate. I slid the same few hangers back and forth, but that didn't change anything. All I had to wear were my bland teacher outfits, accessorized by my wire-rimmed glasses and stumpy blond ponytail. My age and limited wardrobe budget didn't allow for an arsenal of different looks anymore. Not like my college days, when I could alternate between grungy folksinger, disco goddess, and flashy debutante just by changing earrings and a blouse. Tonight, it was either faded jeans with a red flannel shirt or a green flowered dress with unmatching scuffed shoes. Spinster Schoolmarm Builds Log Cabin or Mousy Job Applicant with Ugly Flats.

I pulled on my jeans with one hand while slipping into the flannel shirt with my other. I called to Kyra over my shoulder, "What's happening out there?"

"They're just smoking cigarettes and drinking coffee. Like they think this is Free Slurpee Night at the 7-Eleven."

"I meant your mother. Any sign of her?"

"Nope."

"Where the hell is she?"

"Oh, I forgot to tell you, she said she had to pick up your date from his parole officer, then swing by his AA meeting."

I froze. "What?"

Kyra laughed. "Jeez, you're easy."

"I'm thinking poison in your orange juice, perhaps curare or something equally untraceable. They find your lifeless corpse slumped over the toilet. I cry buckets at your funeral. No one suspects a thing."

"Curare doesn't have any effect if ingested. It has to be injected. That's why the Orinoco Indians of South America dip their blowgun darts in it. You're a biology teacher—aren't you supposed to know stuff like that?"

"You're a hateful child," I said, and hopped into my bathroom, dragging the empty leg of the jeans while fumbling my other arm into the shirt. As I stumbled into the bathroom, I caught a glimpse of my face in the mirror over the sink. A small rash of five white bumps rose Appalachian-like along my jawline. I'd had this kind of stress rash before, but I didn't want one now, not for God's sake now. "Fuck!" I hollered.

"Don't you mean *Fudd*?" Kyra yelled from the other room.

I needed some kind of makeup, foundation or something. Trouble was, I didn't own any makeup except for lipstick. This wasn't a feminist jag I was on, nor did it have anything to do with the fact that my grandmother applied makeup with a basting brush and trowel. My dislike of makeup dated back even to junior high school, when cosmetics had been the drug of choice among my friends. My problem was that makeup reminded me of clowns, the creepy circus clowns I'd always been terrified of since I was a little girl. Their hideous expressions seemed imprinted on their faces like fossilized skeletons on rock. Their flesh was frozen into grotesque parodies of joy and sorrow, as if someone had read each of their futures and tattooed their faces to mirror each appropriate destiny. Like coming attractions for Judgment Day. It scared the crap out of me.

But right now, I was desperate. I dropped to my knees and flung open the cupboard under the sink. Surely there was *something* in this toxic-waste dump. Some makeup samples handed to me while shopping at Nordstrom. I foraged like a raccoon. Panty liners, tampons, toilet paper, two bars of soap. I reached farther back into the dark cupboard, brushed a few hard dry sponges, a can of Comet, a plunger, small nests of hair. And, finally, a small plastic tube. I brought it out into the light. The green tube said Clinique. I couldn't remember buying this stuff. For one thing, Clinique saleswomen with their stiff hair and starched medical smocks always made me feel uncomfortable, as if with each purchase of lipstick they would force me into a complimentary pelvic exam. I tried to twist the cap off the tube. It wouldn't budge. I banged it against the counter a few times and tried again. Slowly it moved, each turn like a cheese grater shedding crusted flakes of dried foundation on my hand. I started dabbing my face clumsily with the tip of the tube. My makeup-applying technique resembled a frantic bingo player with too many cards to mark.

I studied my handiwork in the mirror. Way too much. The beige bumps looked like mud huts.

I wadded some toilet paper, spit on it, and scrubbed my cheek raw. The hell with it. The hell with the whole date. The hell with all of it. Fudd you, world.

I plopped down on the toilet seat and tried to calm myself down. The *People* magazine on the floor next to the toilet stared up at me. The full-page photo on the cover was of Princess Di being escorted to a film opening by a U.S. senator. AFFAIRS OF STATE? the headline wondered. The top of the cover had a bold yellow stripe with a postage stamp–sized photo of me. It had been taken the morning of the prison's press release, before I had even been told about it. Some guy in mirrored sunglasses had walked up behind me in the faculty parking lot while I was rushing to class, my arms bundled with student papers. He'd yelled, "Hey, Blue, did you hear that Paul McCartney's been stabbed to death?" I'd turned with a startled look, mumbled, "What?" and snap, snap, snap. That's why I looked so dopey in the photo. Like I'd just sat down hard on the horn of a saddle. The photo was bad enough, but next to it in bold red lettering was the old familiar headline of my youth: BLUE ERHART—RAISED ON ROBBERY?

A quiet rap on the door.

"Hey, you okay in there?" Kyra asked. She sounded concerned.

"Any sign of your mother?"

"Well, there's a plague of locusts and the tap water's turned to blood. That count?"

I smiled. "Yell if you see her." I listened to Kyra walk away, then returned to the serious task of date preparation. I squeezed a dollop of toothpaste onto my brush and began scrubbing my teeth and tongue. I watched myself brushing, trying to focus on my upcoming date. What should I say; what should I keep hidden? What if he tried to kiss me? Or cop a feel? But I couldn't keep my mind on that high school stuff. My eyes kept drifting to the white foam bunching around my lips like a snowbank. My lectures to my high school biology class replayed loudly in my ears as if they were being broadcast up from the sink drain: *Toothpaste is mostly water and chalk. Yup, the very same chalk I'm using to write with on the blackboard right now. And chalk is nothing more than the remains of dead creatures from the Cretaceous seas millions of years ago. We swish their crushed skeletons around in our mouths like idiot grave robbers.* "*Yeeeech, Ms. Erhart! Gross!*" *The rest of your toothpaste is titanium dioxide, which is white paint, pretty much the same as you'd buy at the lumber store or find in Liquid Paper. That's the stuff that makes your teeth white right after you brush, but it washes off with your saliva. And there's glycerine glycol to keep the paste from drying out; that's similar to the antifreeze in cars. So far all we have is a clump of wet chalk. So, to give it substance, we add some gummy seaweed and paraffin oil. Detergent is mixed in to make it sudsy, even though those suds don't really clean any better. Then some double-rectified peppermint oil for taste. Some sugar simulator to cover the chalky seaweed taste. But now we have a problem, because this is the perfect concoction to attract nasty bacteria, the kind we've been looking at all semester under our microscopes. To prevent that, they add formaldehyde, the same basic ingredient used to embalm corpses. And that's pretty much what you swizzle around in your mouths every morning and night. Yum yum. Happy brushing, kiddies.*

The day after that lecture, a couple of handwritten notes usually are delivered to me by embarrassed students. The notes are on pastel stationery with a lovely bucolic scene of fields of tulips or a sailboat at sunset or a kitten wrapping itself in a giant ball of yarn. At the top it said *From the Desk of . . .* or *Just a Friendly Note.* The note itself was often written in purple ink, the same color used by my girlfriends and me in high school to etch our boyfriends' names into our notebooks like a brand. Seeing that purple ink always made me feel sentimental. The notes, however, didn't: *Dear Miss Erhart, Do you have any idea how difficult it is to get children to brush their teeth? Do you think it's helpful to frighten them with talk about corpses and skeletons? What's that got to do with biology?*

I quickly rinsed the toothpaste from my mouth and tried to compose myself. Maybe all those purple-inked notes from the desks of all those women surrounded by tulips and sailboats and kittens were right. Thing was, I liked those women who took the time to write those notes, who came to all the PTA functions, who didn't know or care that they were the object of so much ridicule and wrath in the world. Maybe they were right; after all, they were the ones paying thousands for their kids' orthodontic work. What did I know about that kind of responsibility? Lately, I'd become much too obsessive about biology. I'd started looking at everything, not as a whole thing itself, not as it appears to everyone, but rather as the sum of its parts—the tiniest microscopic parts. Nothing is as it appears. Everything is made up of something else, something smaller. Smaller things are themselves combinations of other even smaller things. We brush our teeth with the crushed skulls of the dead, for Christ's sake.

My headache suddenly returned, kicking around inside my brain like bikers tearing up a bar. I looked around the bathroom, frantic at what I saw. Everything was getting larger, inflating, as if I had a powerful microscope behind my eyes and could see the tiny universes all around that others ignored. The room was swarming with invisible life and death. I pictured all the creatures crawling, swimming, floating, copulating, digesting, excreting. Everything in the room—the floor, the walls, the counter, the ceiling, the hairbrush, the soap—everything was crawling with microscopic civilizations of living beings. Nothing was solid. I remembered my college field trip to Bracken Cave in Texas, where 20 million bats covered the walls and ceiling, packed so tightly that no rock showed through. The babies were squeezed together two thousand to a square yard. The walls were constantly moving. There was a steady drizzle that you might mistake for rainlike condensation, but it was really the endless downpour of their urine and feces. I'd almost fainted, not from the rancid smell that my classmates teased me about, but from the sheer sensation of overwhelming life all around me. I'd had the overpowering sensation that I was inside some creature's throat, about to be swallowed. Looking around my bathroom now, I felt the same way, as if the zillions of creatures stalking around were about to leap onto me and swallow me in their swarm. I didn't want to see this much. I closed my eyes, knuckled them vigorously. I could hardly breathe the hot, fetid air I shared with all of them. I tried to imagine a white block of ice too cold for any form of life— cold, white, lifeless.

I leaned over the sink and splashed cold water on my face. I refocused on my reflection and the chorus line of blemishes can-canning across my cheek. *That's* life.

These agonizing burps in my concentration had been seizing me more and more often in the past few months. I would stand under the shower, until I couldn't block out the fact that my face was being spattered with billions of living creatures in the shower water, that they were being fired into the pores of my skin as if from a cannon. Sometimes I kept tugging the cosmic thread, imagining the creatures living on the backs of the other creatures we couldn't see, and the creatures feeding off them, and so forth. Down the rabbit's hole of infinity until my mind was flushed into some black vortex and I forgot who I was. Got lost. I came out of these brief trances dazed, like an amnesiac. Like now.

I dried my face with my sleeve and walked back into the bedroom wearing my jeans and flannel shirt.

"You look nice," Kyra said.

"I look like Mr. Green Jeans."

"Who's that?"

"A dead guy. Last known associate: Captain Kangaroo."

Kyra returned to her post at the window, flashlight in hand. "They just keep coming and coming, Blue. There are more reporters out there than neighbors. Why do they stay? What exactly do they expect you to do?"

"Make them money, I guess."

Kyra grinned. "You can do that? How about spreading some bucks my way?"

"Sorry, earth child. I've sworn to use my superpowers only for good." I surveyed myself in the mirror. A vision in denim and plaid. The only thing that could save me from looking like a tow-truck driver was a hat. I rummaged through the closet until I came up with a shapeless black felt hat, which I punched into a bowl shape, jammed onto my head, and wore with the front brim flipped up and the back brim down.

"Does Mr. X know what's going on here?" Kyra asked. "About your new celebrity status? The prison stuff?"

"Your mom says not. He's never heard of me or my parents."

Kyra frowned. "Mom, huh. I hope you got that in writing. Besides, do you really want to go out with some moron who doesn't read the newspapers or watch television?"

"Maybe this isn't the kind of news he's interested in, okay? Maybe he just reads the important stuff. World events. National politics. Articles with strife and turmoil and colored pie charts."

"If he's so smart, then how would Mitzi know him?"

Good point, I thought. Mitzi Rosen was my best friend, an actress with a steady job at the Dana Point Dinner Theater. Whatever the musical—and they are all musicals—Mitzi was in it. Most of the guys she worked with there were too young, too married, too gay, or too obsessed with their noncareers. Mitzi had assured me this guy was different. He'd better be.

"We have movement!" Kyra announced. She slid open the window and leaned out, sweeping the flashlight beam on the people below like an obsessed warden trying to foil a breakout. "The nipple from *People* is chasing Mr. Prichard's dog with a newspaper. I think the dog took a dump next to his Jeep. The bleach job from the *Enquirer* is smoking a cigar the size of a pickle and talking on the car phone in her Mercedes. Some black chick with hair sculpted into the shape of Alaska is setting up a tripod outside the front door." Kyra turned to me, a nasty grin on her face. "You want, Blue, I can go down there and jam a zucchini in the bleach job's tail pipe. The way I'd do it, four hundred bucks damage. Minimum."

"Forget it, Dillinger."

She steepled her hands into prayerful begging. "Please, Blue. A moonless night. A Godless enemy. And a brave child on a daring sabotage mission into hostile territory. It's so cinematic."

"No."

"It's not dangerous. You could signal me from here when the coast is clear. Then when her tail pipe blows, all the other reporters will gather around and snap pictures and interview one another. Just think: reporters . . . reporting . . . on reporters. It's poetry."

I belched loudly. "So's that, Sylvia Plath."

Kyra belched even louder. "There's your rhyme, Emily Dickinson."

I laughed. "God, I'm a bad influence."

Suddenly, a bright flash like a flare filled the window, outlining Kyra in pure white light. Kyra's reflection in the window glowed with a fiery aura, the way movies with low special-effects budgets depict the soul departing the body. Still, for that first moment of blinding light, the way Kyra seemed to melt away in it, I thought, *Jesus, the Bomb! We're all dead.* Then the glare dissolved into blackness and someone outside shouted, "Save your film; it's just the fucking kid."

Kyra staggered blindly a few steps, rubbing her eyes. I noticed the quivering at the corner of her mouth, her eyes magnified by tears. She'd been frightened, too. Sometimes it was too easy to forget she was only thirteen.

"Why are they here at our house?" Kyra asked, her voice cracking. "Why aren't they out at the prison? That's where the story is."

"There's nothing to see there. Not until Saturday. They'll all be out there Saturday, I promise." I hugged Kyra's shoulder. "Meanwhile, they hang around here worshiping Satan and playing their Black Sabbath albums backward. That's what all journalists do."

Kyra returned to the window and checked her pocket watch. "Mom's late."

"As usual." I walked over to the window and peeked out with Kyra. The bastard in denim was still there, smoking a pipe. I lifted my arm and pinched the tuft of hair under there through the flannel. How had he found out that I stopped shaving? Ex-beau Dale? Ex-husband Lewis? And why would anyone care where hair grew on my body? Actually, at first I'd had a good reason for letting it grow. As retaliation against Lewis after our last big fight six months before the divorce. That's when he'd given me, for my thirtieth birthday, a gift certificate to A Better You, the plastic surgery clinic down the street, between Taco Bell and Blockbuster Video. He'd wanted me to get my breasts enlarged.

"Not enlarged," he'd explained. "Firmed up." His cupped hands had hovered away from his chest, forming imaginary "firmed-up" 44D breasts.

"It's dangerous," I'd told him. "Haven't you read the government reports? Those bags leak. Women get sick."

"That's bullshit," he'd said. "A few hysterical women. Accidents happen. A truck could clip you crossing the street. They have new methods now. Scientific methods." He'd been wearing his cop's uniform, having just come off duty. His gun and holster were hanging on the bedroom doorknob. I was sitting cross-legged on the bed, staring at the gift certificate and brochure that displayed before and after photos of drab-chested women suddenly thrusting their inflated chests out at the world with confidence and pride.

Hairy armpits had been my response. I'd stopped shaving them. Legs, too, though my hair there was too blond and fine to be noticeable. But the underarm hair came in mysteriously dark and thick, like exotic underbrush from the Brazilian rain forest, the extract of which might cure cancer. He'd wanted a change, he got one: a better, hairier me. At first he'd tried to ridicule me into shaving: "I've arrested junkies with better hygiene." Then he started berating me, calling it my "grassy knoll," claiming that it was thick enough to have hidden the second gunman who'd shot JFK. After that, it was just a matter of time.

I flopped back onto the bed. Already, I was too exhausted for my date. I would be little more than a lifeless blob slurping soup and mumbling about how I loved my job and how fulfilled my life was. I had to move. I was supposed to meet him at a restaurant that Mitzi would smuggle me out to in the trunk of the car. At least, that was the old plan.

I struggled to get up off the bed, but the best I could muster was to raise my head a couple of inches. From this angle, I could look down my own blouse and see my 34B breasts shifting abruptly as if they were scoops of ice cream melting out from under the upended cones of my bra cups. I plucked my blouse up into a tent so I could look down and measure what damage age and gravity had done to me. Each breast reminded me of the oversized gelatinous head of an octopus. Maybe breast implants weren't such a bad idea. Some of the women at school had them and seemed happy. Mitzi had them. I nudged my left breast with my fingertip, like poking a corpse's cheek. My boobs sagged in a way that reminded me too much of my sagging life in general. The way people start to resemble their dogs after a while. Perhaps perkier breasts would make my whole life perkier. Breasts that can stand up to the onslaught of life reflect an owner who can do likewise. Bulletproof boobs. Tits with a mission. I grabbed both of my flannel-covered breasts, one in each hand, and said aloud, "Shape up, guys. It's a big world and you've got your whole life ahead of you. You've come in here boobs, but you're leaving here knockers."

I started to laugh, but when I looked over at the doorway, I saw Mitzi standing there. Next to her was a handsome, young uniformed cop. They stared at me.

Mitzi applauded. "Is this your new ventriloquist act? I love your dummies." She laughed. "Blue, meet your blind date, Dave. Dave is a god among men. Dave, isn't she everything I said she was? Shy, demure, conservative."

I released my breasts, stood up, walked across the room—said, "Hi, Dave" as I passed them—went into my bathroom, shut and locked the door. And refused to come out.

I sat on the edge of the tub and stared at the tumbleweed of hair in the corner. When was the last time I'd vacuumed? Or dusted? Or scrubbed grout?

"Let me in or I'll huff and I'll puff and so forth," Mitzi said through the closed bathroom door.

"Go away," I said.

"I'm not going away. I'm staying right here."

"Suit yourself. I'm taking a bath." I turned on the faucet.

"You don't come out in two minutes, I start singing every Ethel Merman song I know." She began belting out "Anything You Can Do, I Can Do Better."

I'd heard Mitzi send Dave downstairs with some excuse about my just getting over a bout of stomach flu. Kyra had taken the cue and led him to the kitchen for tea. He'd gone, but he didn't sound fooled.

Mitzi stopped singing. "Come out, Blue; this isn't like you. When did you suddenly turn into Doris fucking Day?"

I looked across the room into the mirror. A ponytail, for Christ's sake. I was Doris Day! I pulled off the rubber band and shook my hair.

"Blue. Blue, honey." Mitzi tapped a single fingernail against the hollow door. It sounded like a code, a secret women's code. Mitzi's nails were long and perfectly shaped, curved like the beak of a tropical bird. I looked at my own nails, short, with ragged cuticles. No wonder I couldn't break the code. I didn't feel like either a woman or a man. I was at a point in my life where I was between sexes, the way some people are between jobs. Sometimes when I looked at my own body naked, I wondered what I was doing with useless breasts and an empty womb. Like I was wearing a costume.

"Come out before I set the fucking door on fire," Mitzi said.

"You know I will, too."

"Tell him to go home. Date's over. I had a lovely time. Ciao."

"I'm getting the lighter fluid. Blue?"

I walked over to the sink counter and picked up my lipstick tube. I smeared some on my upper lip. Red as a child's wagon. There was a time when women of quality didn't wear makeup because red suggested passion and only the lower-class slobs exhibited passion openly. Back in the early 1900s, lipstick was made from crushed and dried insect corpses for coloring, beeswax for stiffness, and olive oil for texture. In 1924, the New York Board of Health tried to get the stuff banned, not to protect women's health (they were sluts for wearing it in the first place) but because they feared men might be poisoned by kissing the women who wore it. I applied more to my lower lip. The main ingredient of lipstick today was acid. The acid begins as an orange color, but when it's smeared across the lips, it literally sizzles into the skin, dyeing it red. Add some castor oil so it can spread smoothly, heavy petroleum-based wax to shape it into a stick, perfume to smother the castor oil, and food preservative so it doesn't go rancid. And, of course, to get that moist glistening effect: fish scales! They buy fish scales left over from commercial fish packers, soak them in ammonia, and dump them in the mixture. That's all it takes to make a woman's lips look like a wet vagina. I blotted my coated lips on a piece of toilet paper and smiled into the mirror. Fish scales glistened enticingly.

"He's nice, Blue," Mitzi said, tapping on the door again.

"He's a cop. You know how I feel about cops."

"He's not a cop. Dave Sorrento's an actor with me over at the theater. He plays Officer Krupke. Remember, *West Side Story?* If you'd have dragged your sorry ass over there, you'd have recognized him."

"Why's he still in costume?"

"Part of the plan. Come on out and I'll explain."

I didn't say anything for a long while.

"I'm sure you've made a good impression." She laughed. Then added quietly, "You're just nervous, Blue."

"I'm okay."

"Yeah, I know you're okay. I'm just saying that after a day dodging those fucking reporters and everybody else's prying, you're bound to be a little on edge. Hell, look at Marlon Brando and Sean Penn. They slug reporters."

I opened the bathroom door. "If you do your Ethel Merman again, I'll slug *you.*"

Mitzi dropped to one knee and in an even more exaggerated Ethel Merman style crooned "There's No Business Like Show Business."

I faked a move to return to the bathroom.

Mitzi grabbed my wrist. "No you don't." She stood up. "He's waiting for you. Go out with him. You'll have fun. In fact, I predict that tonight is going to change your life forever. Trust me."

I sighed. "This isn't the way it's supposed to be, Mitz. All this crap."

"Maybe it is. Maybe true love can be found only through a grueling process of total humiliation and relentless degradation."

"You don't believe that."

Mitzi shrugged. "Shit, girl, I *have* to believe that."

· 3 ·

"Shouldn't we use these?" "Officer" Dave said, unclipping the silver handcuffs from his utility belt and dangling them in front of me like hoop earrings. "Just to be safe."

"I don't think they're really necessary," I said.

He frowned, uncertain. "Gee, I don't know."

"Come on, Blue," Mitzi encouraged. "It'll be cool to see you taken away in handcuffs. Reporters knocking each other over to get to you for a quote. But you don't give them shit, just keep your eyes down, face averted, like a Mafia mobster. Great theater!"

"Cinematic," Kyra agreed from her post at the window.

Dave clutched the cuffs by the chain so that each bracelet stuck out on either side of his fist, like ears. "Come on, Blue, be a sport. I'm dying to actually use these things."

I thought it over. I'd only ever been handcuffed by my ex-husband. Back when Lewis was at the Police Academy, he'd practice his cuffing technique on me nightly, timing himself with a stopwatch. He was determined to be the best cop in his class. He'd spin me around and shove me up against the wall of the kitchen (so we could still keep an eye on the cooking dinner), and he'd twist my arm behind my back and slap them on. I'd wear thick sweatbands on my wrists to prevent chafing. "Up against the wall, motherfucker!" he'd bark, clicking the stopwatch. Again and again.

Sometimes I'd try it, yanking his arms back and bumping him into the wall, shouting, "Up against the wall, you nattering nabob of negativism!" Or, "Grab some wall, you victim desensitized by social pressures brought on by governmental indifference and early childhood domestic violence!" Sometimes after an hour or so, when we were both giddy, he'd push me up against the wall, cuff me, and croon, " 'Desperado, why don't you come to your senses?' " Then there'd be that famous laugh of his. And we'd make love. At first, there'd been a few obligatory jokes and exchanged winks about using the cuffs in the bedroom, but Lewis had never pushed it. He could see they made me uncomfortable. He knew all about my past.

"I'll pass," I said to Dave, pushing the cuffs away. "We'll just have to get by on acting."

"Acting!" David said with a comic flourish, striking the pose of a born ham. "I accept the challenge. I'll have them weeping in the cheap seats."

"Don't you mean *wetting* in the cheap seats?" Mitzi said.

"At least my Ethel Merman doesn't sound like she's just sucked in a lungful of helium."

Mitzi punched him in the arm and he feigned agonizing pain. They laughed, and I couldn't help but think they'd make a better couple than he and I.

"So, what do you want us to do, David?" Mitzi said, using a finger gesture to lasso herself and Kyra. "Run screaming after you guys? Spit on you or something?"

"Spit on me?" David recoiled.

"To give the scene texture. As if you were taking away my best friend."

"I am your best friend," I said.

"Your only friend," Kyra muttered.

Mitzi waved a dismissing hand at me. "This is theater talk, kiddo. You don't understand. We have to spice it up. Heighten the experience. Make it realistic. So, Dave, what do you think? Spit, or maybe a slap across the face?" She slapped her palm, testing the sound effect. "Like that."

"Hmmm." Dave rubbed his jaw, as if in anticipation of her slap.

"I don't see the point," Kyra said. "Why even go through this cheesy charade? Just get in the car and go on your date."

"The point, my 'genius but sometimes lacks commonsense' daughter, is a *distraction*. If Blue and Dave just drove out of here on their little dream date, those reporters would stick to them like earwax. They'd be followed all night. This way, they won't follow them because they'll think they already know where Blue's going. Get it?"

Kyra crossed her eyes. "Duh!"

Dave sighed. "This made more sense backstage a few hours ago."

Mitzi was too hyped on adrenaline to take offense. "Come on, Dave. Don't wuss out on us now."

He looked Mitzi over. She was still in her Puerto Rican spitfire outfit from her role as Anita. Her crinoline crackled with each movement.

"I can change," she said, pulling off her black wig. "How about I put on a bathrobe and come chasing after you? I leave the robe half open. Give 'em a little cleavage. That'll distract them."

"I can jam a zucchini in one of the tail pipes," Kyra offered.

"You will do no such thing," Mitzi said. "That's destruction, young lady, not theater. Subtlety is the key to good staging. Right, Dave?"

"Sure. Subtlety."

Mitzi yanked the bodice of her dress down a couple of inches, revealing ample breasts. "I say we go with cleavage. These'll distract 'em."

"My zucchini is as distracting as your boobs," Kyra said. "And more subtle."

Dave leaned closer to me and whispered, "I think we should compromise with the cuffs. Otherwise, who knows what these two are liable to do for the sake of realism."

I shrugged. I felt as if someone had scooped out my regular brain and stuck in this sluggish loaner. The air seemed too dense to fit up my nostrils. The fish scales on my lips tingled. They longed for the open sea. I looked around the bedroom, yet nothing looked familiar—the bed, the dresser, the poster over the bed of a bright Amish quilt. Who lived here? Outside this condo, ambitious reporters were milling about in the dark, all of them with my face on their minds. Plotting how to steal my image. So many people thinking about me was not flattering but frightening, as if finally at the sight of me they might forget their purpose and just run for me, their teeth bared and salivating, and chew me to pieces.

"I have an idea!" Mitzi said. "This is good. This is very good. How about I microwave some instant oatmeal and hide some in my mouth. Then when I chase after you, Dave can sort of shove me and I'll heave the oatmeal on the ground, just like vomit."

"Oatmeal doesn't look like vomit, Mom," Kyra said.

"We'll mix in some ketchup. Then I'll grab my stomach and say something like, 'God, please don't let me miscarry.' " Tears flooded her eyes as she twisted her face into a tortured expression. " 'Lord, I want this baby so much!' " She sobbed, then smiled. "Like that. What do you think?"

Kyra rolled her eyes. "Subtle."

I held out my wrists to Dave. "Cuff me."

"Ms. Erhart, are you under arrest?"

"Ms. Erhart, what are you being charged with?"

"Officer, what are the charges?"

The reporters huddled in so close to us that I could smell the coffee and cigarettes on their breaths. Someone wore too much lilac perfume and I coughed under its cloying scent.

"What the hell is this?" the man in the denim jacket demanded. He had his cameraman's shirtfront in his fist and was leading him through the tight circle of reporters like a Seeing Eye dog. His swinging elbows hacked a clear path. "There's no arrest warrant on her. I would have heard."

Dave opened the passenger door of his Jetta. He placed his hand gently on top of my head and eased me into the seat, just the way I'd seen it done on TV. He was good.

"Officer, what's going on here?" the man in denim shouted at Dave. "What exactly is she under arrest for?"

"She's not under arrest; she's in protective custody. There have been certain threats . . ." He let the unfinished sentence hang there with sinister implications.

"Since when is someone in protective custody handcuffed?" the man in denim asked.

"And who's she being protected from?" the chubby woman with the fried blond hair wheezed. Actually, her hair was now damp and matted from the night fog that had swooped in from the nearby beaches.

"All I'm authorized to say is that this is not an arrest." He leaned his face close to the man in denim. So close, I guessed, that they could feel each other's breath on their cheeks. Neither backed down. Dave's cold stare drilled the reporter with a ferocity that surprised me. Dave's voice was calm when he spoke, but the intensity of his stare had soaked into his tone. "If you, any of you, were to broadcast or publish that Ms. Erhart is under arrest, I would imagine she'd have justification for a juicy little lawsuit." Dave pushed through the crowd and walked around the car to the driver's side. He opened the door and stuck one leg in.

"This just doesn't make any fucking sense." The man in denim's breath puffed white around his mouth, like a comic-strip character's dialogue balloon.

Dave shrugged and smiled. "I'm just following orders. They told me to bring her in . . . I'm bringing her in. They said use the cuffs for her own protection . . . I'm using cuffs. They said use an unmarked car." He slapped the roof of the car. "This is about as unmarked as they come. You want anything more, call Captain Jerome Robbins of the Santa Ana Police Department. He's authorized to brief you with all the details." More questions were fired at him, but Dave ignored them, climbed into the car, and drove away.

"You were quite good," I said. "I'm impressed."

"I'd like to thank the Academy and of course Mom and Dad for those tuba lessons when I was eight."

I laughed, then rattled my handcuffs. "Now you can take these damn things off."

Dave stared into the rearview mirror. "Hang on a couple minutes. Just to make sure we aren't being followed."

I dropped my cuffed wrists into my lap. I looked around the car interior for some clue to Dave's lifestyle. The car itself was modest, several years old but nicely maintained. There was no cigarette smell, so I was relieved that he didn't smoke. No gum wrappers wadded on the floor. No pencils or pens. No coffee stains on the carpets. No newspapers in the back, no magazines. Nothing. Either he was a neat freak or he had no interests. I rolled down the window. The bitter smell of freshly fertilized fields from the farms up in the hills wafted through the car. Also, someone had planted broccoli. I rolled the window up again.

"This is my first blind date," I said. "What about you?"

"Yup. You got my cherry."

"How nice for my collection."

He laughed. "Mitzi said you were funny. To tell the truth, I didn't want to go at first. You know, a blind date is usually like eating overcooked spinach—some kind of character builder, but mostly a drag. But Mitzi was so persuasive. I'm glad she was."

I studied his face for the first time. Clean-shaven. Boyish, really. No heartbreak lines under the eyes, no disappointment creases around the mouth. He seemed suddenly younger than I'd thought before. Maybe twenty-seven.

"How old are you, Dave?" I asked.

"Twenty-nine."

"Twenty-nine?" I relaxed. Two years difference. That's not too bad. I looked to be about mid-to-late twenties myself. "Twenty-nine," I said again, getting used to it.

"Okay, twenty-six. Mitzi said I should say twenty-nine. She said twenty-six would make you nervous."

"Mitzi said all that?"

"She was just trying to help, I guess. What with all you've been through the past year. The divorce. That guy Dale you were dating from school. The prison announcement. And now this circus outside your home."

My stomach clenched. "Boy, Mitzi really briefed you."

"She was just trying to help. She cares about you."

I didn't say anything. It wasn't this kid's fault that Mitzi liked to meddle, liked to make everyone's life more dramatic. Mitzi wanted life to be good theater, as if she was afraid anything less might get her life canceled like a poorly rated TV show. "Mitzi mentioned you were acting part-time. What do you do the rest of the time?"

"Sell car stereos."

"Oh?" I tried to strangle my disappointment. Not another huckster, foisting overpriced equipment on ditzy teenagers. What was Mitzi thinking?

"Yup," he said. "Tweeters, woofers, in-dash CD players. The works."

"Nice."

"I hate it. But it's paying my way through veterinary school."

I brightened. Okay, he wasn't just a soulless money-grubbing scoundrel; he liked animals. "You're going to be a veterinarian."

"If I can push enough stereos, cellular phones, and car alarms."

I lifted my handcuffed hands to my face and touched the tiny white bumps along my jaw. They felt as big as braille. I wished it wasn't the side that was facing him.

"I hear you're taking graduate classes," Dave said. "Religion or something?"

"Comparative religion." I didn't want to get into details. Most people get nervous when they hear you're studying religion. Either they dismiss you as a religious fanatic or they use it as an excuse to confess their sins. Some get nasty because they blame religion for the world's woes; others get conspiratorial because they think I'm a missionary, out to spread the Word. So I generally dodge the issue.

He laughed. "I had enough of religious studies when I got circumcised."

I nodded noncommittally. His next question would be how Judaism compares with other religions.

"How do the Jews stack up, in your opinion?" he asked.

"How do you mean? We still talking about your circumcision?"

"Philosophically. Which religion makes the most sense to you? That's what comparative religion is, isn't it? Comparing the religions, like three stars for Judaism but five stars for Satanism?" He grinned.

"I don't think I know enough yet to judge them."

"What were you raised as?"

"A Republican. My grandparents considered that a religion."

He nodded. "Mine, too. They thought Reagan was the Messiah. What's your dissertation going to be on?"

I hesitated. Nobody was neutral about this subject. "Thomas Q."

"The Q-balls?" He roared with laughter. Q-balls were what some wits called Thomas Q's followers. "Jesus. That's the guy with his own Ten Commandments, right? The guy in Arizona."

"Yeah."

"He runs that retreat where all these rich people go to get their karma realigned."

"That's him."

"A friend of mine, his sister went. She doesn't talk about it, but my buddy says she's completely changed."

"For the better?"

He shrugged. "She seems the same to me. I think she lost some weight, though."

"Did she want to lose weight?"

"Doesn't every woman?"

I thought about arguing the point because it stereotyped women, but since he was basically right, I let it slide.

"I see those Q-ball Ten Commandments on bumper stickers all the time." He snapped his fingers, trying to remember. "Uh, Show Up is one of them, isn't it?"

"Yes. That's the First Commandment."

"Keep Low. Let Go. Uh . . . What else?"

"Play Fair. Ease Up. Eat Right. Die Well—"

"Die Well. Jesus. Die Well. What's that supposed to mean?"

"Beats me," I said. I wasn't going to spend any more time discussing some reclusive cult leader in Arizona. I'd picked him more out of self-defense than curiosity. So little was known about him that I figured my thesis committee wouldn't have any information to challenge whatever I wrote. Except for reading the few articles that appeared in the popular press, I didn't know much about Thomas Q. I knew that thousands had visited his retreat but few discussed it except to say it had changed their lives. There were no clear photographs of him, just the usual blurred shots taken from such a distance that it could just as easily have been the butt of a buffalo. No one knew what his real name was. Then there were those corny Ten Commandments that kept popping up everywhere. Yesterday, one of my fellow teachers patted my back and said with all seriousness,

"Let Go." I'd smiled and replied, "Die Well." He'd smiled and said thank you.

"How's it look out there?" I asked Dave, rubbing my wrists. "These things are starting to hurt."

Dave adjusted his rearview mirror. "The good news is that they're not following us."

"Great. You can take these off now." I offered up my wrists.

He took a deep breath and frowned. "Well, now, that's the bad news."

I shifted around in the seat to face him, trying to see if he was smiling. "You're kidding, right?"

"No." He shook his head solemnly. "No, I'm not kidding."

I stared at him; I wasn't sure for how long. Time was irrelevant, an elaborate hoax, like horses stomping answers to math questions. "You're kidding," I said. Had I already said that?

He looked over at me, embarrassed. "Look, I'm sorry as hell about this, Blue. But just relax, stay calm. You're safe. Nothing's going to happen to you. I swear."

"Well, your word's certainly good enough for me." I faced forward, staring out the windshield. We were on the Newport Freeway, heading toward the beach. I could yank open the door and roll out onto the dark freeway. Maybe the fall wouldn't kill me. Maybe another car wouldn't crush my skull and pulverize my hipbones into the pavement, leaving me in a wheelchair. A slow burn of panic ignited at my neck and was flaming up my cheeks, across my forehead, singling my hair. My skin was so hot, I expected the edges of my face to blister and peel along my jawbone and hairline like old wallpaper. My eyes were dried walnuts; each blink was like scuffing shoe leather against gritty sidewalk.

"Are you a reporter, Dave?" My voice sounded calm, so I was still okay.

"No, I'm not one of those fuckers."

"Which fucker are you?"

He whipped his cop hat off his head and flipped it into the backseat. "Jesus, Ms. Erhart, I'm just doing a favor for a pal. That's all. You're in no danger, not from me, not from him."

"Who's your pal? Why the handcuffs?"

"I can't say."

"You don't sell car stereos."

"I did in college."

"You're not going to be a veterinarian, are you?"

He shook his head. "Couldn't get into vet school. I'm still pissed about that."

I looked over at him again. "I guess you're an even better actor than I thought. How did you fool Mitzi, though? It's not like her to fall for an act."

"We're almost there. Really, you're in no danger."

I looked at the gun in his holster. Was it real or just a prop? It looked real, just like Lewis's service revolver. What would happen if I grabbed it? I knew how to shoot; Lewis had taught me. Perhaps an elbow to Dave's temple would get the ball rolling, I decided.

Thwump!

Dave's head snapped away from my elbow and cracked into the driver's window. Thin cracks veined down the glass. The car jerked to the left, but Dave quickly recovered and swerved it back into the traffic lane. I dove for the gun.

"Shit! What the fuck . . . !" Dave wrestled with the steering wheel with his left hand and pushed at me with his right. His finger accidentally poked the corner of my eye and tears blinded me. His hand palmed my face like it was a basketball and he shoved me against the door, keeping me at arm's length. I tried to bite at his hand, but my teeth kept sliding off his palm.

"Damn it, relax!" he screamed. "I told you nothing would happen. Christ!"

The whine of the police siren behind the car brought Dave's hand away from my mouth. He looked into his rearview mirror. Red and blue lights strobed through the car. Dave eased to the side of the road. Instantly, I yanked the door handle, shouldered the car open, and rolled out onto the dirt and gravel. "He's got a gun!" I hollered, and kept rolling off the shoulder of the road into a shallow ditch. "He's got a gun!"

When I looked up, my head dizzy, I saw a pair of black-jeaned legs. And cowboy boots. He stooped down, his hand on the butt of his still-holstered revolver under his windbreaker. "What a coincidence, Blue. So do I."

I grabbed a handful of dirt and threw it into his face. "You son of a bitch, Lewis."

Lewis's reflexes were still quick enough to slap away most of the dirt with one hand. A few pea-sized clods pelted his cheek. He offered me a hand up. I spit at it, landing a wet glob on the web of skin between his thumb and index finger. He chuckled, wiped the spit on his pants leg, and reoffered his hand. "Dumb, I know."

I looked up at Lewis's face, which I hadn't seen for seven months. His hair was long and his mustache ragged and droopy. He looked more like the old Don Henley than Don Henley did now. His eyes were filmy and his skin ashen and I knew he'd started smoking again. He looked over at Dave, if that was his real name, and nodded in some male telepathy, acknowledging an owed favor. Dave pointed at Lewis, as if Lewis had just assisted on a slam-dunk. Communications complete, Dave jumped in the car and sped off.

Lewis looked me in the eyes and shook his head. "Come on, Desperado. Why don't you come to your senses?" Then he made a goofy face and laughed his laugh.

I took his hand.

· 4 ·

"You still hate cops?" Lewis asked.

"Just one."

He laughed. "At least you still have feelings for me."

I walked across the dark living room and turned on the lamp next to the sofa. The living room was immaculate. I knew the rest of the apartment would be just as spotless. Lewis was a hell of a house-keeper, much better than I ever was.

Lewis unclipped the gun from his belt and stashed it in the foyer closet. Unlike some of the cops we'd associated with, he was not a gun freak, didn't enjoy having it around the house like a lot of his pals. He was not quick to anger. Read voraciously, though mostly about ancient Greece. As a hobby, Lewis made pictures with mosaic tiles. He never forgot a birthday or anniversary. In bed, he was athletic. He was, all in all, a good guy. How had divorce sneaked up on us? Where had it been hiding?

"So, you're going out on blind dates now?" he said, heading toward the kitchen, grinning.

"This was my first."

"How do you like it so far?"

"Better for me than it will be for you. I imagine your captain isn't going to be too pleased when I file kidnapping charges."

"He'll shit Dalmatians," he called from the kitchen. "Drink?"

"No thanks. The courts might interpret drinking as a friendly gesture on my part, condoning your actions."

"Not if you testify that you were frightened, that you were merely playing along so as not to provoke me. What'll you have?"

I shrugged. "Wine?"

"Diet Coke."

"Ginger ale?"

"Diet Coke."

I sighed. "Got any diet Coke?"

"I'll check."

I heard ice clinking into a glass. I sat on the sofa. A huge book about ancient Greek architecture lay open on the coffee table.

Lewis returned, handing me the glass of diet Coke over my shoulder. He dropped into the chair across from me. He reached into his shirt pocket and dragged out a cigarette, which he screwed between his lips, then lit. "That's how you dress for a date these days? You in mourning for Patsy Cline?"

"What's with the long hair and cigarettes? Last time I saw you, your hair was so short, your scalp shone through like a mirrored ball at a disco."

"I'm out of uniform now. Strictly plainclothes." He struck a dramatic pose, hands on hips. "Undercover cop! Out to save the planet for democracy. Or from democracy. One of those."

"Vice?"

He nodded. "Three more boxtops and I get booted up to Narcotics."

"More money. That'll be nice."

"Yup." He sucked on his cigarette as if it were a respirator. The tip glowed fiercely.

"So?" I said.

"What?"

"Make your pitch, Lewis. You must want something from me to go through all this trouble. I take it Officer Dave is also an undercover cop. You two work together, right?"

Lewis touched the tip of his nose to indicate I was right.

"No wonder he was such a good actor. And Mitzi. What load of crap did you dump on her to get her to go along with this?"

Lewis stubbed out his cigarette, leaned back into his chair, and smiled thinly. "I told her I wanted to get back together with you."

"I'm too tired for jokes, Lewis."

"Shit, Blue. You know when I'm not joking."

"Lewis," I said softly, not knowing what else to say. "Damn it, Lewis."

He nodded. "Dumb, I know."

I looked at him, at his tired eyes. The skin around them was wrinkled, like punched-in pillows. I shook my head. "Lewis . . ."

"Anything can be fixed, Blue," he said, leaning forward, wringing his hands earnestly. "That much I've learned. You know why? You know why?"

"Why?" My voice was barely audible.

"Because nothing changes. All those books I've read . . ." He waved toward the garage, where he kept his books stored in cardboard boxes so as not to embarrass his police friends when they came over. "All that shit about Greece. Socrates. Plato. Aristotle. Everything they said back then, people are still saying now. Nothing changes. Murder, whores, and drugs. Love and betrayal. It was going on twenty-five hundred years ago, and it's still going on now. Humankind doesn't change, but people can. Individual people. See? See what I'm saying?"

I was a little scared. This was Lewis's longest personal speech since we'd been married. Yes, that's where it had been hiding. That's where the divorce had been skulking around during our marriage. In the silences. We could chatter endlessly about our jobs, our friends, movies, food, politics. We could debate current events. He was for the death penalty, I was against it. We could argue for hours on that alone. But I was always a tourist in the Land of Lewis, visiting points of interest, exploring natural wonders, dancing with abandon in the hot spots, but never knowing the natives. I was always shoved aboard a return flight if he felt I'd stayed too long.

That's when the silences started. Silence like a tapeworm growing in our stomachs, eating our words, becoming bloated and sluggish, but still eating, swelling until it choked off the circulation. Things I used to say became things I meant to say. Then things I wanted to say. Then things I needed to say. And all the king's marriage counselors couldn't put us back together again.

I stood up. My legs were shaky, but I managed to walk toward the telephone. "I'll call Mitzi to pick me up."

"Don't, Blue," he said softly. "Talk to me. Turn me down, okay, but at least talk to me."

"What did you think would happen, Lewis? Did you think you'd sweep me off my feet? These feet don't sweep so easily anymore."

"Yeah, well, stealing lines from the Eagles doesn't work much, either. Most of the girls I meet don't even know who the Eagles are. I gotta hum 'Lyin' Eyes' to them before a light goes on." He reached into his pocket for another cigarette. "I haven't gone out in months."

I snorted.

"Okay, weeks. But I haven't wanted to for months. The last few weeks were out of habit, like going to the same restaurant long after you stopped liking their food." Lewis lit his cigarette and puffed a couple times. "I've missed you, Blue. You know I'm not lying about that."

I avoided his eyes. I'd read an article in one of my biology journals about studies showing that women score consistently higher than men when deciphering emotions from photographs and from tape-recorded messages in which the actual words are garbled. The corpus callosum, a bunch of nerves connecting the brain's hemispheres, is wider in women, possibly permitting more crosstalk between the hemispheres. A scientific basis for women's intuition. Whatever. I knew from his voice he was telling the truth. "Your timing sucks, Lewis."

"I know. Once I heard the prison announcement, I knew I had to move fast. With all the shit you're going through now and a ton more you will be going through after Saturday, I figured this is when you could use me most. It was now-or-never time." He spread his arms like a priest welcoming a congregation. "I'm here for the taking."

"Oh, Lewis. Lewis, I . . ." My mouth opened several times to say something, but nothing came out. I didn't know what to say. I wasn't sure how I felt. Yes, I missed him. Splitting up had been a mutual decision, but one I'd first suggested after a week of particu-

larly suffocating silence. A lot of "What's wrong?" "Nothing." "You
sure?" "I'm fine. Nothing's wrong." "Tell me, Lewis." "Nothing's
wrong, really." How much prospecting can you do and keep coming
up empty-handed before you abandon the claim?
   Yet I'd been "out there" for a year. Alone. Out in the numbing
world of dating, like a steady diet of hospital food, tasteless, lumpy,
lacking any nutritional value. Perhaps I'd been hasty. Maybe I'd
fallen victim to the American attitude that everything is disposable,
that it was easier to replace anything broken than repair it. Maybe
Lewis was right: Anything broken can be fixed. I just hadn't tried
hard enough.
   Suddenly, Lewis was at my knees, one arm around my hips, his
head on my lap. His other arm hugged my legs. The hand behind
me dug into my buttock and slid me forward a few inches tighter
into his hug. My legs felt bound, like a holdup victim tied to a
chair. I reached out and touched his hair. It was thick and shaggy,
the way it had been when we'd first met. Six years ago. I had been
in my first year of my present job, teaching biology at Irvine High
School. In the evening, I had attended a graduate class called Birds
Do It, Bees Do it—But How? at the university. The course examined various sexual methods throughout the animal and insect kingdom. I was at the snack bar during the class break, going from empty
straw holder to empty straw holder searching for a straw for my
7-Up. Finally, I made the fry cook dig one out of the back for me.
When I turned around, Lewis was standing there in his leather
bomber jacket and a Dodgers baseball cap. Under his jacket, he
wore the whitest T-shirt I'd ever seen. Across the chest in small
black letters was the word NOTHING.
   " 'There's gonna be a heartbreak tonight, I know,' " he'd said to
me.
   "I was thinking of something a bit lower," I had replied coldly.
   He'd made a goofy face and laughed his laugh. The laugh made
the heads of several other women who were standing around turn
to look at him. They were smiling. Then I had noticed I was smiling,
too. The bastard.
   "What's with the T-shirt." I'd pointed. "That an existential statement or a personal evaluation of you by your former girlfriends?"

He'd handed me his heavy textbook. "Here, use this. A blunt instrument would be faster. Plus you'll get to actually see the blood." I'd looked at the book's cover, *The Feminist Manifesto: Writings in Feminist Thinking.* I'd handed it back with a snort. "Give me a break. Does carrying this book actually help you pick up women?" "No. But it helps me get through my sociology class." He had hooked a thumb over his shoulder at one of the classrooms. "People Under Pressure: Theories of the Oppressed." He smiled and patted my shoulder. "Relax, O Sister, I feel your social pain."

I had laughed. "You do have a certain crude charm. Like cave paintings." I'd started walking away. "But this ain't gonna happen. Too much social pain. Sorry." I'd waved over my shoulder and hurried back to my classroom.

Two weeks later, after many snack-break chats, we went out. We moved in together seven months later. A year after that, we got married. Four years later, divorced.

My fingers combed through Lewis's hair. I noticed whole patches of gray I hadn't seen before. Suddenly, I was hugging him back. He pulled me to the floor. I went so quickly, so lightly, it was like a moment of flight. I landed on his chest. My thigh rested on his crotch and I felt his hard penis through his jeans.

I should stop now, I realized, stop right now. But I kept thinking, Anything can be fixed. Anything.

Sex was somehow different.

The technique was the same. He did the same things; I did the same things. Hands went to familiar locations without any thought, like old horses returning to the stable. Lewis and I rolled around on the living room carpet, a weary mustard-colored shag that had endured how many renters, how many sweaty bodies depositing body oils and fluids into its ancient fibers.

Lewis's lips were kissing a trail to my crotch. When he got there, his hands scooped under my buttocks and lifted my pelvis up off the carpet for better access. He buried his face in my pubic hairs and licked and nibbled enthusiastically, like a man in a pie-eating contest. That image made me smile, though I hid it from him. It felt good. But not great. Different. Not like when we first lived together, not that rabid passion. But also not like when we'd been married a while, the sex less urgent but somehow an act of confirmation, as if each time we screwed we were hammering another nail into the foundation of our relationship, keeping it strong. Each deposit of semen was like a deposit into a joint account for our retirement. That's how I sometimes visualized our time together; each anniversary excited me because I visualized our marriage as a house in progress and each act of sharing, each passing year, every drive into the mountains or along the coast added another brick to the wall, another bush to the landscape. Sex fit right in. There was a feeling of accomplishment that went along with the physical sensations, as if at the end we might hug and congratulate each other for a job well done.

I didn't feel that now. Not anymore. I felt the physical sensations, the hot flush of my skin as his tongue worked up and down my slickened crevices, flicked across the tip of my swollen clitoris. My breathing became shallow and labored, as if for every breath I inhaled, he sucked it out of me through my vagina and I had to pant to keep my body from deflating. My shoulders burned raw from rubbing against the rough shag carpet. I started to think about my shoulders, each rub scraping dead skin from my body, the dead skin floating like leaves down past the forest of shag to the woven floor of the carpet. And waiting there right now, their heads tilted up, their mouths open like children catching snowflakes on their tongues, were hundreds of thousands of dust mites. The Great Goddess Blue providing manna for my devout followers.

Lewis was inside me now—when had that happened?—and we were rocking back and forth together. His arms were great hydraulic pistons planted on either side of my head. His eyes were closed and his head rolled slightly like Stevie Wonder playing the keyboard. I'd forgotten how large his penis was, thick as my wrist, filling me up so completely, I felt no light or air or sound could squeak in. My womb was now as soundproof as a recording studio.

But my mind drifted back to the dust mites, the color slides of dust mites magnified a thousand times that I would show my students as I lectured, each fact punctuated by their collective *yeechs!* and *oooouuus!* of fear and disgust. Just about everything I taught them lately frightened and disgusted them. The mites looked formidable, like subcompact cars with crab claws. But they were gentle creatures, grazing on the dead human skin that flakes naturally from the body. Lewis's bed would be no haven, I knew; 2 million dust mites were roaming beneath the sheets for the bits of skin that filter down through the fibers. *Yeech!* my students would groan. *Change your sheets,* someone always yelled out. And I would tell them that cleanliness had nothing to do with it. Dust mites lived in nearly every home; they had been discovered sixteen thousand feet high on Mt. Everest, in the Antarctic, under the Pacific Ocean, and even living in fungi on the back of New Guinea weevils.

"Unnnnff," Lewis huffed, his hands grabbing my buttocks again and lifting them.

I heard my own moans, and they were honest moans, because I could feel my orgasm alarm bell warning of an impending meltdown. But at the same time, my moans sounded distant, as if I were overhearing them through a motel wall. My mind could focus only on the mites surrounding us, beneath us, dancing a hallelujah because so much activity meant that much more food for them.

Not all were eating, I realized. Some of them were also having sex, in their peculiar way. The male will have deposited his sealed packet of sperm, like a silicone bag used for breast implants. Then he'd leave. The female would wander over and sit on the bag. Or if she's one of the species with her genital opening on her back, she'd roll backward onto the packet. *No way, Ms. Erhart! You mean they don't even do it?*

I arched my back. Oh God oh yes don't stop don't come . . . I grabbed fistfuls of his long hair, the tips damp from brushing his sweaty shoulders.

But still I saw the dancing mites. Because I knew they weren't just on the ground. Sated with food, they would be defecating their tiny pellets, so microscopically small that they floated. Even now, my shoulders and buttocks were thumping the carpet, stirring the air, disturbing the millions of dust mite turds that swirled around our bodies. And mixed in with those pellets were the hollow, mummified corpses of generation after generation of dead mites flying around us as if they were ascending to heaven.

I climaxed. My vision of the dust mites orbiting me and Lewis faded. Let them dance, I thought hazily. Let them worship the gods of their choice. It's the American way.

Lewis rolled off, pulling the plug of his penis and dragging it across my thigh as he flopped beside me, knocking his head on the coffee table. Semen flushed out my vagina. I didn't have the energy to imagine what the dust mites might do with that.

Lewis kissed my cheek and pulled me close. He smelled my hair and sighed. "This is nice," he said. "I could get used to this again."

"Let's eat," I said.

The waitress shuffled over to the table and flung down our plates. She had a purple birthmark on her cheek that reminded me of the ink stain on my bra. Probably not enough to build a lasting friend-ship on. She was in her mid-twenties, bony arms and legs, no butt. Just a hump of a belly that stuck straight out like a hard hat. She might have been pregnant, I couldn't tell.

"What, goddamn it?" Lewis snapped when the waitress left. "What the fuck's bugging you, Blue? Is this some postcoital depres-sion thing or what?"

I shrugged, stabbed a fork into my Belgian waffle. It skidded across the plate like that grasshopper in class earlier. "I'm just hungry, I guess. I was supposed to go to dinner on this blind date, remember?"

"Well, this is your date and you are having dinner."

I stared at the small dry waffle. The crosshatches reminded me of a turtle lying on its back. What I'd really wanted was a burger, a bacon burger well done, but I was trying to maintain my vegetarian status, though I was erratic at it. The longest I'd ever gone without cheating in the six months since Kyra had talked me into giving it a try was one week. A school week, five days. Anyway, tonight I had been fully prepared to blow my last two solid days of strict vegetarianism to rip through slabs of beef with my blind date. Mitzi had convinced me that vegetarianism wasn't a good thing to spring on a first date. It labeled you a kook and a fanatic in your date's eyes. Men are scared enough of women, she'd warned, better not give them any more excuses. Mitzi. She'd had to have been in on this, conspired with Lewis. It would have been good theater for Lewis and me to get back together again. Happy endings.

I poured watery syrup over my waffle and spread it around with the back of my fork. What had gone wrong tonight? Was it the sex? I replayed our lovemaking in my mind: fast forward, rewind, slow motion, freeze frame. Nothing out of place. All the right moves. Heavy breathing. He came; I came. Everything normal.

Yet I felt even more removed from him now than before we'd had sex. Maybe I'd expected too much, let some Mitzi-like fantasy unspool at the back of my mind: sex, reconciliation, rekindled love, renewed vows. Babies.

But this was all wrong. Rehearsed. Not just the sex, but the conversation, everything he did. Like he knew what was expected of him and he knew how to do those specific duties. As if he'd read somewhere "Women like it when you . . ." But he didn't feel it, didn't know why. Anything can be fixed was Lewis's motto. Did he think our sticky secretions from sex would glue our relationship back together? As simple as a cracked vase.

"Hey, I bring you to a fine coffee shop like Denny's, spring for dinner, I expect you to put out." He grinned, cranking up the charm. "So start talking, baby. And talk like you mean it."

"About what?"

"Anything. Just talk to me, Blue. You know what I'm trying to do here. Help me out. Chat, converse, argue, discuss. You like seeing me drown like this?"

"What did you expect, Lewis? One fuck and everything would be okay?"

"No. I just hoped there'd be something, a sign."

"We have a past, Lewis. We have *history*, for Christ's sake."

He dismissed our history with a wave of his hand. "Water under the bridge."

"Hair under the arm."

He laughed and pointed his pickle at me. "God, you were easy to love, Blue. You know that? Right from the start. No period of adjustment. I'd never felt that before." He frowned. "I'm starting to think I'll never feel that way again about anybody. Everyone else takes too much effort. I have to talk myself into too much."

"Everybody thinks that until it happens. And it always happens. It always happens, Lewis."

He looked me in the eye as if he was interrogating me and had just caught me in a lie. I glanced away.

The waitress drifted by with a coffeepot, emptying the dregs into our cups and shuffling away.

"Are you still in school?" Lewis asked. His voice was suddenly tired, as if he realized the evening was not going to end as he'd hoped.

"I'm still teaching, yes."

"I meant grad school. Your master's degree in God."

I smiled weakly. "Comparative religion."

"How long till you're done?"

I nodded at our sullen waitress scooping tips from a nearby table. "About the same time she becomes CEO of this restaurant chain."

"Bullshit. You're too disciplined for that." He bit into his roast beef sandwich, licked a dollop of mustard from his upper lip. "My guess is you know exactly when you'll be done and have already filled out the paperwork for advancing your salary at school."

"Well, that's a little hairy right now. The school board doesn't see where a degree in comparative religion will help me teach biology any better."

"Frankly, neither do I."

I dunked my sourdough toast in the syrup and bit off a small corner. "Yeah, well, neither do I. That's why I've spoken to the head of the philosophy department at the community college about teaching there."

"Teaching religion? You're getting out of the biology game?"

"With any luck. I finish two more courses this next semester and over the summer write my dissertation, which I've already done some research on. By fall, I could be talking monotheism versus polytheism to bored college students instead of vertebrates versus invertebrates to bored high school students."

Lewis shook his head almost angrily, as if I'd disappointed him.
"You love biology. Microscopes and frog guts give you a hard-on."
"I'm broadening my interests."
"Bullshit. You don't even believe in God."
"I'm not becoming a priest, Lewis, just a teacher."
"Why study something you've already reached a conclusion
about? You'd be too biased to teach."
"If I believed in God, I'd still be biased, wouldn't I?"
He looked down at the table. "More bullshit."
I chewed my toast. I liked the sound it made, the sticky pull of it
against my teeth. I looked up at Lewis, in his eyes for the first
time since we'd made love on his shag carpet. "That coffee you're
drinking, Lewis. You know what's in it?"
"Cream and sugar?"
"History. Prehistory, actually. About one hundred and thirty-five
million years ago, there were these tiny marine creatures that floated
on the water. When they died, their bodies sank to the bottom of
the sea, where, if it was shallow enough, dinosaurs stomped them
to pulp. Eventually, they were covered over with lime mud, where
they continued to dissolve into separate little molecules. The water
that was used in your coffee traveled through these various geological
layers, sweeping along with it some of these microscopic fragments.
When the water is heated, the body fragments come out of suspen-
sion and start to stick together again. It's not forming life, just
patching odds and ends of skeleton bits into misshapen lumps. That's
what you're drinking now, Lewis, the skeletal remains of creatures
one hundred and thirty-five million years old."
Lewis took a big sip of coffee and smacked his lips, grinning.
"You know, they taste just like chicken."
I didn't say anything. I lowered my eyes again, like a mechanical
fortune-teller who's told my quarter's worth of fate and shuts off,
awaiting the next coin. He didn't get it. He didn't see the microscopic swirl of life crowded all around us, pushing us this way and
that way without our even knowing we'd been shoved. Right here
in this restaurant, at this table, in his cup of coffee was the collision
of past, present, and future.

Lewis touched my arm. "Jesus, Blue. What the fuck has happened to you?"

"What do you mean?"

"You're so . . . I don't know. Different."

"I guess I need a change."

"Yeah, well, you're about to get one. Come Saturday."

I sighed. "That's not the kind of change I had in mind."

"Have you spoken with them?"

"The prison officials?"

"No, your parents."

RAISED ON ROBBERY. THE BABY BANDIT. THE CRADLE CROOK. That was the legacy of my parents: headlines and nicknames and a life proving that I wasn't them, that biology wasn't destiny.

"What are you going to do about them, Blue? You can't just ignore them."

"It's worked so far." I pushed my glasses up and shrugged. "I don't know yet. I haven't figured it out."

"I've been contacted by some reporters. They want to interview me on TV. Give my point of view."

I looked up at him. "What'd you tell them?"

"Hell, you know me. I'm just a cop. I can't afford a point of view."

I laughed with relief. I should have known Lewis wouldn't talk. He was noble that way.

A man in a white shirt and a skinny brown tie walked up to the table. "Everything to your satisfaction?" he asked.

I looked him over. He was about my age, but his dark brown hair had a spot of white just over his left ear. Did everybody at this place have a birthmark of some kind?

"Everything's fine," Lewis told him.

"Very good." I nodded, waving my half-eaten toast as proof.

"Cool," the man said, and left.

"Do you think he recognized me?" I asked.

"Why?"

"How often at Denny's does the manager come by and ask you how everything is?"

Lewis twisted around in his seat and scanned the room. The man with the skinny brown tie was stopping at various tables, chatting a few seconds, then moving on. "Well, he's talking to others, so you weren't singled out."

"I'm just becoming a little paranoid."

"You're becoming something," he mumbled, giving me a brooding look.

"Come on, Lewis. Let's not spoil it, okay?"

"Spoil what? There's nothing to spoil here. You want to pretend nothing ever happened between us. That we just met at summer camp but now summer's over. Right?"

"No, I don't. I just don't want to pretend something is going to happen between us."

"Something already has, goddamn it!" He thrust the middle finger of his right hand out at me, right under my nose. "Smell! You recognize that? It's you, your own personal musky scent. Essence of Blue. Just so you can't say nothing happened. We fucked. It happened. We have history, right?"

I pulled back. Lewis withdrew his finger, stuck it in his coffee, and stirred. He pulled it out, steam swirling from his reddened skin, and licked the coffee from his finger. "Yummy."

I stood up. "Try to return to human form by the time I get back. Or leave."

I headed for the rest room. What was I going to do with Lewis? After the divorce, we'd agreed that it would be too difficult to keep seeing each other as friends, at least not for a while. Now I felt I was ready to have that friends-only relationship, but Lewis wanted more. It wasn't like him to behave so angrily.

I navigated around tables, past the cash register, between the two-person booths and the counter. The cigarette smoke here was thick and bitter.

"I think her whole Greta Garbo shtick is just an act," a woman at one of the tables was saying. "I think she likes the publicity."

"I don't think so," the woman sitting across from her said.

"Come on. She's just waiting for the right offers to come in. Publishing, TV, an exercise video. *Gams on the Lam with Blue Erhart.*"

The older woman laughed. "Maybe. But that's not how I read her."

I slowed down, folded my hat brim down around my face. The two women were sitting in a small booth across from the counter. I plopped down on a counter stool and tilted my head spylike for a secret glimpse.

"Look at that whole cop scam, some guy taking her off in hand-cuffs. That's the kind of publicity stunt the studios used to pull back in the forties." The woman was tall and thin and the cigarette she was smoking was tall and thin. Late twenties. Her thick long hair went immediately to the top of my Best Hair list. A portable phone stood facing her on the table. Nice Hair's companion was in her fifties or sixties, her face tan and wrinkled. Nice Hair nursed a cup of coffee and puffed on her cigarette. Her older friend was eating a full meal of salad, garlic bread, and spaghetti.

"Plus," Nice Hair continued, exhaling smoke, "who the hell gives a fuck about her parents anymore?"

"They were famous bank robbers. Kind of a hippie version of Bonnie and Clyde."

"Ancient history. This whole thing should be a question in Trivial Pursuit and nothing more. How come every time some old dinosaur from the sixties has a bowel movement we have to wipe their ass with news footage?"

The older woman laughed. "You're going to be good at this, Billie. I mean that. You've got just the right edge, like a buzz saw. They're bound to offer you one of those '20/20'-type jobs soon."

"Yeah, well, fuck 'em if they don't. I want to be in management, anyway. Let some other poor bitch schlepp around the country trying to stay thin on restaurant shit." She stabbed her cigarette into the ashtray. "I'm going to the bathroom." She stood up, grabbed her phone, and marched past me to the rest room around the corner.

"Help you?" the waitress behind the counter asked me.

I shook my head and got up. I couldn't go to the rest room now and risk being recognized. I started back to my table.

"Hey," the older woman said.

I glanced over. The woman was slicing her spaghetti with a knife, not even looking at me. I didn't say anything.

"You want to go out in public for the next couple of days, Ms. Erhart, wear a better disguise. You're too attractive not to be noticed." She chuckled as she twirled her fork in the spaghetti. "Don't fret. Soon you'll be last month's flavor. Somebody always does something worse than you. That's the way redemption works in this country."

I didn't know what to say. Thank you seemed stupid, not enough and at the same time too much. Thank you for what—for not hounding me right now? So I didn't say anything. I just started back toward the table where Lewis sat.

" 'Scuse me." A finger tapped my shoulder and I turned. The man with the white spot in his hair, the manager.

"Yes?"

He didn't say anything. He just handed me a piece of paper. The logo at the top said Disney Studios.

"I knew it!" I said, pushing the paper back at him, unread.

"Ms. Erhart, if you'll just read it through—"

"No." I pushed past him.

"A hundred thousand dollars," he said quickly. "Think it over."

I paused. A hundred thousand dollars is a lot of fuck-you money.

"Think Bette Midler," he said. "Think Goldie Hawn. Hell, think Julia Roberts."

I looked at the paper. "I'm thinking where does it say a hundred thousand dollars?"

"That will be in our contract. This is just a letter of interest. To start negotiations." He smiled and I could tell that he'd probably gotten away with a lot as a kid because of that smile. Lots of big white teeth all in a row. Like Lewis.

"Is this you?" I asked, pointing at the signature at the bottom of the letter.

"Yes. I'm Russell Poundstone." He held out his hand to shake.

I jammed the paper into his open hand, crumpling it. "The word *common* has two *m*'s. *Weird* is *ei* not *ie*. *Tomorrow* has one *m* and two *r*'s, not the other way around."

He uncrinkled it, scanned the page. "Ah. My secretary's been a bit distracted lately. Her boyfriend tested positive for HIV and—"

"A secretary didn't type this. The typeface is uneven, probably typed on a manual typewriter, which I doubt any secretary at Disney Studios would use."

"What are you, Sherlock Holmes?"

"The correct grammar is: 'Who are you, Sherlock Holmes?' " I blasted him with an arctic stare. "I'm a teacher, that's who I am. Who the fuck are you?"

The boyish grin dissolved and his mouth took on a grim expression. "Okay, you caught me in a little lie, but the truth is, I still want to talk movie rights with you. I tried calling you at home, but no one ever answers the phone."

"Did you leave a message?"

"Would you have returned it?"

I turned to walk away. "I've got to go."

"Just hear me out, okay?" There was a tone in his voice, not the greedy one that distinguished everyone else who'd been calling lately. This was desperation. But then, what kind of judge of character had I turned out to be, roped in by performances from Officer Dave and Mitzi?

"I'll pass," I said.

"You don't have to decide anything now," he said. "Just listen. Five minutes. It will be five minutes that will change your life."

"My life has already changed."

"For the better?" he asked.

I started to say something, then forgot what it was.

Lewis walked up, cop scowl screwed onto his face. "What's going on?"

"Nothing," I said. I took his arm and tried to pull him away.

Lewis didn't budge. He grabbed the letter out of Russell Poundstone's hand and read it. A hard smile spread across his face. He tore up the letter and threw the pieces in Poundstone's face. Customers around us were starting to crane around to look. At least we were around the corner, hidden from the two women reporters.

"Come on, Lewis," I whispered. "Don't cause a scene."

Lewis poked Poundstone in the chest, not with the same finger he'd stirred his coffee with, I was relieved to note. "Usually I tell people I'm not a violent man unless provoked. But I'm not going to lie to you. I am a violent man and I don't even need to be provoked. So you can imagine how I feel when I actually am provoked, when some asshole in a tie the color of a skid mark on his underpants busts in on my dinner." Lewis balled his hands into fists. "Wouldn't you call that provoking?"

Russell Poundstone stared at Lewis. I had seen Lewis go into his intimidating mode before and most of the time people crumbled and fled. But this man, slightly shorter than Lewis's six feet, and probably twenty pounds lighter, didn't budge. He just kept staring at Lewis as if Lewis were a rare and curious species he'd wandered upon at the zoo, something on loan from a tiny Asian country. It was the same look I imagined I had when both my eyes were suctioned against my microscope watching the kidney-shaped pseudomonad bacterium wriggling frantically across the slide.

"Have a good evening," Poundstone said. He smiled at Lewis and me, then left.

I turned and watched him walk to the back of the restaurant. He bent over a booth, picked up a suit jacket that matched his pants, put it on, grabbed a briefcase, tossed down a dollar-bill tip, and walked to the cash register. He paid his bill and left.

"Ballsy son of a bitch," Lewis said.

"Will you take me home now, or do I have to call Mitzi?"

Lewis looked at me long and hard. He reached into his pocket and pulled out a quarter. He flipped it at me. "Call Mitzi."

I let the coin drop to the carpet.

He turned and walked back to the table.

I pulled a quarter out of my purse, grabbed the phone, and started punching in my number. It rang. As expected, the answering machine came on and Kyra's voice said, "If you've exhausted all other options, then go ahead and leave a message." Beep.

"Mitzi, Kyra, pick up. It's me."

The receiver at the other end was immediately snatched up. "Blue?" Kyra said excitedly. "What's going on? Mom's afraid to talk to you. What'd she do *this* time?"

A large hand reached over Blue's shoulder and depressed the switch hook. A signal tone hummed in my ear.

"Okay, I'm done sulking," Lewis said quietly. "I'll take you home."

"You're not going to give me any shit, are you?" I asked.

He raised his right hand in a solemn pledge. "No shit."

I hooked my purse strap over my shoulder and started for the front door. Lewis fell in step behind me. I noticed people staring at me, pointing, whispering to each other behind menus and coffee cups, "Is that her? She the one on TV?"

I wished I was the kind of woman who could grab one of them by the ratted hair and snap their forehead into their fish sticks, mashing it around a little, saying, "Keep your eyes to yourself, asshole!" Now *that* would be cinematic. But I wasn't. I was the kind who just pulled the brim of my hat down and ran for the door.

Lewis was quiet as we walked through the parking lot. He kicked at stones, a piece of glass.

"I thought you said you were done sulking," I said.

"This isn't sulking; this is brooding. Big difference."

"You sure it's not moping."

"Could be a little moping mixed in there. But mostly it's brooding."

I punched his arm playfully and he laughed. "Friends, okay?" I said.

"Sure. Pals, chums, buddies, amigos. Whatever."

I leaned over and kissed his cheek. He looked at me, his body tightening as if debating whether or not he should try once more, just grab me by the shoulders and yank me up to his lips and kiss me hard. Anything can be fixed. I flinched at the thought of having to hurt him all over again. Perhaps he read my flinch, understood it, because his eyes sagged, his body relaxed, and he moved away from me to unlock his car door.

"Don't be too hard on Mitzi," he said. "She meant well. She wants you to be happy."

"She expects a little torturing from me. I can't disappoint her."

Suddenly, Lewis pounded his fist on the car roof and shouted, "Fucking son of a bitch piece of goddamn shit!"

"I'm sorry, Lewis," I said. "I really am."

His face bulged with a sudden rush of blood. He walked over to the fender and pounded it, too. "I'll kill him and his whole fucking family!"

I realized he wasn't upset because of anything I'd done. I hurried around the car to see what he was staring at with such ferocity. The front tire was completely flat.

"What happened?" I asked.

"Your buddy, the phony Hollyweird asshole gave me a flat."

I bent down and examined the tire. "Maybe it just went flat. There's no puncture or anything I can see."

Lewis reached over, grabbed my hand, and turned it palm up. He unscrewed the tire's valve cap and tapped it hard against my skin. A tiny chunk of gravel fell out. "That's how! He screwed it in and the gravel depressed the valve, letting the air out. Jesus, weren't you ever a kid?"

"Not that kind." In fact, ever since the FBI raid, I had never been in trouble with anyone about anything. Always on the honor roll. Student council every year. Teachers would smile with relief when they saw I was in their class.

Lewis continued to stare at the deflated tire, kicking it a few times, then cursing Russell Poundstone and every part of his anatomy. I plucked the keys from his hand and opened the trunk. I lifted the cardboard floor of the trunk, unscrewed the jack and spare tire. I handed the lug wrench to Lewis.

"Loosening nuts," he said, his face still furious. "Isn't that your specialty?"

On the drive home, the tiny spare tire caused the car to sag to the side. Lewis spent the first part of the trip plotting revenge on Russell Poundstone, how he would run him through the police computers, send his name to the FBI, whatever it took to get back at the bastard. After a few minutes, Lewis's anger dissipated and we fell into our old rhythm of chatter about the politics of both the police department and the high school. We caught up on some of the gossip about the couples we used to hang out with a lot when we were married but whom neither of us saw much now. It was the same running-in-place conversations' we used to have toward the end of our marriage, the kind both of us could carry on while thinking about something else entirely. In fact, I was thinking about something else: I was wondering why Russell Poundstone had lied to me about representing Disney. More than that, how had he known to find me at Denny's? And how had he known which car belonged to Lewis?

"You okay about Saturday?" Lewis asked.

"I'm okay."

"If you want, I'll drive out to the prison with you. No problem."

"I'm not going to the prison."

He looked over at me. "Right."

"I mean it, Lewis." He didn't say anything, but I knew he didn't believe me, so I repeated herself. "I really mean it."

He shrugged. "Whatever. It's just not like you."

"This is the new me. A less kind, less gentle me."

Lewis wheeled the wobbly car around the corner onto my cul-de-sac. It was after midnight, but the pack of reporters was still there keeping a vigil on the house. White fog swirled around their feet like a restless dog.

"Jesus," Lewis said. "That's a lot of reporters."

"Yup," I nodded. "More each day."

"Time for Cyclops," Lewis said.

"It won't work. These people are like rabid wolves."

"It'll work. It always works."

"Won't work," I said.

Lewis reached under his seat and pulled out his portable flashing police light and slapped it on the roof of the car. The twirling light caught the reporters' attention. They looked over at the car as Lewis drove slowly toward Mitzi's house. Then they all started running at once, straight for the car.

"Shit," Lewis said, and slammed the brakes.

"Try your gun," I suggested.

Lesson #2

Objects in mirror may
be closer than they appear.

· 6 ·

A heavy morning rain pelted my neighborhood with drops as big as spit, pinning the few remaining reporters inside their cars. I watched them from my bedroom window, hunched over their steering wheels, sipping from steaming thermos bottles, wiping the fog from their windows with their fingers so they could keep a vigilance on my house.

I looked out at the circle of houses surrounding my cul-de-sac. I had always thought of them as an impenetrable wall, a circle of wagons huddled together to keep out the hostiles. I'd felt safe. Now that the invaders had broken through and were camping at my doorstep, the houses reminded me of giant squatting mosquitoes. Each driveway sloping down to the circle of black macadam was their strawlike proboscis siphoning black blood from the rain-slicked street. *Not all mosquitoes suck blood. It's only the female that sucks human and animal blood, which she must do in order to mature her eggs. Generally mosquitoes suck plant nectar.* "At least they suck," *one boy had whispered to a buddy.*

Rapid knocking on my bedroom door.

"Enter at own risk," I said.

Kyra opened the door. She was already clad in her black overalls and red Keds. She pulled out a notepad and hopped on my unmade bed. "You want your phone messages from last night alphabetically or chronologically?"

"Where's your mom?"

"She ducked out already. She's avoiding you. What did she do now?"

"Nothing." I finished buttoning my blouse.

"Oh, come on. It has something to do with that guy last night, Dave the cop."

I stopped buttoning. "You mean Dave the actor pretending to be a cop?"

Kyra snorted. "Sure, like you fell for that crap. You didn't, did you?"

I sighed.

Kyra's face flushed a plum red. "God, I'm sorry, Blue. I thought Mom just told you he was an actor because I figured you were hung up about cops. You know, considering Lewis and all. I didn't think you actually believed her. I thought you were just playing along." Now Kyra's expression shifted from embarrassment to understanding. She smiled triumphantly at solving the equation. "I get it! The cop was probably a pal of Lewis. The whole thing was a setup, right? Lewis was behind it all. And that's why Mom is on the lam this morning. She set you up! Wow!"

"Kyra, how did you know he was a real cop?"

"I don't know. Different things." She shrugged. "Like the way he held the handcuffs by the chain. That's the way cops are trained to hold them just as they're about to cuff somebody. Nobody at Mom's theater is a good-enough actor to research that."

I knew that! How many times had Lewis shown me the proper cuffing technique, grasping by the chain so they can be snapped onto the left wrist with one downward motion, then cuffing the other hand, not letting go of the chain but pulling back so the perp is slightly off balance while you search for weapons. This is all information I had but didn't use. Some scientist.

"You want a ride to school?" I asked as I slipped into my penny loafers.

"Nah, I'll catch the bus. That'll give those jerks outside some good photo opportunities of me. Kyra waiting for the bus. Kyra climbing onto the bus. Kyra waving at them from the back of the bus. The whole spectrum of Kyra, her many faces, her changing moods."

"What's with this publicity-hound bit all of a sudden. A few years ago when the press found out about you being a child genius, you acted like a groundhog. You wore your lunch bag over your head for two weeks. Remember?"

"I'm older now. Besides, I'm just the supporting cast here. You're the star. No pressure on me if the show folds."

"Thanks for that thought. I'm outta here." I snagged my briefcase and marched out, down the stairs, and into the garage. Kyra followed behind me into the garage. I turned to her: "Tell your mom I'll kill her later. See you at school."

Kyra saluted. "Aye, aye."

I walked glumly to my car.

"Hey," Kyra said, her face serious. "Today's Friday. One more day and all this will be over. Right?"

I gave Kyra a smile for her concern. "One more day."

There was no point in telling her that tomorrow is when things would get even worse.

"Clear your desks, slaves of science, because it's that most wonderful time of the year. Quiz time!"

A low thunder of groans rolled through the room.

"It's almost Christmas, Ms. Erhart," Heather McLear whined from the back of the room.

"And this is my present to you," I said cheerfully. "The gift of knowledge. Books on the floor. Hurry it up." I clapped my hands twice in encouragement.

"Couldn't you have at least warned us this time?" Joel Simon complained.

"I could have," I admitted, "but I chose not to. Where's the challenge if I warn you?"

"We don't want to be challenged; we just want to get into college."

"Let's talk about you," Michael Perez said. "I read another article in the paper about your folks getting out tomorrow. What's the deal with them?"

"Nice try, Michael." I pointed at his quiz. "You get an A on this test and you can ask me anything you want."

"Anything?" He grinned, trying to look sexy.

"Anything you can imagine." I patted his shoulder. There was no danger there. A C was the best he'd ever done.

I patrolled the rows, watching them scratch their answers, some in a desperate, itchy scrawl, others in bold, triumphant letters. "You've got fifteen minutes left," I said. "If you don't know an answer, move on to the next and come back to it later."

I heard a sound a faint humming, or a whirring. I checked the thermostat on the wall. The heater was off. I walked over to the heater vents and put my hands over them. Nothing was coming out. Still, I heard *something*.

I resumed my patrolling. Cheating had become so rampant at the school lately that all teachers were asked to be stricter in administering tests.

Where the hell was that sound coming from? I looked down at the floor as if I expected to see some giant insect dragging its armored body across the carpet. That's where the sound was coming from— down there somewhere. I paced up and down the aisles, eyes searching the carpet.

I stopped.

A book.

On top of Joel Simon's schoolbooks was an enormous book, too thick to be assigned reading. I bent over to read the cover. A one-volume encyclopedia. It was as thick as a lunch box.

"That your book, Joel?" I asked.

"Uh-huh." Joel didn't look up from his quiz.

I could see an error on question number three. He'd written *protoplasm* instead of *protozoa*. Joel was an A student, not the kind to make stupid mistakes like that. Joel tapped his pencil on the desk while he studied the next question. He scraped his foot on the desk leg; he coughed. Despite his noises, I could still hear the whirring. I leaned over his shoulder, as if studying his answers. But my foot slid across the carpet, the toe hooking the cover of the book. I flipped it open.

Inside, nested in the heart of the book where the pages had been hacked out, was a mini video camera, the lens aimed at my desk through a circular hole in the top edges. The camera was running. Before I'd asked everyone to clear their desks, he'd had it in front of him, swiveling it around as I'd walked around the room.

"Ms. Erhart," Joel said, looking up, his face white, his eyes red, his lips quivering, "I can explain."

I adjusted my glasses. They had slid down my nose while I paced in front of Principal Coltrane, so that when I turned to face him, I was hit with a fuzzy blur where his face should have been. "Something's got to be done, Pat."

"It will, Blue. It will." He pulled open his deep bottom drawer. "Look."

I walked around the side of his desk and looked down. Inside the drawer were two video cameras and half a dozen mini tape recorders. On top of them was the videotape I had taken from Joel's camera.

"These were taken from kids this morning, some of them not even in your classes. I talked to each one. They're all hoping to tape you and sell it to some network news show or something. It's fucking ghoulish."

I looked over at Pat Coltrane's angry red face. He was a large, jowly man a few years older than I, a lapsed Quaker who never got mad and whom I'd rarely heard swear before. "Jesus, Pat, I'm the one who's supposed to be angry here."

He sighed and leaned back in his big principal's chair. "God, sometimes I hate this job."

"No you don't; you love this job."

"Would you let me bitch and moan in my own way, please?"

"I haven't heard you use language like this since they cut the budget last year." I sat on the sofa across from his desk. "What's next? You going to take out a bong and offer me a hit?"

He laughed. His jowls jiggled and some of the red faded from his skin. "This can't go on, Blue. For your sake as well as the school's."

"It'll all blow over in a couple weeks. Certainly by the time we come back from Christmas vacation. Everything will be straightened out by then."

"You going to see them tomorrow when they get out?"

"What is this, Pat, CNN?"

Stung, Pat recoiled. He looked down at his desk.

"Sorry, Pat. Jesus, I'm sorry." I walked around the desk and hugged his massive shoulders. "I'm a little cranky. I can bring a note from home proving it."

"Blue," Pat Coltrane began, his voice low in an oddly controlled way. "I think you should take some time off for a while. Until this thing settles down."

"It is settled down, Pat. I'm not going to see my parents. I haven't seen them, talked to them, or communicated with them in over ten years. And I'm not going to start now. Once everyone realizes that, I'll be out of the loop. No one will even remember my goofy name."

"I think you underestimate the public's attitude about your folks, Blue. It's going to get bigger, not smaller."

I didn't like the way this conversation was going. I felt as if I was being maneuvered into saying something I didn't want to say. I walked to the door and opened it. I felt better having an escape route. "What my parents did in the past or do in the future has nothing to do with me. I'm not responsible and I'm not going to pay for it any more than I already have."

"Blue." He stood up, motioning for me to come back in the room, sit down.

I kept my hand gripped on the doorknob. "No, Pat. I'm not taking time off. Being here has been my choice and I have done nothing that warrants leaving."

"No one is blaming you."

"Then why punish me?"

"We're talking temporary, Blue. A couple weeks."

I looked at him directly in the eyes. "You want me out of here, Pat, talk to the union representative. Meantime, I've got a free lunch hour and some papers to grade." I walked out, not slamming the door, thereby proving I had the rational upper hand here.

"Blue, come back. It's not that easy. Blue . . ."

After a hearty lunch in the cafeteria, I had fifteen minutes before my next biology class began. I mentally reviewed my lesson as I hurried through the halls to my classroom. Some students said hello to me; others just stared. When I got to my classroom and opened the door, a man with a goatee was sitting at my desk.

"Can I help you?" I said with an edge.

"Oh, Ms. Erhart. Hi, I'm Donald Eisenberg." He offered a thin, nervous hand. He couldn't have been older than twenty-four, though he wore a gold wedding band. His suit was dark but hastily pressed, as if he'd just taken an iron to it that morning. Also, it was too dressy, the suit he'd probably been married in. His goatee was new, not fully grown in. He must have noticed my staring at it. "Do you think I should have shaved it? No one said anything about beards."

I looked down at my desk. He had a copy of the roster for my next class. He also had a copy of the textbook I used. "Who are you?"

"Donald Eisenberg."

"I mean, why are you here?"

His face lit up. "I'm your sub, Ms. Erhart. They just called me a couple hours ago and told me to suit up. I felt like I was getting kicked up to the majors. I've been subbing at elementary schools all semester. Finally, I'll get to teach what I was trained for. I can't wait."

"Can't wait?" I repeated mechanically.

"Blue, for Christ's sake, there you are." Principal Pat Coltrane rushed into the classroom, closing the door behind him. He reached over to the bulletin board next to the door and pried a thumbtack and large photograph from the cork. The photograph was a magnified aphid plunging the syringelike stylet that protruded from its head into the vein of a leaf, sipping its sugary blood. Pat Coltrane quickly thumbed the tack into the door so the photo hung over the small window. No one could look in. He turned and faced Donald Eisenberg. "You mind leaving us alone a few minutes, Donald?"

"Sure, Mr. Coltrane. Okay." Donald started to gather his books and papers from the desk, then thought better of it and scurried out of the room.

"What makes you think you can do this, Pat?" I said. I clutched my briefcase as tightly as I could so he couldn't see how my hands were shaking.

"Blue." He walked closer to me. "I have to think what's best for the students here. That's my job. Right now, I think what's going on with you is a distraction to them. Not to mention the reporters hanging around outside the school grounds and interviewing them for any kind of crap they can think of."

"That's not my fault!"

"I know that. The school board knows that, too. That's why this is a paid vacation. A sabbatical. Christmas vacation starts in another week. Don't come back for the spring term. That gives you the spring and summer off. You could finish up your master's and be back for the fall. I'll even make a special plea about accepting that religion degree on the pay scale."

"I need this now, Pat. I need to stick to what I always do, not change anything, just keep going on. That's important to me."

Pat Coltrane sighed. He squeezed his jowls between his thumb and fingers. "I'm sorry, Blue. You know me; you know I'm on your side. But I've got to do what's best for the kids. That's my job."

"The union won't—"

"I've already spoken to them. This is within the guidelines. They're not going to fight us."

I felt the bones in my body start to disintegrate, felt them crumble into a dry powdery dust and be swept along through the bloodstream like Cocoa Puffs. Without my bones, my body would simply collapse on itself into a lump of flaccid parts. I waited for that to happen. When it didn't, I dragged myself across the room and pulled the photo of the aphid from the door. The tack flew off and I pretended not to notice. Let them step on it, the bastards. But then I stooped, searched the carpet, picked it up, and thumbed it into the bulletin board. I tucked the photo of the aphid under my arm.

"You know, Pat," I said without looking back at him, "it's a good thing this isn't the post office. Or I'd probably come back here with a grenade launcher."

"Don't even joke about stuff like that, Blue. Don't say anything I'd have to report, okay?"

I thought of Lisa Drought, the anorexic I'd reported. "Haven't you heard, Pat? Everything I say or do is worth reporting."

· 7 ·

"You're going to the prison, aren't you?" Mitzi said, following me into the bathroom.

"I don't know yet. My Ouija board isn't answering."

"I'll go with you," Mitzi insisted. "It'll be better that way."

"No, it won't."

"Yes, it will. I'm going with you."

"Shut up, Mitzi." I picked up my toothpaste and squeezed a red line of marine corpses onto the bristles.

"You don't want to go to the prison by yourself, Blue. Not with all those asshole reporters waiting there for you."

"Mitzi, I haven't said I'm going. I'm just getting dressed. That's all I can handle right now."

"Then don't go. Stay home. We'll rent sappy videos and order soggy pizza. We'll make obscene phone calls to Pat Coltrane."

"Pat's okay," I said. I leaned over the sink and began brushing vigorously, ignoring Mitzi. I hoped this would encourage her to leave, but I knew better. Mitzi sat on the toilet lid wearing only the French-cut underpants and a plain white T-shirt she'd slept in. She had one leg up on the seat so she could rest her chin on her knee. Her steel-wool pubic hair stuck out of both sides of the elastic so that her crotch looked like a white airstrip lined on either side with dark shrubbery. I, of course, was wearing my traditional winter sleepwear: men's boxer shorts and a ratty flannel shirt.

"You want, I can do something about those zits," Mitzi offered. I spit and rinsed. "They're not zits. They're a stress rash." I tilted my face and stared at the bumps along my jawline. They seemed pointier today.

"Look, Blue, I'm sorry about the whole Lewis thing. Honest. I just thought, I don't know, that maybe you should talk to him once more. He said he loved you and wanted to get back together. He was so damn convincing. Don't be mad at me. I can't stand it when you're mad at me."

"I'm not mad at you."

"Sure you are. I'm still mad at me and you've got more reason."

I turned on the cold water, cupped one hand under it, and threw the handful of water into Mitzi's face.

"Hey!" Mitzi hollered and rubbed her eyes.

"There, now we're even."

Mitzi pulled the towel from the shower door and patted her face. "Then why won't you let me go with you to the prison?"

"Aaaiiiyyeee!" I ran back into my bedroom, jumped into bed, and pulled the covers over my head so that no part of me was showing. "Does that answer your question?"

Mitzi grabbed a pillow and thumped my butt. "I don't know why I love you. You're such a snot."

"I'm just too damn lovable—that's always been my problem."

"If you change your mind, let me know. I mean it, Blue. I'd be happy to go with you."

"I appreciate it. Really. But I'm fine."

Mitzi yanked the covers off my face. "I can tell."

I got out of bed and pulled on my black overalls, a gift last Christmas from Kyra. While I was tying my hiking boots, I heard loud voices coming from outside, like an argument. I stood up and went to the window, peeking out between the blinds. I squinted at the two men standing in the street below. I recognized the man in denim, who seemed to be wearing the same outfit he'd worn since Thursday night. The man he was arguing with had his back to me;

I didn't recognize the clothing, beige chinos and a black polo shirt. His hands were sheathed in his back pockets while he listened to the denim guy rant angrily. Sitting on the curb was the video cameraman who'd filmed my legs the other day. He was wearing fresh clothing. He cradled the video camera in his lap and stared off at the nearby Saddleback Mountains. Yesterday's rain had produced a lot of snow up in the mountains. He had the look of a man who wanted to go skiing.

There were no other reporters around. As I'd predicted, they'd all gone out to the prison for my parents' release. Although my mother had served in Pleasanton Penitentiary, a women's prison up north, she had been driven down to the Terminal Island Penitentiary to be released with my father to make things easier for the press. The governor liked accommodating the press.

I was about to turn away from the window when I suddenly saw Kyra step out from between the two men, where she'd been hidden from my view. Kyra was clutching a huge zucchini in her hand. The man in denim bent over and shouted in Kyra's face. He grabbed the zucchini and pointed it at his tail pipe. Kyra backed away. Then the other guy, the one whose face I couldn't see, snatched the zucchini from the man in denim and bit off half the zucchini in one gulp. The man in denim went nuts, jumping around, hollering. The laminated press pass clipped to his jacket pocket flapped up and down, reflecting sunlight like a sheriff's badge. The other man didn't flinch; he just bit off more zucchini, chewed, and swallowed. Kyra laughed and clapped her hands.

The zucchini man nodded his head at Kyra and reluctantly she turned away and came back to the house. I heard the front door open and close downstairs. Outside, the man in denim continued to yell, jabbing his finger in the zucchini man's face. Finally, the zucchini man walked over to the man in denim's blue Toyota truck and stood facing the driver's door with legs askance. The man in denim started yelling even more, so loudly that I could hear him even through the closed window.

"You son of a bitch!" He turned to the video cameraman. "Damn it, Chomsky, get this fucker on film so I can sue his motherfucking ass!"

Chomsky sighed, stood up, shouldered the camera, and started filming the zucchini man urinating on the truck's door.

I quietly slipped my hands under the blinds and eased open the window so I could hear more.

"You getting this, Chomsky?"

"I'm getting it." Chomsky squatted next to the man and filmed.

Suddenly, the man turned and sprayed a stream of urine at the man in denim, splashing the knees of his blue jeans. I recognized the sprayer's face immediately: the phony Denny's manager who'd let the air out of Lewis's tires.

"You getting this, Chomsky?" Russell Poundstone asked.

"Getting it," Chomsky said, following the action.

"Goddamn it!" The man in denim backed away ten feet, staring at the dark wet patch on his pants. "I'm going to run this on TV, man! I'm going to ruin you!"

"That would bother me a whole lot more," Russell Poundstone said, zipping his pants, "if you knew my name."

"I'm turning a copy of this tape into the cops. They'll find you, asshole. This is indecent exposure. You're going to fucking *jail*, man. You whip it out in there and someone will bite it the fuck off!"

Russell Poundstone walked over to the curb and sat down.

The man in denim pinched the thighs of his wet jeans and plucked them away from his skin. His face was scrunched into an expression of disgust. He was muttering to himself; I couldn't make out the words. Finally, he turned to Chomsky and shouted, "Get in the truck. We'll stop by the hotel to change and head out to the prison. There's nothing going on here, anyway."

Chomsky nodded and climbed into the truck.

I hurried downstairs and found Kyra in the kitchen eating a bowl of cereal. "What the hell were you doing out there?"

"Hey, you're wearing your overalls. We're twins."

"What happened?"

Kyra shrugged. "I jammed a zucchini in that guy's tail pipe, but he caught me. It would have worked better Thursday night when it was dark and there were more of them."

"What's with the other guy?"

Kyra perked up. "Did you see? Man, he ate the zucchini straight from the tail pipe. He didn't wipe it off or anything. Three bites and the evidence was gone. That was so cool."

"What's he doing out there?"

"I don't know. He didn't say anything to me. That butthead in denim had hold of my arm and was shaking me, threatening to call the cops and stuff. Then the other guy walks up and that's that. Like Clint Eastwood or something. Did you see the part where he pissed on the guy's pants?"

"I saw." I walked to the front door and opened it. Russell Poundstone still sat on the curb across the street. He was unwrapping a Tootsie Roll Pop. When he was done, he stuck the Pop in his mouth and neatly folded the wrapper and tucked it into his pocket.

He looked up and saw me staring at him. He took another Tootsie Roll Pop out of his pocket and held it up like the Statue of Liberty torch. "Want one?"

"Come here," I said.

He did, walking quickly, hungrily, like a man going to claim his prize.

"Hi," he said. The side of his cheek chipmunked out in the shape of his Pop; the white paper handle poked out between his lips. He held out the wrapped Pop to me. "You look like a candy person to me."

"I'm not."

He shrugged. "I used to love these when I was a kid. Then Telly Savalas started sucking them every week on 'Kojak' and I kinda lost interest. I mean, what did I have in common with some fat bald guy in a suit?"

"Who are you?" I asked flatly. "No bullshit."

"Russell Poundstone." He reached into his pocket and pulled out a business card, which I refused to take.

"I don't trust the printed word, Mr. Poundstone. Not in your hands. Just tell me what you want. Skip past whatever lies you've concocted, whatever flattery you think is going to work because it's worked on others in the past. Just get to it. Bottom line."

"Film rights to your life."

"You've got the wrong life. It's my parents who've done all the exciting stuff. They're the famous bank robbers."

Russell Poundstone furrowed his eyebrows in what I was certain was his well-practiced expression of concern. "Look, Ms. Erhart, I know I'm not the only guy after your story. So you know that lots of people think it's more interesting to understand the effect having parents like yours had on you than just to exploit the usual bank robbery clichés."

I stared at him while he spoke. His face was an odd mix of mismatched parts. The eyes were narrow and seemed almost Asian, but the nose was wide and long and crooked in a Slavic way. The hair was an unruly thicket of brown curls. The chin jutted slightly with a deep cleft. He looked like one of those character actors who, with a minor adjustment of makeup, could play any nationality, the kind of actor you don't recognize from film to film. The effect was not unpleasant.

"You mentioned a hundred thousand dollars before," I said. "Do you have it yet?"

"I have access to it."

"That means you don't have it."

"I can get it."

"Come back when you've got it." I started to close the door. That should keep him busy for a while.

"Okay, okay," he hurriedly said. "But I need you to sign a preliminary agreement, sort of a letter of intent. Once you've done that, I can have the money here the same day."

I smiled. "You see, Mr. Poundstone, if you were a legitimate producer with the backing of a major studio, you'd have the money available now. I can get on the phone and call half a dozen places and they'd bring the cash right over. That means I don't need you, right?"

"It depends. Do you want your story told right, with the depth and honesty of major writers, directors, and actors? Or do you want Jaclyn Smith playing you in a short skirt and push-up bra during sweeps week?"

"It's hard to have a conversation about artistic integrity with a man who just committed indecent exposure in my neighborhood." He laughed. "There was nothing indecent about it. I didn't do anything sexual. I took a leak. I'll bet there's not a kid around here who hasn't seen a man or boy or dog taking a piss. No one was traumatized."

I thought back for a moment and realized that, in fact, I had not even looked at his penis itself because I was so caught up in what he was doing. "That's not the point," I said.

"Sure it is. Indecent implies some sexual perversion. There was none. You watched the whole thing and I'll bet you don't even know if I'm circumcised or not. Well, do you?"

I tried hard to picture him as he'd turned, but my eyes had followed the stream of urine hosing the man in denim's legs. Still, most men were circumcised. Involuntarily, my eyes flicked down to his crotch. I forced them to look him in the eyes. "Circumcised."

"Wrong."

"Prove it."

"What?"

"Prove it. I think you're lying."

"Okay. Here's the deal. I take it out and prove you wrong, you promise to sign the rights to your life story over to me. Fair?"

"This isn't about a deal; it's about your integrity. Prove your integrity first."

"No, it's about *your* integrity. You claim to have seen my naked penis waving in the breeze. I say you're lying and I can prove it. Do you want me to?"

Kyra walked up with a glass of orange juice in her hand. "Hey, guys. What's up?"

"Go," I said.

She looked back and forth between Russell Poundstone and me. "I'm gone." She went up the stairs whistling something by Mozart.

I waited until I heard Kyra's bedroom door close. Then I turned back to Russell Poundstone and opened my mouth to say something.

"You're going, aren't you?" he interrupted.

"What?"

"To the prison. You're going, after all. I can tell."

"No."

"Look, I can drive you." He pointed across the street at a dented, battered junk heap of a car. "None of the reporters will be looking for my car."

"No one would look for that car."

"I'm serious. No strings attached, no deals. Just a straight offer to drive you."

"Thanks, but I'm not going."

"Look, you change your mind . . ." He scribbled on the back of his business card. "You can reach me at this number. My motel room. I'll wait there just in case."

"I'm not going," I said, and closed the door in his face without taking his card.

I cried.

I sat on the edge of my bed with my favorite pillow on my lap and sobbed into it. My ears were clogged from crying so hard and my eyes felt raw and sticky. The feeling of intense depression had hit with surprising suddenness, as if someone had jumped out from behind the door and swung a baseball bat into my stomach. Nothing made sense. Even the arrangement of my own limbs seemed stupid and arbitrary. I stared at my fingers and wondered, Why five? Why not four or six? Why this big heavy head on such a small scrawny neck? Why a silly crease in my buttocks and another one at my crotch?

I went to my bathroom and splashed some water on my face. Russell Poundstone had wanted to buy my story. Well, *this* is my story, Russ baby. This is it. Not really the stuff of sweeps week. And, by the way, I *like* Jaclyn Smith.

I put my glasses back on. I walked around my room looking for something but halfway through the search forgot what it was I was looking for. I sat back on the bed and stared out the window. This morning, I'd made up my mind to drive over to Terminal Island to watch my parents be released from prison after nineteen years. Now that seemed like a big mistake.

I walked down the hallway to Mitzi's room and knocked on the door. "Hey, it's me."

"Blue?"

"Yes."

"Come on in."

I entered. The bedroom was like Russell Poundstone's face, a hodgepodge of mismatched furniture from various time periods. Brass bed with Early American nightstands. On the nightstands were supermodern black halogen lamps with lots of pulleys and black springs. Above the bed was a poster from *Gone With the Wind*, except a cutout photo of Mitzi's face was pasted over Vivian Leigh's. A contemporary Danish dresser stood against the wall.

"I'm in here," Mitzi called from the bathroom.

I went in and sat on the toilet lid. "You said we could talk."

"Talk. I'm listening." Mitzi was nearly submerged in her bubble bath. Her head was the only part of her body visible. Her hair was whipped high on top of her head like an ice cream cone and secured with a banana clip. Her head was tilted back on an inflated plastic pillow and her eyes were closed.

"I don't know," I began. "I'm feeling a little down."

"That's to be expected." Mitzi sat up, turned on the hot water at a slow but noisy stream, and lay back again, shutting her eyes.

"I'm just so goddamned depressed suddenly. Like I don't have any kind of a life or purpose or friends."

"Thanks a lot."

"I didn't say it was rational thinking. It's just how I feel. Like the best part of my life is over and I never really got to live it. Or something. I don't know what I mean."

Mitzi's upper lip was beaded with sweat. Her mouth kept opening as if she was terribly thirsty. "Maybe seeing your folks will make you feel better, give you a sense of family."

"I don't want to be part of that family."

"I've got news, Blue—nobody wants to be part of their family. Wait till my mother flies out for one of her endless visits. You had the best possible situation, your parents in jail. You could visit them, but they couldn't visit you and screw with your life. Boy, if only my mom would rob a fucking bank. At least attempt an assassination."

I sighed. This wasn't going anywhere. Maybe I should just drive there and get it over with. If I didn't, they were bound to come by here one day. They'd want to rehash the whole thing again, the reason I'd stopped visiting them ten years ago. I couldn't bear the thought of them in my life again, having any kind of cause-and-effect influence. They'd had enough power over my life. I was about to say all that to Mitzi when I noticed an odd twitching on Mitzi's lips. The hot water was still running even though the water was nearly to the brim of the tub.

"Mitzi, the water."

"Hmmm."

"Are you okay? Mitzi?"

"Just a sec . . ." she said a little breathlessly.

I jumped up. "Goddamn it, Mitzi!"

Mitzi opened her eyes. "What?"

"You're masturbating."

"I was almost done."

"Jesus. I'm trying to discuss something important with you."

"I was listening." She lifted her right hand out of the water. A round red rubber device was attached to her hand like a scalp massager. She rinsed it under the water.

"A vibrator. You were using a vibrator this whole time?"

"It's easier for me that way." She shook the water off and set it on the edge of the tub. It squatted there like a crab. "So, go on. You were saying?"

"Nothing! Fuck!"

"Don't pout, for God's sake. I was already in the middle of a good one when you walked in here. I just wanted to finish. What's the big deal?" Mitzi stood up and grabbed a towel.

I looked at my friend. Mitzi was half black and half Puerto Rican, but her skin was so light that she looked neither. Her body was fuller everywhere than mine, which added to her voluptuous stage presence. The only flaw was the white scar across her abdomen from the C-section that had produced Kyra.

"You should try it," Mitzi said. "You want, you can borrow one of mine. Maybe you wouldn't feel so depressed." With her toes, she nudged the crabshaped vibrator toward me. "Go ahead. It's waterproof."

"If I wanted a vibrator, I'd buy one of my own."

"No you wouldn't. You're too chicken to walk into a store and ask for one. And you wouldn't send away for one because you'd be afraid your name would go on some master list of sex perverts. I know you."

This was all true, of course.

"Go ahead and use it. I have three others. Don't worry, I wash them after each use. Our pubic hairs won't get mixed up."

I laughed. "With the size of your bush, I'm surprised you don't shed like a Pomeranian."

Mitzi laughed, too. She wrapped the towel around her chest and knelt next to me, hugging my shoulders. "I can be ready in five minutes, Blue. Take us thirty minutes to drive there. Let's get it over with."

I shook my head and stood up. "I think I'll just go for a drive. If I wind up there, then I do. If not, well, then I don't."

· 8 ·

I climbed into my car and drove straight for the snow-capped mountains, the opposite direction from the prison. Taking my cue from the wistful expression on Chomsky the cameraman's face, I decided some skiing up in Big Bear would take my mind off of everything. I pulled into a gas station to fill the tank and get a Jumbo Gulp diet Coke.

"I'm going up to Big Bear," I told the cashier, a teenage boy with a nasty black mole in his eyebrow. "Do I need chains?"

"I haven't heard anything."

"How's the snow?"

He shrugged. "I don't know. I'm not really into skiing." He pointed down at his feet. "Bad ankles."

I signed my credit-card receipt and started walking away.

He kept talking. "Got 'em crunched playing varsity basketball. First game of the season and some clumsy jerk from Corona falls on them. Snap, crackle, pop and I'm out of the game forever. Forever." He shook his head and started muttering to himself. "Fuck it, who cares, right? It's just a game. A stupid game."

"Sorry," I said. I wondered if I should say something about his mole, suggest a skin doctor or something. It was black and crusty and evil-looking. But I said nothing and walked out. The boy's mole and twisted ankles brought back my depression and suddenly I felt smothered. I couldn't catch my breath. Stepping out of the cashier's office, I felt as if I'd dropped straight down into a dark icy lake and sunk right to the bottom. I stood still and tried to take deep breaths, recapture the bird. But the pressure against my chest was enormous. Small shallow breaths were all I could manage. I was gasping like an asthmatic. I staggered slightly, and a businessman pumping gas into his Land Rover gave me a disapproving glare. Did he think I was drunk? That angered me and I took a step toward him to straighten him out, but my legs buckled. I reached out and caught myself on the nearest stationary object, the pay phone.

"Damn," I said, huffing. A sudden spray of acidic vomit shot up my throat and burned my tongue. My eyes watered from the sour taste. I bent over, waiting for more to bubble up, hoping it would come now before I got back in the car, because no way was I going to drive all the way up to Big Bear with the smell of puke on my upholstery, my head hanging out the window like a dog while I steered.

I leaned my forehead against the metal pay phone, hoping for cool relief. But the metal was hot from the sun and burned my forehead like a branding iron. The shock of pain seemed to settle my stomach, though, and soon I was breathing better.

I fished a quarter from my purse and thumbed it into the slot and punched the numbers. The phone machine came on. "Mitzi, it's me. Pick up—it's important."

"Blue?" Mitzi said, breathless. "Where are you?"

"Gas station. Look, I need the Dave guy's phone number. Lewis's cop friend."

"What for?" Her voice was cautious with concern.

"None of your business."

"I'm your friend. I get to act protective."

"Okay," I said. "I thought I'd ambush him outside his home. Splash some gasoline on him. Strike a match for women everywhere. You got a problem with that?"

"Nope. Hang on." There was a brief pause. When she returned, she gave me the number. "Are you going to the prison or what?"

"Bye." I hung up and made another call. "Dave? It's Blue Erhart, your most recent kidnap victim. I want Russell Poundstone's phone number."

"Who?"

I sighed impatiently. "Don't fuck with me, okay? The only way Poundstone could have run into Lewis and me the other night at Denny's was if he'd followed us to the restaurant. To do that, he would have had to have followed us from Lewis's apartment. And the only person who knew where I'd be, and who would sell us out, was you. Which means Poundstone paid you something for the information. Before you open your mouth and say something to piss me off further, if I hang up this phone and I don't have what I want, I'm calling Lewis next and telling him my theory. Then you can deny everything to him."

There was a long pause. I could hear Officer Dave sucking a long drag from a cigarette, though the length of the drag made me think more of a joint. He exhaled with a chuckle. "You should've been a cop, Blue."

"Just give me the number, Dave."

"I don't have the number. He's staying at the Fairview Motel on Newport Boulevard. That's all I know."

I hung up without a word. I hoisted the giant phone book and paged through the Yellow Pages. I found the number, dialed, asked for Russell Poundstone's room.

"Hello?" he said.

I hesitated. Now that I had him on the phone, I wasn't sure I could go through with it.

"Hello?" he repeated.

I listened to him breathe.

"Blue?" he said.

"Yes."

"You found me."

"It wasn't hard."

"I didn't want it to be hard. I tried to give you my number, remember?"

"Shut up," I said. "I hate it when you talk."

There was a long pause. The silence went on for a minute, maybe two. He was patient, I had to give him that.

"I don't know why I called you," I said. "Sorry." I started to hang up.

"You're going, aren't you? To the prison."

Pause. "I don't know. I haven't decided."

"But you want to go. You're thinking about it." He cleared his throat. "You want company?"

I felt tears squeezing from the corners of my eyes. I'd have to make this quick before I started crying. "Here's the deal, Poundstone. I'm going. You can come along if you do all the driving, help me sneak in, and never, never, never fucking once talk about movie rights to my life. That's the deal. One-time offer. You in or out?"

"In."

"I'll pick you up in fifteen minutes. Be waiting outside."

". . . a new life. A whole new life. Not just the money. Money's money, you know? This will mean a new attitude toward you. A new respect . . ."

His right eye had a thin black line across the pupil, like a small splinter too deep to tweezer out. The kind that had to be dug out with a sewing needle roasted over a match and swabbed with peroxide. I sat next to him in the car and imagined performing that operation on him with glee. He hadn't stopped talking since he'd gotten into the car.

"Within a week of you signing, I'd have a commitment from a name, I guarantee. Not just a name, a huge name. Who would you like to play you? Think big. Geena Davis? Meryl Streep? Annette Bening? They're older than you, but they have box-office pull. Once one of them is attached to the project, we'll have a development deal at a studio in two days . . . ."

I watched his hands on the steering wheel. Large hands with knuckles the size of the hamster skulls back in my lab. He drove at a steady pace, letting cars pass him, never paying attention to the irate motorists who flipped him off or honked or gunned their engines as they rocketed by. He just continued his cheerful prattling.

"I know you're worried about exploitation. You're thinking, I don't want to go into some theater and see Heather Locklear up there shaking her ass in cutoffs pretending to be me. That's not going to happen. I promise."

I couldn't stand it any longer. I reached over and blasted the horn for a good five seconds until he wrestled my hand away. Drivers from other cars were staring in at us. "Our deal was that you would not talk about movie rights, remember? Now, why would I sign a contract with someone who breaks his word one hour after he gives it?"

He nodded thoughtfully. "True. True. That's a good point. But I'm not breaking my word, not really. I'm expanding on it, modifying it a little. I'm adding words to my word, which doesn't change the original intent of my word, only broadens the meaning of my word."

"In other words, you're a liar."

He laughed. "That pretty much sums it up, yes."

"You admit it, then?"

"That's part of my charm, don't you think? Unexpected bursts of honesty."

I sipped what was left of my watery diet Coke. The tang of the carbonation against my tongue sent me drifting again. What was I drinking really, just carbon dioxide dissolved in water? Carbon dioxide attacks the nerves in the tongue, creating pain and causing a flow of saliva. That's what people like. Biologically, you can get the same reaction by biting down on your tongue. I rolled down the window and spit the diet Coke out. It splashed onto the rear door of Russell's car. I smiled. "Answer a question, will you? And make this one of your unexpected bursts of honesty."

"I'll try."

"Why'd you let the air out of Lewis's tire? Back at the restaurant that night. I mean, you did do it, right?"

"Boy, this is the kind of situation where I wish I still smoked. I think my answer would seem a lot cooler if it was punctuated by a steady stream of smoke."

"Didn't that strike you as a weaselly kind of thing to do? Sneak out into the parking lot and let the air out of a tire."

"I prefer chicken to weasel." He smiled.

I didn't respond to his smile. I stared at him and waited.

His smile faded and his face hardened a little. "I don't have any great answer. Nothing profound. He pissed me off, that's all. I'm very childish about some things. I carry a grudge the way some people carry snapshots of their family. He insulted me; I got even. Case closed."

"Why didn't you just say something in the restaurant? I mean, you were so calm then."

Russell laughed. "Are you kidding? Because he could hurt me. He's a cop. I've kind of let myself go since third grade."

I looked at his body under the polo shirt and jeans. His arms were solid, no gut.

"Besides, I don't like bullies. Your husband is a bully."

It was the first time I had ever heard that word in connection with Lewis. I was about to protest, to rise to his defense. But the more I thought about it, the less I knew what exactly I would say.

Russell sped up the car, slipping beside a huge moving van that blocked the harsh sun that had been pounding us for the last ten miles. He stayed beside the truck, keeping the car in the shade. The cool shade relaxed me. I leaned my head back against the seat. He looked over at me, studying me for a few seconds with a curious look on his face. "Why'd you call me?"

"I thought it would be easier to dodge the other reporters if I was with you. No one expects me to be with one of their own, not after the way I've been ignoring them for the past few days."

"I'm not one of them."

"Sure you are. You're a leech who wants to suck my life to enrich your own."

Russell smiled. "You make that sound like a bad thing."

"Don't try to charm me, okay? Eating that zucchini straight from the tail pipe may have impressed Kyra, but not me."

"Me, neither. I spent the last half hour brushing my teeth and rinsing with Listerine. Yeech." He looked over at me. "What would impress you?"

"Maybe eating shit. Maybe that."

"I thought that's what I have been doing since you picked me up."

I shook my head. "I'll bet you have a nickname. Guys like you always have a nickname."

"What do you mean, guys like me?"

"Oh, come on. You know what kind of guy you are. Slick.

Selfish. Ambitious. You probably know a million jokes, never forget a punch line."

The moving van sped up and started crossing lanes to exit the freeway. The sun was relentlessly bright and there were no visible reminders outside of yesterday's heavy rain. The weather in Southern California was like the state, enthusiastic but patternless. Whatever the weather was for that day, rain or sun, it gave a 100 percent, as if it feared this was the last day of weather, ever.

Sweat quilted my skin. Russell reached for the air conditioner, but I stopped him with my hand. "Ozone," I said, pointing up.

"Sweat zone," he said, plucking his shirt sleeve from under his arm.

"Don't be a baby. Sweat is healthy."

"You haven't seen me sweat. It's not pretty."

"You have an unhealthy attitude about your body," I said. "Sweat is very natural. In Shakespeare's time, a woman would clamp a peeled apple under her arm until the apple became saturated with her odor. Then she'd give it to her loved one to inhale. It was called a 'love apple.' "

He laughed. "Love apple?"

"Baudelaire thought a person's soul resided in the scent of their sweat. Napoleon once wrote to Josephine: 'I will be arriving in Paris tomorrow evening. Don't wash.' "

He looked over at me. "You're scary, you know that?"

Another long silence fermented between us. I leaned forward and let the vent air fan my face, thought it was warm and smelled dank.

"Rush," he finally said.

"What?"

"That's my nickname. Rush. You know, short for Russell."

"Russ is short for Russell. Why do they call you Rush? Or did you make it up yourself?"

"No, the name I wanted to be called was Vito."

I made a face. "Vito?"

"Yeah. When I was like ten, I read this book about the Mafia. Vito Genovese was the big Mafia leader back in the fifties. I thought that would be cool, to have a bunch of the meanest men in the world afraid of you, willing to do anything you told them. Besides, it beat my first nickname. 'Poundcake.' "

I laughed. "Now that I like."

"You would. Anyway, a couple fights at the monkey bars and I lost Poundcake by the fifth grade. I played some basketball in high school. I was king of the fast break. I could run the entire length of the court faster than anyone and be open for the shot. Problem was, I was a lousy shot. They'd throw a full-court pass. I'd be standing alone under the basket; I'd shoot. Miss. I'd shoot again. Miss. By now, the other team was all around me and it would be a free-for-all." He smiled, as if thinking of something he wasn't going to share. "Anyway, that's why I'm called Rush."

"I prefer Poundcake."

"Yeah? Meet me at the monkey bars after school and I'll change your mind."

"Okay, Poundcake." I laughed again.

"Hey, anybody named Blue Erhart is living in a glass house, babe. Chucking stones could be hazardous."

"Toss 'em, Poundcake. I can take it."

"Okay. The part I read about in *Newsweek*. Your folks loved the blues, Billie Holliday, I think."

I made a buzzer sound. "Wrong-o. But thanks for playing."

"What? That's what *Newsweek* said."

"*Newsweek*, as usual, is wrong. Believe me, you're a lot less in awe of journalism once you've been written about a few times and see how much is inaccurate. My parents didn't like blues. Well, they liked blues, but that's not how they named me. I was born in the back of a van, all very Age of Aquarius. The inside was painted blue. Hence the name. Very bland story, which is probably why *Newsweek* made up a better one."

"I was named after a child my mom had miscarried before me. They'd already had the name picked out which they'd painted the name on the crib and stuff, so . . ." He shrugged. "I got the dead kid's hand-me-down name."

"Tell it to *Newsweek*, you won't recognize yourself."

"What about the last name? Erhart. Your folks are named Henderson."

"I changed my name when I was fifteen. I didn't want people to remember Blue Henderson as the daughter of the most notorious outlaw couple in the sixties. My grandparents, who I lived with after my folks went to jail, figured I could be whoever I wanted. They were pretty cool. Anyway, I'd just done a book report in school about Amelia Earhart and she was my new hero. She could fly away from all of her problems. My problem was, I used to spell the way you shot basketballs. I accidentally left out the *a* and ended up with the way it is now."

"You kept the Blue, though."

"Grandpa insisted I honor my folks in some way. Besides, all my friends already knew me as Blue. I was used to it."

Russell started edging the car over to the far-right lane.

"What are you doing?" I asked, suddenly feeling panicky.

"Getting off the freeway, Amelia. We're here. Terminal Island Federal Penitentiary."

We swooped around the off ramp. My heart felt impaled on a rib. "We should turn around. This is a mistake."

"Don't be a baby," Rush said. "Fear is healthy. Natural." He reached over and switched on the air conditioning. "This might help."

It did. The cool air soothed me. I'd happily trade a few more inches of ozone just to get through the next few minutes.

The prison loomed ahead. Rush patted my arm. "It's reunion time. A blast from your past."

·9·

I studied the sprawling beige prison as we drove toward it. Everything looked the same as I'd remembered from my last visit, almost ten years ago. Like a Foreign Legion desert outpost—a bunch of boxy buildings, a lot of concrete, and tall metal fences topped with razor wire.

"Home sweet home," Rush said breezily, but I could tell he was affected by the sight. Everyone always was. Everyone trembled a little.

On my last visit—the final visit, as it turned out—I had driven up from college with my new boyfriend, Tim, a bearded performance artist who'd earned some notoriety around campus for once having defecated onstage into a crystal salad bowl filled with Chanel No. 5. The perfume had been red from the food dye he'd stirred in, so it looked like oily blood. Far above in the lighting booth, I had watched fascinated while Tim, his pants bunched around his ankles, had lowered his naked bony butt so far that when his waste plopped into the bowl, it splashed the red perfume up onto his bare buttocks like a wound. The audience was then invited to line up at the bottom of the stage and file past, sniffing the bowl, which about half of them actually did. The performance piece was originally called "Shit Is Shit No Matter How It Smells," but he changed it to "Blood Simple" so that newspapers would carry announcements of his performances. That afternoon over spring break when I had driven us both up to the prison gates, Tim had broken out into a heavy sweat and began to complain of stomach cramps. His clothes were soaked and I could smell the dank odor of fear in the car. I thought he was going to pass out. When I'd asked him if he was all right, he'd nodded and said, "My asshole hurts just looking at the place." Then he'd laughed, "It's a guy thing."

Perhaps that's what Rush was thinking, too—the guy thing.

I wasn't too sympathetic. This seemed to be the only place where guys had to worry about rape, and their chances of going there weren't that great.

Outside the main gates, a few hundred people were crowded together in a festive mood. Some waved handmade signs that said things like GIVE 'EM HELL, HARRY. My father, Harold, hated to be called Harry. My mother used to call him Harry when she was mad at him. She would purposely adopt a nasally Jewish American princess tone and mimic the Long Island accent of her own mother. "Whatever you say, Harrrrrrry. You should live so long, Harrrrryyyy." That always sent him slamming out of whatever remote apartment we were renting while on the run and into the garage to work on what Mom always referred to as the GAC (getaway car). Other signs said CONGRATULATIONS ON YOUR WITHDRAWAL, WE'RE BANKING ON YOU, and other stupid comments that made me want to run the morons over.

"Doesn't anybody have a job anymore?" I said, shaking my head at the crowd.

"Like it or not, Blue, your folks are pop-culture icons. Heroes to a lot of people. More important, marketable heroes. Hell, they could run for office, endorse breakfast cereals."

I looked over at him with a sharp expression. "They were bank robbers, Poundcake. Criminals. Period."

"So? Heroes are hard to come by these days. Anyway, it's not what they did but how they did it. The style or something. I don't know. I was a kid then, too. I can only go by what I read. But look at all these people. They must see something in your parents."

I scanned the crowd. "Ex-hippies who want to recapture the good old days when they ate macrobiotic dirt and screwed themselves dizzy. Kinda pathetic, don't you think?"

He didn't say anything and I settled into a quiet stew. I didn't like how I was acting right now, snotty and petulant. But I didn't seem to be able to stop myself. Any more than I could stop the headache that was now gnawing at the corners of my eyes. I could feel tiny teeth biting into the eyeballs. I rummaged through my purse for an Advil but came up empty.

Rush took a deep breath. "Ready to enter the belly of the beast?"

"Let's park out here."

"They'll let you inside the gates, you know. Your name's going to be on their list."

"I'd rather watch from out here. With the rest of their adoring public."

"Your folks probably won't see you out here, not with this crowd."

"That's the idea."

Rush shrugged. He cruised the rows of awkwardly parked cars in the makeshift lot. Finally, he ended up wedging the car tightly between a BMW and a pickup truck. He'd had to nudge both of their bumpers to squeeze it in.

"Smooth," I said, getting out of the car. My anxiety was churning into anger.

"I worked as a parking valet during law school. I've dented the best of them."

"You're a lawyer?"

He looked away with an embarrassed expression. "Kinda."

"Kinda? How can you be kinda a lawyer? Is that like kinda pregnant? Kinda perverted?"

Rush turned and started walking toward the crowd. "You sure you'll be able to see them through all this activity? We can get closer."

"You're dodging my question, Poundcake."

"Gosh, you're sharp."

"Come on, spill your guts. Maybe there's a movie in it."

Rush picked up his pace, leaving me a few yards behind. "You here to interview me or see your parents?"

"I'll see them." I pulled my floppy black hat out of my overall pocket and jammed it on my head, pulling the big brim down around my face. I wanted to see them but not be seen by them. They must never know I was here, not that they expected me to show. Not after ten years of silence.

Rush and I took our place at the fringes of the crowd. We could still see the main gates, where my parents would be released, about a hundred yards away. Reporters were bunched up at the front, their white vans with cameras mounted on the roofs parked in a row. The men behind the cameras looked anxious, trigger-happy. They looked more like guards than the real guards who hovered with bored expressions near the gate.

I paced around the back of the crowd. I smelled the faint cloying scent of marijuana. A man and woman were changing their baby's diaper on the hood of a car while their other two boys tried to see who could pinch the other harder. It was difficult for me to characterize the crowd. At first I'd thought they were a bunch of yuppie retreads picnicking on their childhood memories, like tuning in to a *Brady Bunch* reunion special. But I could see now that many were lower income, blue-collar types in workboots, sipping beer or hoisting their kids onto their shoulders. Some of the crowd were in their twenties, college students too young to remember my parents' exploits first hand. Their presence surprised me the most.

"Makes you think, doesn't it?" Rush said, nodding toward the tall prison fences. He was wearing dark sunglasses now. "How easy it is to do something, one little wrong thing, and pow you're inside a place like that getting tattooed with a sharpened fork and watching out for your butt. It's like in that Phil Ochs song, 'There but for fortune, go you or I.' "

"Maybe you," I said. "But not I."

He just shook his head and wandered away, slipping into the crowd and working his way toward the front gate. The hell with him, I thought. The only reason he was here was to make money off my misery. People like that deserved whatever treatment they got.

I felt a tapping against my thighs and suddenly realized my hands were shaking. I rubbed them together briskly, but still they trembled.

I balled my hands into tight fists and slipped them into the deep pockets of my overalls like fragile eggs. Okay, I would have to admit I was nervous, a little scared. I stared at the front gate and watched and waited. *Come on, come on, come on.*

"They called a news conference," Rush said, suddenly appearing out of the crowd. He took off his sunglasses and polished them on his shirt. "It's supposed to take place right outside the gate here. That's why the news hounds have all their equipment set up."

"A news conference? What news conference?"

"The one that's about to take place over there. Aren't you listening?"

"Who called the news conference?"

"Who we talking about here? Your parents."

I looked over at the main gate. The anger was gone, the fear, the nervousness. Now I just felt disappointed, tired. "Let's go," I said quietly. I turned and started for the car.

"Wait," Rush said. He grabbed my arm. "Where are you going? They're coming out any minute now."

I shook my head. "It's not going to happen."

"What?"

"There's not going to be any news conference. My guess is they're already gone."

"What do you mean? Your parents are the ones who called it. I just spoke to some guy from KCBS. It's going to be their lead story tonight."

I snatched the sunglasses off Rush's face and shoved them into his shirt pocket. "Listen, Poundcake, my parents never once gave an interview or called a news conference the entire year they were on trial or for the nineteen years after sentencing. Not once. They always said you could manipulate the media if you let them chase you, but once they sat you down in a chair and smeared makeup on you and lit you just right, they owned you. Believe me, my parents know their way around journalists. I mean, how do you think they got to be so popular?"

"Because they were hippie-dippy bank robbers who dressed funny, gave money to weird causes, and had a cute little girl along."

"Yeah, partly. But more important, they were popular because they wanted to be popular. Don't you get it? That was the whole point of the robberies." I pressed my hands against my thighs from inside my pockets. They still shook. "You haven't done your homework, Poundcake."

Rush pointed at the crowd of reporters surrounding the gate. "Yeah, well, nineteen years is a long time to maintain a counterculture attitude. Maybe they've changed. Maybe growing old behind bars with some serious psychos as your neighbors alters your consciousness more than Ravi Shankar strumming a sitar. Maybe they're not thinking 'Give Peace a Chance' as much as 'Give Me a Piece of the Rock.' Maybe they're coming out of the slammer thinking about how to make some money to get them through their twilight years."

"They're both fifty-three. Not exactly old age."

"It is if you haven't had a job, haven't contributed to any retirement plans, Social Security, or anything else. They need a place to live, food, clothes. How they gonna get all that? I mean, they've got to make a few bucks. I bet you anything they already have a public-relations firm on retainer. Some publisher's probably already offered them half a million for their story." He spread his arms, encompassing the crowd, the prison, the parking lot. "This news conference, these people, it's all part of the publicity campaign. Believe me, I know how it works. Thing is, you could be getting your share, too. You've paid the price for having them as your parents, right? All that weirdness when you were a kid. Getting shuffled off to your grandparents. Losing your teaching job."

"How do you know about that?" I snapped.

Rush shook open his sunglasses and jammed them back onto his face. "Friends."

"You have friends? Hard to believe."

"Not my friends, Erhart. Yours."

I was pleased not to show him any reaction. I was used to betrayal. "Who?"

"It doesn't matter who. The point here is that it's your turn now. Isn't it time you got paid back? What's so wrong with me giving you a hundred grand?"

I stuck out my hand. "Show me the money."

"You know what I mean. Sign a preliminary agreement and I'll get you the money. I swear on everything—mother's eyes, father's grave, flags, Bibles. Put it in front of me and I'll swear on it."

I shook my head. "Poundcake, how have you managed to live this long and not get shot?"

"Bullets bounce off my ironclad contracts."

Someone at the front of the crowd started yelling excitedly. People cheered and waved their signs. A small group chanted, "Free at last! Free at last!"

"I don't think this is what Dr. King had in mind."

"Here they come," Rush said smugly. "As advertised."

I faced the gate. A sudden eerie sensation enveloped me. All my senses felt as if they'd been heightened to the millionth power. I could see impossible distances. There, the front gate was so clear that I could even make out the flakes of rust, almost see the process of oxidation as it was happening. Conversations throughout the crowd were being broadcast directly to my ears. I knew what everyone was saying no matter how far away, how low their voices. The young couple in the matching USC sweatshirts standing by the news vans were arguing about where to eat dinner that night. Half a mile away, I heard the flapping of a moth's wings, which sounded like sheets fluttering in the wind. My nose ached from all the aromas around me, as if too many smells were being shoved up my nostrils at once, scraping the delicate membranes raw. I could even smell blueberry muffins from across the prison yard, still strong from the morning breakfast, though breakfast had to have been over for two hours by now. Then I tasted something bitter in my mouth and realized it was my own blood. I'd bitten down on my cheek. All my sudden superpowers disappeared. I sagged against the bumper of a nearby Pontiac and rubbed my face with my palms. Get a grip, Blue. Get a grip.

"Here they come!" Rush said. "Over there!"

I looked up at Rush. It was the first time I'd seen him genuinely excited, not acting. Even he was caught up in the hype. That made me feel even more alone.

"Jesus, a limo," Rush said. "They're leaving prison in a stretch limo. Probably a studio limo. Can you make out the license number? Those bastards at Paramount, I bet. Damn!" The gates opened and the white limo slowly rolled out. The windows were tinted black. Heads craned, but no one could see anything inside.

"It's not them," I said softly. For some reason, I hated telling him that.

"What?"

"It's not them. They aren't in the limo."

"Bullshit." Rush looked down at the scene. The limo idled while cameras were swung into action. Reporters mobbed the car, recorders and cameras poised for the emergence. The crowd cheered and hollered and waved encouragement.

"Let's go," I said, tugging at Rush's sleeve.

"Go? We came this far. Don't you at least want to see them?"

"It's not them. They're not coming." I turned away and began walking back to the car. My hands no longer trembled and my senses were back to normal. All I could hear were my own steps on the gravel; I smelled only my own sweat. I was relieved. Yet I also felt a profound sadness I hadn't anticipated. I'd come this far—I wanted to see them at least. See them under my terms, my conditions. From afar. Like watching Tim's bare-assed performance onstage, me applauding safely from the lighting booth. Another hideout.

"Hold on," Rush called. "Wait a second."

I stopped, turned back. The limo continued to idle. No windows were opened to the reporters, though I could see them boldly knocking on the black glass. One of the prison guards spit out a wad of gum and rushed over to shove the reporters back. The chubby blonde with the fried hair was down there. The man in the denim jacket. A few others I recognized.

Suddenly, the limo honked the horn, a long loud blast like those civil-defense warning tests they're always doing on TV and radio. The sound invigorated the crowd and they began cheering even louder. And then the limo drove off. Reporters jumped back and watched in amazement as the white car sped off down the road. A few reporters ran for their cars, but the crowd was so thick that they were choked off. I expected the crowd to start booing or tearing stuff up to demonstrate their sense of disappointment and betrayal. Instead, they cheered even louder, more wildly, hooting and screaming and laughing. They preferred the unexpected. After all, that's what they liked about my parents in the first place. They were like rock stars.

"Told you," I said. "It wasn't them."

Rush walked beside me toward the car, his face stiff with disappointment. "Could've been them. Maybe they just decided not to talk. You said they wouldn't."

"They wouldn't leave in a limo. They hate limos. The essence of limos."

"You ever ride in a limo?"

"Prom night. And homecoming."

"Then what's to hate?"

I looked at him. "You don't know why my parents would hate limos?"

Rush sighed, started counting on his fingers. "Corrupt bourgeois values. Military-industrial complex. Symbol of ruling class. Environmental rapist. I leave anything out?"

"Bad TV reception."

"When I'm the head of some studio, I'm going to cruise around town all day, holding all my meetings in my customized limo. My chauffeur will pull up to the curb of a No Parking zone and he'll open the rear door to some weaselly producer who'll be standing there trembling with a sweat-soaked script in his grimy hands. I'll just smile, crook my finger, and say, 'Get in.' That's all, just 'Get in.' Like mobsters are always saying to guys they're about to take for a one-way ride to Rigor Mortis Café. And he will. He'll climb right in and thank me for the privilege. Then I'll spit on his script and boot him out at the next intersection. It will be very cool."

"A boy and his dream. How inspiring."

"You need to be more tolerant toward shallow people. You could hurt my feeling."

"Your feeling?" I laughed. "I hate it when you make me laugh. It makes me feel like I've just bought something I don't need."

"Most women wait until we've had sex before saying that."

We arrived at the car and Rush unlocked the door for me. I climbed in, reached across the seat, and unlocked his door. I smiled, crooked my finger, and said, "Get in. Got anything I can spit on?" He laughed as he slid in. "See, you could be a producer, too." He started the engine, put it in gear, and eased the car out of the tight parking space. We fell into line behind other emerging cars crawling for the road.

"Back to this lawyer thing," I said. I wanted talk right now and lots of it. Wall-to-wall talk. About anything, anyone. Something to keep my from thinking about my parents and the cold ache in my stomach. "Tell me about it. The sad story of your fall from grace."

"What makes you think I fell?"

"You were a lawyer; now you're a wannabe producer. Isn't that a fall?"

"Maybe I jumped."

"Jumped or pushed, it's all the same when you hit the ground."

"You've got an answer for—"

A loud thump interrupted, jolting the car.

At first, I thought the sound had escaped from Rush's mouth, some kind of bodily function noise that men often enjoy making. But out of the corner of my eye, I saw the body come flying up over the hood of the car. Saw the woman's face smack against the windshield, blood smearing the windshield from the corner of her mouth. She must have been sixty years old, her long gray hair braided into one thick rope, Indian style.

"Jesus!" Rush yelled, and stomped on the brake. "I wasn't even going ten miles an hour!"

Rush and I jumped out of the car at the same time. The woman lay spread-eagled across the hood of the car. Her long wool skirt was hiked up on one leg so far that a glimpse of panty-covered haunch was showing, pale as chalk. She moaned softly. I tried to tug the woman's skirt down, but her body pinned it in place.

"We'd better not move her," Rush said. His voice was pinched a little higher than usual, but he remained calm. He put his hand to the side of the woman's face. "Can you hear me, ma'am?"

She looked up at him and nodded. "Help me down."

"I don't know if you should move."

Cars began to honk impatiently. We were blocking the road. This made me nervous. I was afraid someone would jump from one of the cars, brandishing a tire iron. Rush ignored them completely. Nevertheless, when the next car honked, I turned and shouted, "Hey!" The guy honked longer in response. These were the kind of idiots my parents inspired. Figured.

"I'm okay," the woman said. She started to sit up, faltered. I steadied her with a hand at her back. The woman looked down and saw that her skirt was bunched around her hip. Quickly, I yanked it down. "You didn't look, did you?" she asked Rush.

He shook his head solemnly.

"You sure?"

Rush winked. "Maybe a little."

She smiled brightly. "Okay, then, you can help me down."

He lifted her in his arms and eased her off the hood of the car like a little girl. She was kind of small under all those bulky clothes, maybe five feet.

"We should drive you to the hospital," I offered. I hoped the woman would say yes; this was the perfect distraction I needed to stop thinking about my parents. Hanging around a hospital with an injured older woman might earn me some spiritual brownie points.

The woman took a couple or wobbly steps, then reached out as if about to fall. Rush grabbed her under the arm. "Maybe if you could drop me off at the emergency room, my husband could pick me up. There's a hospital just down the freeway."

"No problem," I said cheerfully.

"It's really my fault," she said. "I should have been watching where I was going. All the excitement, you know. I don't know where my mind was."

I opened the back door for her and helped her get in. Rush and I returned to the front seats. We pulled back into the caravan of traffic.

"My name's Molly Childress," the woman said. She stretched out her legs on the backseat and brushed some dirt from her skirt. "Molly's bad enough, but then to have Childress added on. Molly sounds like some pioneer grandmother. And Childress is just one letter from childless, which, when you put the two names together, is the double whammy of barren-hag names. Anyway, that's what I'm stuck with. Molly Childress."

"Nice to meet you, Molly," Rush said, without offering his own name.

I turned in my seat, the shoulder strap scraping my neck. "Hi, Molly, I'm—"

"Blue Erhart, of course."

I stiffened.

Molly laughed a youthful laugh. "For Christ's sake, Blue, relax. I'm not a reporter. Your parents sent me."

"Parents?" I said stupidly, the word sticking in my mouth like a scoop of peanut butter.

Rush turned toward her. "Her parents sent you?"

"Now you've got it," Molly said. "Mom and Pop sent me to find you. I have a message. Want to hear it?"

·10·

The street where we parked was dark and smelled of a recent fire. This was an area I recognized from TV news, one frequented by violent gangs. The overhead streetlight was broken, probably shot out. I craned my neck out the car window to see if I could see bullet holes in the telephone pole that the streetlight was attached to.

"Are you sure this is right?" I asked Molly.

"This can't be right," Rush said.

"I ought to know where I live. I may be old, but I saw you sneaking a peek at my ass when I was sprawled across your hood like a fucking deer."

"That wasn't your ass I was looking at," Rush said. "It was the scratch in my hood from your false teeth."

Molly laughed and smacked Rush's shoulder playfully. He pretended to wince under the pain. I was annoyed at how well the two of them were getting along, joking and chatting during my emotional crisis. Not that I wanted them to focus on me; that would be even worse. God, I didn't know what I wanted. Not to be here. Not to be about to face my parents again after ten years. I'd been prepared to see them from a distance, with a crowd anchored between us a as sort of DMZ. But they'd gotten the upper hand again somehow, reaching out even now to influence my life. To make me do what they wanted. So okay, here I was. Now what?

While Rush parallel-parked next to a garbage-choked gutter drain, Molly continued yakking. I studied the deserted sidewalks for signs of street gangs, which for some reason I expected to appear like the Sharks and Jets in *West Side Story*, leaping out from the alley en masse in a perfectly choreographed jeté. I needed to get a grip. This wasn't a movie. My parents weren't Warren Beatty and Faye Dunaway. They were plain old ex-cons. Bank robbers.

"It's been a while since I pulled the bash-for-cash scam," Molly said as we all climbed out of the car. "The fake-accident dodge has been pretty much taken over by the Iranians and Greeks. But back then, back when I started out, the lifted skirt bit was my own twist to the gag. Kinda my signature, you know?"

"Where are my parents?" I said. "Isn't that why we're here?"

"Almost there." Molly pointed down the dark street and walked briskly, leaving the car behind. I hesitated. Leaving the car was like abandoning a life raft to swim for a shoreline you couldn't clearly see. The streetlights that still worked were unusually dim and I could see only ten shadowy yards ahead of me. Molly didn't seem nervous, so I tried not to be either, though I was practically running to keep up. Molly continued to chatter as she led us down the street, Rush at her side, attentive. "I'd be the victim; my husband, Gordon, would be the witness. Maybe we'd threaten to sue or go to the insurance company. Whatever worked. Anyway, after we got divorced, I did the scam by myself for a couple years, got caught, went to prison, met your mom. We kept in touch. Simple as that."

"So who owns the bookstore?" Rush asked.

"Gordon got a little shaken after I got myself arrested. After all, I was one of the best. He could never work any of the gags without me. So he went legit. Bought this place." She pointed at the dirty brick building we were approaching. "Then when they stuck a Crown Books down the street, business got kind of slow for Gordon. He needed some money to keep the place afloat. So he went out and tried to pull the accident scam on his own. Without me."

"You mean he allowed himself to be hit by a car?" I asked.

"Well, you don't actually get hit. That's part of the illusion. Like a magician. You don't think Uri Geller actually bends those spoons, do you?" Molly waved a dismissing hand. "Anyway, Gordo just wasn't as good as he thought."

"Got caught?" Rush asked.

"Got killed." Molly laughed. "I told him it wasn't as easy as it looked." She reached into her drawstring purse and pulled out a ring of keys. She found the one she wanted and walked up to the door of The Book Cell and pushed the key into the lock. She nodded at the store's name in chipped and fading black paint stenciled to the glass. "Gordo's idea of clever. The Book Cell. Now you know why he got eaten by a Lexus." Molly pushed the door open and a bell tinkled overhead. The dry smell of musty pages rushed out into my face. Molly turned on a Tiffany lamp near the cash register. "Anyway, he left me this place in his will. It keeps me off the streets and puts some change in my pockets."

I followed Molly into the store. Rush entered last, closing the door behind him. I noticed he was grinning as he looked around.

"You're getting off on all this, aren't you?" I accused him.

"What?"

"This sneaking around with criminals. The phony car accident. All this bullshit."

"It is exciting."

"This isn't a movie, Poundcake; it's my life."

Rush shrugged, unimpressed. "It's my life, too. I'm standing here, ticking off minutes of my life, getting older. Dying. Is there anything wrong with enjoying myself at the same time?"

The room was filled with rows of wooden bookcases crammed with used hardbacks and paperbacks. A small section by the front counter displayed new books. One metal rack held comic books and New Age magazines.

"They're upstairs," Molly said. She pointed to a spiral iron staircase at the back of the room. "I live up there. Help yourself to a Coke or something from the fridge. Pet the cat at your own risk; the little shit bites sometimes."

"Let me ask you something," I said to Molly. "Other than a flair for the theatrical, why didn't you just come up to me at the prison and tell me my parents were here and wanted to see me? Plain and simple."

Molly laughed. "It wasn't my flair for the theatrical I was concerned with, kiddo. It was yours."

I was astonished. "Mine? I don't have any theatrics."

"Really? That's not what your folks said. They said you'd run if I just did a walk-on and handed you a message." She shrugged, not really caring now that her part was over. "Anyway, it worked, didn't it?"

I started for the stairs, even angrier at my parents because they knew me so little. Rush fell in step behind me. I stopped. "Where do you think you're going?"

"With you."

"Don't you ever stop? This is not going to be a Kodak moment, I promise you. It's not going to be hugs and tears. There's no place for a swelling violins sound track."

His face reddened with anger. "You think you know me pretty well, don't you, Amelia?"

"I know you, Poundcake."

"As the old hillbilly gas station attendant tells Ned Beatty in *Deliverance*, 'You don't know shit.' Turned out he was right."

"Are all your life lessons in film clips?"

He didn't answer.

I looked at him, trying to decide how much of his anger was an act, how much was genuine. I snapped my fingers at him. "Give me the contract. The one you want me to sign."

Rush looked surprised for a few seconds, then pulled a folded piece of paper out, produced a pen. He turned his back to offer a surface. I laid the paper against his back and signed. The pen point stabbed through the paper at the final loop of my signature and left a blue squiggle on his jacket. I handed him the signed contract. "There. You happy now?"

He looked it over and smiled. "Yes, actually, I'm very happy."

Immediately, I snatched the contract out of his hand and tore it into half a dozen pieces. "How about now?"

I had expected anger. Maybe rage. Some curse words. Perhaps even a slap. I was surprised instead to see him stare at the paper, not with the slack wolfishness of somebody who just lost a sale but with true pain. Like a kid who'd just had the sand castle he'd spent all morning crafting stomped on by a bully. It made me feel like a bully. First a bitch, now a bully.

"I take it back," he said quietly with a tight smile. "I guess you do know me, after all."

I sighed. I wanted to apologize, but for what? Rush was the bully. He'd bullied his way into my life, hadn't he? No one had asked him to eat zucchinis or piss on reporters. Still, I wanted to say something to him, something kind. But I couldn't show any weakness now. If I did, seeing my parents would be impossible. I turned away from him and started for the stairs again.

"Here," he said, nudging my shoulder.

I turned back. He handed me a slip of paper with a number on it. "What's this?"

"My number." He reached into his jacket and pulled out a tiny portable telephone that was folded to the size of a wallet. "In case you need help or something. I don't know."

I looked at his face. I'd been conned so often in the past few days that I didn't feel capable of deciding whether or not he was being sincere. It only made me feel more helpless. How could I face my parents now? I folded the paper in half and slipped it into my back pocket.

I started up the stairs. I could hear their heavy footsteps moving about above me. I climbed toward them.

The night before the FBI raid—the TV footage of which Walter Cronkite glumly warned his viewers was "bracing"—I was dancing the hully-gully at my tenth birthday party.

My parents threw the party for me in the motel room where we'd been hiding out for three hot, unair-conditioned days. My mother, Naomi, had pulled the drab curtains closed and slapped a gray strip of duct tape down the middle to secure them. My father had dead-bolted and chained the door and wedged a chair under the doorknob. Their guns had been stored in the padlocked duffel bag under the bed.

The motel was called Night, Angel Motel, with a little neon halo over the *o* in *motel*. The name was what the owner used to whisper to his daughter every night when he tucked her into bed. "Night,

Angel," he'd say, and kiss the air over her bed three times because bad spirits were afraid of kisses and kisses hung in the air like clouds for exactly twelve hours. His daughter couldn't sleep until he'd kissed the air. She drowned at a church picnic when she was twelve, after which he quit long-haul trucking and he and his wife bought the motel with the insurance money. I found all this out years later in the library, reading the news clippings about that night. All I knew at the time, all I knew the night of my tenth birthday party with the taped curtains and wedged door, was that the place was an eight-unit dump squeezed between a Dairy Queen and a trucker's gas station. That the toilet didn't always flush right. That the furniture had so many cigarette burns, it looked like it had been tortured for information. That the diesel trucks hissed and growled all night long, making sleep difficult. And that my hair always smelled like gasoline from the Texaco station and french fries from the Dairy Queen's deep fryer.

But the night of the party, I was so happy, I couldn't stop moving. There were balloons, and streamers. And a carrot cake from the supermarket. The balloons were tied to the bedposts and the tables and the floor lamp with twisties from the vegetable department. The crepe paper was taped to a blurry painting of a ballerina and spiraled across the entire room and into the bathroom, where it was duct-taped to the shower-curtain rod. The clock radio played twangy country and western songs, which kept fading in and out and which I didn't like anyway, but which my mother explained was all they could get in this armpit part of Texas. Nevertheless, every fifteen minutes or so my mother would groan at the sappy song on the radio and try to find some kind of rock station. "I'd even settle for Captain and Tennille," she mock-prayed toward heaven, making me laugh. "Even Neil Diamond, Sonny and Cher. I'm desperate here, Lord."

About as often as Naomi spun the radio dial, Harold peeked out the curtains and scanned the parking lot for cops. Sometimes he'd let me look, too. We'd hunker down and he'd point at a car across the motel lot. "Nope," I would say, "no cops there." For the rest of the evening, we ate cake, drank Dr. Pepper, and played pin the tinfoil crown on Nixon. They let me stay up late and watch Johnny

Carson, who the week before had made a joke about my parents ("Those two make more bank withdrawals than Bebe Rebozo"). I did not get the joke, but the name was funny. I fell asleep shortly after the monologue.

The next day, they robbed the Sweetwater National Bank.

This is how it usually worked: My parents would scout out the bank they wanted to rob, then they'd drive down the road, planning an escape route on the AAA map. Sometimes they drove as far as two hundred miles. When they got to a place they thought would be a safe hideout, they'd rent a room and stay a couple days. The day of the robbery, they would leave me in the room, drive back down the road, rob the bank, then return to me. That way, they figured I was never in danger.

Not that they were always robbing banks. Sometimes they'd go for more than a month or two without a single robbery. My father would get a job on a ranch; having been raised on a ranch in Kansas, he was still very handy in a saddle. I loved to see him in his cowboy boots and big hat. Sometimes he took me riding, and that was the best time of all. My mother, who had studied to be a teacher so she could join the Peace Corps and go to India like the Beatles, instead spent every day tutoring me. My courses pretty much mirrored what other kids were studying, except Mom added World Politics, which consisted of us reading the newspaper together every morning while Mom explained the part of the news the papers left out. The part about the conspiracy between the military-industrial complex and the Nixon administration to crush the poor and the working class. How the people in this country were brainwashed by television to believe whatever they were told because it was easier than figuring things out for themselves. The real genius of it all, my mother explained, was that people still thought they figured it out for themselves. I was surprised how much news the newspapers left out.

Once a week was declared Nature Day and the two of us would drive out to some remote rural area and walk through the woods or fields or by a river or beach and try to name every plant and animal we could. That was my favorite time with my mother. Looking around at all these busy creatures, I was amazed that so much was happening in this world that had nothing to do with Nixon.

Once when my father had gone along with us, he'd picked up a grasshopper, rinsed it off in the stream, and eaten it. "They're very good for you," he'd explained, grinning at his own daring. "Better than the beef and pork that big business is trying to shove down our throats, even though beef diets are unhealthy and use too many natural resources. Someday we'll all be eating like this." Chicken and fish were necessary evils, my parents had both agreed, after several unsuccessful bouts with vegetarianism.

I didn't know about any of that. I just took one look at Daddy shoving that grasshopper into his mouth and burst out crying. I ran away, splashing through the creek, sobbing as my parents ran after me. I couldn't forget the picture of the bug's wriggling legs as my daddy munched it in half. He was worse than Nixon. When they caught up to me, I was slumped by a tree, too exhausted to run anymore. He picked me up and carried me back and swore he'd never do anything like that again. That night, they took me to see *Harold and Maude* for the third time and on the drive home we sang Cat Stevens songs.

The morning of the Sweetwater National Bank robbery, my parents had arisen early as usual. It was still dark outside. Mother kissed my cheek and I woke up.

"We're going now, sweetie," she said.

"Okay."

"You know the rules, right?"

I nodded sleepily, eyes barely open.

"Tell me."

My father was dragging the duffel bag out from under the bed. He pulled out two sawed-off shotguns.

"Tell me," my mother repeated. Her long blond hair was shoved up under a baseball cap. She looked like a handsome teenage boy.

"No television," I recited.

"Right." She handed me two new books. She always gave me new books the morning of a heist.

I lifted my head from the pillow to look at the books. *Where the Red Fern Grows* and *Alice Through the Looking Glass*. I slipped them under my pillow and laid my head back down. "Thanks," I mumbled.

"What else?" my mother persisted. "C'mon, the rules."

"Stay in the room. Don't go out for any reason."

"Not for any reason. Except a fire."

"Okay, Mom, okay."

"Don't answer the phone. Unless?"

I wanted to sleep. My mother's voice was so far away.

"Unless?" she said again, poking my arm.

"Unless it rings twice, then nothing, then starts ringing again. That'll be you and Daddy. Okay?"

"Okay." She kissed me on the cheek and forehead. Her breath smelled of toothpaste and Listerine. Mother was unnaturally obsessed with oral hygiene. At night, we would sit around and read or watch the news and my mother would sit there with a book open, lazily brushing. My father teased that it was the Jewish American princess syndrome, that it would take more than a revolution to break a five-thousand-year tradition of anal compulsion. I didn't get that joke, either, but my mother would sometimes laugh, sometimes just throw her toothbrush at him. Either way, I thought it was great fun and I couldn't imagine better parents anywhere.

My parents left to go rob the bank and I couldn't get back to sleep. Finally, I woke up and read *Where the Red Fern Grows*. At the end, I cried and that put me to sleep for a couple of hours. When I woke up, I turned on the television as I usually did. I figured my parents couldn't really mean for me not to watch, since it was always in the room with me. Besides, I knew they wouldn't be home for a couple more hours anyway, so I'd be okay as long as I shut it off a half hour before they got back, time for the set to cool down to the touch, which was the first thing my mother always did when they walked in.

I knew I had plenty of time, so I watched "Bewitched" and "Big Valley." After that, I planned to turn off the set and let it cool down. When my parents returned, I'd be sitting on the bed reading a book, just the way they liked to see me. My parents suffered a lot of guilt over my lifestyle, so I didn't like to add to their burden. "See," my mom would say, beaming proudly when they came through the door, "she's better off than those TV zombies the rest of middle-class America is hatching."

Meantime, I watched Heath and Nick punch each other, busting up furniture in the house until Barbara Stanwyck came in and made them stop. I thought it was weird that this whole family still lived together, considering how old they were and all, and that they still had to listen to their mom all the time. I liked Heath the best of the sons because he talked the slowest. Nick shouted everything and Jared talked like a teacher. I was looking in the mirror, fussing with my hair, trying to make it look like their sister Audrey's, when the motel door burst open. I was so frightened, I slid off the edge of the bed and landed butt-first on the floor.

Daddy was half-carrying, half-dragging my mother. He leaned to the side so he could support Mom's weight on his hip. Her arm was draped over his shoulder; the other arm hung limp at her side. Her head sagged against her chest.

I leapt up, afraid they would punish me. I started to babble. "I was just . . . I read the books . . . I didn't . . ."

My father didn't hear me. He spoke softly to Mom. "It's okay, sweetheart, it's okay. We're here, we're here." His repeating everything scared me even more.

Mom lifted her head and looked around the room. Her eyes rolled back into her head and she seemed to faint. Daddy kicked the door closed behind them. The sound stirred her awake. "Put me down already, Dillinger."

I ran over to the bed and pulled the covers down. I piled all the pillows, flat and lumpy as they were, into one nest for my mother. Daddy lowered her onto the bed. That's when I noticed the blood. He peeled off the denim jacket that had been draped over her shoulder. The shoulder was a mushy muck of blood, like chili. I screamed.

"Quiet now, sweetheart," my mother said, forcing a smile. "This is nothing. I've had bee stings worse than this. Remember when I got stung by that bee on our Nature Day last month? Remember that?"

I nodded.

"You heard me hollering worse then, didn't you? Remember all those cuss words I yelled, the ones I made you promise not to repeat to Daddy?"

I nodded. I was glad I didn't have to speak; I wasn't sure I'd be able to.

"Well, sweetie, if I was hurt as bad as that bee sting, wouldn't I be yelling like that now?" Mom reached out and stroked my hair. "Wouldn't I?"

I nodded.

Daddy returned from the bathroom with a wet towel, which he pressed against the wound. Mom whispered something to him and he nodded. "Blue," he said, "I want you to run over to that Dairy Queen and buy some ice. Just tell them that your daddy sprained his ankle."

"Don't they have ice here, Daddy?" I knew that most motels we stayed at had ice machines. I loved shoveling the ice into those little buckets.

Mom snorted. "We're lucky this place has water."

My father handed me a five-dollar bill from his pocket. He never carried his wallet when he was out on a job. Not that it mattered; all their IDs were phony, anyway.

"You're going to need a doctor," he told Mom.

"Let's just stop the bleeding for now. Then we can drive over to Houston. Jeremy will know somebody."

Dad nodded. "Right. Jeremy."

I took the money and walked over to the Dairy Queen. Things couldn't be that bad if all they needed was some ice. I didn't know Jeremy, but I was excited about visiting another of my parents' friends. Maybe they would have kids my age I could play with. My parents had friends all over the country, part of some radical underground or something. These friends would hide us out or buy stuff for my parents if things got too hot. Once we got to stay on a commune where everybody lived in tents and ate all their meals together. There were lots of kids there. I liked playing with them for a while, but even that got kind of boring and I missed the motel rooms and television.

When I got to the Dairy Queen, I asked for the ice and two chocolate ice cream cones. That would be all I could carry. But that was okay; I'd surprise my parents with a cone for each. That would cheer them up. And it was even better because I wouldn't have a cone myself, so they could see my sacrifice. And, of course, it might help them forget about the TV being on.

But here was the best part, I thought. Instead of paying with the five dollars my father had given me, I paid with my own twenty-dollar bill they'd given me last night for my birthday. They'd also given me regular gifts and my father played the guitar and sang a song he'd written for me. Mom had given me a photo album with all kinds of different leaves in the plastic windows instead of photographs. These were leaves my mother had collected from every place we'd ever traveled. But the twenty dollars was the start of my college fund. They made me promise not to spend it. I swore I wouldn't. But this was special.

My mother was better by that night. The bullet from the bank guard had just plowed a deep furrow through the skin. She wouldn't need a doctor, after all. Just some rest. We would still go to Jeremy's anyway and hide out. Dad had called and Jeremy was setting things up for us.

Mom was propped up on one of the beds, her arm wrapped mummylike in bandages. She'd taken a lot of aspirin, which didn't help much. She was smoking a joint, which she rarely did anymore, but Daddy had convinced her it would help dull the pain.

They were counting the money from the bank robbery. Piles of cash were strewn across the bedspread. The total haul had been more than twenty thousand dollars, a lot more than usual.

"Okay," Daddy said, "half goes to . . ." He looked at Mom. "Whose turn is it?"

She shrugged, winced from the pain. "I don't know," she said wearily. "Some cancer group maybe. American Cancer Society."

"That was last time," I said. I remembered because I thought it was funny to have the words *cancer* and *society* together, like it was a club for people with cancer. I imagined them all sitting around in tuxedos and evening gowns.

"How about that muscular dystrophy thing?" my mother said.

"Jerry's kids?" Dad laughed. He tried to do an impression of Jerry Lewis. He was always trying to impersonate celebrities, but no one could figure out who he was doing. Except Bob Dylan—everybody always got that one right. Mom looked at me and we both laughed at his impression on cue. Dad grinned with pleasure and returned to the money. "Sure, why not? Jerry's kids." He took half of the cash and shoved it into a manila envelope. He looked up an address in a book they kept of charitable organizations. "Here, punkin', you do it."

I jumped up excitedly and fetched my box of crayons, twenty-four different colors, and carried them over to the bed. I tried to look very businesslike carrying them, the way I'd seen men carrying briefcases. This was important stuff. Daddy scooted aside to make room for me on the bed.

"What color you going to use?" he asked.

I opened the crayon box and studied each color. "Scarlet." I plucked a red crayon and printed the address my father pointed at. After I was through, I traced over the same red letters with a yellow crayon. I liked the way that looked, like fire.

Dad kissed my cheek and licked the envelope shut. Every time they robbed a bank, they would immediately send half of what they stole to some charity or other organization they liked—no matter how small the take. Once it had been the United Negro College Fund, another time the Jewish Defense League, another time the Quakers. There was never a note or anything with the money, but usually the FBI tracked it down. Sometimes an organization had the police check out the money first; some then returned it to the bank it had been stolen from. Most kept it, though.

The rest of the money, my parents kept to live on modestly until they ran out. They never bought anything fancy, no jewels or clothes or appliances. Nothing we couldn't pack up in three minutes and toss into the GAC. Sometimes, if they were particularly outraged by some moral lapse in the world, they would give away all the money. Had the envelopes already addressed and stamped. They'd rob the bank, stuff the money into the envelopes, and drop them into a mailbox during their getaway. Then they'd both take jobs for a while until they had enough traveling money to find another bank.

"The money is nothing," they'd tell me when I used to ask why they didn't use it to buy a house like other people. Or at least a bicycle. "It's not ours to spend on ourselves, Blue. It belongs to everyone. But sometimes the wrong people get too much of it and then the right people don't get enough of it. We're just helping to redistribute some of it to the right people."

Publicity followed. *Time* magazine did a colorful drawing following their "Route of Robbery." It looked like a game board. Editorials around the country varied. Some condemned them and everything they stood for. Others applauded their goals but deplored their means. Some alternative newspapers praised them, dubbing them the "Counterculture Bonnie and Clyde." Nixon refused to comment, saying it was a police matter. Spiro Agnew said it was symptomatic of the breakdown of family values and he prayed nightly for the little girl. He hoped there was still time to save me.

My father had an uncontrollable hatred of Agnew. He hated Agnew more than he hated Nixon. More than he'd hated Lyndon Johnson. He said Agnew was the spiritual afterbirth of the Vietnam War. He even looked like an afterbirth. Mom teased him when he ranted about Agnew, usually while brushing her teeth. Once a stray cat wandered into our motel room in Arkansas and stayed for three days. Mom insisted on calling it Spiro.

Whenever I thought back on those days, I seemed to remember that my entire childhood consisted of driving from bank robbery to bank robbery. I imagined I'd done it for all of my ten years. But, in fact, the whole crime spree lasted only sixteen months.

And it ended just as my father was licking the envelope with ten thousand dollars in cash for Jerry's kids.

That's when the window exploded and tear gas clouded the room. The door splintered with a crash and five big men in bulletproof vests and gas masks charged into the room, shouting and pushing and grabbing. Everyone was handcuffed and dragged out into the parking lot, including me. My eyes burned terribly and my arm hurt where the man had gripped me. But that's not what I was thinking about. I was busy trying to get them not to hurt my parents, who had been thrown facedown on the pavement, shotguns pressed to the skulls.

"Don't hurt them!" I hollered, ripping my throat. "They'll give it all back! They'll give the money back!"

"Get the brat outta here!" someone yelled. I was picked up and whisked away toward a police car.

"Mommy! Daddy! Help!" I wailed. But Harold and Naomi lay pinned to the ground, looking helplessly at me.

"Don't hurt her!" Mom yelled, her teeth clenched. I had never seen her look so angry before.

"Be careful," my father pleaded, and the guys with the shotguns kicked him in the head.

"That's for resisting," the man said. Everyone seemed real mad at my parents, even though it wasn't their money. That's what my parents had always told me. It wasn't the cops' money. Then what were they so angry about?

"Mommy! Daddy!" I could barely hear my own voice, my throat was so raw from the gas and from yelling. "Don't hurt them, please!" I was thrown into the back of a police car. The doors were locked. I watched through the glass.

Another man in a blue windbreaker with big white FBI letters on his back carried out the duffel bag we kept under the bed. He pulled off his gas mask and sliced open the bag with a knife. He pulled out the two sawed-off shotguns, checking each one carefully, then searching the bag again, turning it inside out. "There's no ammunition," he said, almost disappointed. "No fucking shells."

"Where are the shells, asshole?" the guy who'd kicked Dad asked. He poked his shotgun barrel against my father's forehead. I saw the blood bloom.

"The guns were never loaded," Dad said. "Even the firing pins are broken so they can't fire."

Somebody kicked him. An older man in a suit walked up and shouted at the guy who had kicked Dad. "Knock that crap off, Donnely. Somebody get that girl out of here. Now. She shouldn't be seeing this. She's a kid, for Christ's sake."

I didn't see my parents again for a month. After that, I could see them only with a social worker present. The social worker was always telling me how wrong my parents were, how the world didn't hold it against me that my parents were so bad.

I went to live with my grandparents, my father's parents. They were younger than my mother's parents, who had already retired and weren't that enthusiastic about raising another child. According to Mom, they hadn't been all that enthusiastic about raising her, either.

My grandparents stayed alive long enough to see me graduate from college. Grandpa died when he was inoculated for swine flu. Grandma died two years later when her bus to Las Vegas was broadsided by a couple drug pushers on a high-speed chase with the cops. Newspapers pointed out how that was ironic.

A small inheritance saw me through graduate school, until I found a job teaching in a small, obscure high school. And no one even remembered "Little Bandit Blue."

Until now.

A couple of years ago, when for some reason I felt compelled to research my past in the library, the only part of the story that made me sad, that made my cry, was the part about the motel owner's drowned daughter. Night, Angel. The kisses hanging all night over the bed made me sob. The rest of it—the robberies, the arrest, the trial—didn't seem as real as that story.

Now I stood in front of the door. I hadn't spoken to either of them in ten years, hadn't answered their letters or phone calls. What would I have to say now?

I debated whether to knock or just barge in and surprise them, get the upper hand for once. The way the FBI had. Maybe they were inside there, shyly kissing, trying to rediscover each other, but both tentative and embarrassed. Did they still love each other? Maybe they were inside right now, talking about that, tears in their eyes. Would they live together—could they after all these years apart in the company of their own sexes?

I knocked. "It's me."

No answer.

I knocked again, harder. Raised my voice. "Hey! You guys in there or what?"

No answer.

Perhaps this was all a hoax. A ruse concocted by some tabloid. Maybe Molly and Rush were in on it, paid character assassins. I would walk into the room and a dozen flashbulbs would explode in my face. Microphones would lunge at my mouth. Mary Hart's enormous teeth would snap questions at me.

I turned around and started down the stairs.

The door opened.

I swung around, my throat suddenly choked off. I could taste the tear gas in my mouth, the raw vocal cords from screaming. The terror of being locked in the backseat. I felt dizzy and gripped the railing to keep from falling.

"Oh, it's you," my mother said. She was rubbing her short hair dry with a towel. Other than that, she was completely naked. "Come in if you're coming. It's kinda drafty out here."

"So, you made it," my mother said. She turned away and walked across the living room, her bare feet gracelessly thumping the wood floor. As she walked, she unraveled the damp towel from her hair and flung it onto the back of an old ratty sofa of mysterious fabric and color. Mother had always been that way, careless and sloppy and clumsy. Each step was a hammer blow to the floor, each article in her hands, clothing or food or magazines, was to be discarded at the precise moment and whenever she lost interest in it. On my own, I was equally sloppy. But around her, I felt a sudden compulsion toward neatness and order.

I planted my feet and watched my mother lean her naked body over the coffee table and grab a pack of cigarettes from atop a stack of books. Lucky Strikes. Her breasts swayed like potatoes in socks. She struck a match and lit the tip of the cigarette, the whole time her back still toward me.

I didn't know where to look. I stood staring at my mother's naked buttocks, mesmerized by the sight of them. So white! I'd caught sight of her face only for a few seconds—short, straight hair cut in a crude bob, jagged bangs streaked with gray, a few deep wrinkles bracketing the mouth. Not enough to form a clear picture. If asked, I wouldn't be able to describe the face for a police sketch artist. But my mother's ass was indelibly branded into my mind. Nickel-sized dimples above each cheek. Mango-shaped buns. Firm as a soccer ball. The legs, too. The waist was genetically programmed to be short and a little thick, with a patch of mottled cellulite at each hip. But no fat. No jiggling parts. My body was lankier, long legs and torso, thin ankles, wrists, and waist. Like a Barbie doll.

Mother turned around to face me, white smoke ballooning from her lips.

"Since when did you start smoking?" I asked.

"Since this afternoon. You want one?"

I shook my head.

"You can't afford to be a smoker in prison. Cigarettes are currency in there. Like cash." She showed me the pack. "You'd be surprised what this is worth inside, what people would do for it. If you have a need, someone will exploit it. Same as out here, I guess. Human nature." She ground out the cigarette in the saucer of a coffee cup. "That was my third cigarette. Of my life, I mean. My whole life, I've smoked three cigarettes. If you don't count joints, of course, which I don't. My first cigarette was when I was fourteen. I must have told you about that."

"In the girl's lav at school?"

She laughed. "Right. Mrs. Bloom caught us and made us . . ." She waved her hand. "Ancient history. Anyway, my second cigarette was an hour ago after sex with your father. We fucked for forty minutes, which is not bad for his age really, then he lit up one of these things. We shared it. Just like in the movies. He was trying to be romantic, I think. He smokes like a maniac now; you wouldn't believe it. Mr. Organic Rice now eats bacon like it was potato chips." She shook her head, but with an affectionate smile. Then her eyes locked onto mine. The smile evaporated. She showed no expression. "Shouldn't we hug or something? The mother-daughter bit?"

I shrugged. This was a crucial decision. Wouldn't a hug communicate that all was forgiven? I definitely didn't want that.

She opened her arms and walked toward me. "We can get to the accusations later, Blue. Let's just do this and get it over with. I'm still your mother, right? I guess that gives me some hugging privileges."

I stepped awkwardly into my mother's arms. The arms clamped

around me and squeezed. I nested my face in my mother's hair, which smelled of shampoo with honey, and suddenly tears started budding in my eyes, which I fought—I really really fought with all my strength, trying literally to vacuum each drop back into the tear ducts. I fought the cheap sentimentality. Because that's all it was, all it could be, a conditioned response to stimuli. Pavlovian. Ring the bell, the dog salivates; hug your mother after ten years, the eyes tear. Nothing real. After all, what did I owe this woman? This was the same woman who had been offered an opportunity to be released from prison *ten years ago*. The parole board had decided that she was fit for parole but that her husband was not. She had a daughter, they reasoned, and, as a woman, was not totally responsible for the acts committed while under the influence of her husband. Ten years in prison was enough for her, they'd said. Go home to your daughter, they'd said. Be a mother.

Naomi had refused.

She'd made a speech, which was later leaked to the media by anonymous sources. The gist of her speech was that she was as responsible for her actions as her husband was for his. That she would be treated as the same kind of adult as her husband, not as a woolly-brained female unable to distinguish right from wrong without a man's influence. That, unless her husband was also given parole, she would not leave prison.

She instantly became the touchstone of feminist debates. Some women heralded her sacrifice as the kind that were sometimes necessary to achieve true equality between the sexes. Others described her actions as unrealistic and self-destructive, another example of a woman assuming a victim's role. Naomi's face was on the cover of magazines. Her actions were discussed on television. A country-western song was written about her and reached thirty-nine on the Billboard chart.

I was twenty then and in college. Immediately, I was hounded across campus for interviews. What was my reaction to my mother's decision to stay in prison rather than come out and be my mother? they'd asked. How did that make me feel? they wanted to know.

My reaction was to visit my mother and beg her to change her mind. She had listened, had held my hands, had cried with me until we were both hoarse and exhausted. But she would not change her mind. She'd been convinced that this gesture would get my father released sooner. That *both* of them would soon be released. They were not. I tried to get my father to change my mother's mind. He had tried, he'd said, but once Naomi decided something, that was that. Case closed.

So I had to cut them off. Stopped visiting. Stopped writing. Maybe that would bring my mother around to her senses. Maybe then she'd change her mind and take the parole. She did not.

Now I was hugging this same woman. The woman who had chosen to stay in prison rather than be my mother. I tried to imagine my mother as some space monster clutching me in an otherworldly death grip, sucking out all my energy, leaving only the dried husk of the body behind like a locust skin. Soon all of earth would be a devastated wasteland, the leathery shells of barren women freeze-dried by alien/mother look-alikes. It was working; the tears were retreating. Then my mother began slowly rubbing my back while we embraced and the image vanished. No space monster. Just Naomi. Five four. Political hellcat from Long Island who helped storm Columbia University and occupied the president's office, where she had sex on his leather desk blotter with Harold Henderson, the farm boy from Nebraska she'd talked into joining the SDS, which he thought was a film club of some sort. Naomi Klempt, whose own mother had been the president of the local B'nai B'rith for fifteen years and often reminded her daughter that it had been her own "revolutionary" leadership that had brought Sadie Hawkins dances to the synagogue. "Now *that*," Grandma Klempt would say with a cigarette screwed between her lips, "was change for *good*. Positive change. Not this *tearing down* with no idea of how to replace."

Still holding her, I took physical inventory of my mother. Naomi was much shorter than I remembered, our bodies conforming differently than before. The lumpy body parts bumped clumsily. Her breasts seemed larger, mashing against my rib cage; my smaller breasts poked my mother's collarbone. We hugged for exactly twenty-five seconds—I counted—before I let go first and backed away.

Naomi appraised me with a grin. "You okay? You look like you've never hugged a naked woman before."

"Mom, please."

"I didn't mean anything. Just that your expression was so . . . I don't know. Homophobic? That's not your problem, is it? God, I hope not."

"Where's Dad?"

"You're not, are you? You're not one of those AIDS-frightened assholes who wants to kill gays? Please tell me you haven't become born again or any of that crap. You've got that born-again look of disapproval."

I didn't want to follow this line of conversation. Of course I'd wondered what went on in those prisons. About my parents' sex lives there. But whenever such a thought surfaced, I stepped on its throat and held it submerged until the last air bubbles choked from its mouth. My mother had once admitted to me that she'd had an affair with another girl in college, her first roommate. I was fifteen then, listening to all the gross details in a beige room in which the windows were barred and all the exits were guarded by people with guns. Otherwise, I would have made a break for it. "That was back when women were just experimenting with feminism," Mother had said, "trying to figure out what the limitations were. The whole idea that a woman wasn't an appendage to a man was new, at least on a mass level. Just about every woman at college had one lesbian affair. It was trendy. Like not wearing underwear." Tenth grader that I was, I had twitched nervously in my chair. Why had my mother brought this up? All I had said was that I went on a date to the movies—with a boy, Mom, a boy! But every event in my life was an opportunity for my mother to lecture on the world at large. Every action had moral implications. I always felt like a suspect. "So, anyway," she'd said, "what I'm saying is, don't be afraid if you get the urge to try it out. It was a beautiful time for me. If you don't like it, don't do it again. No big deal. And if you do like it, so what. Life won't end. You'll survive."

I had never had the urge.

"You want something?" Naomi started toward the kitchenette. "A drink? You drink alcohol?"

"No. I'm fine."

"Your father will be right out," Naomi said, gesturing at a closed door. "He's in there primping. He's very nervous."

"You look good," I said.

"Yeah?" She slapped her stomach. "I'm okay." She sat on the sofa, propping her feet on the coffee table. The position displayed her crotch directly at me, the thick dark hairs framed obscenely by the potato-pale skin of her thighs. I was determined not to look away, not to give my mother the satisfaction of proving what a prude I was. Naomi raised one leg and flexed her foot to point at an empty chair. "Sit, daughter. It's going to be a bumpy night. You remember that movie?" She laughed. "You got a boyfriend? Husband? Children? Am I a grandmother, for Christ's sake?"

"No. I was married. To a cop." I hoped for some reaction, some twinge of pain or anger to prove I was getting through.

Naomi nodded without expression. "Did you love him?"

"Yes, I loved him. What do you think I married him for?"

"We're not going to get too far if you keep jumping down my throat every time I say something. I'm sorry if I don't say things right, Blue, but I'm out of practice making small talk. Especially with my daughter. I don't mean anything. There's no hidden agenda. I'm just asking."

"Fine. I loved him. He loved me. It just didn't work out."

"Your father and I will have been married thirty-two years next month. Of course, nothing like spending twenty years apart to keep your marriage together."

I knew from newspaper accounts that my parents had written to each other three times a week every week for the past nineteen years. I was jealous of that continuity in their lives. I was jealous of everything, even the bars on their windows.

"Tell me something wonderful about your life, Blue. What's the most wonderful thing you can think of about your life?"

I couldn't think. I looked around the small room for an idea. It had way too much furniture in it, all secondhand stuff that was old but still a couple decades from being antique. Right now it was junk. The cluttered dankness reminded me of the dozens of motels we'd hidden out in. Every shelf, mantel, and table was crammed full of small bric-a-brac, colored glass unicorns, dried flowers jammed into brass shoes, music boxes. Slap a price tag on every item and you'd be in swap-meet heaven. At least there were no bars on the windows, no guards at the doors. I could leave anytime. Like now, for instance.

I got up, started for the door. "I can't do this. I've got to go." Naomi waved. "See you in another ten years. We'll do lunch." I spun around and faced her. My jaw unhinged to let loose the rapid-fire barrage I'd been planning for ten years. Words sharp as spears would impale my naked mother to that cheesy sofa. Let her bleed to death the way I had bled all these years. Then it would be a quick dash out the door and that would be that. Wash my hands of both of them. They could go their way and I could go mine. But as I turned, as my tongue flexed and spread like the hood of a cobra, as my lips pulled tight over my teeth and the first venomous words banged along my throat in preparation of launch, I saw something in my mother's face—a look. It was brief, one my mother hadn't wanted me to see, but she hadn't been prepared for my sudden whirl. I didn't know what-all was in that look, what it meant. Sorrow? Regret? Loss? But it seized my heart in a way I couldn't ignore. The angry words fell back into my throat like slain soldiers. I closed my mouth and sat down.

"I could get you something to drink," my mother said quietly. "Soft drink or water, if you want."

I shook my head. "I'm fine, Mom."

She pulled a pillow onto her lap, covering herself. "Your father will—"

The bedroom door swung open and Harold Henderson stepped through with arms flung wide like Al Jolson delivering "Danny Boy." I was shocked. I couldn't believe how much he had changed.

"Well?" he said, grinning. "Am I the best-looking ex-convict dad a daughter could ever hope for?"

He had gained weight, a lot of weight. When we used to go swimming on Nature Day, Mom and I always teased him about how skinny he was. I used to count his ribs, walking my tiny fingers across the protruding bones. His knees had always looked huge and swollen in those bony legs. Now his stomach hung over his belt like overraised dough and his once-gaunt face was puffy and spongy. I tried to imagine him having sex for forty minutes without needing oxygen. Or a sandwich.

And the clothes! He was wearing a dark suit, white shirt, and silk tie. He looked like the cartoon banker on the Monopoly cards. The top of his head was as bare and shiny as a griddle. What was left of his hair was gray, much grayer than Mother's, and hung around the edges of his bald spot like a dust ruffle. He looked sixty. Naomi, by contrast, looked a rugged forty.

I walked in stunned silence toward my father's waiting arms. We hugged. I could feel his huge body tremble against mine. He was crying. I didn't break away. I held him until he was done and had managed to wipe his eyes before he stepped back. His eyes were still watery, but from this close I could see the mischief was still there. Despite the doughy face, his hawk nose jutted out, crooked from the beating he got when arrested. He still had that sly grin.

"Hi, baby girl," he said.

"Hi."

"Jesus, you look great. Doesn't she look great, Nome?" He looked over at his wife and made a face. "For Christ's sake, Nome, put some clothes on. Your daughter doesn't want to stare at your damn bush."

"Fuck you. She doesn't want to stare at your gut or bald head, but that's what she's got. Might as well get used to it."

He chuckled, slapped his stomach in the same way Mother had slapped her own earlier. "True, I have filled out some. Rounded some of the edges, I guess."

"You're fat, Harold. Fat as a fucking cow." Naomi patted the sofa next to her and Harold walked over and sat down. She kissed his cheek and grabbed his crotch. "Fat where it counts, too."

He jump up as if scalded. "Nome, damn it! Blue's here."

Naomi laughed. "Of course she is, sweetheart. Who do you think arranged it?"

Harold sat back down, looking embarrassed. "I'm sorry about that whole accident thing, Blue. I hope Molly didn't scare you too much."

I sat in the chair. "I'm fine, Daddy . . . Dad."

"You two chat. I'll get decent for our little girl." Mother stood, dropping the pillow onto the ground, and thudded across the floor into the bedroom.

Seconds ticked off silently between my father and me.

"Don't mind your mother. In prison, you can't ever feel comfortable naked. Being naked is a luxury."

I nodded. "You look good, Dad."

"Well, I am fat, that's a fact. Fat and bald."

"Not bald. Not really."

"Balding then. Not the rabble-rouser of yore, right?" He grabbed his gut with both hands and shook. "Not the Young Turk. Not even what you remember of ten years ago."

Ten years ago, I had stormed out of our final visit, tears in my eyes. He had called after me, his large powerful hands reaching, his lanky body hidden in the loose prison clothes, his hair thick and wavy across his forehead. "You're still young, Dad," I said. "Fifty-three is young."

"Not so young, baby girl. Not so young."

"Who wants to be young?" Naomi said, emerging from the bedroom in denim shorts and a sleeveless T-shirt. "You never screwed like that when we were young."

"Are you purposely trying to embarrass me?" I asked.

"When did you become such a delicate flower, Blue?"

"It's just that I didn't come here to discuss your sex life."

"We can discuss yours if you'd like. Getting any, dear?"

"Jesus, Naomi!" Harold said. "Knock it off. Please?"

"No! We haven't seen or heard from her for ten years and now I'm expected to censor what I'm feeling because of her fragile sensibilities. I've already been locked up long enough. I'll talk and act any way I fucking want."

"You always have," he said. "Long before prison."

She shook her head. "I thought I had. You'd have asked me back then, back when we were driving around with unloaded shotguns under the seat, and baby Blue there in the back singing Cat Stevens songs, I'd have said, Yes, I always speak my mind. I always say what the fuck I mean. But I know now that wasn't true. Not really." She looked at her husband and he looked back, and for a moment I could see that I was completely out of the picture. They were communicating on that nonverbal level humans share with some plants, something that takes place in our roots. Only I had no one whom I could speak to like that, through my buried parts. Someone who could sense the parts of me that were never exposed, never above the ground.

Naomi reached over and stroked her husband's arm. I noticed the dark thatch of hair sprouting under my mother's arm. I felt a sudden surge of anger about my own unshaven underarms. Christ, would I someday be sitting around naked, legs apart, chatting with my own daughter?

"Is this why you wanted me to come here?" I snapped. "To rehash what happened ten years ago? Because if that's what you want, if that's what you fucking want—"

"It's not what *I* want!" Harold assured me.

"The only one who seems to want to dwell in the past is you, daughter," Naomi said.

"I don't give a shit about the past."

"Then let's not talk about it," my father said. "The past is prelude, right? Let's just talk about now, who you are, what you're doing. I don't know—tell us anything that comes to mind. We want to know everything."

"I teach." I felt at a loss, as if I couldn't remember what I did. What was it I taught? Where did I live?

"You teach . . ." my father said encouragingly. "Teach what?"

"High school biology. You know, microscopes and skeletons. Name the seven bones in the tarsus, or ankle. That sort of thing."

"A teacher." Naomi nodded, though I couldn't interpret what the nod meant. Approval, disapproval, appreciation, disappointment.

"Do you like it?" my father asked.

"Teaching? Sure. Yes, I like it a lot." Why couldn't I just say, Yes, I love it. I live for walking into that classroom and telling them about the wondrous, treacherous world of nature. The lessons of survival. How the male orb-web spider no larger than a freckle must mate with the female, who is the size of a human hand. *She sits on her web all day waiting for movement. The moment she feels a disturbance, she scurries over and sinks her fangs into her prey. The*

*tiny male, however, feeling in the mood for sex, knows better than
to rush right over and meet the same fate. So he strums on the web,
creating a seductive rhythm that she recognizes is not the same
irregular rhythm of a struggling insect. Once he's soothed her, he
scampers toward her to complete his task. To her, he's so small, he's
beneath her contempt. But he's still cautious, trailing a silken rope
behind him in case she changes her mind and he has to swing to
safety like Errol Flynn.*

But I don't want to tell them about anything I love, expose
anything I care about.

"Do you tell them about the insects?" Naomi asks. "The way I
used to tell you on our Nature Days? Remember?"

"It's nothing like that. This is much more technical. This is
science, not a celebration of spring."

"How technical can it be in high school? You teach how they're
born, how they mate, how they die. Occasionally, you cut one open
to show what makes them tick. We did that once, remember the
bird? The robin?"

I flashed to that afternoon. Pennsylvania. Bucks County. We
were on a walk in the woods. It was after their very first bank robbery,
which had been in California. They'd been so scared, they drove
across the country and hid out for a month before trying again. That
day, we'd come across a dead bird, a robin. Mom had picked it up
and laid it gently on a rock. Then she took out her Swiss army knife
and started dissecting the bird, nudging the organs out of the wound
and naming each of them. I had been so impressed by her courage.
Most women I knew would have been squeamish and made a
disgusted face. Yet, even as she mucked about inside that robin,
she'd been gentle and respectful of the intimacy. Afterward, we
buried it and Mom made me thank the robin for the lesson. I had
forgotten all about that day, even through the endless dissections in
college.

"You remember that robin?" she repeated.

"No. Anyway, I teach them science. Things like imprinting."

"Imprinting?" Harold laughed. "Sounds like fingerprinting,
something I know a little about."

"Imprinting," I continued, my voice flat and pedantic, not at all the voice I'd ever use in my classroom. But this lesson was for my mother. "That's what occurs when certain birds are born. They have a program in their brain to follow the first large moving object they see. If it's a cat, they'll follow it. If it's a pair of rubber boots, that's mom to them. For some, it's not what they see but what they hear. Wood ducks nest in holes in trees. They can't really see their parents very well. So they are likely to follow the first sound they hear and follow it for the rest of their lives. To them, parents are a figment of their imagination, not real at all. Love isn't even involved."

I stared fiercely at my mother, but Naomi's gaze was steady, perhaps even amused. I turned to my father, who shifted uncomfortably. "Or I might tell them about the elephant seal, those cute lumps the world is crazy to protect from hunters. The male gets as big as fourteen feet, weighs about two tons. He lies on the beach and maybe a hundred females come flopping over to be in his harem. He services them sexually and they give birth to even cuter little pups. Then along comes some other male to steal some of papa's girlie action. And papa gets so mad, he attacks, charging across the beach with such fury that he crushes whatever gets in his way, including his own pups. Surviving parenthood is tough work for kids."

My father looked sadly at me. "Well, I . . . I don't . . ."

Naomi touched his leg and he lowered his head with such a pained expression that I wanted to throw myself on the ground and beg forgiveness. To weep in my father's lap and have him stroke my hair and sing the corny folk songs he used to sing. This isn't me, Daddy. This isn't the real me!

Mother reached for the pack of cigarettes, thought better of it, and leaned back. "So that's science, huh? You're right, I sure as shit didn't teach you all that. Nor did I teach you how to insult us with your rudeness. That was my fault. All the time I was teaching you not to trust authority, I forgot that's what we were."

"Not every effect has an obvious cause, Mother. Every jerk who's heard of Freud thinks they've got a license to practice psychiatry. They'll claim I teach biology because my mother cut the heart out of a robin once. But what would they say if I hated the sight of blood? They'd say the same goddamn thing. She hates blood because her mother butchered a bird. If I cheat on my taxes, it's because you robbed banks. If I return an extra nickel given to me at a store, it's a reaction to my parents robbing banks. I mean, when does it fucking end? When am I just the me *I* made?"

"What are you talking about, Blue?" Harold asked. "We're just trying to get to know you again."

"That's what I'm talking about. What's the difference what I am, who I am, what I do, what I think? They don't reflect on you. It has nothing to do with either of you, what you did or didn't do or should or shouldn't have done. Don't take credit and don't take blame. I am responsible for myself. If I'm rude, that's who I choose to be, okay? Okay?"

Naomi sat straight up and pointed at me. "Jesus, I wish to hell I was a fat seal. I'd come rolling my two tons over there and crush the shit out of you right now. Then you could be yourself all over the goddamn floor."

"Then do it!" I hollered so hard, I ripped something in my throat. I could only croak out the next words, but I did it with great force. "Do it, Mother. I wish you would." I leaned forward myself, willing my mother to come charging over so I could throw the first punch of my life. Naomi's eyes were huge, peeled back to reveal more eyeball than I thought possible. She trembled with such rage, I suddenly feared she might simply shoot across the room like a flare. Is this how she'd survived prison? Is this who she'd had to become?

I looked away. This was not how I dealt with emotional conflicts. I discussed, not yelled. I reasoned, not shrieked.

A row of wooden egg holders painted like various fish, their open jaws angled up to hold the egg, lined a dusty shelf against the wall. I named them: Albert, Bartleby, Colin . . . This calmed me. Sometimes, in cases of extreme agitation, I would try to make up names for my children, the children I might have one day. Tucson was a favorite for a son; Sasha for a daughter. These were names for interesting children, bright, lively, studious. Loved. A family that went everywhere together—museums, amusement parks, the Grand Canyon. I stopped myself from thinking of them. I feared, however irrationally, that my mother might somehow sense what I was doing, even read my mind, and use it against me.

My father's hand slipped around his wife's shoulder and a few seconds later Naomi relaxed, as if that chubby arm had sponged up her ferocity. Naomi leaned back against the sofa.

"Look," I said quietly. "You had to know we would all end up like this tonight. Why'd you go to so much trouble to get me here?"

"We're going to have a baby," Harold said. "You're going to be a sister."

I looked at my mother. "You're pregnant?"

"Not yet. We only just decided today."

"Well, we decided a few months ago," Harold said. "We wrote, discussed it."

"Right. But we started the process today."

"You're fifty-three," I informed my mother.

"So's he."

"But you can't have a baby."

"There's no reason I can't have a baby if I want one. I'm still not menopausal. If your dad still has the right sperm count, and I have a feeling he does, we'll be introducing you to a sister or brother in a year or two."

"Mother, that's crazy. It's dangerous. Not just for you, for the baby. All kinds of things can go wrong. Deformities, brain damage. Not to mention the potential to miscarry."

Naomi shook her head angrily. "I hate that word—*miscarry*. It's just the kind of word a male would pick to describe a naturally self-aborted fetus. You're a biologist, right? It's a physical reaction, the body reacting organically. Spontaneous abortion. There's no conscious or unconscious inducement. Miscarry, Christ. Sounds like the woman did something wrong. You miscarried, dear. Didn't carry it properly. Like you dropped it or something. Stupid goddamn word."

"What am I supposed to do with a sibling over thirty years younger? Share my diary? Teach it to do the latest dances and how to be popular at school?"

"Do what you want, Blue. Be as involved as you want. That's

your business. But we are going to have this baby, even if it takes screwing till our brains melt. Even if it takes the entire medical community and every drug and fertilization technique they can come up with. You don't think we intended to stop with you back then, did you? We always wanted more children, Blue."

"Ow!" I jerked my hand, which had been dangling off the edge of the chair. A fat tortoiseshell cat sat beside the chair, looking up.

"Stop it, Chelsea," Naomi said. "She bites. Just give her a swat."

I folded my hands onto my lap. My little finger throbbed where the cat had nipped me. "I don't know what to say. You're right. You should go ahead and do whatever makes you happy." I didn't mean a word of what I was saying. What I meant was: Can you imagine what the media will do with this? Photographs of the baby with the caption "The New Baby Bandit"? Just when my life will have settled down again, a new flurry of attention, phone calls, cameras. As long as my parents were loose to do whatever outrageous thing they wanted, it would never end. I was attached to their actions by a media umbilical cord thicker than any chain.

"Any other plans you have?" I asked. "Anything I should be forewarned about?"

"That's it for now," Harold said.

"You won't have the energy for anything else," Naomi told him with a grin.

"What about work? How will you make a living?"

Harold shrugged. "We've had offers. We might write a book together, a dual biography, alternating chapters."

"Like Jimmy and Rosalynn Carter did," Naomi said.

I nodded. "Carter said their book was the closest they ever came to divorce. Caused more stress than his presidency."

"Can't be harder than robbing banks," he said. "Besides, there are still some things we want to say. Prison hasn't changed our mind about the way this country is heading. Hell, things are worse now than when we went in. Big business is bigger. Poor people are poorer and there're more of them. The Supreme Court is a brothel, selling the Constitution down the river just because they were pimped into the job by conservative Presidents."

"Maybe you're right. Maybe people do need to hear that." See how calm I am, I thought, how reasonable? This is me, folks, the real me. Teacher, scientist, rationalist. Can you see that? Can you? I can make small talk. "I'm sure your book will be very popular. There's a lot of retro interest in the whole sixties thing." I sounded like a talk-show host.

"Maybe we'll write the book, maybe we won't," Naomi said mysteriously. "We'll get by. We still have friends."

"Do you need money? I can give you some money until you get going."

"We're fine," Mom said.

"Where are you staying? Here?"

"Just for a couple nights. Any longer and I'd kill that fucking cat. Besides, Molly doesn't need us underfoot. Maybe we'll get a place down in Laguna Beach. Very quaint. You can come visit, Blue." She paused, her face brightening. "Hey, yeah! We can all go for a walk on the beach. Like a Nature Day, except you can teach me this time. Point everything out, dazzle me a bit. I'd love that, sweetheart."

I saw the thrilled look on my mother's face, the pure joy at the prospect of walking along the beach with me, of having her daughter talk about the sea life, point to flora and fauna and just talk. The past washing out to sea as we spoke. Each step in the sand a fresh print. Had I ever had such power before, the power to make someone so happy? "Sure, I guess I could . . ."

"Yes!" my mother agreed. "We'll pack a picnic lunch, like we used to. And a lot of sunscreen—we're not quite used to the sun yet."

My father, moved by his wife's enthusiasm, reached over and grabbed her hand. They each looked over at me and raised their free hands toward me, inviting me to come over and join the family circle.

It should have been a touching scene, the very Kodak moment I had told Rush wouldn't happen. But something strange was happening to me; something was moving inside me, twisting and turning and kicking at my insides. I was looking into my mother's face, into her jubilant eyes, and I was thinking about my mother weaving a garland of wild flowers and crowning me and dancing around in a circle and splashing barefoot through a creek, kicking water at each other, and I remembered laughing, all the laughing I had done and how safe and warm and loved I had felt back then and have never ever never *fucking ever* felt that way since and probably *never fucking ever* would again and suddenly I was on my feet yelling at my mother, screaming, the soreness at the back of my throat flaring and burning. I didn't care. I pointed an accusing finger at my mother and opened my mouth and the words flew out: "You stole from me, Mother! We could have walked on endless fucking beaches in the last ten years. But you weren't there. You could have been—they would have let you out, would have released you. I was waiting for you. But you let yourself stay in prison for ten years longer than you had to. Am I supposed to respect that? The purity of your ridiculous ideology? The mythic qualities of your Odysseus-like voyage through the belly of the beast? Fuck that bullshit. I was your daughter. You owed me something, too. You owed me!" I tried to speak more. My mouth opened, but all that came out was a great moaning sob. I cried, loud, bone-shaking sobs. I tried to stop, to close my mouth, but I had no control. I attempted to speak with my hands, gesturing with my useless fingers. But they, too, betrayed me and I ended up hugging my own body to keep the sobs from wrenching my body apart at the joints. I turned so I could run out of the room. But my legs wobbled and I dropped to my knees. Mucus bubbled from my nose. Hot tears streamed from my eyes and dripped to the floor.

My father leapt from the sofa like a much lighter man. He started for me. Naomi stopped him with a gesture. She pointed with her chin, gave him a look. He hesitated but finally retreated to the bedroom, closing the door.

I sat on the floor, a limp puddle of body parts. Naomi sat cross-legged next to me. She grabbed my hand and held it firmly between both of hers. "It wasn't just ideology, Blue. I thought it was at the time; I tried to convince myself it was. That I was staying in jail for a cause, the very kind of cause that put me there in the first place. But I was wrong."

I rubbed the tears from my eyes with the palm of my hand. I couldn't speak, didn't know what to say if I could. I waited for my strength to return so I could dash out the door and never see these people again.

"I was weak, sweetheart," she continued. "That simple. No great martyr story here. No flag-waving, bra-burning, Bible-thumping cause." She closed her eyes and I tracked a slow tear as it rolled down my mother's face. "Jesus, why does everything have to be so hard? You think we'd be entitled to just a little . . ." She shook her head, wiped her eyes. "Like I said, it wasn't a Joan of Arc thing. I wasn't fighting for women or oppressed masses or anyone. I was scared. I knew with me outside and your father inside for another ten years, I would never have waited for him. I would have tried, tried hard. But I wouldn't have made it. I would have found another lover, another man. Maybe had another child. I wanted children, Blue, more babies just like you." She squeezed my hand hard. "It wasn't strength that kept me inside, sweetheart; it was weakness. You're so right—I owed you. But I owed him, too. I don't know if what I did was right, if it was for him or for me or for you. I just did it. That's all. It's done."

I rasped, each jagged word scraping my throat. "What kind of insight is that? You 'did it and it's done'? Now you want to raise another child with that kind of thinking? How do you know if you'll be there for it? Be there when it needs you. How do you know what other weaknesses you have that might force you to abandon it?"

"You mean the way you abandoned us ten years ago?"

"That was different. You'd already made your choice to stay inside. You'd already abandoned me."

Naomi looked down at the floor. She didn't say anything for a long time. Finally, she shook her head sadly. "It was our fault. We taught you how to imagine a perfect world but not how to survive in this one."

"I know how to survive. What do you think I've been doing for twenty years?"

"Hiding. That's not the same."

"I'm not the one who got caught and sent to prison. I didn't abandon my daughter. I didn't rot for nineteen years because I was stupid enough to trust some underground freak named Jeremy who turned you in to beat a dope bust."

Naomi looked into my eyes again. I returned the stare, vowing not to back down from this hippie "the eyes are the windows of your soul" crap. But my mother's stare was different, as if she was struggling with something inside, some awful secret.

"What?" I said. "I hate these staring contests. Just say what's on your mind."

Naomi took a deep breath. "It wasn't Jeremy who led the FBI to us, Blue. That was a lie the feds put out in exchange for our plea bargain."

My skin turned icy. "What . . . How'd they find us?"

"You."

I had no reaction. Someone could have come by and started sawing off my leg and I wouldn't have noticed.

"I'm sorry, sweetheart. We didn't want you to know. But if we're ever to get by this place where we're all stuck, this logjam of bitterness, something has to be done. Your father's going to go through the roof when he finds out I told you." She laid her hand on my arm. "The twenty-dollar bill you used to buy the ice cream that day I was shot. It was marked. That's how the FBI found us. You led them to us."

Lesson #3

Harmful if swallowed.
Induce vomiting.

·12·

"You should come in," Rush said. "At least to wash off the blood." He held open the door to his motel room for me. "You could get infected or something."

I rooted for the keys in my purse and pointed with my chin at my car in the lot. "I should get home. Miles to go before I sleep and all that."

"Just to wash the blood off." He touched my torn sleeve. "You're a mess. Yeech."

I looked down at my arm, the long purplish scrape from elbow to wrist. The blood matting my fine blond hairs was mostly dry. The pattern of bruise, shredded flesh, and crusted blood made it look as if I'd just gotten a fresh tattoo. It looked like it should hurt like hell, but it didn't. I didn't feel anything.

"I've got some peroxide," Rush said.

"You travel with your own peroxide?"

"I'm a lousy shaver." He rubbed his stubbly chin with his palm. "My ex-girlfriend used to call me Nick N. Bleed." He chuckled wistfully. "It seemed funnier then." He looked inside his room as if for something embarrassing he might have left lying around. "Anyway, you could disinfect it or something. I've also got Band-Aids and gauze."

"You're quite the prepared Boy Scout. I'm surprised; I pictured you sloppier."

"Nope. I brush, floss, and vote." He gestured to me to come closer. "Now, let's look at that scrape."

"I'm fine," I said. "Thanks anyway."

"Whatever." Rush shrugged and backed into his room. He started closing the door. "I'll call you tomorrow, okay?"

"Yeah, sure." Then suddenly, I was brushing past him into his room, not even knowing why. "Where's the bathroom?" I asked.

He pointed with one hand while using the other to snatch a twisted pair of his underpants from the king-sized bed.

"Don't clean up for me," I said. "There's not going to be any fucking."

"Christ! Who said anything about fucking?"

"I'm just making that clear. Just in case. I don't want any misunderstanding."

Rush angrily slammed the door. "You're uncanny. How quickly you caught on to my ploy. For years now I've been inviting women to my motel room to wash the blood off their skin just so I can jump their bones. I feel so exposed, Geraldo."

"No need to get pissed. I'm just being direct. Save us both some embarrassment later." I walked into the bathroom and closed the door. I don't know why I'd said that to him. I'd never said anything like that before. It was something Naomi would say.

I ran the hot water in the sink and looked around for a washcloth. A worn white one was folded neatly on a shelf below the medicine cabinet. I opened the cabinet: bottle of Tylenol, can of shaving cream, two Bic disposable razor blades, Polo after-shave, hydrogen peroxide, Band-Aids, gauze, red toothpaste, blue toothbrush—everything in a neat line, like soldiers at attention awaiting his orders. I should have figured him to be a neat freak, in control of every object.

I heard the TV go on, channels being flipped.

I dunked the washcloth into the hot water, rubbed on some motel soap, and dabbed at my arm. Some of the scabbing tore away. Diamond-shaped chunks of gravel rolled out.

"Hey." Rush knocked on the door. "I'm out here fucking. I know we agreed not to, but I couldn't help myself. Hope you don't mind. I'm almost done."

"I didn't realize how sensitive you are, Poundcake."

"Next to you, everyone seems sensitive. Saddam Hussein is a weeping sissy. Stalin was a goddamned wallflower."

I wrung out the washcloth and dabbed at my arm again.

"What exactly did I do to you?" he asked. "Okay, I was obnoxious about the whole contract thing. Yes, I wanted you to sign. Yes, I'm a nobody trying to weasel my way into the big time in Hollywood and I was hoping you'd be my ticket in. I admit all that and more. But I haven't mentioned a damn thing about movies or contracts or any of that crap since you talked to your folks. Have I? Have I, Blue?"

"It's just a matter of time."

There was a long silence. I draped the hot washcloth over my wound. The heat felt good.

"Fuck you, Blue. Okay? Fuck you. To make a movie of your life, they'd have to bring Boris Karloff back from the grave." I heard him stomp away. The TV volume grew louder. The canned laughter of a sitcom filtered through the door.

I wrung out the washcloth. Blood dappled the water in the sink. How many times in the past twenty-four hours had I ended up locked in a bathroom? Before today, I had never done that before, not once.

Boris Karloff. I laughed.

I looked at my face in the mirror. Isn't that what characters in the movies always do at a dramatic climax. Jack Nicholson in *Five Easy Pieces*. They always seem to see something in the mirror, some Dorian Gray reflection. The essence of their souls. Something. I saw none of that. Just my face. Eyes red and swollen from crying. Blond ponytail. A small puffed scar on my lip from the time I'd fallen against the monkey bars when I was six. My grandparents had offered to pay to have the blip of a scar surgically removed when I was in college. I'd refused for some noble reason I couldn't remember now. Maybe it was time. Inflate my chest, remove the scar. What else? Hair extensions?

I submerged my hand in the sink and splashed water up onto my arm. Scabs melted away. Probably leave another scar.

Oh, Mom, I thought. Naomi Klempt, who had been philosophically opposed to taking on her husband's last name at marriage but had hated her own so much: "Klempt!" she used to say, making a sour face. "It's like kleptomaniac. When people say my name, it's like they're accusing me of something." She'd compromised. Couldn't I compromise, too?

After Mom's revelation about my part in their capture, I couldn't stay there in that apartment any longer. I'd muttered good-byes and something about calling them and I'd hurried out the door, scrambling down the spiral staircase and bolting out the front door, with Rush running to catch up. I'd taken about three lunging steps out the bookstore door when I tripped over a raised lip of sidewalk and fell hard on the pavement.

"You okay?" Rush had asked, helping me to my feet.

"Fine. Fine, thanks." I'd brushed the dirt and gravel from my clothes. In the dark, I hadn't noticed the scrape on my arm. When I gave it a slapping brush with my palm, pain had jolted me like ice picks through my eyeballs. I'd let out quite a howl.

"Can you move it?" Rush had asked.

"Why would I want to move it? It hurts."

"It might be broken."

I'd flexed the arm a few times. Most of the pain had been from the shock. Now I was used to it. "It's not broken," I'd said. "Just a dull ache. Like life."

Rush had guided me down the street toward his car. "Maybe I should take you to the hospital, get some X rays. Just to be safe. You have insurance, right?"

"I don't need X rays. It's not broken. I'd cartwheel to the car, but the change would fall out of my pocket."

He'd laughed. The sound had struck me as odd, as if I'd never heard laughter before and didn't understand how it worked. Like in sci-fi movies, cyborgs never laugh; that's how we know who they are. Robot brains can't understand laughter. That's how I felt; I was the robot now. I couldn't imagine myself ever laughing again. I'd have to spend the rest of my life in my room, wearing white starched clothing, growing fat as possible on an exclusive diet of Dairy Queen ice cream. Penance for my sins.

I'd sent my parents to prison for twenty years because of a chocolate ice cream cone.

Now I was locked in a motel bathroom. I held Rush's razor in my hand.

The blue plastic made it almost weightless. I pretended I was an astronaut, like Sally Ride, floating around the space shuttle, sneering at gravity. I watched myself in the mirror, my exaggerated slow-motion movements imitating weightlessness. I waved at myself in slow motion. Then I gave myself a slow-motion thumbs-up.

The image of my naked mother smacked me like a meteor and I crashed back to earth. I was no longer in space orbiting a decaying planet; I was part of the decay. My mother's festive armpits reminded me of the vegetation growing at the bottoms of ponds. The black hairs waving in the murky current. And feeding there on each vegetation was the miraculous amoebae, specifically the versatile *amoeba proteus*. A truly remarkable being, students. It has no mouth, no anus. It absorbs food and excretes waste anyplace on the cell surface. Hemorrhoids are no problem for the wily amoeba. And if the outside environment becomes unfavorable, it simply secretes a cyst membrane and surrounds itself with an outer protection. A room of one's own. When trouble passes, the cocoon dissolves. But even more sinister is its method of reproduction. It merely divides in two, splitting its internal food-processing mechanism in half. Like magic: Where once was one, now are two. And each half is younger than the original. Theoretically, the amoeba is immortal, can live forever. No need of heaven and hell. No Judgment Day. Just enough tetracycline to feed itself and it is forever young. A god, really.

I slipped out of my blouse and raised my arms. Puffball tufts of blond hair with dark roots. Everything inside the body is dark when it first emerges—hair, urine, feces, blood, babies.

Five minutes later, my armpits were nude again—slick and pale as a halved pear.

"Not that I care," Rush said through the door, "but if you've killed yourself, I hope you did it in the tub. I hate mess."

I rinsed Rush's razor and replaced it in the medicine cabinet.

Then I put my blouse back on, feeling much better. Weightless
again. No clone of my mother now, I didn't have to hide out
anymore in my cyst enclosures.

I opened the door and saw Rush kneeling on the floor beside a
large golden retriever. He threw his arm around the dog's neck and
held him in a headlock.

"Hold still," he said to the dog.

I took a couple steps closer and saw that Rush was brushing the
dog's teeth. "Jeez, you're sicker than I thought," I said.

"His gums are shot. We're taking heroic measures just to keep
what few teeth he has left." He shook a scolding finger at the dog.
"I warned you about sweets, didn't I? Neighborhood kids are always
feeding him jelly beans and crap. He loves candy." He grabbed the
dog's enormous stomach and shook it. "As if you couldn't tell from
his gut."

I looked around the room for a cage. "I didn't see him when we
came in."

"I left him with the manager for the day. She has a couple dogs
of her own, so she let him run in her backyard while I was gone."
The dog tried to squirm out of Rush's headlock, but he held firm
and continued swiping the toothbrush across the dog's yellow teeth.
The dog let out a dull growl. "Relax, damn it. Why do we have to
go through this every time?" Rush nuzzled his nose against the dog's
neck, which seemed to relax the dog. He peeled back the front lip
and scrubbed gently. The dog whined pathetically. "Okay, okay.
You've been good. Good boy." Rush released him and the dog ran
into the bathroom, stuck his head into the toilet bowl, and started
lapping loudly.

"You teach him that?" I said to Rush.

He didn't laugh. He screwed the lid onto the toothpaste tube and
dropped it in a paper sack. He stood up and gave me a cold look.
"Since there wasn't going to be any fucking, I thought I'd do the
next best thing—brush my dog's teeth."

"Okay, okay. Maybe I should have kept my mouth shut. I was
upset. I'm sorry, okay?"

The dog trotted out of the bathroom, mouth open, tongue hanging, face dripping toilet water. He brushed my leg in passing and almost knocked me down. "He's very big."

"He's old."

"What's his name?" I asked.

"Russell."

"You named your dog after you?"

"Easier to remember that way." Rush walked past me, deliberately ignoring me, and went into the bathroom and rinsed his dog's toothbrush. Then he placed it in the medicine cabinet next to his own. There was something about that, about how he placed it next to his own, so neatly, at exactly the same angle. I don't know, it got me somehow. It was such a domestic gesture, a genuine act of love. Maybe there was more to him than I thought.

When he came out and tried to swerve around me to avoid looking at me, I quickly stepped into his arms. Actually, I pulled him into my arms. I kissed him on the mouth. Nothing sloppy, just some minor lip mashing. Junior high stuff. He was too surprised to participate much.

He pushed me away. "What are you doing?" He patted his pocket. "Hey, where's my wallet?"

"Okay, I deserved that."

"Which? The insult or the kiss."

"Where's your contract?"

"You tore it up, remember? That little lesson in psychology I'm still grateful for."

"You must have copies. You're the type."

He gave me a skeptical look. "What's going on, Blue?"

"You want me to sign or don't you?"

"Sure. I just want to know if this is going to be another opportunity for you to make a speech and give me third-degree paper cuts at the same time."

"Trust me, okay?"

"Trust?" He said the word as if he'd never heard it before. Then he shrugged. "Just give me a chance to put on my hockey mask before you throw it in my face, okay?" He went over to his briefcase and opened the lid. The little leather loops for pens each held a pen. The calculator pocket hugged a calculator. Very organized. "What made you change your mind? And what was that kiss all about?" He handed me a copy of the contract and a pen.

I signed it and gave both back.

"Do you have condoms?" I asked him. "Have you been tested for AIDS?"

"Well, it was more like a quiz really . . . ."

I started for the door. "You want to play games, play with yourself."

He flopped onto the edge of the bed. "I'm not running after you, if that's what you're expecting. You've got some movie going on in your head here and you're writing it as you go along. Tell me the plot, who I'm supposed to be, I'll jump in."

I turned around and faced him, my voice crisp and businesslike as I could make it. "You want to have sex or not?"

"Have you been tested for AIDS?"

"Yes. I'm clean."

"Clean." He laughed at the word. Then his face got serious. "Why you doing this, Amelia? A minute ago, you wanted to eat my liver."

"I don't want to go into explanations, Poundcake. You want to have sex or not? Not hypothetically, not sometime in the future. Right now. Right here. Actual fucking."

"Sure. Okay." He got up and grabbed Russell by the collar, ushering him into the bathroom. He closed the door and started pulling off his shirt.

I hesitated. I wasn't sure what I'd expected him to say or do. I wasn't even sure what I was going to do. I'd seen something in him a moment ago, seen the potential for trust. He was attractive—I'd felt that right from the beginning—but seeing him put his dog's toothbrush next to his own, it made me want to trust him. And why should I care if I sold my story to Hollywood. Rush had been right about that. Didn't I deserve a little something back for all the suffering I had gone through, anyway?

I pulled off my blouse. The air-conditioned air stung my shaved armpits. I kept going, matching him clothing item for clothing item—shoes, pants, underwear.

We stood naked on either side of the bed. The TV was still on, as if he figured I was going to back out at any second and he didn't want to miss the end of the show if I did.

"I'd read that you didn't shave your armpits," he said, nodding at my arms.

"You were misinformed."

He laughed. "Bogart. I should have figured you'd quote him about now. Who am I supposed to be, Lauren Bacall? 'You know how to whistle, don't you'?"

We stared at each other across the bed, daring the other to feel ashamed and either get dressed or jump under the covers. He put his hands on his hips and looked over my body. I went him one better, folding my arms behind my back. Nothing to hide here, pal.

His body was thin and almost hairless, except for a diamond-shaped patch over his sternum and a woolly circle around his penis. His arms were toned and his stomach lean, but there was a hint of a little growth around the middle, like the wax gathering at the bottom of a candle. His penis was semierect, not fully trusting of the situation.

He made a move toward the TV.

"Leave it on," I said. "I like the noise."

He shrugged, returned to his side of the bed, facing me.

"What's your plan?" he said. "We do it from across the bed without actually getting on it? You overestimate me, Amelia."

I pulled back the covers all the way, stripping them from the bed into a pile on the floor. This was going to be a lights-on, no-covers screw. I didn't want any soft music, dim lighting, snugly covers. Nothing romantic. Just biology.

I climbed on top of the sheet. He did the same.

"One thing," I said. "I'm not going down on you, okay?"

"Got it. And I'm not doing my animal calls, so don't even ask."

"I'm serious. If I've learned one thing about sex, it's that if you swallow a man's come, he right away takes that as a validation of everything he believes in. Like you also have to swallow all his bullshit, too." I was thinking about Dale. Until we'd had oral sex (I was the first actually to do it), he'd pretty much treated me as an equal. Once I'd swallowed his sperm, though, he assumed I agreed with him about everything and always looked surprised and hurt when I didn't. "This is just straight intercourse, okay?"

"Okay, no sucking. No swallowing. No eye gouging or hitting below the waist. Now go to your corners and come out screwing." He pushed a pillow against the headboard and leaned back on it. "Now, here are my rules. Maybe you're doing this because you're going through some kind of emotional turmoil. Maybe deep down you think that at the last second I'll get up and say I can't do this or some kind of gentlemanly bullshit like that. I won't. Not unless you tell me to. You say stop, I'll stop." He looked over at me, waiting.

I didn't say anything.

"Okay," he continued. "Maybe I'm taking advantage of the situation. No, I'm definitely taking advantage of the situation. You've had a huge emotional shock tonight. Tomorrow, you'll probably regret this and be pissed at me. Thing is, I don't care. If you weren't trying to prove something right now, we'd probably never have sex. And I want to have sex with you, I really do. I just wish I was smart enough to figure out what it is you think this will prove."

"I'm not trying to prove anything. All you amateur analysts raised on TV psychology think you know so much. It's kind of pathetic, really."

He laughed. "Nothing gets me hotter than being called pathetic. Ooooh, baby!"

I looked down at his penis, which was even less stiff than before. "Is this going to be a problem for you?"

"You referring to my being pathetic or my being limp."

"I didn't know men could use the word *limp* within a two-hour window of having sex. Some sort of superstition thing, like step on a sidewalk crack breaks your mother's back."

He shrugged. "Maybe if we just shut up and see what happens, it won't be a problem."

"Okay." I slid across the sheet next to him and threw my leg over his hips. We kissed, this time with our lips lightly brushing, tentative and gentle. We did that for quite a while, and I have to admit, it was nice. The next thing I knew, his hard penis was pushing against my leg like a dog fighting a leash. We began to move against each other more vigorously. And somehow I found myself sucking him and he started doing his animal calls.

·13·

"So?" Mitzi asked when I walked into the house. "So? So? So?"
"What? What? What?" I tossed my purse on the kitchen table,
where Mitzi sat sipping tea. The sweet peppermint smell made me
nauseous. "Why don't you ever drink the orange pekoe I got you
for . . ." I tried to remember the occasion.

"Valentine's Day," she said.

"Right. I got you the tea and those chalky scones from that fancy
bakery. Way too expensive, considering you only got me a jar of
popcorn."

"It was just Valentine's Day. We're not lovers, for Christ's sake.
If we were, I'd have thrown in some lingerie or smelly soap."

I flicked her teacup with my fingernail. "I hate the smell of that
stuff. Like hot mothballs."

"Breathe through your mouth."

I licked my finger and rolled it in the crumbs on the empty plate
in front of her. I stuck my finger in my mouth. "Yum. Cinnamon
doughnuts. Don't make me beg."

Mitzi sighed, got up, and went to the cupboard. She smacked a
doughnut on a plate and threw it in front of me. The doughnut slid
off the plate. "So?" she repeated. "So? So? So?"

"Stop saying that."

"Then tell me what happened. With your parents. You think I'm sitting up this late because I like tea? I'll be pissing peppermint for hours."

I bit into the doughnut and chewed and kept pointing at my mouth while she waited for me to answer. I chewed until the doughnut was the consistency of oatmeal.

"That bad?" she said, squeezing my hand. "Oh, Blue honey, I'm so sorry."

"It wasn't that bad."

"How bad?"

"I drove up to the prison. Hit an old lady with the car. I saw my folks. My mother was naked. My dad got fat. Mom has a boxy ass, by the way. Also, I found out I was responsible for them getting arrested and spending almost twenty years in jail. Plus, I'm going to have a baby sister or brother. They're probably grunting away even as we speak. Also, I signed away my life story with a shady wannabe Hollywood producer who has lied to me about a zillion times since I've met him. Then I tore up the contract. Then I fucked him." I bit into the doughnut and continued talking with my mouth full. "Oh, and I met his dog, who has the same name as he does but has bad gums. That was pretty much my day."

She shrugged. "I watched TV."

I took another bite of doughnut. I was famished, ravenous. I could eat this plate, the table, Mitzi's arm. "Did I mention my mother's boxy ass? Looks like a cracked cement block."

"Don't you want to know what I watched on TV? I mean, I listened to your evening."

"Sure. What was on?"

"Who cares!" she hollered. Her eyes rolled toward the ceiling as she remembered Kyra sleeping upstairs. She lowered her voice. "You come in here at almost three o'clock in the morning, lay all that shit on me, and pretend like it's business as usual around here? I want *facts* and *details* and I want them *now!*"

I went to the cupboard and fetched the rest of the doughnuts. There were three left in the package. By the time I'd finished eating all three of them, I'd filled Mitzi in on everything I could remember.

"You cried in front of this guy?" she asked.

"Yes."

"How come? You never cry in front of me."

"Before this week, I haven't cried since my divorce. Now every time the breeze changes direction, the floodgates open. It's humiliating. Like rehearsing for menopause."

"I don't usually cry in front of a new guy until the second date. After I've seen him naked."

"It wasn't like that. Not like a date or anything. At first it was just business, then it just happened. I was upset, angry, guilty. I just did it, that's all."

"Well, do you like this guy or what?" she asked.

"What do you mean?"

"What do I mean? You just screwed the man and then you run out of his room and come home. You're becoming more like a guy every day."

"Forget Poundstone. He's not important. He's not even the point here. This isn't high school, Mitzi. Everything isn't always about guys. Didn't you hear the part about my parents? What I did to them?"

"Sure, I heard it, but that's bullshit and you know it. I mean, so what? You didn't know what you were doing. You were a kid. That's not real. This guy is real. I mean, he's real if you like him."

I laughed and some cinnamon crumbs clinging to my lips sprayed across the table. "He's not real, Mitzi. He's a liar. He'll say anything to get a movie deal. Besides, what kind of guy would sleep with a woman as obviously distraught as I am?"

"Are you kidding me? Any guy who could get it up."

"My point exactly. I've already been hustled enough lately. People have been lying to me and conning me left and right lately. You, for instance, the other night with Officer Dave."

She threw up her hands. "Christ, I knew you wouldn't forgive me about that. I told you so. You carry a grudge like it was a bullet lodged in your spine."

"I'm not mad; I'm just stating a fact. You tricked me, Officer Dave tricked me, Lewis tricked me, Rush tricked me, that Molly woman tricked me, and even my parents. I'm just saying that maybe I'm not in the best state of mind to be making any judgment calls, emotionally speaking. I'm having a little trouble telling what's real and not real. You know what I mean?"

"Yeah. Maybe you're right. If Poundstone is as big a liar as you say, you're better off without him."

"Exactly."

"Can I have him?"

I laughed. Then I licked my plate. Then I licked her plate.

"You're disgusting." Mitzi went to the refrigerator and came back with a white carton from a Chinese restaurant where we'd ordered takeout a few days ago. She brought back two forks and dropped one in front of me. "Here. Before you embarrass yourself any further."

I took the carton and sniffed. "What is this?"

"Some left over moo shu pork. And some sweet-and-sour chicken on the bottom."

"Mixed together?"

"Saves room. I don't like clutter in the refrigerator." She reached over and jabbed her fork blindly into the carton. She withdrew it with a bright red piece of battered chicken on the tip. She put it in her mouth and chewed.

"Does it taste okay?" I asked.

She made a face. "Tastes funny. Fishy."

"Maybe it's gone bad."

She shrugged. Swallowed. "If I get sick, at least I'll puke up all the junk food with it."

I shoveled a forkful of moo shu into my mouth. It tasted like burnt cork, but I chewed and swallowed. We passed the carton back and forth, quietly eating.

Finally, Mitzi looked me in the eye and said, "I've been thinking about what you said. Sorry to be the one to tell you this, Blue, but you're really fucked up."

"No kidding."

"The thing is, you've got no priorities. To you, everything is equally awful. But some things are more awful than others. And some aren't all that awful."

I made an exasperated spare-me face. "Gee golly, Veronica, you mean like who's taking me to the prom—Archie or Reggie?"

"It's not about guys or even this particular guy. Hell, you're probably right and this Rush is a jerk. He's a guy, so odds are he is a jerk. But you don't know *for sure* that he's a jerk. Not for sure. That's all we've got."

"That's it? That's your big insight, your life philosophy, Master Wing Nut? *Maybe* the guy's not a jerk?" I slammed my fork down and glared at her.

She glared back. "Yeah, that's the whole thing right there. Okay, maybe it's not something out of all those thick, musty books from your grad school classes. It ain't St. Augustine or Kirkguard—"

"Kierkegaard, not Kirkguard. He didn't captain the goddamn *Enterprise*."

"Look, don't get snooty with me, okay? I'm just saying that I've lived a little and I've learned from my experiences. Everything smart doesn't have to be translated from some foreign language first, you know."

I let my forehead drop with a thump on the tabletop. It hurt. "I'm being a rag, Mitz. Ignore me."

She went to the refrigerator, came back with an aluminum container of Sara Lee cheesecake. She peeled off the lid and revealed a third of the cake still left. We dug our forks in at the same time. "All I'm saying is that it's all maybe," she said. "If you think about it too much, really consider the odds and angles of everything, nothing should ever work out for anybody. But it does. Sometimes. That's the Maybe Factor. Maybe people aren't as bad as we know they are capable of being. Maybe that unshaven man mumbling to his shopping cart won't whip out a gun and shoot me and a dozen other shoppers in aisle three. And maybe this guy Rush, unlike all other guys you've ever known, will have the balls to hang in there. Maybe things will work out."

I stole a bite of cheesecake off her fork and gobbled it down. "God, you're sick."

She laughed. "Whatever works, right? Anyway, here's something that's not a maybe. I've got sixty-five hundred dollars in my savings account. Cold cash, baby. Tomorrow morning, you and I are going down to the bank and I'm withdrawing five grand. You're going straight to the airport and hopping on the first plane to Hawaii and you're staying there until this shit blows over." She forked another bite of cheesecake. "And I don't want to hear any arguments."

"Who's arguing?"

She smiled in surprise. "You'll go, then?"

"No. But I won't argue." I leaned across the table and kissed her cheek. "You're the sweetest friend. I promise never again to mention the Officer Dave treachery. Unless you piss me off or I need a favor."

"Why couldn't we just be lesbians. That would solve most of our problems."

"Because your breasts are too large and your feet too small. I can't wear your clothes or your shoes. If I were to pick a lesbian lover it would have to be someone my size. Sex is one thing, but doubling my wardrobe is more important."

"It's a good thing we aren't given a choice, like if they could just give you a pill and you could be a lesbian. And on a woman's twenty-fifth birthday, after she's had a few dating experiences, some government guy comes around and says, 'Well, you want to remain straight or be a lesbian?' I wonder how many women would grab the pill?"

I shrugged and finished off the last bite of cheesecake. Mitzi went to bed. I ate a bowl of Sugar Smacks and an English muffin with grape jam. Then I went to bed too. I dug out a battered copy of St. Augustine's *City of God* and read it until I fell asleep.

I couldn't stay asleep. I kept thinking about Rush, about what we had done. It wasn't like me. Nothing I was doing lately was me. Even the sex.

Sex is never what I expect it to be. The moment I anticipate it being like one thing, it turns out to be something else entirely. Sex is like a secret code, a made-up language created silently from the movements and interactions of the body. Skin against skin. Lovers like mad scientists mixing their body chemicals to form some entirely new compound, to create a Frankenstein creature neither can control.

If sex were a movie, everything the couple on the screen said before sex would be in English; but afterward, everything they said would be unintelligible, would require subtitles for the audience. Only the couple on screen, the ones who have just had sex together, could understand their language now.

I'm not being romantic here. I'm talking science, basic animal behavior. It's like, when you're done screwing and you both roll apart, your skin making that sweaty peeling sound like plastic wrap, you should feel as if you did something foolish, shared a silly risk that adults wouldn't approve of. But because you took that risk anyway, you know the world is better for it. Somehow because you had sex, you've justified humanity's existence for one more day. Literally saved the world. That kind of feeling.

That's what I'd been thinking earlier as I straddled Rush's bony hips.

I wasn't sure how I'd arrived at this position atop him. Did I maneuver myself there on purpose or had he pulled me onto him? I remembered penetration, the nudge of his rubber-clad penis as I'd lowered myself and suddenly slurped him in whole. Straddling him like that, knees splayed, the point of his hip bones digging into my thighs, I felt awkward, like I was riding a wobbly seesaw. Even as I rolled my hips back and forth, feeling his penis rubbing inside me, I was too nervous about losing my balance, afraid I'd suddenly pitch forward, maybe crack his nose with my skull, and send a gusher of blood splashing across both of us. Worrying about that made it hard to enjoy myself.

The thing is, I find all sexual positions to be physically challenging, marvels of balance and engineering akin to those human pyramids cheerleaders and acrobats are always forming, standing on one another's shoulders three, four, five tiers high. I know sex doesn't have to be that complicated. One could simply flop on one's back, spread one's legs, anchor butt and feet and arms to the bed, and imagine you are the backseat of a car on a bumpy ride down a dirt road. Up, down, up down, thump thump, finished, park. But with someone new, there's always the hope that the physical challenges of the act might influence its meaningfulness. Sort of a Puritan work ethic applied to sex: The harder you work in the here and now (read: in bed), the more it pays off in the afterlife (read: relationship).

That's my problem right there. I think of sex as a means rather than an end. It's like a tool, a saw, a hammer, a drill. As if I were wearing a tool belt with my appendages hanging from it. "Looks like we'll need to reinforce the penis here, maybe use a number two vulva." Sex as a bridge to get from point A to point B. Toward the end of my marriage to Lewis, when things were really Advil-popping tense, he started to want to have sex more and more often. The worse it got between us, the more we screwed, practically daily. I guess that was Lewis's way of trying to fix things, as if we could keep pounding into each other like that until we softened like clay and finally blended into one solid intertwined lump of flesh.

At the time, it was difficult to keep having sex with Lewis. Yet I'd felt that at least he was doing *something*, making some kind of effort. To help myself get through those times when I considered our frenzied sex life to be too desperate, I used to pretend we were trying to make a baby. I was faithful to the pill, evangelical in fact. I knew I didn't want children then, if ever. But my fantasy was that we'd been told we couldn't have children. Doctors from all over, specialists with dour faces and bad complexions who had studied hard in school because they couldn't get dates, just shook their balding heads sadly at us and said, "It's futile. Nothing the medical community can do. There are limits to science, dear people." But there we were, flying in the face of all the experts, humping like mud snails to prove them wrong, joined in this noble quest to transcend the limits of human knowledge. Each thrust of my pelvis was a stake in the heart of the false god Science. Science isn't God; human will is. Mothers have been documented lifting two-ton cars to save their child. People have fallen from airplanes without parachutes, hurtled a mile through the air, bounced against the ground, and gotten up, walked to the road and hitched to the nearest hospital, suffering nothing worse than a sprained wrist. Willpower can overcome physics, circumvent known cause and effect.

Sex was hope, the hope that the whole is more than the sum of its parts. After all the sweating, licking, sucking, grinding, bouncing, and slamming, there ought to be something to show for it. Even if it's nothing more than that hope.

"Mmmmmm," Rush had moaned, startling me. I'd kind of forgotten he was there.

His eyes were closed, his head turned to the side. His mouth was drawn tight with concentration. He seemed to be enjoying himself. I decided I should concentrate too. Stop connecting dots to find the big picture, Blue. Forget the cosmic and the microcosmic. Deal with one dot at a time. To focus myself better, I used the imaging technique I'd read about in some of those articles on relaxing I'd been swamped with lately. I pretended I was a pro athlete, a tennis player. "Imagine the ball contacting your racquet," my coach droned. "Block out everything else. Forget the crowd. The endorsements. The next shot. The stupid skirt and panties outfit they make you wear. Even the pain in your elbow. Think ball and racquet. Picture it and freeze it in your mind. Walk around it, look at it from every angle." I thought about Rush's penis plugged up into my vagina. I pictured them together like a cross-section drawing in a health textbook, each part labeled in Latin. I walked around it, looking at it from every angle. Capillaries, hair follicles, epidermis. Too clinical. I erased that image. I imagined just his penis. Long and sleek, curving a little to the side as if it was straining to look around a corner. Next I pictured my vagina, pink and soft as if lined with moist rose petals. Then I pictured his penis inside of me, pushing and arching. Like a bloated weasel caught in a too-small tunnel, struggling to desperately dig and squirm its way out. Mashing my rose petals under its furious feet.

I laughed aloud.

Rush opened his eyes. "You okay?"

"Uh-huh." I kept moving. If I stopped, I'd start laughing again.

"I didn't hurt you, did I?"

"Nope. I'm fine. Really. A little cough, that's all." I cleared my throat as evidence.

He looked at my face and I smiled and closed my eyes, rocking back and forth a little more vigorously, trampolining the mattress with my knees. I opened my eyes again a few seconds later and his were closed. I stared at his face. His lips twitched in pleasure. He shivered briefly. It was a sweet face, really. The white birthmark in his hair looked like someone had dropped a powdered doughnut on his head.

I realized I was slowing down, so I just kept picturing him with his dog, brushing its teeth so intently. What kind of man hauls his dog all the way down here so he can keep an eye on its dental hygiene?

Rush's eyes snapped open. "You sure you're okay?"

Startled, I nearly fell off. "Yeah, sure. Why?"

"I don't know. You seem . . . distracted. We can try something else if you are."

"No, this is good."

He lifted me by the waist and, in one of those deft gymnastic moves I was marveling about before, rolled me over until he was on top, his arms on either side of my head. His penis was still snugly lodged inside of me. He lowered his head and kissed me. It made the tops of my ears tingle.

He pushed himself up and looked at me. He was smiling.

"What?" I asked. "What are you thinking?"

He hesitated. "I was just . . ." He shook his head and kissed me again.

What was he thinking? Was he thinking about baseball so he could keep his stamina up? Maybe he was imaging too, or pretending to be making babies. Perhaps he imagined my ovaries, the eggs all lined up, neatly, like the items in his medicine cabinet. Why hasn't she had children yet? he wondered. He imagined my eggs to be clumsy slow-footed children at a playground waiting to be picked for the team, any team.

He was nuzzling my neck, his hand was cupping my breast, his hip rotating against mine.

I pushed roughly at his shoulders.

He lifted himself up and looked at me. "What?"

"What were you thinking? I want to know. If we can do this . . ." I nodded toward our hips. ". . . you should be able to tell me."

"It's nothing. Silly thought. Stupid, really."

"Tell me anyway."

He sighed, looked at my breasts. "You have extraordinarily long nipples. They're very beautiful. But they are the longest I've ever seen. That's what I was thinking. Are we going to fight now?"

I laughed. "They are a bit long."

He leaned down and took my right nipple in his mouth. They

are very long when aroused, as long as the tip of my pinky finger. Mitzi saw them once when I was drying off after a shower in which I had allowed the shower head to linger a little too long on my crotch. "Jesus," she'd said, jumping back in mock terror, "they look like a dachshund's pecker." In college when I'd gone braless as part of my feminist awakening, I'd been forced on occasion to tape Band-Aids over them to avoid any embarrassing tent-pole effect.

The gentle tugging of Rush's warm mouth made them seem bigger than ever. I leaned my head back and let them grow. Grow like Jack's beanstalk. Like Pinocchio's nose. Like my parents' prison sentence. Year after year stacked like milk crates up to the sky. I had stacked them there. One by one. Me and my marked twenty-dollar bill.

Suddenly, I pulled Rush's head against my chest, mashing my breast, feeling the involuntary bite of his teeth. Then I grabbed his buttocks and pulled them hard. I flung my legs around his waist and locked my ankles. My urgent burst of energy seemed to excite him, because soon he was holding my buttocks in his hands and moving against me at a dizzying pace. But nothing short of dizzying would do for me. I wanted dizzying. I wanted unconscious.

Sweat dripped onto my cheek and I opened my eyes. He was staring at me, his eyes fierce with intensity. Sweat covered his face and back and legs. Mine, too. A small stream of sweat from my breasts funneled down between them, ran down my sternum, and pooled around my navel.

Rush eased my legs from around his waist and lifted them up until they were straight in the air, propped against his shoulders. He scooted closer and I felt his penis push an extra inch or so deeper into me. He began to move slowly. I pushed down on my forearms so I could lift my hips toward him; my scraped arm ached with each thrust, but I liked the ache, wanted to feel it stronger to see how much more pain I could withstand. The pool around my navel spilled down my side. I could smell us both, the sweat and the sex and something else, something raw but sweet, like newly discovered tropical fruit at the height of ripeness we'd just sliced open and were smearing the pulp over our bodies. I dug my nails into the mattress and slammed my body toward his while he thrust upward toward me. My scalp went neon. The slow, heavy footfalls of the orgasmic runner were pounding right above my pelvic bone. My pubic hairs felt like a brushfire that he was trying to tamp with his body. His fingers slipped deep between my buttocks and stayed there, not venturing forth, merely a presence, a threat, a possibility. I pounded harder. The footfalls grew heavier, faster. The runner was sprinting now, climbing the hill. Climbing. I clenched my body into a fist and shook like an epileptic.

"Jesus," he whispered.

I opened my eyes, my body still twitching. I felt the warm rush of my guilt escaping through every pore of my body like the excretions of an amoeba. Rush wasn't moving, just staring into my face with an expression of wonder. "Jesus," he said again, and suddenly came.

Afterward, we laid side by side, staring at the ceiling. The sheets were wet with sweat.

"Did you know that ninety-seven percent of all mammals are polygamous?" I asked.

"Really?" he said.

I nodded.

"Refresh me," he said. "Are we mammals?"

I looked over at him, incredulous. "Are you kidding me?"

"Yes." He dove to the foot of the bed and pulled the covers up from the floor and hoisted them over us. "I know what a mammal is, Blue. Gotta have mammaries, right?"

"Basically."

"Well, don't ask me any more wild kingdom stuff. That's the only thing I know."

"Why would that be the only thing you'd know?" I asked. "Are you obsessed by mammaries?"

"Sometimes I'm downright possessed." He laughed, leaned over, and kissed my nipple. When he looked up in my face, he stopped smiling. "You're being serious?"

"I'm just curious. Men seem to be obsessed with boobs. When you stop to think about it, why would a grown man find large breasts more attractive than small breasts? Why would he find breasts attractive at all?"

"You don't have small breasts."

"That's not my point. What if I did? What if I was completely flat-chested? Not even a bee-sting swelling, calm as a lake. Would I still be as attractive to you?"

"Yes," he said without hesitation. "Absolutely."

"Maybe. But you'd be the exception."

"I am exceptional, true."

I pushed his head away from my breast. "The point is, when a grown male gets hot because he sees big balloon tits, is that because he's been taught they're sexy or because he has a biological imperative to seek out buxom babes? See what I mean? Big breasts have no function to the adult male; they neither impede nor enhance copulation, nor do they indicate a more fertile breeder. They're superfluous. Therefore, the only reason he could find big breasts attractive is because they trigger his original response to what must have once seemed like enormous blimps of nourishment—his mother's breasts."

Rush made a face and shivered. "So he gets hot because big breasts remind him of his mother's breasts? I hate this Freudian shit."

"It's the only logical explanation, from a biological perspective. Every time some guy leers over a couple hooters, he's really thinking of mom. Kind of makes guys seem pathetic, doesn't it?"

"For the record, I was the one who said I didn't care about size. Remember that, okay?"

"Have you ever seriously dated or been in love with a woman with very small breasts?"

He sighed and pulled the covers over his head like a cadaver. "Did I do something wrong? Did I say something insulting to you?"

"No," I said.

"Then why are you bringing all this up now? Why are you cross-examining me as if I was a child molester or something?"

"I didn't mean to." I scooted up until my back pressed against the bed board. I kept the sheet tucked under my armpits to cover my breasts. Our conversation made them seem on display. "I'm feeling chatty. Is that okay? Did you want to roll over and go to sleep or you want me to leave?"

"No. Chatty's fine. But can we find a more neutral topic?"
I nodded.
He pulled the covers off his head. We lay side by side like convalescing patients. Finally, he reached over and placed his hand on
mine. I rolled my hand up and grasped his. I wasn't sure what I felt
right then. I liked him, but something was gnawing at me. I felt
antsy and squirmy, like any minute the FBI was going to bust down
the motel door and slap handcuffs on us.
He rolled onto his side and laid his arm across my waist.
"It's just that lately I've been thinking a lot about breasts," I said.
"The essence of breasts. What effect they have on behavior. They're
everywhere—every magazine, every movie, every fashion. We
should get rid of the eagle as our national symbol and stick a tit on
our money. United Breasts of America."
He laughed. "Our army could go topless."
"Our flag could be shaped like a bra. That would make for a hell
of a Flag Day."
"Give new meaning to the words *Old Glory*." He kissed my
shoulder.
I cupped my left breast in one hand and lifted it up. "Why the
breast, though? The Nama tribe of southern Africa prefer dangling
vulvar lips. Mothers massage their infant daughters' genitals, stretching them so that by the time the girls are teens, the lips hang
enticingly down like tongues."
He made a face. "Ouch."
"See what I'm saying, though? About love and desire. Attraction
seems universally to be based on a perversion of a woman's natural
body. Giant pendulous boobs. Flapping vulva. Thirteen-inch
waist." I rolled over on my side and faced him. The arm he'd had
around my waist slid south, his hand massaging my butt. "That was
true what I said before, about mammals being mostly polygamous.
Not much romantic grow-old-together monogamy among our class
of animal. That's four thousand species of adulterers."
"There's always that upright three percent to inspire us."
"You misunderstand me. I'm not making a moral judgment. Just
stating an intriguing fact. Which brings us back to that whole breast
thing again. Some biologists theorize the reason mammals can't be

monogamous is because of the female breast. Mothers feed their offspring from their breasts, which causes a unique and powerful bond between child and mother. Plus, mammals generally have longer pregnancies and their offspring take longer to raise to maturity. Some whales have been known to wean for thirteen years."

I paused, expecting some wisecrack. He didn't say anything, though.

"Thing is," I continued, "the male mammal is excluded from this mother-child bond, isolated from his own offspring, and he starts to think he would be better off investing in a whole new brood. Starts looking for another mate." I paused again, waiting.

"What?" he said.

"Nothing. I just expected you to say something. A joke."

He sighed. "Well, you are making me feel like I'm some kind of promiscuous slug in search of the Great Giant Tit. At least let me get out my Iron John handbook for a good comeback. Maybe it's some kind of man-wilderness-hunter thing. There could be a reason, something very majestic and spiritual and life-affirming."

"Metaphysical," I said.

"Exactly. A whole yin-yang, holistic, uh, existential, uh . . . thing."

I laughed. "A whole horndog thing."

He laughed and pulled the covers back over his head. "I can't win this argument."

I whipped the covers from his head. "We're not arguing. We're discussing human nature and its relation to animal behavior."

"Who said there's a relation?"

I snorted. "You're not going to tell me how superior we are to animals, are you?"

"All I know is that we're the ones with the Super Bowl. You figure it out."

I poked him in the side. "Great closing argument, counselor."

"I never said I was a *good* lawyer." He rubbed his rib where I'd poked him. "You're going to strike oil next time."

I gestured with my finger as if to poke him again and he twisted away. I saw something odd on his back.

"Hey, what's that?" I said, climbing over him to see his back.

"Nothing. Scars."

Scars indeed. Two long parallel scars like a trail of melted wax ran down each shoulder blade. "Jesus, Rush, what happened?"

"No big deal. I was in a fire when I was a kid. Some burning wood fell on my back. I think it makes me look tougher, more manly. What do you think?"

I ran my fingers along the hump of each scar, tracing it over the curve of his shoulder blade. "It just looks like you had your backpack on too tight."

"In some countries, a tight backpack is very manly."

I pressed down on the scar. I couldn't get over how satiny it felt.

"My mother used to say that those were the buds of my wings. That one day they would grow and I'd become an angel."

"I hope you didn't tell that to the other kids."

There was a long silence. Rush looked far away and pensive, a man who had to come to grips with never growing angel wings. He rolled onto his back, suddenly embarrassed. He forced a smile and said, "Don't you know any *good* animal stories?"

"Do you mean good stories about animals or stories about good animals?

"Good animals. Upstanding animals admired by all."

"Most birds are monogamous," I said cheerfully. "Some geese couples stay together as long as fifty years. Penguins hug and kiss all the time. And they're like the ultimate parent. Once the female lays eggs, they have to worry about them freezing in the Antarctic blizzards, where it gets more than sixty degrees below zero. To protect the eggs, the father penguin stands immobile on the frozen snow, with the eggs resting on his much warmer feet. And he stands there without moving or eating for two months."

"Two months?"

"Meantime, the mother is away at sea eating everything she can. When she gets back, she takes her mate's place. The eggs hatch on her feet and the infants stay there until the weather becomes warmer."

"Ah ha!" he said.

"What?"

"Following your breast logic, the adult male penguins should be attracted to the female's feet, because that's what keeps them alive. Do they nudge each other, point a flipper, and say, 'Yow! You see the flippers on that babe? I'm in love, guys.' "

"You're not taking this seriously. There's a lot we can learn about ourselves from observing animals. A lot of humans' superior attitude was the result of observing animal behavior in the zoos. But that was abnormal behavior. Once biologists started going out into the fields and recording behavior in natural habitats, we discovered a whole new world. It's like going to another planet and discovering life. Nothing was as we thought. Maybe that's true of a lot of the way we look at human behavior, what we think is normal and abnormal."

"Yeah, but we can know that only by observing humans in their natural habitat. What is our natural habitat? The city? The jungle? The shopping mall?"

I shrugged. "Maybe that's why we have so much trouble figuring out how to behave. You know of any other species that requires rule books like the Bible or Koran? You know of any other animals that feel guilty?"

"Dogs. Russell gets that look when he's done something he knows he shouldn't."

"That's my point. Contact with humans instills guilt. On their own, out in the wild, there is no guilt. Every act is natural. When the female praying mantis is having sex, she bites off the male's head during the act. But the male's nervous system allows the lower part of the body to keep pumping into her. Next, she bites off the shoulders. But he keeps going. Seems cruel to us, but she's merely getting the nourishment that her body requires to endure pregnancy and feed her offspring. No guilt."

He raised his hands in surrender. "Sex with you is very informative."

"What do you usually talk about after sex? With other women."

He thought for a while. "I don't really know. If it's somebody from the business, we talk about movies and deals and what jerks everyone else is and how much taste we have and how we would run things. Like that. You?"

"I can't remember. Isn't that weird. Never this stuff. I've never talked about all this before, not even in my classes." I felt kind of funny, light-headed. I forced a smile. "This isn't really like me. Nothing I've done lately is like me."

"Okay, then let's try to talk about what other couples would talk about."

"All right. Let's pretend to be normal." I reached over and tugged the covers down his chest. I touched the triangular patch of hairs on his sternum. I swirled my finger as if stirring icing. "I forgot to ask, Poundcake, are you married?"

"No, Amelia, I'm not married."

"They think they found Amelia Earhart's remains. Did you know that? Some scrap metal and a size nine shoe."

"I know. We bid on the movie rights."

"Who's we?"

He sighed deeply and sat up farther. My fingernail scratched his chest as he suddenly shifted position. I sat up, too. I sensed a confession coming.

"Okay," he said, "suppose you had a choice. You could live the rest of your life paralyzed from the neck down. Completely immobile except for your face. No sex. You piss and shit and never know it. Can't even change your own bags of feces and urine. That's one choice."

"Is this the stuff normal couples discuss after sex?"

"Or you could live your life as you do now. Mobile. Free. Have sex. Eat and drink what you want. Play tennis, go to the movies. But there's a catch. Every day you had to kiss the ass of someone you hate."

"Come on, Rush."

"I'm serious. What would you do? Honestly."

"I'd kiss his ass like it was sugar."

"What if you had to do it in front of a crowd, or on television? Every day you show up at the studio, he drops his pants and bends over, and you—in front of the whole world—plant your lips on his rancid fat butt."

I shook my head. "I can't believe we're having this conversation. Is this your idea of postcoital sweet talk?"

"Hey, I listened to your breast lecture."

I sighed. "Okay. Go on."

"Thing is, I was a lawyer. And I was married. A minor lawyer for a major law firm. My wife kind of came with the job, I guess. She married me because I was a responsible citizen, the ultimate adult. I had a house, a briefcase, and a cellular phone."

"Why'd you marry her?"

"I married her because . . ." He reached up and touched the patch of white hair at his temple. "I wish I had a witty answer. I wish I had any kind of answer that made sense. Or that didn't make me seem so stupid. I mean, I've thought about it a lot, but it all seems very fuzzy now. I can remember that at the time everything seemed so perfect. I was a million bucks in potential. Top of the world, Ma. That sort of thing."

I nodded encouragement. But I was thinking about my own failed marriage. Back when Lewis dreamed of one day becoming chief of police, maybe mayor. My dreams were never that big. Just teach until retirement. Travel with my husband. Occasionally maybe I would be out shopping and some man or woman dragging a kid or two behind them would come up and say, "Remember me, Ms. Erhart? You were the best teacher I ever had." Small dreams.

"Anyway," Rush said, "within a couple years I hated my job, my wife hated me for hating my job, and we hated each other for being unlucky. I was paralyzed in my life and couldn't budge."

"Until somebody offered you an ass to kiss."

He laughed. "Well, it didn't look like that at the time. I don't know how to explain it. It's like you wake up one day and suddenly you realize you're not very good at your job and there's nothing you can do to be better. I was the best attorney I could possibly be and that just wasn't very good. I was hired because I had great potential, but what I soon found out was that I'd already peaked, I'd already reached full potential. And that peak wasn't very high. New people were being hired all the time and I could see they were better. They were younger, with less experience, but they were better. One of our clients mentioned there was a training program at CAM, Creative Artists Management. I applied, was accepted, and I've been kissing ass for two years now."

"CAM handles a lot of big stars, right? I read about them sometimes."

"Actors, directors, producers. We're the biggest and the baddest."

"Then you got what you want? Happy ending."

"Yes, I did. It was like I molted, shed some dead skin—there, I do know something else about animals—and everything that was clinging to that other skin, every parasite, just stayed with it. But I was gone. My wife married somebody else in the same firm, a much better attorney. My income dropped to half. No house, not much of a car, and a stolen cellular phone. And so far, all I've been doing is running errands—picking up dry cleaning, delivering messages, making lunch reservations, that sort of crap."

"Puckering up."

"Exactly. But the thing is, I like this business. I really like it. It's exciting as hell. I've learned a lot from hanging around. But I'm ready to move out on my own. I figured if I could just snag one good story, make one deal by myself, I'd be on my way. That's how it's done. You've got to break the rules, you know, jump out in the middle of traffic and grab the loose change. Those who wait around for something to happen to them just end up with a lot more asses to kiss."

"So when you stop and think about it, you expect me to be your savior."

"I hope so. A couple days ago, I came across a memo on the desk of one of the top agents. She makes the megabuck deals. Several top actresses and directors within the agency wanted to know about the rights to your story, what kind of package we could put together. That was my chance. I stole the memo and came straight out here. Since you weren't answering your phone, I figured I had as good a chance as anybody once we got face-to-face."

"Well, we just spent forty minutes face-to-face."

"Pretty nice forty minutes." He smiled, stroked my cheek. "Pretty nice face."

"What kind of movie will they make?" I started thinking about my mother again. About my traitorous twenty-dollar bill. Ice cream melting on the back of my hand under the hot Texas sun as I trotted back to the motel, a motel just like this one. Mother lying in bed with a bullet wound, me with the all-important ice. Not to mention my special treat for her. I'd licked the melted ice cream from my hand when I'd arrived. I could remember the exact taste of it even now. It swelled up in my mouth, sweet syrupy chocolate. It was so good that I was doubly thrilled not to have bought any for myself. Knowing what it was I was forgoing made the sacrifice all the more delicious. As it turned out, though, I was sacrificing more than I even knew.

He reached over, started massaging my hand. "Once I've sold the rights, they'll probably send a writer around to talk to you, get some facts about your life. Not that they'll use facts if making it up works better. Still, research makes everybody feel like they have artistic integrity."

I pivoted away from his grasp and sat cross-legged facing him. "What if I asked you to give me back the contract?"

He paused. "Are you asking?"

"No. I'm just curious."

"Curious, right." He made a hurt face. "I'm not some animal to keep prodding so you can observe my responses."

"We're all animals, Poundcake. Why do you think we're in bed right now? Animal urges."

"Maybe so. But we try to treat each other with a little respect, too. Besides, this motel room isn't my natural habitat." He closed his eyes for a moment, then sighed. "You want to tear it up, tear it the fuck up. You know where it is. This isn't my last stand. If not your story, I'll snag somebody else's. Some other baby bandit will come along sooner or later. It just means kissing ass a little longer. My lips have calluses, anyway."

"I'm sorry," I said. "I don't know why I'm acting like this." I threw the covers off and got out of bed. I found my clothes and hastily dressed. My torn sleeve was stiff and crusty with dried blood. "I don't know what I'm doing here, anyway. This isn't like me. I don't do this."

"Do what? Have sex?"

"Have sex with strangers. Lie in motel beds and discuss my personal life. Fuck while a dog with bad teeth sits in the bathroom."

"Bad gums, not bad teeth."

"I don't do any of this stuff. It's not me. This is not me."

"You keep saying that. But if you're doing it, maybe it is you."

I pushed my feet into my shoes. "Fine. Whatever you say. But just because you crammed your penis inside me doesn't mean you know me. It's not a space probe, Poundcake, gathering information. It's just a muscle." I grabbed my purse and slung it over my shoulder.

He climbed across the bed and sprang up in front of me. "Why are you doing this, Blue? What are we even fighting about?"

"We're not fighting," I explained. "I just want to go home. I'm tired."

He stepped aside and gestured at the door. He frowned sadly. "Then go."

I walked across the room and opened the door.

"Congratulations, Amelia," he called after me as I left. "It was a clean heist. And an even cleaner getaway. The baby bandit strikes again."

I closed the door and ran to my car.

·14·

I woke up because my pillow was wet and matted and I figured I must have been crying all night in my sleep. I had lots of reasons to cry, good reasons. My poor old parents' lost years in the big house, separated from each other by an uncaring society and a moody daughter. My own mangled life and the damage I've inflicted on myself and anyone I ever loved. The children I would never have. Students I'd never reached. Pets who have died, none of which I could remember burying.

I had enough sorrow to saturate a dozen pillows.

I wondered if I should continue my cry now that I was awake. That would probably show some sort of emotional growth. I'd be coping, hugging the child within. Then I brushed my chin with my hand and realized I hadn't been crying; I'd merely been drooling. I laughed and flopped back down on the bed. I crossed my hands on my chest like a corpse, my fingers fanned out as far as they would go.

I tried to sleep. I turned this way and that way, flipped my pillow to a dry side, folded it in half, sandwiched my head between the folds. I pulled the covers up, then kicked them off, then tugged them up again. Without Rush in it, the bed seemed too big and too demanding. An empty bed looks like a palm, the way the sheets wrinkle into lifelines and such. Sometimes I think I could tell my own future just staring at them. Not just mine but every woman's. Just show me your bed, pull back the cover and let me see the bed's skin. Where the feet had spasmed during the night and ripped the bedding lose. Where the hand had wrung the top sheet into a twisted knot. The floral patterns on the sheets, flannel or cotton, dust ruffle or not. The future spills its guts. It's all there.

After drifting in and out of sleep, I finally sat up, looked at the clock, and sighed. This would have been one of those perfect times to be a smoker. Lying in bed wide awake at 5 A.M. with a smoldering unfiltered butt pinched between my fingers, gazing tragically out the window, the winter sun nibbling at the bleeding horizon. A cigarette would give drama to my insomnia, depth to my moodiness.

Being in bed with Rush had been different from being with anyone else. Not the sex part, but the actual being in bed. Rush had been a presence, not just a body. Lying between those worn sheets with him in his $24.99-a-night motel room, his rotting-gummed dog listening at the bathroom door, I'd felt as if we'd completed a long, treacherous drive together rather than just made love. We'd talked and argued and I'd gone a little insane, but I'd felt he was there with me the whole time. Not slipping out through some mental window where guys go sometimes when you raise your voice and talk about personal stuff that makes them feel helpless. Had I ranted that way with Lewis, he would have been taking notes, like the auto mechanic with the clipboard writing down what needs to be fixed.

I closed my eyes and hugged my pillow, feeling the wet drool spot against my cheek. It made me feel creepy, like I was kissing myself. Maybe I should get a fresh pillowcase. Change the sheets. Turn on the TV. . . .

I sat straight up in bed again and looked at the clock: 6:11 A.M. An hour had passed. I had fallen asleep without noticing. I pushed the covers off and spilled out of bed. I was wearing a sleeveless T-shirt and underpants. The elastic on one of the legs had ripped apart and some of my pubic hairs crowded through the opening like unruly weeds pushing up through a sidewalk crack. I tried to tamp them back into place but ended up tearing the pants even more. I pulled them off and fired them like a rubber band across the room at the wastebasket. I missed and they toppled the pencil canister on the desk. I dug out a fresh pair of underpants and nested a pad in the crotch. My period wasn't due for two days, but I wanted to be safe. Stress sometimes knocked me off schedule, so I'd stopped on the way home at a 24-hour convenience store and this was all they'd had. One brand, one box. The box said these pads had "wings" to fit better. I didn't like the word *wings* associated with my crotch. I pictured a small sweaty bird down there, bunched up and struggling to fly before it suffocated.

Using my toes as pincers, I lifted my jeans off the floor and climbed into them. My shirt was too trashed to wear again so I tossed it into the wastebasket with my panties. My scraped arm looked nasty, crusty little scabs had already formed. I noticed some bloody brush strokes on the sheets from my wound. I pulled on a black long-sleeved sweatshirt.

Outside my window the reporter in denim sat on the curb beside his truck, the one Rush had pissed on, and drank from a Styrofoam cup. He was alone, not even a cameraman. All the other reporters were out hunting my folks, but this lone Ahab was obsessed with me. I hid off to the side of the window, peeking secretly through the blinds. Nevertheless, he suddenly looked up at me, made a gun with his thumb and finger, and fired. He laughed and poured his coffee into the gutter.

I had no idea why I was getting up and dressing this early. But I didn't push myself for answers. I just kept going groggily through the motions, figuring my body would eventually reveal its plan to me.

I slung my purse over my shoulder and tiptoed down the stairs.

"Hey," Kyra whispered behind me.

I turned and whispered back, "Hey yourself."

She stood sleepily at the top of the stairs, picking at the corner of one eye. She wore an oversized T-shirt, sweatpants, and thick white socks. The sight of her standing there groggy and wobbly gave me a jolt of maternal feeling. Sometimes that would happen. I'd see her doing something inane, like drying dishes or reading the newspaper, and my stomach would tighten down through my womb and

I'd feel an overwhelming compulsion to get pregnant. Now! That day, if possible. I'd think of likely candidates for a while and the feeling would pass.

Kyra sat down on the top stair. "What's going on?"

"Nothing's going on. Go back to bed."

"What happened yesterday? With your folks. You see them?"

"Yup, I saw them. We talked for a while. It was very nice."

She nodded and yawned. "Where you going? It's only six-thirty."

"A drive. To think. Clear my head."

"So, who's the guy?"

Startled, I forgot to whisper. "What guy?"

She smiled. "It's that man, isn't it? The one who ate the zucchini and pissed on that reporter's truck. He's cool."

"What are you talking about? There's no guy."

She pointed to my face. "The skin around your mouth is a little red and swollen. Just a little. Like you've been kissing a lot, probably someone with a five o'clock shadow. Plus, whenever you have sex, you walk funny the next day. Your back's all stiff and brittle, like Hester Prynne in *The Scarlet Letter* walking out among the towns-people. Like you think everyone knows. Mom noticed it, too. It's funny."

I turned and continued down the stairs. "Go to bed."

"Glad things worked out okay with your folks," she called after me. "We were worried. We love you, you know."

"I love you, too."

"Are you going to see that guy again?"

"Go to bed." I didn't look back.

This was very wrong. Worse, stupid. To sit in a parked car and stare at a curtained window for over an hour was not rational. Not me. I felt like a Peeping Tom. No better than the sleazy reporter in denim.

The bookstore across the street looked different in the dim morn-ing light, less sinister. But shabbier, like a storefront mission. The plateglass window was dirty. The books displayed there were faded and curled at the edges from the constant pounding of the sun.

The streets were empty. No cars. Everyone was sleeping behind their deadbolts and barred windows, the bars designed to look arty, like decorator items.

My parents were up there. Up the stairs, in their bed. Beneath them were thousands of volumes of books, knowledge collected by humans over many centuries, often at the cost of millions of lives. Chronicles of triumph over adversity as well as dreary tales of failure, anguish, lost hope. But were any of those stories as bizarre as their own?

Right now I could get out of my car, ring the bell, and talk to them. Not confront them like last night. Just talk. Tell them I was sorry. Sorry I'd got them caught. Sorry I'd stayed away for ten years. Sorry I didn't have a cause worth robbing for, a love worth going to jail for.

Maybe they were up there making love. Maybe they'd stayed up all night having sensible sex. Catching up. Mom's boxy buttocks squatting atop Dad's wide hips, her hands placed on the hump of his stomach for balance. Relearning each other's changed bodies. Maybe they were wondering whether this explosion of pent-up passion would endure for the rest of their lives, or whether, now that they no longer had the safety of prison, they would drive each other nuts like most of the couples in the world. The prison of love gone bad was much worse than any real bars. Perhaps at the same time Rush and I were climaxing in his squeaky motel bed last night, so were they. Mom making that yipping noise that I remember as a child, though at the time I hadn't known what it was. I thought she had chronic hiccups. I myself made no noise during sex, no sounds. I have stealth sex.

I closed my eyes and leaned back against the headrest. Mothers and daughters. Sounded like ingredients to some volatile explosive: a pound of mother and a pinch of daughter, mix very carefully. Highly unstable. Dispose of properly.

What kind of mother would I make? Was it even possible to be loved by your daughter after she's reached puberty? My own model for understanding the typical mother/daughter relationship comes right out of nature. When I think of motherhood I think of the *Miastor* genus of the gall midge, a tiny fly with a sinister reproductive style. The mother gall midge produces female larvae within her without the need for male fertilization. No courtship, no sex. Miraculous virgin births. However, almost from the moment these nasty daughters stir to life they begin to consume their mother from the inside out. They eat all of her internal organs, dining on them in a specific order that allows Mom to live as long as possible, thereby keeping the food fresh. Once they've eaten all of her insides, they burst through the dead husk that was their mother and begin life on their own, like little Mary Tyler Moores tossing their hats in the air and singing, "She's gonna make it after all." Except for one thing. They are already growing hungry little daughters inside of them.

The first time I taught the reproductive methods of the gall midge, the next day the school received a dozen phone calls insisting I stop. Girls had come home announcing they would never have children. A few wanted their mothers to take them to the doctor for birth control pills. The head of the department called me into her office for a discussion. Science shouldn't scare children away from fulfilling their natural duties, she said. Which duties would those be? I asked. She said, Finding a mate. Raising children. Being happy. She looked at the framed photo of her husband and three sons on her desk. We both glanced at my left hand to see the conspicuously naked fingers. I teach biology, I told her, the facts of life. I don't judge those facts. What about swans? she kept saying, teach about swans. They mate forever and are adoring parents. I do teach about swans, I told her, along with owls who, when food is scarce, feed only the older offspring, starving to death the younger ones. Which they then eat themselves. Would you like little Jimmy's head, dear? No, no, I'm busy with Suzie's guts right now, sweetheart. Swans, she said stonily. Teach swans.

I had a good view of Rush's erection.

Not his best effort, I knew. But, after all, he was still sleeping. Since men have about three erections a night, perhaps the other two had been more reflective of his true capabilities. The whole erection-while-you-sleep thing is kind of spooky anyway, confirming some medieval dogma about demons taking over while we sleep. Anyway, it looked funny just jutting out there, hard and smooth and shaped like the rubber handle grip on a bicycle. Hang a couple colored streamers from it and I'd be the envy of every kid on the block.

At the foot of the bed, his pooch, Russell, slept, drooling almost as much as I had. Suddenly, the dog opened his eyes and looked straight at me. He lifted his head and a thread of drool stretched from his mouth to the bedspread. He stood up unsteadily on the mattress, revealing that he, too, had an erection. What was with these two?

I turned away from the window of Rush's motel room. The curtains were drawn, except for a sliver that I'd been able to peek through. Jesus. Now I really was a confirmed Peeping Tom, a pervert who watched sleeping men and their dog's erections through grimy motel windows. I didn't even know why I had come here, though I was pretty sure it wasn't to do this.

"What the hell are you doing, lady!" a man yelled.

I looked down the sidewalk. A man with greasy black hair and enormous sideburns was coming out of his motel room. He started walking toward me.

I stepped out from behind the sparse shrubbery that lined the motel wall. My shoes left muddy prints on the sidewalk. Evidence.

"I asked you what the hell you were doing there!" He must have just shaved, because he was surrounded by a toxic cloud of Brut. Plus, he'd missed a little patch along the jawbone where a dozen black whiskers huddled. He was tall and lanky and looked both angry and excited, as if he'd been waiting all his life to catch somebody doing something perverted so he could kick the shit out of them.

"You deaf?" he asked.

"What's your name?" I asked him.

He looked startled. His anger drained away. "What?"

"Your name?" I concentrated on scraping the mud off my shoes, not bothering to look at him, as if no answer could matter.

"What's that to you? You're the one diddling around that window there."

I looked past him to his room. "Number twelve. I guess the clerk has it on record."

He reached out and grabbed my arm. "Why don't we just march

over to the clerk, then, and see whether he has your name on record. Or maybe the police do." He stared at me. "Don't I know you?"

This wasn't working out. Why couldn't I run a bluff and get away with it? Just once. What was I lacking, some basic ingredient for self-survival?

Rush's door opened and he stepped out. One hand held a bath towel around his waist, the other scratched his mussed hair. He yawned and nodded at me. "Hey."

"Hey," I said.

The dog brushed by Rush's leg, almost taking the towel with him. He ran over to the patch of grass and began sniffing. He squatted and began a bowel movement that, from the tense expression on his face, must have been excruciating.

"Jesus," Sideburns said, wincing at the dog. I understood his concern. Something to compete with his Brut.

"What's going on?" Rush asked.

"You know her?" Sideburns asked.

"Yeah, she's my ex-wife."

He gave me the murderous look of a man behind on his alimony payments. "Well, I caught her peeking in through your window." He pointed at the window. "She was leaning over, staring in. Just watching."

"Not again. I told you, Gladys, I'm not sleeping with your sister anymore. It's your mother I love." He leaned his head into his room and hollered, "Mom, you want your daughter to join us this time?"

Sideburns looked startled again. Then an angry red flush brightened his cheeks. He scowled at Rush. "Very funny, pal. Fuck you both." He marched to his car, got in, flipped us his middle finger, and drove away.

"He was just trying to help," I said to Rush, compelled for some reason to defend Sideburns. "What if somebody really was trying to break into your room?"

"I'm not a very nice guy. You've shown me the error of my ways." He waved toward the street where Sideburns was driving off. "Sorry, pal. Give peace a chance."

I stood there, trying to think of something to say. Why had I come back here?

"You wanna come in?" Rush said. "Go out for coffee?"

I shook my head. "Just for the record: I wasn't peeking in at you."

"Consider the record clear."

"I'm serious. After I left your room last night, I got in my car and closed my eyes for a second, just to rest them. I guess I was pretty tired, because I must have fallen asleep. I just woke up a couple of minutes ago and thought maybe I should call my roommate, tell her what happened. She worries. I just wanted to use your phone."

I waited for him to laugh in my face or something. When he didn't, I said, "So, that's what happened."

He pointed to the phone in his room. "Go ahead, help yourself."

"Well, now that I'm this late, I guess it doesn't matter. I might as well go. Thanks, though."

"Anytime." He looked over at Russell, who was frantically digging up grass in a futile effort to cover his monument. "Give it up, pal. It's way too late for that."

I turned to go to my car.

"You're even more compulsive than I thought," he said to me. "Managing to change your clothes last night before you fell asleep in your car."

I looked down at my outfit, the black sweatshirt and jeans I'd put on this morning. I tried to think of an explanation. I couldn't. So I didn't say anything. I turned away, walked over to my car, climbed in, and started the engine. Rush hip-hopped with bare feet across the gravelly parking lot, still clutching his towel in a knot at his hip. He leaned down at my window. "This is stupid, Blue. You're acting like a maniac."

"Who said I'm acting?" I reached into the glove compartment and pulled out a peanut butter cup. I gobbled it down in two bites.

He reached in, plucked a piece of chocolate from my chin, and ate it. "I'm happy to see you, Blue. For the record."

I shifted into gear, popped the clutch, and drove away.

I was almost home when I drove through the first stop sign of my life.

I couldn't believe I'd done it. I had never deliberately broken the law before, not once. Running traffic signs wasn't me; looking both ways before crossing a living room was me. Slogging through life turtle slow and steady while cocky rabbits napped, gathering winter acorns while grasshoppers fiddled—that was me.

The sky had become heavily overcast in the past hour and I needed my headlights to navigate the fog. But I didn't slow down.

It rattled me, this outlaw behavior—Peeping Tom, scofflaw driver. I felt so guilty that I was sure my name must be popping up on FBI computer screens across the country. Agents were grabbing their hats and guns and running for the door, yelling, "Get the bitch!"

Yet a block later, I zipped past another stop sign.

Didn't even slow down.

It was as if I was strapped into some amusement park ride in which all the car's controls were realistic but nonfunctioning props. The car couldn't be stopped nor the course altered until the ride was over. I was just a passenger. I hurtled down deserted suburban streets, litter-free black rivers that fed a hundred cable-ready cul-de-sacs.

I tried to think responsibly. I worried that my mini crime spree might traumatize future generations of my family yet unborn. Because of me, children and grandchildren to come would endure crude taunts over by the swings from bloated guppy-faced bullies. I would be the family black sheep. Someone to live down.

By now I'd goosed the car up to about eighty and was blowing past my third stop sign. Screw the next generation. Let 'em hate me. Stop signs whizzed by. True, it was overcast and foggy, but I saw the signs. Each red metal hexagon flared like a match head in the glare of my headlights. The fourth intersection was guarded by a fat black traffic light suspended above the intersection like a hanged man. Its iron-lidded red eye bulged.

What am I doing? I wondered, even as I nailed the gas pedal to the floor and wheeled sharply through the red light. I turned too hard, though, locking the wheels and sending the car sliding at an angle toward the corner. My right-front tire bumped up over the curb and bounced down hard, clacking my teeth together. The rear tires fishtailed with a scream, painting the pavement with rubber graffiti. *Jesus Jesus Jesus*, I thought, then punched the gas pedal again, sending the Honda squirting down the foggy street at seventy miles per hour. Eighty. Ninety. Sweat blistered across my forehead and along the back of my neck. My hands choking the steering wheel were numb. I ignored them. I rocketed straight ahead until suddenly my headlights spotlighted an obese brown opossum waddling across the street directly in front of my car, a scrap of someone's garbage stuck to his back foot like a snowshoe. I jumped on the brake pedal so hard, my body lifted up off the seat. The car dragged to a smoky stop. The opossum, only inches from death, scurried into the dark gutter.

I took my first breath in three miles. The shock of cold air caused my stomach to spasm and I vomited this morning's candy bars out the window.

I let the car idle there in the middle of the empty street while I dabbed my mouth. I rummaged through the glove compartment for Breath Savers. Bright headlights washed over me and I froze. An enormous car the size of a parade float approached from the opposite direction. The cloud of white exhaust hunkering around my idling car swirled away as his car neared. The driver, a frail, elderly man in an Angels cap, barely able to see over the steering wheel, smiled as he braked.

"You okay, young lady?" he asked. He had a couple of dark scabs on his cheek where it looked like skin cancers had been burned off. His glasses were as thick as beer mugs.

"I'm fine, thanks," I responded. I didn't look directly at him on the chance he might recognize me from the papers or TV news.

"You sure?"

"Yup, I'm sure. Thanks, though. You're very kind."

He wagged a blunted finger at me that looked much too short for his hand, as if the tip had been bitten off. "A young woman should be careful these days. It's that kind of world."

"Yes, sir. I'm careful."

He touched the bill of his cap in a salute. "Okay, then. Merry Christmas."

"Merry Christmas."

The big car sailed on, the man continuing to smile and wave at me with his uneven fingers.

I returned to my glove compartment. No Breath Savers. I stuck a Tootsie Roll Pop in my mouth and drove on. The white paper stick poked from between my lips like a frozen tampon string. Suddenly, everything I did was tainted. Even my candy was sinful. I drove more cautiously now to make up for my earlier recklessness. I slowed at school crossings even though it was Sunday and there were no students. A couple of times, I stopped at intersections that had no stop signs.

The old man's kindness had been a sign, not that I believed in spiritual signs or anything otherwordly like that. I didn't. I believed in physics, science, cause and effect, biological imperatives. The *tutti di capo*, the boss of bosses: Mr. DNA. No gods, no Great Spirit, no Holy Father. Just gravity. The old man wasn't a burning bush; he was a road sign. Like the stop signs I'd ignored earlier, I'd been ignoring Mitzi's Maybe Factor. Maybe the old man in his iceberg of a car was a genuinely nice guy. They are rumored to exist, like unicorns and the Loch Ness monster. On the other hand, I couldn't stop thinking about his finger. Stunted fingers were sometimes a sign of schizophrenia. Maybe the old man was driving home right now on the verge of a psychotic episode, an Uzi on the seat next to him. Maybe the next car he pulled up to, he'd blow her head off. Had he pulled beside me five minutes later, his brain's dorsolateral prefrontal cortex reacting to choked-off blood flow from the shrunken hippocampus, could have resulted in my brains splattered inside my Honda like chili overcooked in the microwave. You never know.

·15·

That evening during "Entertainment Tonight" I started throwing up. A steady stream hobbled me to the bathroom floor for three hours, barely able to lift my head to the bowl. My ribs ached and my teeth hurt and just when I was sure there wasn't anything left inside of me not attached, I'd lunge for the bowl and choke out another few tablespoons of orange goop.

Mitzi had already left for the dinner theater and Kyra kept knocking on the bathroom door, which I had locked. "Blue, let me help."

"I'm fine," I said. "Go away."

I didn't deserve help. I deserved to keep vomiting until my large intestine uncoiled out of my mouth into the toilet. I made a mental list of my sins between each spasm of puke, starting with my gluttony from last night. Add to it not honoring my mother and father. Fornication. Greed, in signing that Hollywood contract. Staring at a man's erect penis through a window (not to mention his dog's, though I wasn't sure which sin covered that). Plus reckless driving. Not that I really thought there was any relationship between these acts and my current condition, except of course for the gluttony, especially the highly suspect Chinese leftovers. This wasn't divine punishment. I just listed them to pass the time between spews. That and brushed my teeth a lot. My gums were sore.

Finally, it stopped. I staggered to my feet. I filled the sink with cold water and stuck my face in it. I cleaned my teeth once more just using toothpaste on my finger because the toothbrush bristles hurt too much. I stripped off all my clothes because they smelled of vomit. Then I took a hot shower, washing my hair and scrubbing my skin, though I did all this bent over, holding myself up with one hand against the wall, the other clutching the shower head.

I opened the bathroom door and started shuffling toward the bed.

"You need anything?" Kyra asked. She was sitting in the dark on my bed. She must have been here for the whole three hours.

"Bed," I whispered hoarsely.

"You mean me or you?"

"Both."

"You want a T-shirt or something?"

My skin was extraordinarily sensitive. Even the air touching it felt like sandpaper. I shook my head. "No shirt."

"You never sleep naked, Blue. You want underpants?"

"Go . . . to . . . bed."

"I put some water by your bed. And a bell. Just ring it if you need anything. I'll leave my door open."

I nodded. Speech took up too much energy now. I'd used up everything crossing the room. I lowered myself into bed.

"Good night, Blue." Kyra waited at the door.

"Night."

She left.

I lay my head on my pillow.

My stomach rumbled once, then again, then a stream of bile pumped out of my mouth and nose onto my pillow and sheets.

I rang the bell.

When I woke up the next morning, I was sleeping on clean sheets. The window was open and the cold fog carried the salty smell of the ocean. Everything smelled clean and fresh and outdoorsy, like that laundry detergent commercial where a woman is running through a hillside meadow à la *The Sound of Music*, only she's carrying a basketful of just-washed laundry. It made me want to run on a hillside, too. I tried to ease my torso up, but my stomach muscles still ached and my ribs pinched. Planting my legs against the mattress, I pushed myself to a sitting position. I noticed Kyra asleep beside me.

My heart swelled and my face flushed as I had another one of those maternal moments. She looked about eight when she slept, her little fist on the pillow next to her mouth, a leftover habit from her thumb-sucking days. Her red topknot sprouted straight up, but sleep had flattened it somewhat. The covers were pulled right up to her chin because she hated to have any part of her body except the head exposed. If the covers slipped over her shoulder during the night, she would wake up and readjust them. She had cared for me, stayed with me when I was at my worst. Like a loving daughter. I felt that nudging pressure again in my womb, that need to run out and get pregnant. But combined with my general queasiness, this longing threatened to make me ill again. I started to lose that maternal rush.

I wanted it back. I stared at her, trying to conjure the same feeling, that enveloping tingle of love. But it was futile, like trying to get back to a great dream from which you've awakened. Suddenly, I felt very uncomfortable being a naked woman in bed next to a young girl. She had a T-shirt on; I could see a part of its neck. Still, I was naked. Even Mitzi might secretly wonder if she popped in on us now. With great effort, I swung my legs over the side of the bed. My feet landed on something soft. I looked down and saw a neatly folded T-shirt and a pair of clean underpants. Kyra's work. I put them on. The effort exhausted me and I flopped back down to rest a minute or two.

"How ya feelin'?" Kyra asked sleepily, raising her head from the pillow.

"Better." I started to get up.

"Where you going? I can get it for you."

"Clean the toilet bowl. I don't want it smelling all day."

"Did it already. Comet and Lysol. Also, I took your clothes down and washed them last night, but I forgot to stick them in the dryer."

I looked over at her. She sat up and yawned mightily. "What have you done with Kyra, stranger?" I asked.

"She's in a safe place. Want to speak to her?" She belched loudly. "Recognize her voice?"

"Yup, that's her. I'll pay the ransom."

She pushed some pillows behind me so I could sit up. "You hungry? I could fix some soup or something."

"Maybe some toast," I said. "Dry."

She came back with toast and tea and a can of diet Coke. I sampled each. She climbed back into bed next to me and opened the newspaper. She was a news junkie.

"Don't you have school today?" I asked.

"I'm staying home. I haven't taken a sick day all semester." Since Kyra was already far ahead of the rest of her class in every subject, Mitzi allowed her three sick days each semester, whether she was sick or not.

She stole a slice of my toast and munched it. "I'm giving up on vegetarianism," she said. "Not that I'm rushing out to tackle a cow and eat it, but I'm not going to be strictly a vegetarian."

"What happened? Watching me spew give you a taste for blood?"

"No. I've been thinking about something you said about plants."

"How it was your turn to water them?"

"Hardy har har. Remember, you said that plants are the same as humans."

I reached for my glasses. "I never said that."

"Don't be a teacher for a second, okay? Just listen. You said that plants have the same basic activities as humans: They eat, eliminate waste, produce offspring."

My masticate-defecate-procreate speech. I use it on classes to foster a greater appreciation of life-forms other than themselves and their puppies and kittens. I must have dumped the speech on Kyra at some point, though I didn't remember doing so. Maybe I'd just taken to lecturing everyone about the threat to all creatures great and small, like those doomsday soothsayers with placards that read THE END IS NEAR!

"I've been thinking about that. I mean, you're right, of course, plants reproduce; they have babies for the same reasons humans do, to continue the species. All other reasons we give for having kids are bullshit, rationalizations so we don't feel like robots programmed to perform sex. Plants eat, they eliminate waste from their bodies, and they have children. Same as us. That's it. We can talk about our ability to think and reason, but those are tools to allow us to be more efficient at eating, excreting, and procreating. So, eating a plant isn't any more morally righteous than eating an animal. That's just more self-righteous crap. Every living creature eats something else that's alive. We all murder to stay alive. The fine distinctions are just to make us feel better about the blood on our hands."

"I'm pretty sure I never said all that. Much too long-winded for me."

"But that's the implication, right? That's why you brought it up. The body is basically nothing more than a food-storage unit that feeds other living creatures from conception until death—long after death, actually. We're an elaborate can of beans."

I didn't know what to say. She was smart, yes, but she was not my daughter. Mitzi had certain values she wanted to instill, it was not for me to screw with them. "You should discuss these ideas with your mother," I said lamely.

"Aw, Blue. I can't talk to Mom about stuff like this. You know how she is. She'd think I'd joined some satanic cult if I told her what I told you."

She was right, of course. Mitzi was the sweetest friend in the world, but she didn't like to think about certain things. Sometimes I would tease her with tales of the horrible cruelty animals inflict on one another. She would flinch and make a face and say, "That's why God made them animals and us people."

"I can talk to you, Blue," Kyra said. "Just you."

That rush hit me again, that maternal longing. I wanted to cuddle her and kiss her and take her out shopping and buy her tons of outfits and enroll her in college and get her a car and teach her about the world and warn her about heartbreak and show her how to cook the two dishes I knew. My scalp tingled. I wanted this feeling to last. I remembered Mitzi telling me how when Kyra was six and helping to set the table for a formal dinner, Mitzi had told her to set out the "special napkins," meaning the good linen ones. When Mitzi entered the dining room, she found Kyra slipping Kotex under the silverware. To have been there, to have that wonderful moment in your memory, that would be worth anything. My mother had missed all my wonderful moments. Did that bother her? Was I any different than Mom, locked away from these same experiences?

"Does my talking make you nervous?" Kyra asked. "You look funny."

"I'm still a little woozy. Go ahead, spill your guts. I spilled mine all last night."

"You sure did." She laughed. "You make the worse sounds when you're upchucking. Like an elephant charging or something."

"How sweet of you to notice."

She paused, looked at me blankly, as if about to recite a poem. "You're my closest friend, Blue."

"I hope this doesn't sound phony, but you're my closest friend, too."

"Even more than Mom?"

I nodded. "In some ways, yes. There are things I talk about with you that I wouldn't mention to your mom."

"That's kind of sad, though. I mean, even though I'm mature for my age, I'm still only thirteen. Wouldn't you be happier with friends your own age?"

I stared at her. "You're starting to piss me off."

She blushed and forced a laugh. "I'm just teasing you."

But I knew she wasn't. She'd really been curious and a little pitying. Now she felt guilty because she'd been caught. She threw her arm over my waist and scooted up next to me. Transparent ploy, but it worked. Even being conned made me feel maternal.

"Hey, what's going on, you two?" Mitzi padded into my room and plopped down on the bed. Her eyes were puffy from last night's stage lights and cigarette smoke and her voice raspy from singing. "Why isn't everybody sleeping, like normal people?"

"It's after nine, Mom," Kyra said. "We've been up for hours."

"Why aren't you in school?"

"Sick day."

"You sick?"

Kyra shook her head no.

"Okay." Mitzi wore a nubby blue bathrobe. When she reached across the bed for a wedge of toast, the robe gaped apart and one bare breast fell out. She stuck the toast in her mouth and tucked the breast back into her robe. "This is good." She looked at Kyra. "Did you do this?"

Kyra nodded a little guiltily, I thought.

"Very nice. Maybe you're not such an evil daughter, after all."

An odd silence ensued, odd because when the three of us were together, one of us always had something to say about something. Mitzi was busy with her toast. I didn't know what Kyra was thinking about. But I was a little miffed that Mitzi had come in. Here I was having this great breakthrough with Kyra and now it was over. I felt cheated. This was probably as much mothering as I'd ever get to do, and now it was cut short. I knew these thoughts were irrational and petty, but there they were. All mine.

"This could be fun," Mitzi said. "We should make it official, kind of a girls' day home. Whata ya think?" Mitzi got very excited at that thought. "Yeah, that would be neat. Kyra, honey, why don't you nuke me a cup of tea and I'll be right back and the three of us can kick back together and squander our lives. How's that sound, girls?"

Kyra and I nodded in unison. Kyra got up and headed for the kitchen. She was wearing her usual red T-shirt and black underpants. Mitzi took off, too. Now that everybody was up, I wanted to get up, too. And do what? Go where?

Kyra returned with steaming peppermint tea, the smell of which caused my stomach to rumble. She handed me a fresh diet Coke and climbed into bed next to me. Mitzi appeared in the doorway and struck a pose. Now she was also wearing a T-shirt and underpants, though she always slept in the nude. She'd also managed to slap some makeup on; she never could go more than twenty minutes in the morning before she smeared or dabbed or drew something on her face.

"Look," she said, "now we're all wearing the same thing. Like a team uniform or something."

Kyra laughed, and I wasn't sure if she really thought that was funny or she was being polite. After all, she and I had shared something a few minutes ago. If Mitzi knew how close we'd become here, it would crush her. That knowledge made me feel powerful and cruel.

Mitzi pulled a videotape from behind her back, shoved it in my VCR, and climbed into bed on the other side of Kyra. The three of us stared at the screen.

"What is it, Mom?"

"You'll see." Mitzi rubbed her hands gleefully.

The Rocky Horror Picture Show came on.

"Oh, Mom, not again."

"It'll be fun. Trust me."

"We've seen it a billion times."

"Not like this we haven't. On a weekday, a school day. In the morning. All of us in the same bed. This is so cool!"

It turned out Mitzi was right. The three of us had a great time. We shouted out lines at the usual places, laughed at the same old gags. We stopped the tape at one point and all went downstairs to make scrambled eggs and popcorn, which actually wasn't all that bad. I only had a bite, though, because my stomach was still very tender. Mostly, I ate toast. Mitzi hammed it up, playing all the parts, ad-libbing asides to the audience. She was hilarious. Kyra and I laughed so hard, we spilled some of our diet Cokes on the bedspread. We were all having such a good time, we just mopped up the excess with a pillowcase I'd pulled from one of the pillows and let it go at that.

Mitzi was trying to be scary and was tickling Kyra's ribs. Kyra howled with laughter, her feet kicking frantically under the covers. I laughed harder than both of them.

"Mrs. Erhart?" a man's deep voice asked.

I was surprised and disoriented. I looked over at the TV screen, thinking maybe I'd misheard some line of dialogue.

"Mrs. Erhart!" the voice repeated firmly.

We all looked to the doorway, where three men in suits stood. The spokesman had his ID wallet open so I could read it. FBI. Agent Mason Bigelow. He was black. The Asian man beside him held a pistol in a two-handed grip, the barrel pointing up at the ceiling. A third man, fat and white, stood behind them, but I couldn't make him out too well.

"What the hell are you doing in my house?" Mitzi screamed. "Do you have a warrant?"

"Yes, ma'am, we do," Agent Bigelow said. He leaned to the side and the third FBI man in the back reached between the two in front and waved the warrant.

"Are you Mrs. Erhart?" the third man asked.

"Not Mrs.," I said.

"Ms., then?"

"Yes." All I could think of was that I had been right yesterday. While I was speeding through those traffic signals, my name was popping up on FBI computer screens.

"You need to get dressed and come with us," the spokesman said. He looked over at Kyra, saw her staring at the man with the gun. He nudged the armed man, who quickly holstered his weapon.

"What's this about?" I asked. "Am I being arrested?"

"No, ma'am. We will need to search the premises, though. That's why the warrant. We knocked downstairs, but no one answered."

"We were watching a movie," Kyra said.

"I don't understand what you want here," Mitzi demanded. "This is my house. I own this house. Lemme see that warrant."

The third FBI agent produced it again. Mitzi studied it. She turned to me. "You want me to call Lewis?"

"I don't know." I turned to Agent Bigelow. "What did I do?"

"Nothing that we know about. But your parents just robbed another bank."

"I don't believe that. They just got out on Saturday. This is Monday."

He reached into his jacket pocket and pulled out a videocassette. He tapped it on the palm of his hand. "Seeing is believing."

Mom held a red shotgun shell up to the fluorescent light like it was a test tube of youth elixir she might drink from. She looked down at the people sitting on the floor with their hands tucked under their butts and said, "This is a shotgun shell. What I am about to say is like a consumer warning. I know you may have read that my husband and I used to favor unloaded guns. That was true." She looked over her shoulder, then at her watch. "One minute!" she shouted. Then she returned her attention to her captives. "But before any of you get the idea to play hero and come charging toward one of us . . ." Mom lifted her sawed-off shotgun to her chest and pushed the shotgun shell into the chamber. She pumped the gun, the harsh metallic sound causing the people on the floor to flinch. "Well, this is the nineties, folks, and the times they have a'changed."

I couldn't see Dad yet. The videotape was black-and-white and very grainy, as if it were shot through an aquarium by some film noir nut. It had been clumsily edited together from several different cameras to give the events some continuity. In the lower corner of the screen, a digital clock counted off the time.

Mom wore a bulky wool coat that hung to her knees with a Native American zigzag design. She checked her watch again and called over her shoulder. "One minute, twenty seconds!"

"Almost done," came Dad's voice, confident but winded.

Behind Mom, bank patrons continued to sit on their hands. Some squirmed uncomfortably. "I have to scratch," one of them said. "I really have to scratch."

"Scratch where?" Mom said.

"My face. Just my face. I have very dry skin."

Mom nodded and he pulled his hand out from under him, flexing his fingers. He vigorously scratched his cheek, then tucked his hand back under his butt. I couldn't make out the faces of the people too well. They were just fuzzy grayish lumps.

Mom glanced at something offcamera and started walking in that direction. The tape cut to her walking up to a heavy woman bank patron with a baby stroller. The baby was asleep. The mother sat in a chair in front of a desk with a gold sign on it: LOANS. An older woman with very severe taste in suits sat behind the desk; she looked scared. The woman with the baby didn't seem scared, just annoyed at the inconvenience, as if this was nothing more than a stalled car on the freeway.

"What's her name?" Mom said, pointing at the baby.

"James," the woman said.

Mom laughed. "The pink clothes threw me."

"Hand-me-downs. He's got a sister a year older." She spoke with a slight southern twang.

Mom leaned over and touched the baby's face. "I'm going to have a baby."

The woman looked at Mom's stomach.

Mom shrugged. "Well, we're still trying."

The woman snorted. "I didn't have to try too hard."

"You're lucky."

"I guess. But I'd be luckier if I'd have picked tomorrow to come to this here bank."

Mom laughed a deep, throaty laugh. She looked so calm and relaxed. My heart was thumping as if I was watching some Hitchcock thriller. Run, I silently urged. Hurry! Get out of there!

Dad rushed into the scene, pulling a backpack onto his shoulders. The backpack was bulging, presumably with cash. He tucked a shiny revolver into his waistband under his thick sweater. "Let's go."

Mom turned toward the people on the floor. "Statistically, this is the time when most people get hurt. In thirty seconds, we'll be gone. Resist any foolish impulses until then and you'll have a merrier Christmas."

They jogged in unison toward the front door. Mom stashed her stubby shotgun into the lining of her coat. The videotape cut abruptly to the camera above the front door. Dad opened the door for Mom, but she stopped suddenly, turned, and looked straight up into the camera. She smiled and waved. "Hi, Blue. We love you, honey."

Lesson #4

To reduce risk of shock,
do not get too close.

·16·

I threw some clothes in my suitcase for my trip.

Kyra appeared at the door, holding a small package wrapped in brown paper. She watched me pack for a couple minutes, stunned. "Jesus, Blue, what are you doing?"

"Open-heart surgery." I laid a stack of out-of-fashion blouses into my suitcase, right next to the threadbare slacks and jeans. I looked up at Kyra. "Your mom was right. I need to get out of here."

"What happened with the feds?"

"The 'feds'? Who are you now, Ma Barker?"

"Okay, okay." She pursed her lips and affected an English accent. "Did your chat with the gentlemen from the Federal Bureau of Investigation prove productive? Were the minions of evil thusly thwarted? That better?"

"Eminently." I wedged socks around the edges of the suitcase. "Nothing happened. They asked me some questions about my parents and I answered." I pointed at a sweater on the dresser next to her. "Toss me that sweater."

She did. I snagged it out of the air, folded it, and laid it in the suitcase. Kyra sat on the bed next to the suitcase, fidgeting with the package in her lap. Occasionally, she would reach into the suitcase and neaten something.

"Did you lie to them?" Kyra asked.

"No. Well, not exactly. I'd told them that I'd seen my parents. I just didn't tell them where. We met in a park, I told them. They didn't look as if they believed me."

"Where you going?" Kyra asked.

"I don't know yet."

She made a disbelieving noise.

"I really don't, Kyra. Maybe I'll just get in the car and drive."

"That doesn't seem right. This is kinda like *High Noon*. The bad guys are chasing you out of town."

"Only it wasn't the bad guys who wanted Gary Cooper to go. It was the townspeople. They didn't want to stand by him. Remember?"

Kyra shrugged. "He didn't go, though."

"Yeah, but he should have. Grace Kelly was right. I mean, the bad guys wouldn't have done anything to the town if he'd have gone. And if they did, well, that's what the town deserved for being such wimps. Grace Kelly was the most logical person in the town. But nobody listens to us blondes. We have a rep for being dumb." I folded a couple belts against my pants. "Anyway, they won't have Blue Erhart to kick around."

Kyra chuckled halfheartedly. "Jeez, Blue, it's almost Christmas. It'll be a drag around here without you. Mom will get all lonely and end up inviting those jerks from the dinner theater. They'll form a Marlene Dietrich chorus line again and sing, 'See What the Boys in the Back Room Will Have.' Maybe you should wait until after the holidays. You can go then just as easily as now."

"I can't wait, sweetie. I really can't."

"Wherever you go, somebody will recognize you. You know that. Especially now that your folks are robbing banks again."

"I'll wear a disguise."

"What made them rob another bank? I don't get it. They just got out of prison after nineteen years. If they get caught again, they'll never get out."

"I don't know why they did it. They aren't exactly Ozzie and Harriet." I heard some loud noises outside the window. I walked over and looked down. News vans were arriving. Cameras were being unloaded. Reporters were sharpening their teeth. Neighbors were being interviewed on their doorsteps. I wondered what they would say about me. Quiet woman? Friendly? Always suspected there was something about her, something not right.

The phone started ringing. I unplugged my extension. We could hear the other phones in the house ring four or five times before the machine picked up. Every couple of minutes, the phone rang again. Word was definitely out about my parents' latest adventure.

I just stared out the window without reaction. I didn't take it personally anymore. Reporters were a natural phenomenon, like wind or bladder infections. I returned to my packing. "Where's your mom?" I asked.

"At the store shopping for some food. Looks like you and she cleaned out the refrigerator last night. Left this poor child with nothing to eat." She batted her eyes waiflike.

I bounced a ball of socks off her forehead. "Begone evil demons. Leave this child's body." I bounced the socks off her forehead again. "Out, Satan! I command thee!"

Kyra laughed so hard, she fell against the suitcase, knocking it to the floor. My clothes spilled out in a jumbled pile. "Oh, Blue! I'm so sorry. I'll fix it. Let me fix it."

"It's okay, Kyra. No big deal." I hefted the suitcase back onto the bed and the two of us began refolding and repacking. Heaped together like that, my clothes looked like the three dollar bin at a thrift shop. The colors were mostly beige and olive green and khaki brown. That ridiculous drab pile represented the pattern of my buying choices over the past five or six years. It wasn't until I saw them all tangled together that I could see the color pattern of my life. Clothes choices represent how you see yourself, how you want others to see you. My clothing indicated someone who didn't wish to be seen at all—camouflage.

Kyra picked up each item, shook it gently, laid it flat on the bed, smoothed it with her palms, then folded it with razor creases as if it was new in the stores. Every article of clothing she placed in the suitcase received a comforting pat, as if wishing it farewell. It was such a touching gesture that my dormant maternalism swelled again. I leaned over and kissed the top of Kyra's head.

"I haven't washed my hair in three days," she warned.

"That's okay; I haven't brushed my teeth in a week." I lifted a loose strand of her hair. "In fact, a little flossing might be in order right now."

"Blue!" She pulled away, laughing, smoothing her topknot. There was something about her laugh right then, something about each note that rang out so clear and tony, like the bells you hear in some Christmas carols. Her face was scrunched with joy as she laughed, the bed bouncing under her. Her eyes glistened with tears. My heart felt so big that it actually hurt. I thought that this must be what devout Christians feel when they see the plaster baby Jesus in those nativity scenes.

"I love you, Kyra," I said, my voice trembling more than I had realized.

"I love you, too," she said. She hugged me hard. Then even harder. "I bet I could squeeze you till you pass out," she said. "I'm pretty strong."

I grabbed hold of the tops of both her ears and tugged. "I read a book once where this spy tears the ears off some assassin. He said it was a lot easier than people think." I pulled a little harder.

"Owww!" She let go and backed away, rubbing her ears. She was smiling. "Please don't go, Blue. Please?"

Suddenly I had a brainstorm! Of course! There was no need for me to slink away into hiding in some remote town in Montana, freezing my ass off, watching talk shows all day. I would ask Kyra to go with me on my trip. It wouldn't be a retreat then; it would be a journey, a quest. We could go anywhere. We would travel around like mother and daughter. We already shared secrets, more than she did with her own mother. It was a natural next move, an evolution of sorts. You weren't stuck with your biological families; you could create your own. We didn't have to be gall midges, consuming our mothers in order to be born. We could live with them, learn from them, love them.

"Kyra," I said, "I've got a great idea. How about you come with me?"

I expected her eyes to widen with delight. Maybe she'd jump up and down, which she actually did sometimes when she was exceptionally excited. She did neither now. She stared at me, confused. "Go with you?"

"Yeah. On a trip. It wouldn't be that long. I'm sure we could talk your mom into it. It could be very educational." I kept blathering away, trying to sound convincing. I hadn't expected to have to persuade her.

She looked down at my suitcase. The clothes she'd packed were so neat that there was now extra room in there. I could pack more of my beige life. Maybe that's what she saw, staring into my suitcase. A life wrapped in camouflage. A life she should stay away from.

"It's okay, Kyra," I said, forcing a smile. "Just an idea. A dumb one."

"It's just that I can't leave Mom. Holidays are tough enough on her. She really needs me."

So do I, I thought. But I haven't earned the right to. I didn't carry you for nine months, didn't nurse you through sicknesses and divorce. Didn't endure your scorn and hatred when you were throwing tantrums. I waltzed in, rented a room, and tried to steal your love. A worse thief than my parents.

The genes know. Far beneath every action we take, every blast of emotion we experience, every alliance we make or break, in a twenty-four-hour-a-day world we can't even see, our own genes beat the tom-toms and we dance. Regardless of what Kyra and I had shared, she and Mitzi communicated through the silent vibrations of shared genes. Next to that, words were meaningless.

We are all gall midges, every one of us.

I walked into the bathroom and gathered my toothbrush, tampons, shampoo, antiperspirant, hairbrush, and dental floss. I dumped them in the plastic-lined pocket and zipped them in.

"You know, it's too bad your folks can't come here for Christmas," Kyra said. "That would be so cool."

"We'd be aiding and abetting fugitives. Felons." Horny middle-aged felons trying to make a baby between bank jobs.

"I'd like to meet your mom someday. I mean, if this all works out somehow."

"Works out? How could it possibly work out?"

"Like if they stop robbing banks and the statute of limitations runs out or something."

"By then, you'll be too old to care. Besides, why do you want to meet my mom? She's a criminal."

"Sure, but she's also a hero."

"Hero? Because she robs banks?"

"No, because of what she did with your dad. Going to jail, staying there even though she could have gotten out. That must have been the hardest thing in the world. I don't think I could have been that brave."

"Let me tell you something, Kyra. Naomi didn't stay in jail out of principles. She stayed out of fear. She was afraid if she got out, she'd end up leaving my father. Instead, she left her daughter."

"She did a Gary Cooper. She probably should have listened to Grace Kelly; that would have been better. But I still admire her for recognizing her weakness and doing something about it. She's like some of those overweight women who, out of fear of relationships, eat until they've made their bodies so grotesque that they never have to deal with men. These women imprison themselves in fat. Your mom did it for real. Don't you see the heroics in that?"

"What about her daughter, Dr. Brothers? Didn't she owe something to her daughter?"

"Sure, I guess. That's the part that confuses me. I mean, who do you owe more to, your spouse or your child? It's like that moral dilemma I read about: What if you're in the jungle and a tiger starts chasing you? Now, you're carrying your baby. You start to run, but pretty soon you know the tiger will overtake you. Your husband and other child are waiting for you back at camp, but too far away to hear your cries. What is the best choice here? You could toss the child into the brush and keep running, hoping that the tiger will ignore the child and keep chasing you. Of course, he could catch and eat you, then return for the baby. Or the baby could be dragged off by some other animal. Or just die of exposure. That choice leaves both of you dead. Second choice: You could toss the baby to the tiger, right in his face. That's easy food for him and there's a chance you can get away while he's devouring your baby. If so, you will be reunited with your husband and you can always make another child. Of course, would he ever forgive you for sacrificing his child? And even if he agreed with your decision, could you live with what you've done, knowing you murdered your own child to save yourself. To me the answer to this question reveals the true nature of intelligence."

"I don't want the nature of my intelligence revealed. It's too embarrassing."

"C'mon, Blue. What would you do in this situation?"

"Am I the mother or the baby? Because if I'm the baby, I'd grab Mom by the throat and say, 'Listen, bitch, I go, you go!' "

"You're the mother."

I sighed. "I hate these kinds of questions. I'll never be in a jungle."

"It's metaphoric."

"Maybe I could just throw the diaper and scare the tiger away."

Kyra shook her head. "Why don't you want to answer the question?"

"It's a stupid question. People are always giving these hypothetical questions, elaborate situations that you never find yourself in."

"You're in an elaborate situation right now. Your parents are bank robbers. You're being watched by the FBI. Reporters chase you everywhere. I think there's another reason you're not answering." She picked up a pair of my sandals from the bed and fit them snugly into the suitcase. "Me, I'd toss the baby to the tiger. I know that's easy for me to say right now because I haven't given birth and had all those goofy feelings for the kid you're supposed to have. Still, it's the only choice that makes sense. You toss the baby to the tiger, then you have another one with your husband. Your family still goes on; you are alive to give and receive love. I'd like to think I'd be able to overcome all the sentimental brainwashing crap and do the smart thing. The function of having babies is to continue the DNA. Any decision that does not promote that end is less than intelligent."

"Some animals have practice babies," I said. "Because they aren't taught how to raise their offspring, the first baby they have is for making mistakes. Usually, they accidentally kill it. Then they have the real baby. Some gorillas do that."

"Wow. The way we have dolls, huh?"

"Yeah." I looked at Kyra sitting there, fussing with the contents of my suitcase, and I very much wanted to cry. My plan for the two of us traveling together had excited me so much, I wasn't prepared to deal with her rejection. I remember overhearing two women in a restaurant. They were talking about a mutual friend. One of them said, "There's no human being more alone in this world than a childless mother." I'd laughed to myself, thinking that it sounded like a line from an old spiritual or something. No human being needed another to fulfill her.

But right now, standing there in front of my packed suitcase, the world yipping at my butt, I had a different perspective. Form follows function. A woman's body is constructed to bear children. That's its function in the physical world—perpetuation of the species. Perhaps the body protests when it isn't allowed to fulfill its function. Like if you score high on all your tests and get all A's and everybody keeps talking about your great potential. But you end up thirty years old without a job, a lover, a family. Potential unfulfilled is the heaviest failure of all. Nature abhors a vacuum, especially in the womb.

"What?" Kyra asked.

"What?" I said.

"You said something about a vacuum. You want me to vacuum?"

I shook my head. Stop talking to yourself, Blue. A bad sign. "Let's go wait for your mom downstairs. There's got to be a talk show on some channel."

I closed the suitcase and lifted it off the bed. A few articles of clothing I decided not to take littered my bedspread. I snatched them up to return to the closet. Under one green sweater was the package Kyra had brought in with her. "Hey, your package," I reminded her.

"Oh, right. That's for you. A messenger delivered it while you were out with the feds."

I picked it up and examined the wrapping. Just brown paper with my name and address. No return address. It was about the size of a thick paperback book. I tore off the wrapping.

Inside were two stacks of money. Tens, twenties, fifties, and hundreds.

The attached note said: "This is clean money, sweetheart. Untraceable. So spend however you want. Happy Sweet Sixteen. We're working on the other significant events we missed. Love, Mom and Dad."

Kyra touched the stacks of money and whistled. "Man, I've *really* got to meet your folks."

The phone rang twice, then stopped. Rang twice again. Stopped. "That's Megan," Kyra said, leaving the bedroom. "Our tricky code. I've got to call her back or I'll lose my only friend at school with a car. Don't spend any money till I get back, okay?" She ran out the door.

I counted the money. I made neat little piles of a hundred dollars each, then counted up the piles. Ten thousand dollars. I swept my hands through all the piles and mixed the bills together into one big pile. I sorted the money according to denominations. Then I recounted. Still ten thousand dollars.

I stroked the pile of hundreds. The bills felt dry and rough like grandparent skin. Why had they sent this to me now? A peace offering? Or a way to make me an accessory after the fact? Was this an act of love or an attempt to suck me back into their depraved lives?

"Jesus, where'd that come from?" Mitzi said from the doorway. "You rob a bank?" She laughed. "Get it, rob a bank?" She hovered over the money and rubbed her hands greedily.

"Don't even think about raising my rent."

Mitzi knelt down beside my bed and tapped each pile of money with her sculpted fingernail. "How much?"

"Ten grand."

"Jesus."

"Amen." I knelt on the floor next to her. We looked like we were about to say our prayers before bed.

"Are you going to see them again?"

"Who, the FBI?"

"No, your parents."

"I don't even know where they are," I said. "The bank they robbed is in Nevada, so they could be anywhere by now."

"Maybe they'll ask you to join their gang," Mitzi said. "You'll need a nickname like Machine Gun Kelly and Mad Dog Morgan. How about Anal Retentive Erhart? It's got a ring."

"Don't even joke. It wouldn't surprise me if they showed up here one night and asked me to do just that. Shotguns in hand, the motor revving. The radio blaring Crosby, Stills & Nash. Maybe a new baby strapped into a car seat with a tiny ski mask over its head." I shook my head. "I'd like to think of them as wacky, colorful characters, playful banditos with hearts of gold, the way the rest of the world seems to enjoy them. Like they were performance artists and these robberies were just another form of entertainment for the masses. But when they get caught and maybe killed, or go to prison for the rest of their lives, the rest of the world will forget them and go back to poking into Princess Di's bedroom. Meantime, they'll still be my parents." I laid my head on the bed and closed my eyes. "God, Mitzi, they're crazy fucks."

Mitzi put her arm around me. We knelt beside the bed and stared at the money.

"You want some?" I said, offering her a stack of twenties.

She took it, fanned herself with the bills. "From the velocity of the breeze, I'd say there's about two thousand dollars here."

"You want more?" I slid a stack of fifties across the bedspread. She shoved it back and tossed the twenties back down. "They meant it for you, Blue. I wouldn't feel right." Mitzi nodded at my suitcase. "Besides, Kyra told me you're taking a trip. This money will come in handy."

"I guess." I laid my head down on the stack of hundreds as if it were a tiny pillow. I could hear the ocean, the expensive part of the ocean, the Riviera, the Caribbean. "You think my parents knew I'd need to leave town?" I asked her. "Maybe that's why they sent this?"

"Yeah, I do. I think this is their way of helping you out."

I snorted. "They've helped me enough, thank you. If it hadn't been for them, I wouldn't need to leave town in the first place."

"True." She got off her knees, brushed her pants, and sat on the bed. "Did they say anything about why they did it? Why they robbed that bank?"

"Nope." I handed her Naomi's note.

She read it, turned it over. "That's it?"

"That's all she wrote."

"It doesn't make sense," she said. "They could have made more money by writing their memoirs than from robbing a stupid bank. I don't get it."

"They're not doing it for the money."

"They do know the sixties are dead, don't they? I mean, you did tell them that, didn't you? Bob Dylan ain't gonna write a song about them."

I was tired of thinking about them. "Fuck 'em," I said, standing up. I started stacking the smaller piles of money into one big stack. "I can't live my life as a reaction to whatever they do anymore. They aren't gods."

"So few of us are these days."

I looked over at her. Did she mean something personal by that? Had Kyra told her about my attempt to steal her daughter away? My head throbbed with guilt for trying. My heart ached with loss for failing.

"What are you going to do with the money?" Mitzi asked. "Not something stupid like give it back to the bank?"

"I don't know. Maybe. I don't know." Giving it back would sure send a message to Mom to keep me out of any future plans. Who was I kidding? They weren't doing this for me. They were used to giving away their money to charities. This time, I was their charity. I was one of Jerry's kids.

I popped my suitcase and stuffed the money inside. "I'm off. I just hung around to let you drool on my cash. Don't rent my room out, okay? I'll be back."

"You'll call, right? Every day?"

"I'll call, Aunty Mitzi. But not every day. When I do, don't ask me where I am. Chances are your phone will be bugged by the FBI. Those guys are serious."

"They can do that? Tap my phone? Jesus, that makes me mad." I hefted my suitcase and started for the door.

"Promise me you'll be miserable without us," Mitzi said.

"I'll be miserable."

"Okay. But if you meet some new guy and fall madly in love, I'll hunt you down and kill you, I swear. I'm older and I deserve to fall in love first."

"Much older," I said.

She laughed. "Do you have any idea where you're going?"

"Someplace with a good library. I figure I may as well work on my dissertation on Thomas Q while I've got the time. It'll keep me from going crazy."

"But the guy you're writing about is crazy. Thomas Q! What the hell kind of name is that? That's one name."

"Like Cher. Madonna. Prince."

"Exactly! He's all show biz."

"Jesus. Confucius. Buddha. Moses. Muhammad."

"Jesus had a last name. Christ. Jesus Christ."

"Christ isn't a name—it's a title. Like King or Duke. It means one who's accepted as the Messiah."

"Really?"

"Really."

"Well, I don't care about any of that. All I know is that I read about Thomas Q in *People*. He's crazy."

"His followers say he's the new Messiah. Which is crazier, to let people think you're the Messiah or to be someone who thinks Thomas Q is the Messiah?"

Mitzi made a face. "I hate the way you mix me up." She yanked my suitcase from my hand and slammed her body into mine in a powerful bear hug. She lifted me off the ground. She was crying. Now I felt even worse for trying to talk Kyra into going with me.

"Thanks for realigning my spine," I said, stepping out of her bear hug. I kissed her on the cheek.

She laughed and kissed my cheek. "Go, my child. And sin no more."

I grabbed my suitcase in one hand and my leather bomber jacket in the other and headed out the door. Mitzi followed. "By the way," she said, "there are about fifty reporters out there right now and more coming all the time. I heard about ten different languages as I drove in. You're now international news."

"Not if they can't find me."

"You may have trouble shaking them."

I thought about my wild ride the previous morning. The stop signs whooshing by. Tires screaming. My foot nailing the gas pedal to the floor. "I'll shake them."

The doorbell rang downstairs. I stopped in the hallway before my foot hit the top stair. The front door was not visible from here.

"Don't worry," Mitzi assured me. "Kyra has strict orders not to let anyone in she doesn't know."

I heard the front door open. "Oh, hey!" Kyra said excitedly. "Blue's upstairs. Go on up."

Footsteps padded across the foyer, up the stairs. Because the stairway curved away from where I stood, I couldn't see who it was. Just body parts. A big hand sliding up the banister. The top of a head. Brown hair with a white patch at the temple.

Rush.

"Hi," he said. He was smiling. Something was up.

"Hi," I said. "What are you doing here?"

He held out his hand to Mitzi. "I'm Russell Poundstone."

"Mitzi," she said, shaking his hand.

He looked at my suitcase. "Where you going?"

"A trip. Visit some friends."

Rush looked at Mitzi, then back at me. He had a giddy look that made me nervous. "Can we talk?"

"About what? I'm in kind of a hurry."

He pulled some scraps of paper out of his jacket pocket and waved them at me. "Money. Lots and lots of money."

* * *

"How much do you hate me, Blue? I need to know."

"I don't hate you and you know it. I just don't trust you. Huge difference."

"All right, how much don't you trust me? Be precise."

"Which measurement do you prefer I use," I said, "cubic miles or light-years?"

Rush closed my bedroom door behind him and grinned. His eyes actually sparkled. "All that's about to change. You're about to fall in love."

"Love, huh?"

He tossed his scraps of paper onto my bed. Then he reached into another pocket and pulled out more paper. Other pockets and even more paper. Envelopes with notes scribbled across them. Toilet paper with phone numbers and names. A corner of the Yellow Pages with tiny writing. They made a thick lump of confetti on my bed. He stirred the papers together with his finger like a little boy sampling fudge. "These are the names and numbers of hot producers, directors, and studio executives who want to meet with me about you. I faxed everybody I could think of this morning after you left and told them I had the exclusive rights to your story."

"Did the earth move for them?"

"Not exactly. At first, I got no response. At least not from anyone who mattered. Just a couple calls from peripheral players. Grunters and squeezers."

"Grunters and squeezers?"

"Movie lingo. That means they're financially constipated. Takes them forever to grunt up financing before they finally squeeze a movie out."

"Lovely image." I pointed at the scraps of paper littering my bedspread. "If the others are constipated, who are these guys? The diarrhea gang?"

"These are the real things, Blue." He circled the bed while pointing at the pile of papers. There was an odd ritualistic feeling to his movements, like he was conducting some voodoo rite. I kept expecting flames to shoot up from the bed. "These are the guys I couldn't get to take my calls this morning. Everybody was in a goddamn meeting. Their secretaries all took my name, but I know no one had any intention of getting back to me. Who knows why? Maybe they all thought this thing with your parents was a retro-sixties thing and that fad has passed. I don't know. All I know is that I'm sitting in my motel room in my underwear, covered with the rancid sweat of failure. I'm brushing Russell's teeth, trying to figure out the best way to plead temporary insanity at the agency to get my old job back. I'm already imagining the line of appropriate asses I'll have to kiss."

I didn't say anything, but he seemed to know by my expression what I was thinking. "You've never really wanted anything badly, have you, Blue? I mean, you never wanted to do something or be something because you knew deep down that you were meant to do it. You never punched a wall in frustration or threw a toaster in anger because you were afraid you'd never do anything in your life that you gave a flying fuck about. You've never risked everything. Not like the real Amelia Earhart. Am I right?"

He was right, of course. I had never dreamed of being anything in particular. Biology hadn't been my passion. I had taken some career-guidance tests and they said I'd be good in sciences, medicine, biology, that sort of thing. And I *was* good at it. I read it, studied it, lived it. But was I spiritually fulfilled by it? If anything, my current obsession with the microcosmic universe was eating away at me with a sinister intensity.

I went over to the window and looked out. I didn't try to hide behind the blinds. Cameras suddenly swung up in my direction. Flashbulbs popped. Reporters waved to attract my attention. They shouted questions I couldn't hear. I turned back to Rush. "You think you're so noble, Poundcake? That you have some moral superiority because you're willing to lie, steal, and kiss ass to be a movie producer? A movie producer? Gosh, I feel so shallow."

He sighed. "Look, I don't want to fight with you, Blue. I've come with good news, damn it. Just let me finish, okay?"

I could hear the reporters outside calling my name. Just barely, like the voices a schizophrenic must hear. "Okay," I said.

"I started this morning scared I'd blown any chance at a career.

Then this thing with your parents breaks. They rob a bank! It's all over the news. They interrupt 'Donahue' with a special bulletin, for Christ's sake." Rush was pacing now, gesturing wildly as he spoke. He was excited in a nervous way, like a man who's just received a stay of execution giving him twenty-four hours to prove his innocence. "Suddenly, I'm getting calls and setting up meetings. And not with the soldiers, but with the generals, the people with the power to *write checks*. By the end of this week, I guarantee you that I will make a deal for you worth six figures, minimum. Maybe three hundred grand. If your folks hit another bank or two, we'll be at six hundred easy. Are you in touch with them at all?"

"My parents? Sure, I'm in touch. Why, you want me to coordinate a bank job with one of your meetings? Any special branch you want them to knock over?"

He ignored my answer and started gathering up his slips of paper. He treated them as preciously as I had the ten thousand dollars I'd just counted. "Anyway, that's why I want to know how much you hate me. Do you hate me enough to blow half a million bucks? Because once I make this deal, before they sign the check, you're going to have to talk to these people. And you can't go nuts on them and start tearing up contracts. If you hate me, fine. Get it out now. Kick me in the nuts, gouge out my eyes. I can live with that. But once we're in Los Angeles, we're business partners. Okay? We act civil, even friendly. They sense any animosity between us, it'll cost us money. It's good that you're already packed. We can swing by my motel and pick up Russell. We'll be in L.A. in an hour."

"I'm not going to L.A."

"Didn't you hear what I just said? We're very close to a deal."

I didn't say anything. We just stared at each other.

Finally, he sighed. "Where are you going?"

I shrugged. "Away."

"Look, if it's money, you can stay with me. No strings or anything. You want your own room, I can kick Russell right out of his. He never cleans it, anyway."

I shook my head. "I've got to get away a few days, Poundcake. Bury myself."

"Believe me, once you enter my apartment, you're as good as buried. You're practically entombed."

"I can't. Really."

He fanned out the slips of paper in front of him like a magician about to do a card trick. "Any one of these could be our ticket, Blue. Any one. You'll have plenty of money to go live wherever you want as long as you want. You can tell your parents, your school district, and the rest of the world to fuck off. That's what this deal can do for you."

"And what will it do for you?"

"I'll have a shot at being a real producer. My shot at the bigs. That's all I want."

I looked at his face. Fear had acid-washed the charm from his expression. His features looked harsher, edgier, hungrier. He had taken a chance with this deal, risked his job, his whole dream. And it had almost failed. Still might. He'd walked to the edge of the precipice and looked over and there was no bottom, just darkness and a howling wind. It had scared him. I admired him for risking so much.

"You make the deal, Poundcake," I said. "I'll come and sign. I'll even be nice to you." I reached out and touched the slips of paper in his hands. I trailed my fingertips across them. They made a twicking noise like a card in a bicycle spoke.

"Go ahead," he urged. "Read them. You'll recognize some names. These aren't just nameless corporate types. Some are production companies of famous actresses who want to play you." He plucked a piece of paper from the rest and showed it to me: Sigourney Weaver's name, followed by a phone number. He picked out another piece of paper, a restaurant receipt with a phone number across the back. "Jane Seymour." He crumpled the paper and tossed it on the floor. "Who needs her?" He handed me a napkin with some red sauce on the corner, as well as a name and phone number. "Jane Fonda's people called. They want her to play your mom and her niece Bridget Fonda to play you. They're talking Jack Nicholson to play your father." He grinned. "And I would be the producer. Me and Nicholson and Fonda." He banged on the strings of his air guitar. "Yes!"

I snatched another piece of paper from the pile and read it, then another. I couldn't help myself; I kept plucking them like I was cracking open fortune cookies looking for just the right fate. I couldn't believe all these famous women were somehow associated with my mundane life. They knew my name.

Rush laughed. "Admit it, you're impressed."

"I'm impressed."

"But you're not happy. You're not thrilled. I was expecting a little thrilled here."

I took him by the arm and led him to the bedroom door. "Ever hear of the empid fly, Poundcake?"

"No, and I'm not much interested in hearing about it now. Can't you just admit you're thrilled and let it go at that? Do you really have to locate its twin in the natural cycle?"

"The female empid fly is not receptive to male sexual advances," I said. "So, to distract her, the male wraps up a piece of food for her in a silky package made from his own glandular secretions. The wrapping is very elaborate. The female accepts the gift and begins unwrapping it. While she's engrossed in unwrapping the gift, he has sex with her. But by the time she finishes unwrapping, he's already screwed her and is on his way to brag to his fly buddies. Hey, after all, he paid her, right? But some species of this fly don't even have any food in their package. It's all wrapping, all show. She unwraps the thing and there's nothing inside. Zip. By the time she realizes she's been tricked, the male's already used her and is long gone." I handed him back his pile of papers.

"What is it with you, anyway? What is this rain-forest-oat-bran-all-God's-creatures trivia kick you're on? You're not exactly Margaret Mead or Dian Fossey, you know?"

"Margaret Mead was an anthropologist; she worked with people. Dian Fossey worked with apes."

"My point is that all this bug behavior is warping your perception. You can't distinguish between animals and humans. You need to get out in the real world more, Amelia. Interact."

"That is the real world, Poundcake. All human actions, all our sins, are mirrored by nature. Not just mirrored but necessary for survival. Cannibalism, incest, rape, sodomy, murder, infanticide, abortion—these behaviors aren't deviations; they are prerequisites for existence of the species. Once you realize that, human behavior is much clearer. And a lot less scary."

He smiled. "So you think I brought all these notes and phone numbers over just so I can have sex with you?"

"Screwing can be metaphoric."

"True," he said, frowning. "But I wouldn't worry about that if I were you. You're already totally screwed up."

I punched him in the stomach. It was a pretty hard punch, plus it caught him by surprise. Me, too. Air oomphed from his mouth and he doubled over. His eyes watered with pain and anger. I had never punched anyone before, never struck another living being in my entire life. I didn't feel good about doing it, but I didn't feel bad, either. I felt kind of pleased that I'd done so well my first time, like a novice bowler rolling a strike. Rush seemed to be in real pain. His teeth were clenched and his face was contorted. And I had caused it, deliberately. I wasn't usually the one who caused pain; I was the one who endured it. I was like a shock absorber bouncing down the highway of life, while the people I loved drove over every pothole and railroad track they could find. This was new.

Suddenly, Rush reached out and grabbed a fistful of my hair and yanked my head back hard. "Don't hit," he hissed. "You can call me anything you want, any name you can think of. But don't hit. Okay?"

"Yes." I winced and he released my hair.

He eased himself onto the bed and massaged his stomach. "I warned you you'd be pissed at me for sleeping with you. I told you that you couldn't handle it. You'd blame me just because you couldn't control yourself. If you're mad about the sex, blame yourself for not listening to me."

"I'm not mad about the sex." I sat beside him. "Okay, I'm a little mad about the sex. But I definitely don't blame you. And I don't regret it, either."

"What then? Why are we always fighting?"

Because I can fight with you. That just popped into my head. I hadn't thought it through before, hadn't run a CAT scan or carbon-dated it to find its source. I wasn't even sure what I meant.

"I may seem very prudish and small-town to you," I said, "but

I'm too old for just sex. I mean, sex for the thrill of it. I have nothing against that, for others. I'm just talking about me, who I am at this stage of my life. Right now, I see sex as a way of getting to know someone better, but it has to be with someone I *want* to get to know better. See?"

"And you don't want to get to know me better."

"What I already know is enough," I said. "I don't mean that as an insult. I'm attracted to you and you know it, so I'm not pulling some romance-novel bullshit here of pretending I don't like you."

"But . . . ?"

"But you're not what I'm looking for in my life right now. You're not what I want or need."

"Ouch," he said. He made a sucking sound and mimed pulling an arrow out of his chest. "Bull's-eye."

"What I mean is, I don't see us making grocery lists together. Arguing about whose turn it is to take out the garbage. Debating the pros and cons of scented toilet paper."

"Scented. I know it costs more, but it's worth it."

"Don't ridicule me," I snapped. "You wanted serious, I'm being serious."

"Sorry, but it's hard to keep up with you," he snapped back. "You go from accusation to execution in twenty seconds. Isn't there supposed to be a trial in there somewhere? Isn't that what dating is, a trial? We each present our evidence as to why we're so wonderful and cool, then the other person's jury decides. Sometimes the jury is friends and family; sometimes it's just the other person." He pointed his finger at my face. "You're not looking at all the evidence."

I put my hands over my face and sighed. This was the most intimate conversation I'd had with a man for years. I'd forgotten how exhausting it could be. Maybe Lewis with his epic silences had been onto something. I patted Rush's knee. "Look, Poundcake, be honest here. Other than a ticket to making movies, what else do you see in me? You don't even know me. Other than biblically."

"I know enough to know I want to know more. Plus, I just used *know* three times in one sentence. A guy who does that *has* to be serious."

I laughed. "Don't make me laugh, okay? I've been charmed before. I don't want charm anymore."

"What do you want, Blue? What?"

I didn't know what to say. How can anybody answer that question without sounding like some lame Miss America contestant. Peace on earth? Goodwill toward fellow humans? True love? I'd had love and it went bad the way it always goes bad, because everything mortal has a shelf life. Repetition diminishes everything. After a few times through the vending machine, love is no longer the bright coin of hope it once was.

I looked over at Rush's face. I liked his face. Rugged and angular. It looked like it had been drawn with an Etch-A-Sketch. I liked sex with him, too. And he was funny. In a parallel universe where Harold and Naomi weren't bank-robbing fugitives but regular aging parents who played golf together, we might all be sitting around a dinner table laughing our asses off. Mom would argue politics with him all night, but she'd crack up at his jokes. Dad would nod and grin, talk about movies, about which Dad was aggressively opinionated.

But in this universe—the one where the FBI picked me up, reporters hounded me, I was suspended from my job—I needed someone with a lot less voltage than Russell Poundstone. He'd pissed on the reporter's truck. He'd let the air out of Lewis's tires. He'd walked around Denny's pretending to be the manager. He'd faked a letter from Disney Studios. This is the kind of crap that, taken individually, can look wacky and charming, the same as my parents' bank jobs. But looking at the big picture, the cosmic pattern, these were reckless actions. Antisocial behavior can be contagious. Since knowing him, I'd broken traffic rules, peeped into windows, lied to the FBI, sport-fucked, punched a man in the stomach. I needed to pull back, reset the moral gyroscope.

"Listen," I said. I faced him, looked him right in the eye. "I have behaved badly, I know. You deserve better. This really isn't me. It really isn't. It's just that I'm not in a place right now where it makes sense even to think about dating or juries or anything else. Okay?"

"Okay," he said quickly. He started stuffing his papers back into his pockets. He held a couple of them up to me. "And by the way, these aren't empty wrappings like that fly you were telling me about. This is the real thing. You'll see." He reached into his pocket and pulled out a bulging legal-sized envelope. "This, however, is the empty wrapping." He tossed it to me.

I opened the envelope. Pages and pages of handwriting. It looked like a play. Across the top in big printing was the title: *Tito Vermillion, the Most-Feared Man in Chicago, Explains the Nature of Romantic Love.*

"What is this?" I asked.

"Something I wrote last night. For you."

"You wrote a play for me?"

"It's a screenplay. A short screenplay. A five-minute movie, very low budget."

"You wrote a screenplay for me? I don't think I've ever heard of that before."

"Well, I'm not really a writer, you understand. I don't know anything about poetry or stories, and my personal letters all sound like I'm about to take legal action against the person. But I do know scripts." He shrugged. "I'm not a writer—I really want to stress that, okay? I'm a producer. Remember that when you read it."

I should say something now, I kept thinking. He stood there expectantly. I stood there dumbly. I refolded his script and placed it back into the envelope. All my movements were slow and excruciatingly deliberate. Even *he* had to see I was stalling. I couldn't think of anything to say, either encouraging or discouraging. I tried to calculate his reaction to whatever I said or did. Then I had to consider what my reaction to his reaction should be. And so forth. Where, in the end, would that leave me? In a place I wanted to be or in a place I wanted to run away from?

I couldn't decide.

So I stepped up to him and kissed him hard on the mouth.

We fell onto the bed.

Throw the baby to the tiger, you idiot, I thought. The baby, not yourself.

He sat beside me and softly kissed me. We eased backward across the bed, still kissing. It was a lazy kiss, not as if it was obligatory

222 · LARAMIE DUNAWAY

foreplay in preparation for the next step but as if that was all he wanted to do at that moment, just kiss me. Very unusual. My hand curved around his back and slid over his burn scars as if they were fleshy speed bumps. I pulled him closer.

The kissing went on for a while, along with some random fondling. His tongue was in my mouth, his hand on my breast, his fingers in my vagina. I felt like a sexy accordion. My nipples were so hard, they hurt. I was the one who wanted to move on to the next step. I wanted him inside of me now.

He seemed to know. He lifted up on one elbow. I thought he would just climb on top of me, but instead he placed a hand on my hip and rolled me over facedown. He swung around behind me and lifted my hips up until I was on my hands and knees. Suddenly, he was inside of me, his hips slapping my buttocks.

The bed creaked with each thrust. Slap, creak. Slap, creak. It was an imitation Shaker bed from Sweden that I'd bought when I moved in with Mitzi and Kyra. True to the spirit of the original Shakers, who had rejected sex and therefore died out as a religion, this was the first sex this bed had experienced. It didn't seem to like it much. I realized it was the first sex I'd had in this house, at least with a partner. I had come home here every night, undressed, showered, used the toilet, somehow filled a couple hours until bedtime, and then slept. Rush had been right—this room had been like a prison cell. Not a place where I spent time but, rather, a place where I *did* time.

I lived like a recluse here, as much a prisoner as my parents had been. Lewis had been my arresting officer and Dale, the one guy I'd dated after the divorce, had been a parole officer. There was no need to throw away the key; I carried it with me, locking myself in every night. But I was here on a bum wrap, trumped-up charges, false evidence. My life so far wasn't the result of anything I had done, any kind of plan; it was all a reaction to other people's actions. Why? Just because my parents had broken the law, did I have to live the rest of my life making amends? Just because they were bad, did I have to keep proving I was good? Even now that they were out of prison, everything they did relentlessly impacted me. They commit a crime and everyone shows up at my door to put me under a microscope. They go on the run and now I was about to go on the run. Exactly where were my choices free of their choices? Even marrying Lewis could have been a reaction. Did I pick someone in law enforcement as a public statement that I supported the laws and rules of our society? I felt like a Jew in Nazi Germany whose parents had been dragged off to a concentration camp while I stood outside in the streets watching and pretending not to be a Jew. At rallies against Jews, I screamed loudest for their blood.

How did anyone live with the consequences of their actions on loved ones? I couldn't. I didn't want my actions to carry so much weight. Same reason I shouldn't have kids. Every act, every statement can injure a loved one. People go on shooting rampages after being dumped by a loved one. Children turn to a life of drugs because a parent didn't help with geometry homework or pushed them into toilet training too early. Wives hurl themselves out windows because husbands don't like new haircuts. Husbands take mistresses because wives complain about soap scum buildup in the tub. I don't want my actions to have that much impact on anyone. Make your own mistakes, world, and don't point any fingers my way. Love is just another word for blame.

A tear dripped from my eye down to the back of my hand. I was on all fours with a sexy, smart, ambitious, funny, attractive man lustily writhing away behind me. A man who had written a script for me. Alone in his motel room with his bad-breathed dog, he'd thought of me and was moved to write it all down. Already our actions together had started chain reactions. We started with a car drive; now we are in business together, having sex together, and he was writing scripts to me. The weight of responsibility settled in on my back like a leather saddle.

I lowered my head to the pillow and left my rump, which was otherwise engaged, still pointing up in the air. Rush rocked slowly behind me, back and forth. His hands slid around and cupped my breasts. His fingertips brushed my nipples, which sent a hot copper wire straight to my vagina.

This wasn't love. I was positive. This was sex. People got into trouble when they confused the two. Need caused the confusion. But I had no needs now. I could do something that had no effect.

I could walk the high wire without a net. I could have the hottest, wildest, sweatiest sex I'd ever had and walk away without looking back. Without any consequences. Without any responsibility for whatever actions Rush might take afterward. He could write a fucking opera if he wanted. I was proving it was possible for the caboose to break free from the pull of the thundering locomotive. I was a scientist, I reminded myself, and this sweaty thing we were doing right now was nothing more than an empirical experiment in free will.

To demonstrate, I reached back between my legs and held Rush's dangling scrotum. This seemed to invigorate him. I wanted him invigorated, I wanted him so laser-hot that it would vaporize any lingering romantic notions of love. He would recognize this as nothing more than the instinctual passion for reproduction that all animals share. It wasn't me, Blue Erhart, he was interested in; it was just my rump in the air. Any rump. Nor was he interested in making *my* movie, *my* life story. He was interested in making *any* movie that would give him some power in the industry. He wasn't choosing me; he was reacting to me. I wanted him to see that, to know. I stroked his balls, fondled them, bounced them lightly in my palm like loose change. He moaned with pleasure, pounding against me harder and harder.

I let my hand slide back even farther, my finger touching his anus. He jerked slightly and hopped against me, driving me forward. The pillow slid into the headboard, followed by my head into the pillow. He didn't notice. He had both hands on my hips and was lifting me up and down on his penis in a frenzy of lust. My knees were bouncing off the mattress.

The experiment was working.

Suddenly, inside me small explosions detonated. One. Then another. Another. Small cluster orgasms bursting like helium balloons. I'd never felt that before. I jerked and strained and curled my lip. The strange thing was, usually after coming, I was too sensitive to even be touched there. But right then, I felt as if I was just starting. I pushed my buttocks right back at him as if I was parallel parking my body. He slammed forward into me, fighting me for the space. We continued jousting energetically for several minutes. After a while, he slowed down. He was panting.

"You don't have to hold back for me," I said. "You can come. I did."

"I'm okay," he huffed. "I was just trying to remember if I took my heart medication." He clutched his chest and made a pain-stricken face. Then he smiled.

I laughed. I reached back and took hold of his hand resting on my right hip. I brought it around between my legs and pressed it against my clitoris. He began slowly massaging. I rotated my hips against him. Then I slipped my hand under his and began rubbing myself. This was not part of my usual sexual repertoire. I'd read about it in a magazine while married to Lewis, but it still took me a year to try it with him. But I was making a point here. This wasn't for me; this was for science.

Rush's penis, which was still inside of me and a little fatigued, suddenly perked up. It swelled up like a blowfish. I rubbed myself some more, then reached back and wiped my moist fingers across his lips. And he was off. He began pounding into me again with an urgency just short of demonic possession. I needed both hands on the mattress to brace myself and keep from going through the wall.

Phase two of experiment complete. Subject responding well to olfactory and taste stimuli.

Our sweat plucked at each other's skin with each contact. The sheets were soaked.

". . . M . . . MMM . . . MMMMM . . ." I moaned, losing my stealth status.

Wait, I wanted to tell him. Hold on a second. I started gasping. Wait. This sensation was different from what I was used to. I was dizzy. My skin felt hot and raw, as if I'd been dragged naked across a mile of pavement. But I wanted it to burn even more. I wanted to combust spontaneously. I threw my body backward against him each time he drove forward. The collision of body parts jolted me with agonizing pleasure.

"Ahhhhhyyyyuhhh . . ." Rush said. I felt his penis discharge, his condom-encased muscle spasming uselessly in search of my buried treasure of unfertilized eggs. His fingers dug into my hips and lifted me off the bed.

"MMMMMMMMMMMM," I responded. Then, "Jesus Jesus jesusjesusjesusjesus . . ." I came so powerfully that I blacked out for a moment. My body went limp beneath me as I sank deeper into the mattress and disappeared beneath the surface, drifting down into the dark universe inside matter. I could hear the sound of Rush rolling the condom off, a muffled "Ow" as the rubber plucked at his pubic hairs.

Rush's jostling on the bed beside me revived me back to consciousness. His head plopped into the pillow and he pushed his sweaty body up against my sweaty body. Even the chill of my evaporating sweat felt delightful. He kissed my neck.

"I'm sure I'll be able to walk again in a day or two," he said sleepily. He kissed my neck again.

I wanted to say something, something witty and dismissive, to show this was all just good clean fun. Finally, I said, "I have to go to the bathroom." I slid out from under his arm and got up.

"I admire your energy," he said, and closed his eyes.

I quietly grabbed the envelope with the script he'd written for me and tiptoed into the bathroom. I locked the door behind me. The mirror revealed a rather tousled me with pale skin and nipples so long, they could pick up Radio Free Europe. I turned and observed my backside in the mirror. My buttocks had two red splotches from hammering against Rush. My cheeks heated with embarrassment and I turned away. I smoothed my hair and pulled it back into a ponytail, which I held with one hand while searching for a rubber band. When I found one, I bound it, sat on the toilet, and began to read.

Fade in.

·18·

Dear Blue,

We just made love for the first time.

(Do you realize how optimistic that sentence is?)

Anyway, we just made love. Now you are gone and Russell is lying at the foot of the bed. Drooling. I am glad he's here, because when you left I had the distinct conviction that the bed had suddenly become too light to be affected by gravity and that soon the whole bed frame and mattress would begin floating upward, squashing me buglike against the ceiling. Fortunately, the weight of Russell's drool anchors the bed to the floor. He's a lifesaver.

I was not a very good lawyer, Blue. I am a worse writer. In high school my single claim to artistic fame was making up dirty limericks. I could create one using anyone's name. Guys used to pay me a buck to make one up using some girl's name they wanted to impress. Some guys paid me a buck not to use their girlfriends' names. But that's the extent of my creative background. I don't know why I chose to write to you now. I don't even know how the damn thing will end. If I don't figure out an ending, you won't be reading this, anyway.

The thing is, I have been thinking about you ever since you left and I don't want to stop thinking about you just yet. Scribbling these words, imagining you reading them, helps me keep thinking about you.

Well, here goes. . . .

TITO VERMILLION,
THE MOST-FEARED MAN IN CHICAGO,
EXPLAINS THE NATURE OF ROMANTIC LOVE

FADE IN

INTERIOR VERMILLION'S TAVERN—NIGHT

A seedy bar with seedier customers. People don't come here to chat, talk sports, or otherwise socialize. They come here to drink. A lot.

ANGLE ON BARTENDER

Behind the bar is its owner, TITO VERMILLION, 40s, big and confident-looking. Has thin white scar that curves halfway around his throat before descending down the front of his chest, lost in the thick brush of his hair. Tito has a reputation as the baddest of the bad, though he seems gentle-enough standing there wiping beer mugs.

ANGLE ON TWO MEN AT POOL TABLE

In the back of the room is a coin-operated pool table. Two young men are lazily shooting pool, just as they have for hundreds of nights together since high school.

DANNY, 23, still wears his car mechanic clothes from work, still has some grease under his fingernails. Looks confused.

HIGH DEUCE, 23, dresses like his idea of a dandy. Most people would just snicker and think he's a bad Elvis impersonator. He doesn't look like he's ever done a day's work, but he's obviously the kind of guy who always has a few bucks in his pocket. He gave himself his nickname.

High Deuce shoots a tough bank shot, sinks the ball. He slides around the table in search of his next shot the way a cat circles an insect with a broken wing.

> DANNY
> So, okay, I'm sitting there on the sofa with her, makin' out—

> HIGH DEUCE
> Where?

> DANNY
> The sofa, like I said.

> HIGH DEUCE
> Yeah, I know the sofa, asshole. I mean whose sofa, hers or yours?

> DANNY
> Hers. Her old lady's out of the apartment visiting some sick aunt or something.

> HIGH DEUCE
> She's a widow, though, the old lady?

> DANNY
> Right. Her old man kicked off, I dunno, eight, ten years ago. Some lung or kidney thing. Cancer maybe. Something like that.

> HIGH DEUCE
> So you're porkin' the daughter on the old lady's sofa—

> DANNY
> I didn't say porkin', I said makin' out.

High Deuce shoots another tough shot and sinks the ball.

> DANNY
> Son of a bitch! Lucky son of a bitch!

> HIGH DEUCE
> (laughing)

I'd rather be lucky than good, man. Fortunately, I'm both.

> DANNY
> Fuck you, man.

> HIGH DEUCE
> So you was on the sofa . . .

> DANNY
> Makin' out.

> HIGH DEUCE
> Which means what exactly? You were ramming your tongue down her throat? Tickling her pussy? She was suckin' the chrome off your gear knob? What?

> DANNY
> Geez, you're an asshole sometimes. I just said makin' out. Kissing and stuff. You know.

> HIGH DEUCE
> Was your hand on her tit? At anytime was your hand actually touching tit?

> DANNY
> Forget that, okay. I'm not talking about that. I'm getting at something else. Something entirely else.

> HIGH DEUCE
> Man, there ain't nothin' else.

Danny angrily tosses his pool cue on the table, scattering the balls, and starts to walk out.

> HIGH DEUCE
> Hey, man, I'm sorry. What're you so uptight about?
> Jesus.

> DANNY
> Fuck you, okay? I'm trying to talk about something
> here, okay?

> HIGH DEUCE
> Then talk, jerkoff. Talk all you want. Talk till your
> goddamn tongue drops out. Can't you talk and shoot
> pool at the same time?

Danny looks angrily at his friend, then shrugs it off and grudgingly returns to the table. He really needs to talk about what's bothering him. They return to the game. High Deuce keeps knocking the balls in, rarely missing. Danny snicks in an occasional ball or two. He's too distracted.

> DANNY
> Anyway, like I was saying. We're sitting on the sofa
> kissing and such. Then she turns to me out of the blue
> and says, "Danny, do you love me?"

> HIGH DEUCE
> (stops in mid-shot)
> Fuck, no.

> DANNY
> Yeah, man, I'm serious.

HIGH DEUCE

What'd you say, man? You said yes, I hope. I mean, you'd better have said yes if you wanted any nookie.

DANNY

I didn't say anything at first.

HIGH DEUCE

Big fucking mistake, man. You can't hesitate. You can't show weakness. They hate that, man. You got to answer right away. You got to jump right in and say, "Yes, goddamn it, I fucking love you." Like treating a snake bite, you gotta suck the poison out right away. I'm serious, man. Right away.

DANNY

I don't know. I just sat there, thinking. Finally I said something like, "Sure, I think I love you."

HIGH DEUCE

You said what?

DANNY

I said, "I think I love you."

HIGH DEUCE

You said fucking what?

DANNY
(quietly)
"I think I love you."

High Deuce shoots a ball harder than necessary. It cracks into another ball and sinks with a wump.

HIGH DEUCE

I can't believe you. You are not to be believed.

DANNY

What else could I say? I don't know if I love her. How are you supposed to know a thing like that?

HIGH DEUCE

You serious? I mean, I'm asking you straight right now if you're serious. Is this a serious question?

DANNY

Yeah, it's fucking serious.

HIGH DEUCE

I ask 'cause I've never heard so much shit at one time. Major shit. The shit meter is going off the scale, man.

DANNY

Fuck you. I don't even know why I talk to you.

HIGH DEUCE

Listen, pal, you want to know about love, I'll tell you about love. If a babe you've never fucked asks you if you love her, the answer is always the same. Yes. Afterward, it depends on whether or not you want seconds.

DANNY

It's not like that with her, man. She's different.

HIGH DEUCE

None of them are different, jerkoff. That's what's so cool. They all got holes between their legs.

DANNY

You don't understand.

HIGH DEUCE

Well, do you looovvve her?

DANNY

I don't know.

HIGH DEUCE

What're we talkin' about here, son? Marriage?

DANNY

No. Maybe. I don't know. I'm mixed-up.

HIGH DEUCE

(disgusted)

Shit, man. Love fucks up more guys like you. Man,
love don't even exist. It's just a word invented by
women to make men stick around longer. Guys feel
guilty because they don't feel it the way babes do.
Guys just use the word to make women feel good. It's
like being polite or something.

DANNY

Haven't you ever been in love, man? Marcia Holmes
in eleventh grade?

High Deuce reacts. A sore spot. He bluffs his way out.

HIGH DEUCE

Me and Marcia had a few laughs, man, that's all. A
few laughs is all you can expect. They say count your
blessings, I say count your laughs.

DANNY

I don't know, man. I have these feelings . . . .

He hesitates, unsure how to express himself.

HIGH DEUCE

You're just horny.

DANNY

Fuck you.

HIGH DEUCE

Wait till I bend over. I told you you were just horny.
(smacks Danny good-naturedly on the arm)
Right?

Danny laughs a little, but he's obviously still disturbed.

Tito Vermillion walks over to the pool table. His size makes the
room seem much smaller. Danny and High Deuce are obviously
a little afraid of him. Maybe even a lot afraid.

TITO

Heard you boys talking.

HIGH DEUCE

Were we too loud? Sorry, Tito.

TITO
(ignores him)
Heard you boys talking about love. Right?

DANNY

Sure, yeah. About love.

TITO

That's what I said. About love. You boys want to know
about love?

DANNY

I don't . . . know . . . .

TITO

Hey, love is nothing to fool around with. You treat

love with respect, boys, or someday all you'll have is
some memories and old letters that make you cry.

> HIGH DEUCE
> (laughing because he thinks Tito is joking)
> Yeah, right. Cry.

Tito gives him a look to crack marble. High Deuce stops
laughing, pretends he's coughing.

> TITO
> Love don't come around like the seasons. Fucking,
> that comes around and around. But love? Love is like
> a rug burn over your heart.
> (to Danny)
> You feel like that when you kiss your girl?

> DANNY
> Feel like what?

> TITO
> Feel your heart. Feel like a rug burn across your heart.
> When you kiss her.

> DANNY
> I don't know. Maybe not a rug burn. More like a
> football somebody sat on, you know? Compressed kind
> of.

> TITO
> Okay, that's good, too. Like a rug burn or a football.
> Don't matter which. You just made poetry, kid. If a
> kiss makes you think like a poet, that's gotta be love.

> HIGH DEUCE
> (feeling threatened, like he's losing an argument
> and a friend)

Poetry! That's faggot bait.

Tito gives High Deuce a look that backs him up, scared. Tito approaches him.

> TITO
> You know all about love, High Deuce?

> HIGH DEUCE
> Some. A little.

> TITO
> No, you're too modest. You know a lot about love.
> You know everything there is to know. Only thing is,
> you just don't know that you know. You think love is
> something you can refrigerate, that will keep until
> later. Or it's like city buses—you miss one and another
> comes along right behind it.
> (shakes his head)
> Ain't like that, boys. Love is strong but also fragile.
> Like a hand.

Suddenly, his hand lashes out and clamps onto High Deuce's wrist. He pins High Deuce's hand against the top of the pool table.

> TITO
> See how strong the hand is that can lift so much
> weight and build so many wonderful things? But it is
> made up of very weak little bones, like love is made up
> of weak little people. They are strong only when they
> form a whole hand. You see? You guys see my point?

> HIGH DEUCE
> (terrified)
> Yeah, sure. I understand. I really do.

> TITO
> I don't think so. Not yet.

High Deuce squirms; in a panic he tries to pull his hand free.
Tito keeps it pinned with little effort. Tito reaches over and picks
up the eight ball from the table.

> TITO
> This ball is very hard. It bounces around the table and
> crashes into other balls. Even the best players, even
> players as good as my buddy High Deuce here, even
> he sometimes misses and the ball does something to
> mess up his game plan. Right, High Deuce?

> HIGH DEUCE
> Right, Tito. Everybody misses sometimes. Nobody's
> perfect.

> TITO
> That's my point. Exactly my point. No matter how
> much you plan, sometimes the eight ball comes along
> and fucks things up. But you can't let that lose the
> game for you. You have to readjust, rethink your
> plans. Accept change. Hell, sometimes that change is
> for the better and you end up with an even better shot.
> Am I right?

> HIGH DEUCE
> Very true. I seen it happen lots of times. Absolutely.

> TITO
> You love pool, don't you, High Deuce?

> HIGH DEUCE
> I don't know. I never thought about it much. I'm
> good, that's all I know.

TITO

Good? You're great. One of the best. You come in
here what? Five, six nights a week and shoot for three
or four hours each time. Isn't that love?

HIGH DEUCE

Love? I don't . . .
    (looks at his trapped hand)
Sure, I guess. Love.

TITO

I mean, if you had an accident or something playing pool,
you'd still come right back and play, right? Maybe you'd
wait until you was healed, but you'd be back playing, even
though you were hurt playing. Right?

HIGH DEUCE

I don't know. I never been hurt playing pool. It's not
that dangerous, you know. Unless you bet with the
wrong guy or something, ha, ha.

TITO

I'm just speaking hypothetical right now. Maybe.
What if. That sort of thing.

HIGH DEUCE

Okay, sure. What if. Well, then, yeah, I guess. I
suppose I'd come back and play again.

TITO

After you was healed.

HIGH DEUCE

Right. After I was healed.

Tito smashes the eight ball down on High Deuce's index finger,
crushing it. High Deuce howls. Tito releases the hand. High
Deuce stumbles backward in agony.

TITO

I figure that'll take six weeks till you can hold a stick
again. You'll be back then, won't you, High Deuce? I
mean, you'll be right back here playing at this very
table again. Right?

HIGH DEUCE
(eyes watery, voice weak)
Back. Sure. Yeah.

TITO
(to Danny)
Now that's love, kid. That's what love is all about.
You think that over, Danny. You think about that the
next time she asks. You have to have the same courage
as your buddy here. You understand? Life doesn't have
assigned seating. You know what I mean?

DANNY
Yeah, sure.

Tito walks away, back to the bar.

HIGH DEUCE
Get me to a fucking hospital, man.

Danny helps High Deuce toward the door. But he's thinking
about something else.

DANNY
Why did Tito do that, man?

HIGH DEUCE
He's fucking insane, that's why! Now get me to a
fucking hospital!

DANNY
Why'd he do that? Why'd he smash your finger like that?

HIGH DEUCE
I told you. He's nuts. Life doesn't have assigned
seating! What the fuck's that? He's nuts!

DANNY
I guess. Thing is—and this is really weird—thing is, I
love her, man. I know I love her. I know now for
sure. But I don't know how I know. I gotta tell her,
man. I gotta tell her tonight.

HIGH DEUCE
Fine, fine! Tell her any fucking thing you want. But
take me to the goddamn hospital first.

Danny escorts High Deuce out the door. High Deuce moans in
pain. Danny looks unnaturally happy. His confusion is gone.

I leafed through the pages again, not to reread but just to look at
the words. Sometimes he had crossed out a word or a line or several
exchanges of dialogue between characters. Sometimes he penciled
in new words above the crossed-out ones. I compared the old words
with the new ones. The new ones were better. On the first page,
his handwriting was neat and curvy, the letters small but firm. He
knew what he wanted to say. As the pages progressed, the handwriting began to unravel—gaps between letters in a word, alternating
between writing and printing. At the end, where Tito makes his
speech about love and crushes High Deuce's hand, the writing
became neat again. He must have rested before writing that part in
order to think about what he would say.
   That scared me.
   He had stopped, rested, perhaps brushed his dog's teeth, then
come back and written about a man crushing another man's finger
with a pool ball. Okay, I was flattered by the attention, by the effort
spent on my behalf. And I guess I was impressed by the writing. I

didn't know whether it was good or not by general literature standards, but it affected me. I hadn't expected anything so powerful from him. I figured him for something well-meaning but sappy. Still, the whole broken finger thing bothered me.

I refolded the pages and tucked them back into the envelope. What could be possibly want from me? What did he think I could do for him? How did he expect me to make his life better? Was he breaking my fingers or was I breaking his?

I leaned back on the toilet seat. All my sweat from lovemaking had evaporated and now I was cold. I pulled a towel down from the rack and draped it across me. I tapped the thick envelope on my knee. This script had not existed before I'd had sex with Rush. Now it did. It was like we'd had a child, an offspring from our union— something in existence that wouldn't have existed without us. Cause and effect: Every action, no mater how innocent, how casual, results in reactions. Rush had spent hours writing this, writing with a stub of a pencil until his hands cramped. Now I had a responsibility to his feelings. From now on, I'd have to watch what I said or did. My experiment in sex without effect had failed.

I cracked open the bathroom door and peered out. Rush was asleep. I crept across the room, grabbed my clothes, suitcase, and car keys, and sneaked out of the room. I quickly dressed in the hallway, then hurried downstairs. I hugged and kissed Mitzi and Kyra good-bye. I told them not to wake Rush until I was gone.

As I eased my car out of the garage, the crowd of reporters swarmed around me. There were more of them than ever and they were even more insistent. They pounded on my car. Someone broke off the radio antenna. I laid on the horn in a long, unbroken blaring that startled them. They fell back as if they thought the car was about to explode. I floored the gas pedal, rocketing past my house, past the mob, past Rush's old heap of a car. Past my past life. Past everything.

I switched on the radio, figuring some loud rock 'n' roll would add the right touch of rebelliousness to this gesture. But the broken radio antenna left me with nothing but speakers filled with tinny static and garbled words as if spoken in tongues.

Lesson #5

Do not remove cover.
No user-serviceable
parts inside.

·19·

"Where are you now, Blue?" Mitzi asked.

"Can't tell you."

"Blue, talk to me, damn it. Where are you?"

"Ask me something else," I said.

Mitzi paused, then remembered. "Ooooh, right. I forgot. The FBI is still sniffing our bicycle seats. Oops. You boys didn't hear that, did you?" She sniffed loudly. "Erk-jays."

I laughed. "Mitz, I think they can break your inscrutable pig latin code."

"Uck-fay em-thay."

"It's nice to have a second language," I said.

"Oh, before I forget. Geraldo's people called. They want you to come on their 'Troubled Children of Celebrities' show. Bing Crosby's kid will be on, too. And Oprah wants to do something on—hold on, I've got to find the slip. Here it is. On 'Adult Survivors of Criminal Parents.' Want their number?"

"No," I said. "How's Kyra?"

"Terrific. She wants to know when you're coming back."

"I don't know. Really."

There was a long pause. Mitzi only allowed pauses in conversation when she was depressed. She used the pause to regenerate her buoyant good cheer. When she spoke again, her voice was light and breezy. "Guess what? I just got a call. We're doing *Oklahoma!* next at the theater of the damned. For the millionth fucking time."

"What's your part?"

"What else? The schlub, Ado Annie. My boobs are too big and my legs too short and my ass too round to play leading ladies. That's the word from our sainted director, Meg DeSoto. According to her, people who come to dinner theaters just want to see the movie highlights after stuffing themselves. That skinny blond bitch Shirley Jones ruined my life. So instead of singing love songs, I get all the spitfire/sidekick/bimbo songs for the rest of my life."

"And a wonderful bimbo you are. So lifelike."

"Thanks a heap." She sighed. "Blue, speaking of holiday moods, I've been thinking. Maybe Kyra and I could join you for Christmas. You find some clever secret way to let me know where you are and I promise I'll shake the feds. Bunch of pud-tuggers anyway, right boys?" She laughed.

"I can't think about Christmas right now. My life's too strange."

"It's only a few days away."

Actually, I'd forgotten about Christmas. What would I do for Christmas? People should have some special plans for Christmas. I hadn't even shopped yet, hadn't bought Kyra or Mitzi anything. Or Lewis. I popped open a can of diet Coke I'd bought from the machine outside. I took a deep breath and asked what I'd called to ask: "What about Rush?"

"Nice guy."

"I mean, did he say anything when he got up? About me leaving him there while he was sleeping."

"Blue, honey, you've only been gone an hour. We just got him out of the here twenty minutes ago."

I looked around my small motel room. The walls trumpeted bright yellow. The paintings on the walls were also bright colors, blues and reds and greens. The bedspread was fire red, the lamps candy purple. It was like a child's room. I had pulled in here after only forty minutes of driving, too depressed to go on. Already I missed my old life, my friends. I was like a little kid who'd just run away from home, afraid to cross the street. On the bed beside me was the envelope with Rush's script. I nudged it with the edge of the Coke can. "Was he mad?" I asked. "How mad?"

"You sure you want to discuss this over the phone? Prying ears and all that."

"I don't care anymore. My life is an open wound."

Mitzi sighed. "Blue, I know you're going through a lot of shit right now. I know that. But driving off while the guy was still lying in the wet spot on your bed? I don't know. Isn't that the kind of thing we used to want to castrate guys for doing to women?"

"There was no wet spot. We used a condom."

"You know what I mean."

"You don't understand," I said. "It's complicated."

"Everything's complicated for everybody. That's why we have manners."

"Gosh, Mom, you're right. If only Jimmy will give me a second chance, sob, sob."

"Fuck you very much. Anyway, Rush left for L.A. Meetings with big-shot studio people and all that. He can be very intense. He said he's going to make you a star."

"Look outside your window. See all those reporters? I am a star."

"No, you're famous. Not the same thing at all. Trust me, I know all about *not* being a star. I know about being second banana, onstage and in life. The star is the one everyone wants to be like, look like, live like. Worship. Madonna's a star. Bette Midler's just famous."

"Since when did you become such a social philosopher?"

"I've always been wise beyond my measurements."

"You're full of it-shay. Anyway, I'm not looking to be a star or famous. I just want to get through this circus and come out on the other side with enough money to disappear for good."

"So, what about Christmas? Shall we synchronize our watches and pull a 'Mission Impossible'?"

"Let me think about it," I said. "That's why I took off, right? To think about things."

"So think. Figure some way around the assholes listening in. It would make my Christmas to screw them up."

We said good-bye in pig latin and hung up. I hoped the FBI had been listening, because then they could see what a normal person I was. I had a close friend, someone who cared about me, a noncriminal.

I sat on the bed and looked around my room. The bold colors seemed like a desperate attempt to elevate a small boxy motel room to some greater dimension of fun. Maybe the owner thought of himself as an innkeeper, the kind on some sitcom who was always butting into people's lives, making things better. A stationary Love Boat with guest stars every week. But all he could afford was this tiny twelve-unit barracks building next to the 91 Freeway in Riverside, where the once flourishing orange groves have mostly been choked out of existence by the smog rolling inland daily from Los Angeles. Perhaps he was of the I'll-slap-a-coat-of-paint-on school of optimism. Bright colors. Happy decor. A family motel. Anyone could be happy in a lemon-yellow room. So. Here I was. Riverside, California. Next door to a Jiffy Lube garage and across the street from a wilted shopping mall. I was in yet another motel. Were Harold and Naomi holed up in a similar motel right now, too? What was the view from their window? Had they taped the curtains closed, propped a chair in front of the door? Were their shotguns sitting on the bed while they read Sartre aloud to each other?

I went over to the vanity and dragged a chair across the carpet, wedging it under the doorknob. I returned to the bed and flicked my finger against the envelope containing Rush's script. It made a crisp popping sound, like gunfire. I needed a destination. I couldn't just wander aimlessly. I wasn't good at that. I'd been on the road only one hour and already I felt lost.

· 20 ·

They tried to arrest me in the shopping mall—in front of a crowd of frightened shoppers.

I had just spent two thousand dollars on clothes. Cash. More money than I'd spent on clothes in the last five years. I'd practically thrown the money at them. Two grand on vests, boots, sweaters, blouses, jeans, underwear, socks, belts, earrings, a copper bracelet, a garter belt and fishnet stockings I'd never, ever wear. All from one store. The salesgirl, Melissa, was so caught up in the shopping frenzy that when I couldn't decide on a peach bra, she pulled open two buttons of her blouse and showed me hers. I bought the bra. I gave Melissa a fifty-dollar tip. She rang me up on a separate register, away from the other customers. I was treated like a god.

I was leaving the store, lugging about eight plump shopping bags in each hand. To keep from being recognized, I wore sunglasses so dark that I could barely see where I was going, as well as my floppy black hat with the brim pulled down all around my face. Looking every inch the mysterious big spender. Somebody's bored wife with time and money on her hands. I had receipts for two thousand dollars' worth of clothing from their store, plus another eight thousand dollars in cash in my purse. It was like being in a movie.

I was shuffling along under the weight of my bags when some enormous pregnant woman who looked like her water was about to break ran out of the store and clamped a heavy hand on my shoulder like a vulture's talons. My knees buckled from fright.

"Excuse me, ma'am," she said firmly.

"What?" I responded, trying to regain my composure.

"I'm afraid you'll have to return inside to talk to the manager."

"Why, did my cash bounce?"

"Pardon?"

I put my bags down because the plastic handles were already cutting deep into my fingers. I rubbed the circulation back into my hands. "What's the problem?"

"I'd prefer to talk about it inside, please." She was about twenty-five and very pretty beneath her dour expression. Her Prince Valiant haircut and bovine eyes made her look like a former cheerleader still adjusting to the disappointing awareness that popularity in high school rarely carried over to the job market. During history class, she probably used to sketch the clothes she would one day model on the cover of Vogue.

"Ma'am," she ordered, "please step inside the store."

"No," I said, reaching for my bags.

Her bulging stomach nudged up against my hip. "I must insist," she told me, tightening her grip on my arm.

"Are you really pregnant?" I asked her. "Looks fake. Like padding."

"Ma'am," she said. "You need to go back inside the store. Immediately."

"Because if you are pregnant," I continued, smiling calmly, "you'd better release my arm and step back. Otherwise, I'm going to kick you in the stomach so hard, your little baby is going to pop out your mouth like a phlegm ball."

"That would be adding assault and battery to shoplifting," she said.

"Shoplifting? Is that what this is about? Are you crazy? I just spent two thousand dollars in there!"

She did not release her grip. I saw two more women from the store hurrying toward us. One was my salesgirl, Melissa.

"Please come inside and we will discuss the matter in private. Mall security has already been notified, ma'am."

"Uck-fay ou-yay," I said. I pulled my arm and was surprised at how easily I broke her grip. She seemed surprised, too. She didn't try to grab me again. The other two women from the store joined us. One woman was about my age, dressed in the same ultrasoft cotton turtleneck dress I'd just bought (with dropped shoulders and ribbed trim at the hem and cuffs). Mine was iris, hers patina. She walked with a crisp stride, like someone in charge, so I assumed she was the store manager. Melissa, who had helped me throughout my shopping spree, was in her early twenties and looked frightened. Perhaps she thought I'd ask for my fifty dollars back.

"Janis," the manager said to the "pregnant" woman, "what's going on?"

"I saw this lady take a watch and slip it into one of her bags."

Everybody, including me, looked down at my bags. No watch was immediately visible.

"That's ridiculous," I said. "I didn't steal a watch." I pulled up the sleeve of my bomber jacket to reveal the clunky black Casio watch on my wrist. "See? I have a watch. Besides, if I'd needed a watch, I'd have bought one. Right, Melissa?"

Melissa's eyes widened. She couldn't speak. Perhaps she feared allegiance to me would mark her as a heretic and she would be burned at an adjoining stake. She waved her hands uselessly.

"Can we just go inside?" the manager asked me sweetly. "I'm sure we can straighten out this whole thing inside."

The mall wasn't very crowded this early in the day, but shoppers were starting to bunch around us, anxious for some distraction from their shopping routine. Some pretended to be looking in windows of other stores but watched us in the reflection. Perhaps they were so used to seeing conflict on a screen, that's the only way they could watch it in real life.

I stood on the gummy mall tile, my shopping bags surrounding me like Stonehenge. The counter boy from the cookie stand next door came out to see what was going on. He wiped his hands on his apron, leaving smears of chocolate like the silhouette of a dead tree. He grinned at me and said, "Free cookies if you beat the rap."

The manager lowered her voice to a whisper and leaned toward me. "I'm sure this whole thing can be straightened out very easily. Janis has probably made an honest mistake—"

"I did not make a mistake," Janis insisted.

The manager ignored her. "But we have to check out her accusation. Otherwise, there's no point in paying all this money for security, right? The point is to keep costs down for the customer. Sometimes that means a little inconvenience and cooperation."

No wonder she was boss. I found myself nodding along with her just like Melissa. Had someone shouted out, "Hang the shoplifting bitch," I'd have gotten the rope.

My cookie boy, perhaps sensing my defeat, hurried back to his ovens.

"No!" I said loudly, as if I was in a classroom. "I will not go inside. Let's settle it here. If you attempt to move me back into the store, I will have you arrested for false imprisonment and kidnapping. And I will physically defend myself."

A security officer in a dove gray uniform with the impressive patch of the mall sewn on his sleeve walked up to us. He was in his sixties and didn't seem to care which way this thing went as long as he clocked out on time. The new member to our cast excited the onlookers; the stakes had been cranked up a notch.

"Update me, Janis," the security guard said. His voice was raspy like Eli Wallach's.

"Did you call the police?" I asked him. "Have you notified the police?"

"This the shoplifter?" he asked Janis.

"Yeah, Bob. She boosted a watch." Janis pointed at my bags.

"Have you instituted a search?"

"Call the police," I demanded. "I want the police present during these proceedings."

"Look, lady, you know and we know that when we search your bags, we're gonna find a watch you didn't pay for. Why put yourself through that embarrassment? Just go inside and settle the matter."

"Because, Bob, I want every action witnessed for evidence in court later. When I bring a lawsuit against each of you and this store."

"Lady, don't be telling me my job. Every person who gets caught shoplifting threatens to sue, so that goes about as far with me as a goddamn lead balloon. You wanna sue, then go ahead and sue."

"Gee, Bob, if you're so sure of yourself, then I suggest you go right ahead and start searching my bags. Dive right in there. Meantime, I'll be walking around getting names and addresses of these witnesses." I opened my purse and pulled out a pen and pad of paper from the motel. "Let's see who finishes first. On your mark—"

"Show me some ID, lady. A driver's license will do."

"Sure, Bob. But first, show me your penis. You have as much right to see my ID as I have to see your dick."

Bob stared at me, uncertain. His hand went to the heavy flashlight attached to his utility belt. I knew from Lewis that this was meant to intimidate me.

"Get set—" I said, raising my pen.

He turned to the store manager. "She's nuts, Ms. Gilford." He pulled his walkie-talkie from his belt. "I can have the cops here in five minutes and throw her ass in jail. Let them deal with her. They love people who threaten to sue."

"You," I said, pointing at Melissa. She stumbled backward as if I'd just struck her. "How much did I spend in your store?"

"Over two thousand dollars," she said sheepishly.

"How much is your most expensive watch?"

"Uh, seventy-nine ninety-nine."

I turned to Bob. "Duh."

"Doesn't prove anything. You coulda run out of money."

I opened my wallet and pulled out the rest of my parents' legacy. I wagged the cash back and forth. Shoppers who had been watching us in window reflections turned to gaze upon the cash directly. I waved it about so they could all see; their heads followed the wad of cash. "This is eight thousand dollars," I said to the manager. "Do I look like I need to steal a watch? An eighty-buck piece-of-shit watch?"

"A lot of shoplifting ain't because of need," Bob said. "Lots of rich and famous people shoplift. They get some perverse thrill out of it. Like that Bess Myerson, the former Miss America. And Hedy Lamarr, the actress. Remember her? They had money, too."

The manager, caught in the middle of our courtroom drama, seemed stunned. She was no Solomon.

I put my money away. "Okay, you've convinced me. Here's the

deal. You want to search my bags, go ahead. Only for every bag you search and don't find the stolen watch, you can take that bag back into the store, because I'm returning that merchandise for a full cash refund. If you do find the watch, I'll keep all the stuff I bought. So, if you search every bag and don't find the watch, you owe me two grand. By the way, Melissa, how much of the two thousand dollars I just spent is profit for the store?"

Melissa shrugged. "I really don't know."

I did. At least a thousand dollars was profit, probably more. I stepped back from the eight bags and sat on a bench next to some potted plants. I crossed my legs and smiled. "Dig away, Bob. We all want to see how this will turn out."

The four of them stood in front of the bags and stared at me. Melissa, Janis, and Bob turned toward the manager for their cue. Janis adjusted her phony gut.

The manager smeared a phony smile across her face. If her eyes had teeth, my face would have been gnawed to the skull. "I'm so sorry for the misunderstanding, Ms. . . . ?" She waited for me to fill in the blank with my name. I didn't.

She clapped her hands cheerfully. Her voice rose as she projected her words so that all the faithful gathered could hear her forgiveness. "I'm sure Janis made a mistake. We've had to be so careful with all thefts. You realize we end up having to pass those losses on to the consumer, so this is really for everyone's good. Again, please accept our apologies. We thank you for shopping at Smart Shoppe."

I stood up, hooked my hands through the bags, and walked away. The bags were heavy, but I fought the weight to maintain a righteous posture. I could feel their eyes stuck to my back like porcupine quills. I walked up to the counter of the cookie stand and slapped my hand on the glass showcase. The kid looked up from his cookie tray.

"Gimme my free cookies," I said.

Back in my motel room, I sat on the bed eating cookies, my new clothes spread out all around me. They were arranged in coordinated outfits and draped over the edge of the bed like worshipful supplicants. And there at the foot of the bed, the crown jewel of my collection: my new $79.99 watch.

* * *

By one in the morning, I had found the head of Richard Nixon, Lyndon Johnson, and Jimmy Carter. The last one was tough. The stucco ceiling swirls leant themselves to images of thick-nosed, jowly men and big-haired women. Marilyn Monroe had been easy. Brigitte Bardot, Sophia Loren, Dolly Parton—child's play. All three formed a constellation around the heating vent. Twiggy had taken some time. Big eyes and no hair were a challenge. Men who wore glasses were easy. I found Malcolm X right away. Aristotle Onassis hovered over by the bathroom. I started to think of the ceiling as my own private glimpse into heaven, a giant window where I could now see all the souls of dead people floating above who'd been voyeuristically peeping at me.

Not everybody I saw was dead, but in a way they were. They were famous, their faces so familiar that I was able to pick them out of pimply spackle. But the famous part of a person was only a compilation of selected information, not really the actual person. Maybe when you became famous, your real soul died and went to my little heaven while the famous part took over your body. You became what was reported, like some "Entertainment Tonight" twist of *Invasion of the Body Snatchers.* Anyway, I didn't really believe in souls or heaven or afterlife. We were merely matter in motion, teeny bits of agitated particles clumped in a dervish of activity. The rest was the fevered illusion of hope and fear.

I couldn't find Rush up there. Once I thought I saw him near James Dean, but that turned out to be Janis Joplin. Lincoln seemed to be everywhere. Other people kept turning into Lincoln. I'd just picked out Marvin Gaye, exactly the way he looked on the cover of *What's Going On,* when he suddenly turned into Lincoln smoking a cigar. Lincoln was starting to annoy me.

I turned off the light and tried to sleep. I couldn't. I looked up at the ceiling. All the faces now had bodies and were dancing with each other. Elvis cha-chaed with Jimi Hendrix. Gandhi did the dip with Joan Crawford. Lincoln did the twist with another Lincoln. I closed my eyes. I saw them through my eyelids.

I turned on the light again and got out of bed, careful not to disturb my new clothing, all of which was still carefully arranged around my bed. I felt light-headed and giddy, like a teenaged drunk. I grabbed my new cosmetics bag, stuffed with all my new makeup. I plopped down in front of the TV screen, less than a foot away. On top of the set, I lined up the twelve different shades of lipstick I'd bought. I turned on the set while I applied lipstick number one to my lips. My plan was simple: Every time I spotted a man I wanted to have sex with, I would kiss him. This was much better than just picking out heads from spackle. More personal, I thought. Like a video game.

By 3:00 A.M., the TV screen looked like a car windshield that had splattered a couple dozen colorful butterflies. I'd planted a sticky kiss on James Cagney, of course. Then William Powell in one of his *Thin Man* movies, the one costarring Jimmy Stewart, who also got a big smooch, even though I hate his right-wing politics. Audie Murphy, lame actor, but heck of a soldier. He got the magenta lipstick, closest I had to a purple heart. I laid one on Alan Hale, Jr., during a "Gilligan's Island" rerun because I thought he'd be funny in bed, maybe grab one of my boobs and say, "Let's have sex, Little Buddy." I kissed a few guys I didn't know, bit actors in "MacGyver" and a badly dubbed Italian gangster movie.

Sometimes when I kissed the screen, a little spark of static electricity would crackle, which, when I was a kid and had never kissed anybody, is how I thought all kisses were supposed to be. I looked at the pattern of colored mouth prints across the screen and wondered what the maid would think when she cleaned the room.

I turned off the TV and climbed back into bed. I switched off the light and closed my eyes. I saw myself back in the shopping mall, surrounded by Janis, Bob, Melissa, the store manager. I had faced them all down, I had told them a lie and, for the first time in my life, I'd gotten away with it. In this new version, Rush was in the crowd, having tracked me down by speaking to Mitzi and then calling every motel and hotel within a one-hour drive of my house. Kyra was there, too, concealing a Mother's Day card in her bib overalls. Mitzi was there, dressed as Eliza Doolittle, waiting for a chance to break into song and show she could handle lead roles.

I opened my eyes.

I pulled the Bible out of the drawer and began to read. King James

Version. Bad translation, nice poetry. One of my religion courses in grad school had been to read and compare all the translations of the Bible. Muslims didn't encourage translations of their holy book, the Koran, believing that since God's words had been spoken in Arabic, that's how they should be learned. Translations only opened the way for mistakes. I began to think about translations, the ramifications of getting it wrong. Talk about cause and effect and chain reaction. I imagined a desperate man, blood streaming from his empty eye sockets, stumbling up to some priest. "What happened, my son?" the priest asks. "The Bible says 'If thine eyes offend thee, pluck them out.' So I did." "My son, that was a clerical error. The new translation shows that what the Bible really says is 'Don't offend someone near a tree. You could put an eye out.' "

I laughed and rubbed my eyes. They offended me by not going to sleep. I rubbed them until they hurt. My eyeballs were raw.

I snagged my new purse from beside the bed. I dug Rush's card out of my new wallet and punched his number. After all, we were partners. I'd told him I'd keep in touch. His script lay on my lap, under the phone.

It rang a long time. Finally, he picked up.

"Wha . . . ?"

"Are we rich yet?"

"It's four-thirty in the morning. People aren't rich until after ten." He yawned. "Where are you?"

"Riverside. A charming motel room that reminds me of you."

"I sense a verbal trap here and I'm too sleepy to be clever. Call me back in a couple hours and we can have sparkling repartee."

"I liked your script."

He didn't say anything for a long time. Then said, "Good. That makes me happy."

Silence.

"Did you want me to say more?" I said. "I don't know how to critique these things. This is the first one I've read."

"First what?"

"Script."

"Is that what it is? A script?"

"What do you mean? What else is it?"

"A valentine, I think." His voice had tightened a notch.

"You're kind of a mushy guy, aren't you? I wouldn't have thought that about you."

"You think I'm mushy?"

"Maybe *mushy*'s the wrong word."

"What's the right word?"

I thought about it. I sensed the nature of our conversation was taking a bad turn, a hairpin curve over an emotional cliff from which there was no return. "Never mind."

"No, tell me. I'm curious."

"I can't think of another word. Let's stick with *mushy*."

"Do you know the last time I did something like that for a woman, wrote something? Guess. Go as far back as you want. Guess."

"This conversation isn't going like I'd wanted."

"*Never* is the correct answer."

"I appreciate that," I said. "I really do. I'm not unappreciative here. I am very appreciative. It's just that we have this business relationship now. Makes it hard for me to trust you. How can I be sure you're not doing all this mushy stuff just to keep me signed with you?"

He sighed. "What are you saying? To prove my affection I should burn our contract, preferably in front of an audience, so when I make my speech about how you're more important than any career, they can weep and applaud? Jesus, how many Patrick Swayze movies have you seen?"

"I didn't ask you to do anything like that."

"Why do I have to sacrifice my big chance to prove I care? Why can't you just be happy for me that you gave it to me? Christ, movies have fucked up this whole dating/love thing. Every woman needs some big gesture, the grand show. Songs dedicated over the radio. A blimp with your name in flashing lights. Skywriters puffing out a cloudy marriage proposal."

His anger surprised me. I didn't know how to respond, what to say. Finally, I tried to lighten the mood. "Courtship rituals in nature are often very elaborate and dangerous," I said.

"Well, fuck nature, okay? I don't live in nature; I live in Los Angeles. Here we just say how we feel and go from there. Kind of like this: I like you, Blue. I'm attracted to you. I want to have a relationship with you beyond sex and movies. See? Easy. Now you try it."

I thought about it for a long time. He waited patiently without saying a word, though I could hear his breathing. I also heard his dog stir, the sound of the mattress springs squeaking as the dog scratched himself. I kept listening for more sounds rather than focusing on my response. How did I feel? I cared about him or I wouldn't have called at this hour. Couldn't he figure that out? I guess I'd made his life better because now he had his shot as a big-time producer. But I'd also made his life worse because he was sitting in his apartment at 4:30 in the morning being agitated at me. Why should I have such power over him? It made me feel contagious, some kind of Typhoid Mary of love, a carrier of relationship death.

"Blue?" he said. "You still there?"

Gently, without a sound, I hung up.

Still, I couldn't sleep.

I rearranged the outfits on my bed, putting this sweater with those pants, this belt with that dress. These shoes here, those boots there. No help.

I closed my eyes and tried to sleep. My body couldn't relax. My body felt alien, like ill-fitting borrowed clothes. I needed sleep. Anything for sleep. I tried to masturbate, thinking that would make me sleepy. But it seemed too therapeutic; I couldn't think of anything sexy. I replayed Rush and me making love, but he kept looking at me and saying, "What do you feel?" My fingers cramped, my vagina felt raw, and I was more awake than ever. Plus sore.

The problem was, I had no plan. Nothing to wake up to. I needed to know where I was going next, what I would do when I got there. Then I could sleep.

I sat up excited. This was good. I had analyzed my problem, reasoned the cause, and logically induced a solution. That thinking process was the goal of civilization, the pinnacle of all human achievement, distilled in my simple struggle for sleep.

I reached over my tea rose tapestry vest with the striped floral motif and the brass-tone buttons and snagged the phone from the table. I began punching in numbers. I knew the number from my previous research. A twenty-four-hour line: 1-800-THE-BEND. The Bend was the name of Thomas Q's retreat in Arizona. It was named after a Creedence Clearwater Revival song. In fact, his whole movement had a certain sixties and seventies retro-feel about it, though it had a scrubbed and moussed nineties image. The Bend did not advertise, offered no brochures. Yet its rooms were booked for over a year in advance. How much a person paid for those rooms was determined personally by Thomas Q. Some paid a fortune, others nothing at all. And, from what I'd read, the amount was not based solely on income. *Newsweek* reported that a grocery store checkout woman had been charged an astronomical seven hundred dollars a day for a week, wiping out her entire life savings, while some millionaire desk manufacturer had been charged one dollar a day. But this was not a pattern of soaking the poor; each price was fixed based on some mysterious formula known only to Thomas Q. No one complained, not even the checkout woman. Entry to the retreat was just as mysterious. An application was required, with final determination decided by Thomas Q. Here, too, there seemed to be no pattern. Wealthy and poor alike were both welcomed and rejected. Famous movie stars applied and were refused. Others were accepted. Even clergy from other religions applied. Some were accepted, some rejected. *U.S. News & World Report* tried to generate a computer readout that would reveal the pattern of Thomas Q's secret agenda. But no pattern could be found. This led to some conjecture that he just threw the applications in the air and those that landed on his desk were accepted.

The phone rang twice before being answered.

"Hello, this is James. Can I help you?" Very cheerful. A twenty-four-hour friend.

"Is this The Bend?"

"Yes," James said, "this is The Bend. What can I do for you?"

"Do? I want to visit." For some reason, I was nervous and breathless. I could barely get out a short sentence before I was panting for air.

"We don't give tours," he said in a helpful tone.

"Not a tour," I said. "To visit. Stay."

"Have you sent in your application?"

"No time." I took a deep breath. "Can I come now?"

"I'm sorry, but there's currently an eighteen-month waiting list." His voice deepened with concern. "However, if this is an emergency, we do have a procedure to override the general application process. Kind of like instant credit at a department store." He laughed in a kind way. "I can help you do that right now. Is this an emergency?"

I hesitated. I could lie. After my shopping-mall triumph, I felt confident in my ability to pull off yet another whopper, especially with some cheerful New Age Q-ball from The Bend. But if I lied to get in, once I was there they would discover the lie and I would never get access to Thomas Q.

"Not an emergency," I said. "I'm a grad student in religion, writing my dissertation on Thomas Q. I'd like an interview."

"What is your name, please?" His voice had hardened with a protective edge. Kindness evaporated. "What school do you attend?"

Giving my name would be a big mistake. I was already covered with the rotten stench of publicity. Surely they wouldn't want that to follow me to their retreat. "Why is that important?"

"Without your name, I'm afraid I will have to terminate this conversation."

"Blue Erhart."

"Blue Erhart?" He was unable to hide his surprise or delight. "The daughter of the bank robbers?"

"Yes."

"Oh." He cleared his throat, trying to find his calm, unflappable voice. "Well, I'm afraid, Ms. Erhart, I can't help you. Thomas Q does not give interviews. You should know that."

"He has in the past. He gave one to that high school girl for her school paper."

"That was the exception that proves the rule."

"The what?"

He cleared his throat again. "The exception that proves the rule."

"I'm sorry. What does that mean, exactly?"

"Pardon?"

"What you just said. What does that mean?"

"You know, every rule has an exception. You've heard that before. It's a saying."

"A saying? Every rule has an exception? I'm confused. If every rule has an exception, why not include the exception in the rule? Kinda sloppy not to, right? But then, for your saying to work, you'd need yet another exception. Which means, theoretically, there would always be an exception to every rule, no matter how many times you changed the rule to accommodate the exceptions. If so, then there must already exist not one but an unlimited number of exceptions to every rule. That makes more exceptions than rules. Which makes rules pointless and futile. On the other hand, if your original premise is correct and there is an exception to every rule, then your rule about there being an exception to every rule would also have an exception, which means that some rules do not have exceptions. Which would negate your original argument. Is that what you mean? Is that what Thomas Q is teaching out there? I want to get this right for my thesis."

I heard a man's deep laughter through the receiver, but it was background laughter, not from James.

"Look, I was just saying . . ." James stopped, flustered, took a deep breath. "I'm sorry, Ms. Erhart, but our policy is that we cannot have you—" He stopped abruptly. I heard muffled talk in the background.

"What's going on?" I asked.

"One moment, please." More muffled chatter. A deep sigh. When James spoke again, his voice was courteous but formal. "Ms. Erhart, you are welcome to come. When do you expect to arrive?"

I was stunned by the sudden reversal. "Tomorrow?" I blurted.

"Fine. Lodging will be made available. You are welcome to stay as long as you wish as our guest. All accommodations are at no charge to you."

"No charge? As in free?"

"Yes, free."

"And my interview with Thomas Q?"

"Possibly. He will be informed of your request."

"Is he there right now? In the room with you? Did he just personally okay my admission?"

A long pause.

"Tell me, Ms. Erhart," a deep voice, not James's said. "Are you the exception or the rule?"

I had heard his voice before on "60 Minutes." They'd played an audiotape someone had smuggled out. It was Thomas Q. I felt uneasy, as if he could look right through the phone line and see me sitting on my bed, my clothes surrounding me like some satanic ritual, the lipstick smears on the TV screen, my face hagged out and eyes puffed up from lack of sleep. I pulled the covers over my lap, covering my underpants. "Which rule?"

"Pick one. Which rule might you be the exception to?"

"Survival of the fittest."

He laughed again. "You're a hoot."

"A hoot? What're you, Grandpa Walton or something?"

"I never did trust him. He had a weird look in his eye, don't you think? Like he had some very racy magazines stuffed under his mattress. Am I nuts or what?"

"It's almost five in the morning," I told him. "I'm not too good at pop culture quizzes at this hour."

"What are you doing up at this hour, Ms. Erhart? Aren't all people with clear consciences asleep by now? Remember what Cervantes says in *Don Quixote*: 'Now blessings light on him that first invented this same sleep! . . . 'Tis the current coin that purchases all the pleasures of the world cheap; and the balance that sets the king and the shepherd, the fool and the wise man even.' Pretty nifty stuff, huh?"

"Hardly a match for 'The exception that proves the rule.' "

He laughed another deep, rumbling laugh that obviously had nothing to do with what I'd just said. He had his own private joke going.

"What do I call you?" I asked. "Thomas? Thomas Q? Mr. Q?"

But the line was dead.

·21·

My windshield was smashed and dented and I was pretty sure those smeary pink splotches on the shattered safety glass were my blood.

I sat behind the windshield and stared. I didn't move. I couldn't decide what move to make, which limb to activate. Or if I even had a choice.

Where was the highway I'd been driving on? Through the massively cracked windshield, I saw only beige desert dirt and scrub brush. The smeared blood on the glass filtered the scenery, giving it a dusky pink hue, like a painted backdrop in those old cheapie cowboy movies shot on soundstages.

And what was that horrible noise, like screaming?

A slight movement in front of my eye caused me to twitch. As if a tiny suicidal person had leapt from the top of my head and plummeted past my left eye, splattering his hopeless body on my cheek.

I felt an itch on my cheek where he'd landed.

I scratched.

My fingers came away covered in wet blood.

"My goodness," I said aloud. I tried to move, but I didn't seem to have enough strength. My forehead throbbed and another red jumper took the plunge past my eye.

"Rush," I said, but I knew I was alone. Rush, I thought . . .

There it went again, that terrible sound, that agonized wailing. I looked but couldn't see anyone through the fractured windshield. I closed my eyes. I could sleep now if I wanted. Finally. Sleep would be easy now. So easy.

But first I had to remember how I'd gotten here. I saw myself hanging up the phone after speaking to Thomas Q, immediately packing my new clothes, throwing everything into my car, and driving straight for Arizona at five in the morning with three candy bars and a forty-four ounce cup of diet Coke.

There I was. Right there. That was my car zipping through the Arizona desert in the bright morning light about fifty miles past Phoenix, about twenty miles from The Bend. The only car on this desolate back road. That was me behind the wheel. Those were my candy wrappers on the floor. My Coke stain on the upholstery.

I was driving ninety-five miles an hour. I was practicing the art of holding my breath.

Willie Nelson sang "Always on My Mind." His voice quivered huskily like a grown man asking his parents for a loan.

I took a deep breath that inflated my chest and puffed out my cheeks. I held my breath and started counting silently. I was going for a personal best.

. . . ten . . . eleven . . . twelve . . .

I picked up the plastic tape box to see how long this song was. It didn't say. Maybe I could hold my breath through the rest of this song and into "Blue Eyes Crying in the Rain." That had to be more than two minutes. Two minutes was my goal. Two minutes was a survival zone.

. . . fifty-three . . . fifty-four . . .

A small burp of air escaped from between my lips. I pressed them tighter. My chest was burning for oxygen. My eyes watered.

I tossed the cassette case onto the floor among the crumpled Payday wrappers. I'd bought the tape at a gas station because I was tired of hearing the same stupid Christmas songs over and over on the radio. As a child, I'd alternated Christmases between my parents' prisons, visiting Dad one year and Mom the next. We got to bring in a picnic basket and watch a talent show put on by families of the inmates. The prisons played Christmas music during these visits. I

associated Bing Crosby and Tony Bennett not with white Christmases and roasting chestnuts but with concrete walls and razor wire.
Anyway, all the other tapes the gas station carried were serious country stuff sung by guys with big cowboy hats or women wearing Dale Evans blouses and—

Whooooosh.

Ninety-three seconds. I was getting better.

Suddenly, I felt light-headed. The road blurred for a moment, then came back into focus. I shook my head, rubbed my eyes under my glasses. Perhaps I should have napped before beginning this drive. I hadn't slept in almost twenty-four hours. And my candy bar-and-cola diet wasn't helping. But after my brief chat with Thomas Q, I'd been so excited, so charged up, I had to move, had to do something.

I had a goal, damn it. A destination.

For the first time since my life had begun to unravel, I had purpose. I felt energized. I would study the people at The Bend, interview Thomas Q, and write my dissertation. I was a scientist again, a sort of anthropologist entering the exotic world of desperate seekers of spiritual fulfillment. I would live among them, mimic their ways, learn their rituals, and in my dissertation explain to the rest of the world what truths they discovered there—the rest of the world consisting of my five-person thesis committee. Perhaps my thesis would eventually be a book, get published, receive some small acclaim among the academic community. I would become known and respected for my intellect and deep insight rather than being notorious for my outlaw lineage. Through sheer willpower, I could overcome the momentum of familial doom and change the course of my life.

I was more curious than ever about this mystery guru in Arizona. Why had he suddenly decided to let me come to his holy retreat? And what was he doing up at that hour? I had no life—that was my excuse. But he was worshiped, adored. Some of the interviews I'd read with Thomas Q devotees after they'd left The Bend were filled with evangelical fervor for the man that lasted for years. They thought of him as a godsend—if not a god.

I sucked in another deep breath and held.

. . . six . . . seven . . . eight . . .

This breath-holding thing was not just a frivolous game. It was a form of self-defense, biological judo, inspired by something that had happened to me while packing my bags in my motel room. I'd been off the phone with Thomas Q for maybe only five minutes when I was packing up my toiletries and saw a patch of fuzzy fungus on the bathroom wall. I hadn't noticed it before. The bright yellow walls only highlighted the dark mossy gunk. Fungus on the walls was not news to me. I was well aware that the air was filled with fungus spores. Millions float through the air, resembling those clunky round World War II mines they still find in the ocean after fifty years. Ironically, some of those spores are just as old and have traveled just as far. They ride the wind currents, too small to be seen by the naked eye, but swirling around every room in everyone's house like asteroids. It takes about a week for spores to travel from Texas to Minnesota, faster than some who drive. Once they arrive, they drift into homes and knock up against walls. If the walls are dry, they bounce off and move away like pinballs. If the walls are moist, they attach. And since the average house absorbs about a pound and a half of water just from morning washing and brushing, a lot of the spores stick. Once they stick, their shells break open and the fungus begins to grow arms, then more arms. These arms attach to the wall and begin feeding. Some species dine on the sulfur grains in concrete; others slurp up the metals in paints. Some get high on the glues in wallpaper. And some munch on the antibiotic poisons produced by the wood. The problem they all face in this buffet style of eating is that they often absorb a lot of miscellaneous poisons. To keep from being killed, they spray the excess poisons into the air like an aerosol room freshener—everything from carbon dioxide to hydrogen cyanide to ethanol fumes.

And they are in almost every room we enter. Guaranteed.

Generally, they are harmless. Sometimes, they can be deadly. In older houses from the 1920s, fungi clinging to those walls and sucking up that pre-EPA paint will be guzzling the arsenic they used back then as an oil binder. Then these little invisible creatures will begin farting arsenic poison into the room. People used to die from it. Of course, to produce enough poison to be lethal, the fungi colony would have to be large enough to be visible.

By then it may be too late. Who knows what kind of new chemicals and poisons are being used in paints, with effects on humans that we won't know about until millions have died or had their internal organs eaten away, as with asbestos? Everything around us, seen or unseen, was potentially life-threatening. Maybe they were the same source as Legionnaires' disease or chronic fatigue syndrome.

You can see now how holding one's breath could come in handy. You're in a room, you spot the furry splotch on the wall, and you hold your breath and run out of there. Don't take chances.

That's just what I'd done. Thrown everything in the car and sped away from those thriving fungi as fast as I could.

I took another deep breath.

. . . three . . . four . . . five . . .

Something ran across the road.

I jumped on the brakes. I flew off the seat and smacked my head into the windshield, then was dumped back into my seat with a wump. For the first time in my life, I had forgotten to wear my seat belt and shoulder harness. Figure the odds.

Beneath me the car kept skidding, began to fishtail.

Thumped something.

The car hopped up as a tire rolled over something.

A shrill howl of pain.

The clock showed 8:23 A.M.

The car spun around and around like the Mad Hatter's teacup and I blacked out.

The howling woke me.

I felt relaxed, rested. As if I should be whistling. As if I'd just had twelve hours of sleep.

The clock showed 8:25 A.M. I'd been out for two minutes.

I looked out the windshield, but it was too webbed to see properly.

Another drop of blood dripped past my eye, but it didn't clear my glasses. I took them off and cleaned the lens with my T-shirt.

I touched my forehead. It hurt. My fingers slid around on the wet, oily skin. I looked at my hand. More blood. Lots of it.

The howling outside had become whimpering. Soft mournful sounds of despair.

What had I done?

I pushed my door open and stepped out. Immediately, I dropped to the dirt. Apparently, my legs weren't as rested as the rest of me.

The highway was about fifty feet away. My car had left frenzied tire tracks in the desert dirt, uprooted some shrubbery, and knocked over a tall cactus. On the highway, the whimpering figure was lying very still. I couldn't make out what it was exactly, but it had fur. Not a person.

That knowledge didn't make me feel much better.

I crawled for a few feet, then tried the legs again. They were weak but serviceable. I staggered toward the body. As I shuffled closer, it's howling grew louder again, more accusatory. It looked like a coyote.

"Oh, Jesus, I'm sorry. I'm terribly sorry."

I hurried, dragging my right leg a little. Finally, I stood over it. She wasn't a coyote; she was a dog. Part German shepherd and part something wild. She wore no collar and there wasn't a house in sight, hadn't been for the last twenty minutes. Probably she'd been dumped in the desert by someone who no longer wanted a dog and she'd managed to survive out here ever since, survive the sinister onslaught of nature. Until she met me and my Honda. She couldn't move her body, but her single remaining eye followed me as I walked around toward her head.

The damage was massive. Blood puddled around her hind legs, darker than I'd ever seen red before. The black tire mark across her crushed chest was the hieroglyphics of blame. There was cause and effect, right there. My actions had at the very least crippled this dog, and she had done nothing. I had been irresponsible, not gotten the proper sleep, had not eaten balanced meals from all the food groups, had not driven at the legal posted speed. I had acted as if were above the physical laws of the universe, as if I could transcend them. Now someone else had to pay the price. I wanted to reach out into every home across America and grab their children by the scruff and say, "Clean up your room, damn it! That's where it all begins!" The dog stopped whimpering and closed her eye.

"Oh no, please don't die. Please, please, please!" I knelt down beside it. From down there, I could see the gash in her stomach, her bowels uncurling through the opening. I'd been around dead creatures before, having dissected a few hundred. But those were prepackaged corpses killed and preserved by someone else for my educational purposes. This was my first kill.

Flies the size of bumblebees arrived like a posse. Some circled around the body. Others landed and began hiking the length of the body. The dog's tail flicked weakly, barely lifting from the blood slick it was lying in.

I held my breath. Not because the smell was bad but because it was oddly sweet, not at all what I'd expected. The scent was rich and compelling, like wildflowers. I found myself inhaling deeper to take in more of that delightful aroma. Jesus, Blue! I thought, suddenly repulsed by myself. So I held my breath. See, it had come in handy, after all.

The dog's eye was closed; her chest barely moved. I reached down and stroked her head, tried to offer her some final comfort.

She opened her eye and bit my hand.

It was a weak bite, having taken all her strength, but it was powerful enough to have punctured my skin and drawn blood. Almost instantly, her eyes closed again and her head flopped to the pavement. She was dead. Her last act had cost her the rest of her life, and it had been an act of retribution, not love. The need for justice went deeper than the need for comfort; perhaps it was even stronger than the need to survive.

These insights—part of that whole new insightful me—did not come without a cost. The dog had died with her teeth still locked onto my hand.

I tried to pry her jaw open, but it wouldn't move. That was unusual. Rigor mortis wouldn't set in for at least thirty minutes. Perhaps her jaw had been dislodged by the accident and this one final act of vengeance, though causing her excruciating pain, had forced her jaw to lock shut.

I looked up and down the highway. No cars. I hadn't seen one since taking this isolated road that led past a cemetery, a ghost town, and ended at The Bend. I was alone and the morning sun was getting hotter.

At first, I was as delicate with her as if she were someone's dead child. I pushed at her lips, then the snout. It was difficult working with only one free hand. The puncture wounds weren't deep, but they were bleeding and there was danger of infection. Still, I was unable to budge her mouth. I looked around for some sort of tool. A few feet away was a stick about the length and thickness of an arrow. I stretched out to reach it with my hand. Couldn't. Tried to snag it with my foot. Failed. Finally, I grabbed the dog by the back of the neck and dragged her a couple feet. The flies came along, though some of the dog's intestines didn't.

I picked up the stick and tried to leverage the mouth open. The stick broke. I bundled the two halves together. Both halves broke.

I was getting mad at the dog. "Okay, I made a mistake. I admit it. But I can't undo it. Let go of my hand, you bitch."

I dragged the dog another couple feet, smearing blood across the highway. My hand was aching so much, I forgot about my throbbing forehead and my bad leg.

"This is your last chance to let go," I pleaded. There were tears in my eyes.

I picked up a rock the size of a melon. I kneeled over her head. I smashed the rock into her jaw. I repeated hammering the jaw until teeth and bone were pulverized, freeing my hand.

I wrapped my hand in the bottom hem of my T-shirt. The bleeding had stopped by the time I was almost to my car.

That's when I noticed the small fire in the passenger seat.

I ran as fast as I could, kind of hop-running on my wounded leg.

I looked through the window and saw what had caused the fire. My spare glasses, an old prescription that I kept clipped to the visor, had been dislodged during the accident and had dropped onto the dashboard beside a candy wrapper. The desert sun glared through the lens, pinpointing on the candy wrapper until it burst into flames. A part of the burning wrapper had dropped to the floor, igniting other wrappers and my unread copy of the *Phoenix Sun*. Now the seat itself was on fire and spreading to the backseat. In a few minutes, it would reach my suitcase and all my new clothing, not to mention my purse with all my money.

I pulled open the door and began hand-scooping dirt onto the flames.

That seemed to work.

Then I had another epiphany, an insight so clear and brilliant that I could understand how Joan of Arc, if this was anything at all like she'd experienced, could willingly roast at the stake in trade for one of these. Every color of the desert was suddenly more vibrant, every smell painfully acute. I could distinguish a hundred different scents in one inhaled breath. It was similar to my previous experiences with the microcosmic universe, only this time it didn't scare me. This time, I marveled in its beauty. I was in such a state of clarity or grace or euphoria that I knew even the dead jawless dog would forgive me now if she could.

I stopped throwing dirt on the flames.

I walked around the car, opened the door, popped the hatchback. I pulled out my purse and tossed it ten feet to safety.

The fire was spreading across the backseat.

I leaned into the trunk and opened my suitcase. I pulled out my new clothes and tossed them into the backseat fire. The fire flared, rejoicing at the addition.

I walked away from the car and sat on the ground next to my purse, watching the fire spread and grow. I cocked my head to the side and made a face. I felt like an artist evaluating my work in progress. It just wasn't right yet.

I went back to the car, tossed a thousand dollars cash into the flames. The fire jumped on the bills in a copulating fury. As I watched the bills ignite, I felt a sudden rush of adrenaline surge through me, as if the soul of each bill had entered me. I threw in the rest of the money, all eight thousand dollars.

I backed away and watched, giddy and impatient.

The clothes were in flames; the money was gone. I was entering this part of my life purified from the causational elements of my past. When I walked into The Bend and faced Thomas Q, I would have nothing to hide.

Then I remembered. There was something I wanted to keep. Two things.

I raced back to the car. The flames whooshed from the hatchback as if it were an out of control barbecue. It couldn't be too long before the gas tank ruptured and blew up. I grabbed a stick from the ground and quickly poked through the open suitcase. What I wanted was at the bottom. I lifted the flaming underwear with my stick and darted my hand into the suitcase. A flame nipped at my hand, singing the skin. I dropped the stick and backed away.

In one hand was my stolen watch; in the other, Rush's script.

·22·

They were talking about me on television. My name was being heard by millions of beer-slurping, crotch-scratching, nose-picking, ear-drilling, child-swatting, chip-munching Americans exercising their First Amendment right to know.

I thumbed up the volume on the remote. I wanted to hear every word.

"Well, they are at it again," he said. "Husband-and-wife bank robbers, Naomi and Harold Henderson have struck for the fifth time since being released from prison after serving nineteen years for a similar string of holdups in the early seventies."

The screen behind him fills with a grainy black-and-white photo taken from a bank surveillance camera. Des Moines, Iowa. Their faces are unrecognizable blurs, but clearly visible are the backpacks of money slung over their shoulders and the sawed-off shotguns they are furtively stuffing under their overcoats.

"Even as the banks' coffers are being emptied, sizable cash donations have begun arriving anonymously at such organizations as Amnesty International, Greenpeace, the Los Angeles Literacy Center, the Chicago AIDS Hospice, Farm Aid, and others. Ironically, following the public announcement of each anonymous donation, contributions from private donors to these same organizations almost double in each case. As one charity worker said, "Getting a donation from those bank robbers is better than getting a telethon from Jerry Lewis."

Cheers and enthusiastic applause from the studio audience interrupt. He waits, his face deadpan.

When the applause dies down, he continues: "Law enforcement officials seem perplexed as to how to stop this modern-day Bonnie and Clyde."

A photo of pop-eyed Don Knotts dressed as Barney Fife appears, his uniform pants puddled around his knees as he tugs furiously on the gun in his drooping holster.

Laughter and applause.

"Meanwhile, recently uncovered early family home movies from the Hendersons show their young daughter, Blue, asking her parents for a raise in her allowance."

An old silent movie from the 1920s fills the TV screen, the film scratchy and erratic. A pale-skinned little girl in an old-fashioned white dress with a giant bow the size of a buzzard perched in her hair skips into a living room, licking an enormous lollipop. Her parents, old codgers with permanent scowls, are sitting on the sofa, reading thick leather books. The portly father is dressed in an old-fashioned banker's suit; the mother looks embalmed and ready for burial in her neck-high, floor-length black dress. The little girl mouths something to the father, smiles sweetly, and holds out her open hand. The screen cuts to a caption card with an ornate border in the tradition of silent films. The card says: "Can I have more allowance, Daddy? I'd like to make a contribution to that nice Mr. Nixon's campaign." Smoke shoots from the father's ears. The mother faints. Father angrily wags a scolding finger at the little girl. Card says: "Nixon! Why, when your mother and I were at Woodstock—" The little girl starts screaming and jumping up and down in a tantrum. Card: "Not that bulls—t Woodstock story! Pleeeeease!" Suddenly, the little girl has a rope in her hand and is running frantically around her parents, trussing them up. She pulls out a six-shooter, aims it at her parents, rifles his pockets then her purse, stashes the cash down the front of her dress. She bonks her dad on the head with her lollipop. She strikes a wooden match across her mother's cheek and lights up a cigarette. She pulls out her cash, waves it at her folks, and laughs hysterically. Card: "Nixon wants to eliminate capital-gains tax, damn it. That's why I'm giving it up for Dick."

Throughout this scene, the audience is laughing hysterically. At the last card, they begin to cheer.

I stabbed the MUTE button. I thumbed open the Tylenol bottle and shook three more tablets into my palm. I'd been popping them like breath mints since showing up here. Despite the five stitches, my forehead still throbbed from cracking into the windshield. Two of my fingers were wrapped in gauze to protect the blisters I'd gotten from reaching into the burning car. Band-Aids covered the dog bite. The scabs on my arm from my fall with Rush a few nights ago itched like crazy. At this rate, I wasn't going to survive until Christmas.

I wondered what the plot of that old film was before the writers at "Saturday Night Live" went to work on it. How did that story end? How did the family reconcile? Did the parents see the error of being too harsh and distant and, after a group hug, forgive their little pumpkin? Did the despondent little girl, realizing the extent of her antisocial behavior, do herself in with the six-shooter? I wondered if anybody who'd had anything to do with that old film was still alive. Was the little girl now a caved-in old woman lying in her own excrement in some nursing home?

One spooky coincidence: Though I had never dressed or looked anything like that little girl, sometimes when I thought back on my childhood, that's how I remembered myself. I'd picture me as a little girl in some nice party dress just like that one, thick crinoline crackling around me like static electricity with every step. A huge pink bow pertly atop my head. Black patent-leather flats. Then I'd remind myself that I'd never worn a dress like that in my life, or endured any goofy ribbon. My parents had been philosophically against encouraging that kind of gender stereotyping, and my strait-laced grandparents, though they tried to give me dresses, couldn't get me out of my jeans. Still, if somebody walked up to me right now and said, "Blue, what were you like when you were eight?" a mental image of myself in that dress and bow would pop into my mind. Weird.

The skit was over, so I hit the MUTE button again and restored sound.

"I'm Kevin Nealan and that's news to me."

G. E. Smith played his guitar. They cut to a photo of guest host Michelle Pfeiffer in a baseball uniform, blowing a big chewing-gum bubble. Miller Lite commercial.

I looked around the television room. Except for myself, it was empty. That didn't surprise me. I'd been here every night for the three nights I'd been at The Bend, and I was usually the only one watching TV. Except Tuesday, when about twenty others showed up for "Roseanne." They'd watched, they'd laughed, then left immediately afterward as a group. Very strange, I'd thought at the time. Later, I ran into one of them in The Bend library and asked her what that was all about. Turns out they were all part of some seminar conducted by Thomas Q himself. "Thomas Q told us," she explained to me as we shared slurps of water at the library drinking fountain, " 'look deep into Roseanne Connor and you will find yourself.' "

"Sounds like horseshit," I said.

"Doesn't it?" She laughed, wiping water from her lips. "But everything around here sounds like horseshit. Until you get into it. Then it works." She shrugged. "Don't ask me how."

I didn't. I was saving my questions for Thomas Q himself. The only problem was that I still hadn't seen him. I'd gone to the administration building six times already and requested an interview appointment. They kept putting me off. They were all friendly as hell, but it was still the runaround. "Thomas Q will contact you when appropriate," they'd said.

"What does that mean?" I'd asked. "When is appropriate?"

"When he decides to, I suppose," one young man behind a computer said, then laughed. He wasn't being mean. That's how most of the long-term residents I ran into acted. Kind of giddy, like junior high school girls after receiving their first French kiss. It was hard to stay mad at anyone. I tried, anyway.

I had questions. Questions about the philosophy of this group. Was it more pseudopsychology like est or pseudoreligion like Scientology? The library hadn't helped. There were no books or articles or even pamphlets by Thomas Q. When I asked the old librarian in the straw cowboy hat about that, he nodded sympathetically. "Weird, isn't it? But Thomas Q believes that he hasn't yet said anything worth writing down."

"What about his Ten Commandments? Show Up. Keep Low. That stuff."

"Well, he didn't exactly write that down. That was the Outreach Board, which he doesn't really sit on. It gets kinda complicated. You should ask Thomas Q hisself."

"But you don't believe that he hasn't said anything worth writing down, do you?" I said, frustrated. "I mean, you're working here. I understand he only hires people who have lived here at least a month as guests first, right?"

"That's right. Before I came here, I had a job. . . ." He laughed. "Shit, I almost forgot what I used to do." He shook his head at himself. "Easy to forget some things when you're here. Unimportant things. Guess that's why I decided to stay on."

"But what is it that he's said that's changed your life around so much? What does he preach?"

"Preach?" He laughed again, a real hearty Santa Claus ho-ho-ho. "Shit, girl, I don't think I ever heard Thomas Q preach. Not once. It's not like that around here. He doesn't advise, doesn't tell people what to do or how to act. I ain't never heard him say Show Up or Keep Low or any of that crap. He just does. Or is. You know?"

I shook my head no.

"I'm not good at explaining these things." He scratched his bald head under his hat. "All I know is that I'm happier now than I have been in years. At peace, I guess you'd call it. Maybe it's something in the water." He laughed.

"Just don't drink the Kool-Aid," I said.

"Huh?"

"Jim Jones? Jonestown?"

He shrugged. I didn't explain.

"Saturday Night Live" was over. The cast gathered around Michelle Pfeiffer. She thanked everyone, waved, wished the world a Merry Christmas and Peace on Earth. Theme song. The cast milled around on stage, waving and whispering to each other, probably planning which hot spot they were going to party at while the poor schlubs at home clicked around the dial for a late movie to fall asleep to. I switched off the TV and stood up. I stretched. Tomorrow was Christmas Eve. You couldn't tell from this place. There were no lights, no nativity scenes, no Hanukkah menorahs. Nothing. I'd asked a woman in Administration about the lights. They offered to buy some for me and string them around my cabin that afternoon. I declined.

"Don't you guys celebrate Christmas here?" I'd asked her.

"We're nondenominational."

"You don't believe in Jesus then," I pried, digging for scraps. "That He was son of God?"

"That has nothing to do with what we're about here."

"What are you about? Specifically?"

She smiled as she pressed the FAX button. "You have to find that out on your own."

"That's what I'm trying to do right now."

She gestured at the outside. "Walk around. Meet people. Enjoy yourself."

"Show Up. Keep Low. Scratch Hard. Wash Hands. Curb Dog." I'd stormed out frustrated, but for the past three days I'd been following her advice. Walking. Meeting. Relaxing. No one I spoke to could articulate what the dominant philosophy around here was. Some tried, but they would always fall back on terms they were familiar with—New Age jargon, Christian terminology, Eastern mysticism. Even if it wasn't edifying, it was interesting talking with the amazing variety of people who were staying here. There were a lot of minorities. African-Americans. Latinos. Native Americans. Old and young alike. Gay and lesbian couples. Newlyweds. Families complete with children. We were like some cruise ship in a movie. Slice of life. Bound for disaster. *Poseidon Adventure III.*

I walked outside the TV cabin, shaking my Tylenol bottle like a maraca. It had been shocking to hear my name on "Saturday Night Live," to know that people spent time thinking about me, people I didn't know. Michelle Pfeiffer knew my name, just as I knew hers. The desert air was cold but cheerfully so. People were walking around all over the place, even though it was after one in the morning. The Bend was a twenty-four-hour place, with over five hundred people staying here at any one time. A fifties-style diner stayed open all night serving up burgers (beef, chicken, turkey, or vegetable) and fries and malts. There was a video arcade, a bowling alley, and even a twenty-four-hour movie theater. The buildings were made from straw bales covered with adobe. Each resident had his or her own bungalow. Some had big-screen TVs and bars and saunas, some nothing more than a cot and a desk. Whatever you wanted was provided.

I walked by a couple lying on the ground, looking up at the stars. They stared straight up, but they were talking about a blueberry cobbler recipe. They were trying to piece together the ingredients her mother used but refused to tell them.

"Nutmeg, I'm sure of it," he said. "Nutmeg and something else."

"Eye of newt," she said, then laughed.

"Nuts of newt," he said, and they both laughed.

Not everybody was that nauseating. Mostly, they were just average people on a budget, not religious nuts or desperate kooks or cult groupies. Some were addicts trying to get straight, couples on the verge of divorce, kids with sexual-identity problems. Most were just people who'd heard there was something here, something good, and they were curious to experience it. And many had. Everyone I'd talked to had met Thomas Q, gone on a walk with him, swum with him, bowled with him, chatted about basketball with him. Thomas Q conducted occasional discussion groups, like the "Roseanne" one. They were never prepublicized or scheduled. When he got an idea, he'd post it and those interested would attend. He hadn't posted any since the "Roseanne" seminar.

"What have you learned here?" I asked one woman my age as she was packing her car to leave. I'd followed her out into the parking lot. "What are you taking home with you from this place?"

"Two towels and a washcloth," she said. "Don't tell." Then she laughed. "I'm kidding." I asked her again, giving her a serious look. "Well," she said, climbing into her car. "I didn't find a man. I didn't get laid. I still had a good time. That's a first. That's what I'm taking home." She looked up at me. "Tell you the truth, I kind of expected some sort of orgy-type atmosphere. The Garden of Hedon—type thing, you know? Some of that goes on here, but not that much. It's not discouraged or anything. It's just that people end up doing things they didn't think they would. Like me. I didn't think I'd end up playing Scrabble every night with some nun from France. But I did. Couldn't wait to see her the next day. Kicked her ass, too."

Not everybody staying here was a peppy convert. I ran into a few grumblers who thought the whole thing was a monumental waste of time. They'd been dragged here by their spouses, or they'd come hoping for a more directed spiritual program, meetings or lectures or something tangible, printed programs and schedules. They couldn't overcome the panic of waking up in the morning and realizing they had nothing they were obligated to do.

Sometimes people recognized me. I could tell from their reaction to seeing me, or if I got cornered and had to introduce myself. But no one said anything. No one asked about my parents, probed for details. Maybe because there were many people around more famous than I—actors, writers, artists, musicians, politicians. In fact, after my car had blown up in the desert, I'd managed to hitch a ride into The Bend with Mike Nesmith, the skinny guy in the wool cap from the Monkees. After a few miles of glancing over at me, he'd recognized me. He said he knew how hard it was having famous parents because his mother had invented Liquid Paper. "Really," I said. "I didn't know that." He nodded and asked me to pick out a CD to play. I picked Tom Waits. We didn't speak for the rest of the drive and I hadn't seen him again since we checked in.

The coffeehouse was open and packed with cappuccino sippers. Somebody was on the tiny stage, playing guitar and singing an old Bob Dylan song that had been playing on the car radio when I broke up with Lyle Dieter in the tenth grade. He was a senior and as such had not been satisfied with merely rubbing my breasts as if he was polishing doorknobs.

I'd been looking forward to some strong coffee, but the place had too many people and I was feeling too restless to wait. I drifted on to the movie theater. I walked inside. It was dark, the movie already in progress. One other person was here and he sat in the front row.

I didn't recognize the movie, probably because it hadn't yet been released. Some hotshot studio boss had come here once, turned his life around, and ever since has been sending movies here before they are released to the general public. This one had Harvey Keitel and Christian Slater. They were walking through the woods, carrying a red rowboat. I think Harvey was supposed to be Christian's father. I had the feeling the movie was almost over.

The theater was small, with a seating capacity of about fifty. But it was clean and new and air-conditioned. No snack bar, just a few vending machines that required no money. I went over and punched a button. A diet Coke dropped noisily. The man didn't turn around. He was eating an ice cream sandwich, peeling back the chocolate wafer part and eating the ice cream like a banana. Then he'd fold the sticky wafer part into a small square and pop it into his mouth as if he was at Communion.

Harvey dropped his end of the rowboat, ran to the other end, and slapped Christian Slater in the face. I'd missed what had been said.

I sat down in the back row and watched Christian punch Harvey in the nose. They wrestled around and I closed my eyes for a second. Suddenly, I fell asleep as if someone had whacked me on the skull with a shovel. I slept hard, without dreaming.

"Hey. Hey." The man from the front row was shaking me gently. He pointed to the screen. "You want me to start it from the beginning?"

I blinked at him. The room was still dark, but a shaft of light from the exit lamp wedged across his face. The eyes were buoyant with good cheer. The mouth curled at the corners like apostrophes. It gave him a permanent smile. His jaw was dark with a day's worth of unshaven stubble. His two front teeth were crowded so tightly, they were a little crooked.

"Stop undressing me with your eyes," he said, smiling.

"Thomas Q?" I croaked hoarsely, my throat still numb with sleep. I don't know why I said that. I wasn't even totally awake.

"Bingo," he said, touching the tip of his nose.

"What am I supposed to do?" I asked. "Bow or curtsy or what?"

"Can you do handsprings across the lawn?"

"I'm not wearing a dress, so what's the point?"

He laughed. "Oooh, you've got a nasty streak in you. I'm going to have to be careful around you."

We continued walking across what he referred to as "the campus." Everyone we passed said hello to him and, by extension, me. My old celebrity status was eclipsed by his greater celebrity. I was no longer the daughter of notorious bank robbers; I was the companion of a revered spiritual leader. Kind of like dating the high school quarterback. People walking by would look at his face and smile, then they'd look at my face, glance up and down my body, then smile. Even here, in the midst of attempted enlightenment, gossip superseded all other thoughts. Who's screwing whom? will always be more interesting than What is the meaning of life?

"Gee," I said to him, "if many more people look at us that way, you're going to have to give me your frat pin."

"The people who wonder if we're sexually involved haven't been here long. Lots of people come here thinking we're some kind of free-love commune or something. A bunch of painted VW vans circled in the desert, incense burning everywhere, black lights shining on Day-Glo posters of Jimi Hendrix. Cream and Led Zeppelin broadcast from loudspeakers."

"Aren't you? I mean, intellectually. Isn't this place just est with bathrooms? What do you actually do here that qualifies you as a spiritual leader? What is your canon, your teachings?"

He stopped walking, looked at me in the eyes. Lamps lined the walkway, so it was almost as bright as day. I saw his face clearly for the first time. I couldn't deny that he was good-looking. I'd hoped he wouldn't be. Having a homely, even ugly, leader might have given depth to this movement. Instead, this was probably nothing more than the usual flocking to some face and worshiping its appearance. Jim Jones, Reverend Moon, David Koresh, Marianne Williamson.

His hair was black and clipped short like a gulag escapee. His face was a little long, the nose crooked as if broken a few times, the chin extending a little farther away from the face than it should. Still, it all came together in a compelling arrangement. The mouth, however, was the danger zone, with lips so intricately formed that they looked as if they'd been created separately from the rest of him. As if the face had been sculpted, then a lip expert was called in, an artist obsessed with perfection. He was also quite tall, maybe six four. He was dressed in baggy khaki shorts, a white sweatshirt with a pinkish tinge on one side that indicated he did his own laundry, and ratty rubber flip-flops like mine. The sleeves on his sweatshirt were pushed high on the forearms, revealing muscles as massive as the ones on his legs. He could have been a mountain climber. The only flaw in the package was his left eye, which was discolored with white smears like a soaped window.

"I'm blind in that eye," he said, startling me.

"Blind?" My voice was barely audible, my face flushed with embarrassment. Still, I couldn't help but stare at it.

"Childhood accident. Disagreement with the little girl down the street. I told her she threw like a girl and she hurled her baseball into my eye."

"Jesus."

He shrugged. "I whacked her with my bat, broke her arm. After that, she really did throw like a girl."

"You say 'throw like a girl' once more and I'm going after the other eye," I said.

He laughed. "This is fun. I'm glad you were able to join us here."

"Why did you let me? To say nothing of paying for everything."

He looked off into the dark desert. "I'm not sure yet."

"You're not sure?"

He nodded. "Not yet. I'll think more about it."

"Are you kidding me?"

"No."

"What if I write this really critical thesis about the place, exposing you as a phony?"

"I am a phony. I'm a phony if I don't live up to your expectations, right? If you think I've promised something and not delivered on it after taking money. That's what a phony is, right?"

"Right."

"Well, not everybody leaves here feeling they got what they came for. I certainly make no effort to find out what they want, nor do I make any effort to give them what they want. To those individuals,

I will always be a phony. You must have talked to a few unhappy residents by now."

"One or two. But I talked to a lot more who have received something from you. They just aren't sure what." I looked up at him, into his good brown eye. "What do you give them?"

"Nothing, really."

"Do you mean that in the existential Buddhist sense? Like people should strive to become 'no thing,' abandon their ego, which emphasizes differences and keeps them clinging to the materialism of existence?"

"Sure, if you want. Sounds cool."

I sighed with frustration. "Are you playing dumb now or are you really dumb? I can't tell."

"You mean, did I have any idea what you were talking about?"

"Exactly. Nobody knows anything about you, where you grew up, where you went to school. Did you study philosophy or what? Do you have any kind of religious background? How were you raised?"

"Anything else?"

"Yes, but let's start with that."

He smiled, leaned his face toward me. For a second—I thought he was going to kiss me. "Hit me," he said.

"Hit you?"

"Yeah, hit me. Hard as you'd like."

"Is this going to be some kind of moral lesson, like snatch the pebble from my hand, grasshopper? I hate this kind of thing."

He tapped his chin, daring me to strike him.

"Look, I'm a teacher, an adult woman quite able to understand any theological concept you want to articulate. I don't need crude demonstrations or primal screams or role reversals or hand puppets. Just tell me what you have to say."

"Hit me," he repeated. His perfect lips formed the words so grandly, it was as if he was speaking a foreign language. "Come on, don't be afraid to throw like a girl. Just reach out and hit m—"

So I hit him. I slapped him smartly across the cheek. My palm stung from the impact.

"Ouch," he said, rubbing his cheek. "That hurt."

"Okay, now what's the point? What's the moral? That I can write whatever I want in my thesis and can't hurt you? That whatever I write is a reflection of my own hostility and failure as a woman? What?"

He was still rubbing his chin, wincing. "That really hurt. Really, really hurt."

"Good. So what was the point?"

"I wanted to see if you hit like a girl." He laughed. "I'm kidding."

"Then why did you have me hit you?"

"I didn't 'have' you hit me. I said hit me and you did. The question here is, Why did you hit me? Just because I said to?"

"Bullshit," I said. But I felt an uneasy rumbling in my stomach. The back of my neck felt spiny and cold.

"Look, Blue, I ain't Satan. If you're looking for some symbolic hook for your thesis, you'll have to keep digging. I'm not David Koresh or Elizabeth Clare Prophet. I don't seduce people by promising them either eternal paradise or some dark forbidden pleasures. I don't do jack shit."

We walked silently for a few minutes. I kept forming questions in my mind, but just as I was about to ask them, my mind kept reeling back to the one most nagging question: Why had I hit him?

· 23 ·

We ended up in my bungalow. He'd given me permission to interview him and I wanted to get right to it before he changed his mind. I dug around through my drawers for my tape recorder and my notes.

"I had some questions prepared," I said, searching furiously. I felt like a high school student who didn't bring a pen for the test.

"Ask me about my stupid name," he said from the sofa. He did a very good impression of Mike Wallace: "Thomas Q? What's with the Q? Your mother frightened by a Q-Tip when she was pregnant?"

I abandoned my search for my notebook and just clicked on the tape recorder. I sat on the sofa beside him. "Okay," I said. "What's with the stupid name?"

"I think it looks cool. That big Q after my name. Very mysterious." He grinned. "Don't you agree?"

"Isn't there some symbolic meaning behind it?"

"Symbolic? Like what?"

"I don't know. Like some ancient Egyptian myth attached, or runic sign. Some I Ching message."

He shrugged. "It's not my real name; that's kind of symbolic in itself. Don't you agree, Ms. Erhart?"

"Well, I changed my name for obvious reasons. Unwanted family ties."

"I had my reasons, too."

"So, you've got something to hide. What is your real name?" He clamped his hands around his throat. "The trap tightens. She shows no mercy."

I laughed. I tried not to—I wanted to be professional here, scholarly. But he was sitting there, pretending to choke himself, bugging out his eyes. I had to laugh. In an effort to regain my composure, I resorted to picturing him in high school, imagining what type he had been there. This is a trick I use to keep me from being intimidated by people. I figured him for the folksinging radical type, the first kid to grow a goatee. Played guitar, wrote songs that sounded like Donovan. He sat by himself in the school cafeteria, eating an apple and reading French poetry. He dated older girls from the local college, girls who looked like Judy Collins. He called movies "cinema" or "film."

Rush, on the other hand, was the popular type. He'd had friends. He'd been invited to all the parties. There were more photos of him in the yearbook than anyone else. He did his own homework, but some girl in penny loafers with a crush on him, but whom he would never ask out, always volunteered to type his papers for him. He felt guilty, but he always let her. He belonged to every organization— newspaper, football, basketball, student council. He wasn't the leader in any of these, but he made all the meetings more fun than they would have been without him. Teachers figured he'd go into politics.

Thomas Q pulled a folded newspaper from his back pocket. "Present for you." He handed it to me. It was a copy of today's *Hollywood Reporter*. An article on the front page had been circled.

"I didn't know you read the show biz trades," I said.

"I love to read. I subscribe to twenty-two newspapers and magazines. *Discover, Time, TV Guide, People, Entertainment Weekly, National Geographic, The New Yorker, Utne, MacUser, Premiere, The Wall Street Journal, U.S. News & World Report* . . ." He took a deep breath. "Should I go on?"

I shook my head and looked at the paper. The circled article was about me. Rush had sold my story to a producer for a reported $600,000. "Jesus," I said. "Holy cow."

"Congratulations," Thomas Q said.

I was stunned. More than half a million dollars. It wasn't just a possibility anymore. It was real. I don't think I really thought it would happen. If I put the money in the right place, I would never have to work again. I could go anywhere, do almost anything. My head felt light and cottony.

"You okay?" he asked.

I shut off the tape recorder. I needed a moment to compose myself. Rush had actually done it; he'd actually pulled it off. I looked up into Thomas Q's face. He was smiling, but it was hard to tell what that smile meant. Happiness at my good fortune? Pity for my shallow values?

"I suppose you're going to want me to start paying now," I said.

"Not at all. You're my guest for as long as you want to stay." He took the paper from me. "The producer is a good one. He just finished filming *The Fourth Stooge*, about some steelworker back in the fifties who's obsessed with the Three Stooges. He quits his job and travels to Hollywood to try to become the fourth Stooge. John Goodman's in it. It'll be out this summer."

I looked at him, at the frosty glaze of his blind eye. Was he making fun of me?

I thought about calling Mitzi and Kyra and telling them. I hadn't phoned them since I'd arrived. They were probably worried about me. Perhaps they could come out here and visit for Christmas. We could spend lots of money. I took a Payday out of my pocket and offered some to Thomas Q. He shook his head no, so I took a massive bite and ended up biting my own lip. "Oowww!" I said, jumping up.

"You okay? Bite yourself?"

I nodded and ran off into the bathroom, where I spit out the wet clump of Payday. I could taste the blood in my mouth. I pulled my lip down and looked in the mirror. There was the puncture. The lip was already swelling. I sipped water from the faucet, but I couldn't rinse the blood taste out. I brushed my teeth and gargled with Scope. But I could still taste it, like sucking on a copper penny.

"Do you want me to go?" Thomas Q called from the sofa.

Did I? Was I even going to bother with all this graduate school crap anymore? Why bother? Still, even if I dropped out of my current life, I needed to do something with my time. I had the perfect opportunity to interview one of the most elusive figures in the news. Who knew when I'd get that chance again? "Stay," I said, emerging from the bathroom. My gums were raw from brushing. "You have any gum?" I asked.

Thomas Q rummaged through his pockets and pulled out half a pack of Trident cinnamon. He tossed the pack to me.

"Sugarless?" I said. "How sensible."

"Four out of five dentists recommend sugarless gum to their patients who chew gum."

"Sure, but what I'm wondering is, what does that fifth dentist recommend? Does he say to his patients, 'Screw it, chew the sugar gum. What's another cavity.' Shouldn't that guy's practice be looked into by someone?" I popped two sticks into my mouth and chewed furiously while Thomas Q stared at me with a huge grin. "What?" I said. "What?"

"You look cool chewing gum. Very Barbarella. I have to be careful chewing gum. My teeth get very excited if I chew gum. They start biting my lips and tongue and cheek, just like what happened to you. It's like having a small animal living in my mouth."

I chewed loudly, my mouth open for effect. "I feel like a biker chick. Is it my imagination or does the act of chewing gum seem to drop IQ by twenty points?"

"I think chewing gum is some kind of secret psychedelic. Sometimes when I'm chawing away, I get the impulse to hot-rod over to the record store and dig on the groovy chicks." He slouched into a cool James Dean pose.

"See, that's your problem—there aren't any record stores anymore. Just CD stores."

"No wonder I can't find the groovy chicks."

"You don't have to find them. They come to you." I gestured to include the entire Bend complex. "I'd bet that there are plenty of great-looking women throwing themselves at you every day. Am I right?"

"Define throwing."

I snorted. "The only question is, Do you catch them?"

He didn't answer.

"Do you?" I repeated.

"That wouldn't be ethical, would it?"

"Don't ask me about ethics—I'm the daughter of bank robbers. Besides, aren't you the authority around here on ethics? You're the guru."

"I'm just a resort owner, Blue. Nothing more."

"Oh? Is there a Mrs. Resort Owner?"

"No. I'm alone."

His answer surprised me. He was idolized by thousands, living in the middle of a daily ego massage of adoration. He could have said he was single or unmarried or divorced. But he said he was "alone." This seemed a good place to resume the interview. I clicked on the recorder and thrust it toward him. "Janis Joplin used to sing this song. I forget the exact title, but it was something like 'I Just Made Love to Fifty Thousand People, but I'm Going Home Alone.' In the midst of all this adulation, why are you alone?"

He laughed. "You don't interview, you interrogate."

"Give me a break. I'm new at this."

He went over to my bed, sat on the edge, and bounced up and down, testing the springs. "New mattresses. We just replaced all of them last month. Comfortable?"

"Like floating on a fucking cloud. Now, are you going to answer my questions?"

"Sure, as soon as you tell me why you picked me for your thesis?"

I clicked off the recorder. "Come on, I already told you. I had lots of reasons. I wanted something contemporary, something fresh, without the thumbprints of a thousand other grad students on it. I don't know. Temporary insanity? Easy grade? Satisfied? Anyway, this interview is about you."

"It's just hard for me to imagine you doing anything without a better reason."

"Why? You don't know what I've done in the past, what I'm capable of doing. You don't know me."

"I think I do, Blue."

My scalp tingled with anger. It was something Lewis might say, or any fucking man I'd ever known. They always think they know you—after all, you've got tits, an ass, and a pussy—how different can you be from all the other women they've known who have the exact same equipment?

"Are you okay?" he asked, looking concerned. "You look a little flushed."

"I can't believe your arrogance. You may be the head Lost Boy here in Never-Never Land, but I am not looking for a personal guru or savior or therapist or even a shoulder to cry on. I'm here for an interview and nothing more. You said you'd give me an interview. If you're not going to live up to your word, then be honest enough to say so up front and I'll phone a taxi and get the fuck out of here."

He went over to the small sofa, sat down, and crossed his legs in a formal pose. "Snatch the pebble from my hand, Ms. Erhart."

"Fine," I said. I pulled up a chair until I was sitting directly in front of him. Our knees were six inches apart. He stared straight at me, but I wasn't fazed. He didn't know me; he was looking at a mask. A made-up me, like the Phantom of the Opera. I could stick my tongue out at him right now and he wouldn't see.

I leaned forward to set the minirecorder on the arm of the sofa where he was sitting. I smelled cherries.

"Life Savers," he said, opening his mouth and showing a red Life Saver lying on his red tongue. "Want one?"

I shook my head and wondered how he knew what I'd been thinking. I adopted my teacher pose. "Why are you so reclusive with the media. Are you afraid of bad publicity?"

Thomas Q: Do you mean reporting or publicity? I have nothing against reporting. It's just that it's such an inaccurate science. It's more distorting than reporting. It's not the reporter's fault, though.

Me: Whose fault is it?

Thomas Q: No one's fault. Once a human being experiences something, no matter how wonderful and uplifting, the moment he or she tries to describe it to someone else, that experience becomes filtered by that individual's own life experiences and prejudices. Even by their vocabulary. Then you're no longer describing the experience; you're interpreting it, you're translating it. Like trying to paint a brilliant sunset with only two colors, black and green.

Me: That's the nature of language, isn't it? A fatal flaw in human communication. Tower of Babel and all that.

Thomas Q: That's why some things shouldn't be communicated. Just experienced.

Me: Isn't communicating an experience to another part of that experience. Sharing thoughts gives depth to what otherwise is merely sensational.

Thomas Q: [*Applauding*] You're so quotable, Blue. Maybe we should switch places. [*Pauses*] What happens here at The Bend is an individual experience, completely unique for each person. The goal here is *the experience itself*, not the analysis of that experience. We don't talk about it. That defeats the whole purpose, trivializes it. That's what I'm against. [*Leaning toward me, excited.*] It's like someone who has never had an orgasm but who has read about them in books trying to describe what one feels like to someone else who has never had one.

Me: So you'd liken the experience of staying here to an orgasm?

Thomas Q: That's just an example.

Me: Yes, but a very quotable one. The kind guaranteed to create more publicity.

Thomas Q: Okay, it's not like an orgasm. It's like a tooth extraction. A splinter under the fingernail. Lancing a hemorrhoid.

Me: Aren't you afraid I'll do the same thing in my thesis? Won't I be just another outsider trivializing the experience? A virgin describing orgasms to other virgins. I haven't had the local equivalent to orgasm here.

Thomas Q: [*Laughs*] You haven't left yet.

I clicked off the tape recorder. I got up and went to the kitchenette for a glass of water. "Want something to drink?" I asked.

"I'm fine," he said.

As I filled my glass, I looked over at him. I was barely scratching the surface with him. He seemed to know what I would ask and had an answer ready. I had to find my way past the veneer. I had to get personal. I drank the water I hadn't wanted and returned to my chair. I turned the recorder back on.

Me: Are you happy?

Thomas Q: Right now? Right this minute?

Me: In general. Most of the time. Do you consider yourself a happy person?

Thomas Q: *Happy* is such a tricky word, isn't it? Everybody wants to be happy, but no one really knows what it is.

Me: The absence of sadness.

Thomas Q: Okay. But if you take percentages, most people admit that they spend much more of each day either unhappy or neutral; that is, functioning in a zone that is neither happy nor unhappy. Very few minutes of the day are designated as happy, rewarding, or fulfilling.

Me: But it's important?

Thomas Q: Happiness is the currency by which we judge how successful our lives have been. It's the best revenge, isn't that what they say?

Me: Do you think you promote more happiness among your followers?

Thomas Q: You want to know what they get for their money? Is that it?

Me: Yes.

Thomas Q: If most people experience ten minutes of happiness a day and I help make it eleven minutes, wouldn't that be justification enough for what goes on here?

Me: Drug dealers and pimps could use that same reasoning.

Thomas Q: Rightfully so. But we're more cost-effective. More yucks for your bucks. Plus, I don't promise anything. I don't heal, don't see the future, don't read minds, don't talk to God or the dead.

Me: What do you do?

Thomas Q: I run a resort. Haven't you seen the shuffleboard tournament?

Me: Why are you avoiding my questions about substance? Why don't you want to talk about ideas, your ideas?

[*Long pause. Thomas Q leans over and shuts off the tape recorder.*]

Thomas Q stood up and walked over to my dresser. "Would you like to see God, Blue?"

"See God?"

"Sure. Look right into God's face. See what all the fuss is about around here."

I looked at him, leaning against the dresser. "Is God in my dresser?"

"As a matter of fact." He whispered, "Wanna see?"

"If God is bullshit, I'm staring at Him right now."

"Hey, it's your choice. I'm not twisting your arm."

I tried to figure the angles. What was the trap he was laying for me? Somehow I was going to come out of this looking like an idiot. Still, I was intrigued by his act. "What the hell," I said. "Bring on God."

I activated the tape recorder.

Thomas Q bent down and opened the bottom drawer. I didn't have enough clothing left after the car fire to fill even the first drawer, so I'd never opened the fifth one. "You know how every hotel has a copy of the Bible in it? Well, this is our Bible." He pulled out a paddleboard attached to a rubber ball by a rubber string. He tossed it to me.

"Yes, of course," I said. I touched the paddle, string, and ball, naming each: "The Father, Son, and Holy Ghost?"

He pointed at the paddle. "Go ahead. Give it a try."

"Are you serious?"

He nodded.

"This is God? This is how you people get orgasms?"

"Try it and see."

I smacked the ball once with the paddle. I fanned my face. "Goodness gracious. Was it good for you?"

He was smiling, but I could tell it wasn't at my joke. It was more like an adult smiling at the antics of a precocious child. That pissed me off. I dropped the paddle on the bed. "I came here as a serious student to ask you serious questions, not to be treated like a child learning to walk."

"I'm sorry if I gave you that impression, Blue. I can see you're angry. Tell you what, just hit the ball fifty times without missing and I'll answer anything you want to know. I promise. No questions refused. Even ones of, gulp, substance."

"If this explodes or makes farting noises, I'll kill you." But I found myself picking up the damn paddle and smacking away at that little red ball. I hit it twenty-three times in a row before missing. "I was never very good at this as a kid," I explained. "Got any jacks? Couldn't we see God in jacks?"

"Try again. You almost had it."

I started in again, *whack whack whack whack*. Thirty-eight times before missing.

And again.

Thirty times.

I had a couple more false starts, but finally I hit fifty. I didn't stop at fifty, though. I kept whacking the ball and it kept flying off toward the wall then snapping back at my paddle. I got to where I was anticipating that little thump into the paddle, the little quake of motion against my hand and tug on my wrist before I fired the comet back into space.

Seventy-five.

I tossed the paddle onto the bed, smiling, slightly breathless. "There. Now, where's God?"

Thomas Q walked over to my bed and sat down. He picked up the paddle and began wrapping the rubber string around the handle. "How do you feel?"

"Fine. Thanks for asking. Where's God?"

"I mean, how do you feel, exactly? Describe it."

"Whoa. You mean translate and trivialize my orgasmic experience?"

He nodded. "Just this once."

"Okay. I feel . . ." I searched for a word, but nothing fit. *Happy* was too strong and I didn't want to give him the satisfaction. *Content* was too mild. *Victorious* too ridiculous. "I don't know. Good. I feel good."

"But you didn't feel good before, right? Before you did this. You were thinking about a lot of things. About your parents. About me. Whether I am as big a fake as you think I am. About this Rush guy in the *Hollywood Reporter*. Right?"

"Not to mention my car, my job, my thesis. And I think I might be getting a bladder infection. People think about a lot of things. The nature of the beast. So what?"

"But not while you were paddling. While you were paddling, none of those things were important. You weren't thinking about yourself. All you could see was the paddle and the ball, the rhythm of the motion, the snap of the wrist. That's the face of God."

I was not at all impressed. For all his good looks and charm, all he had to offer was day-old bread of life. No revelations. No burning bushes. I tried not to look too disappointed. I didn't want to say anything to insult him. I was here to write my thesis, not make judgments. I looked down and fussed with the recorder, not wanting him to see my disappointment. I adopted a professional demeanor. "Is this paddleball thing part of a ritual here? Or can you use a Rubik's Cube or computer chess, something like that?"

He looked at me in the eyes with an intensity that unnerved me. His frosty blind eye glared. I tried to remind myself about my whole Phantom of the Opera mask thing, but that wasn't working.

"I know you think this is just boiling the shoes of other philosophies and religions," he said. "You're right, it is. All religions are rehashes of earlier thoughts."

"The only thing new is the packaging, is that it?"

"Don't underestimate packaging. Would Christianity have spread if not for that catchy logo of a man nailed to a cross? Where would Buddhism be without a roly-poly Buddha? Judaism without Moses carrying those tablets? Islam without Muhammad? These are like celebrity spokespersons, like Michael Jordan stumping for Nike. Without them, you've got no sales appeal. Without their face on the cereal box, nobody's buying."

"So there's nothing new under the sun."

"What Christ said wasn't new. What Moses said wasn't new. It was just new to them."

I walked over and picked up the paddle. "So—and correct me if I'm trivializing here—God is happiness and happiness is achieved through distraction and misdirection."

"Basically."

"*Distraction. Misdirection.* Isn't that the vocabulary of the magician, the illusionist?"

"Also the con artist," he said, smiling. He wiggled his eyebrows.

"I'm curious, where does pain and disappointment and tragedy fit into your happiness scheme?"

"Happiness is the absence of pain. Pain is an illusion."

"So if a person loses a loved one, their mother or spouse or child dies, their grief is an illusion."

"Yup."

I held the recorder directly in front of him, making sure I got each word. "A woman in a car crash wakes up in the hospital, to be told her husband and daughter have been killed. You're saying her screams of pain are an illusion."

"Yes. She chooses to feel pain."

I made a face. "That's going to be a tough sell here in the USA. We pride ourselves on our emotions. Mothers, puppies, the flag— if they don't choke you up, then you're a goddamn Communist."

He shrugged. "I'm not out to convince anyone. The Buddhists teach that the way to enlightenment is to throw off the shackles of passion. The only way to escape misery and suffering is not to be attached to anything worldly. If we can accept that all things end, that ending is part of the natural cycle of things, and train ourselves not to take death or pain personally as a direct insult, then we can be happy."

"Are you saying that humans shouldn't love, shouldn't marry, shouldn't have children? Doesn't that contradict what you said earlier?"

"There are two roads a person can take, though they eventually converge and become the same road. A person can either love nothing, disdain all things of the flesh, remove themselves from the interactions of human beings, from which come all pain and suffering. Or they can love all people equally, love each individual the same. Love your spouse and children, but no more than any other person known or unknown to you. You can still limit your sexual activity to one person if you wish, you can raise your children as best you can, but you must not love them any more than anyone else in the world. To do so is an act of egotism. Of pride. It's saying they are more valuable because they are related to me and I am the center of the universe. That starts that whole pain and suffering cycle again."

I looked at him, studied his face to see if he was putting me on. "Most people couldn't follow either of those roads."

"That's why most people are unhappy most of the time. As a species, are humans any happier now than they were five thousand years ago? Do people suffer any less now? Are you any happier than Mrs. Caesar was or Madam Curie or Virginia Woolf?"

"Possibly Virginia Woolf," I said.

He laughed.

Love nothing. Or love all things equally. Those were the two roads to happiness. Or, if not happiness, then to eliminating suffering. I'd read it all before, though I had to admit, it had more impact somehow coming from him rather than from an ancient text. I guess he was right about packaging.

"Blue, what do you say we take a break?" He tapped his watch. "If we hurry, we can catch 'Dennis Miller's Christmas Special.' I'll provide the candy."

"What about the interview? We were talking about being happy."

"Happy schmappy. Let's watch TV and zone out."

I turned off the tape recorder. My movements felt stiff and clumsy. Happiness seemed far away, like a place I always dreamed of visiting but realized now I never would. Like China.

Thomas Q stood up. "We can watch in the TV room or my room. Your choice."

I turned toward him. Was this a come-on? Was all this religion-philosophy-psychology babble merely his seduction routine? *You want happiness, baby, I got paradise eight inches long.*

"Do you think a lot of sex goes on here?" I asked him, gauging his reaction "I mean, on a daily basis. More than average. Like tonight, for example. Are most of your flock humping their way to enlightenment?"

He looked at his watch. "If they are, they'll miss Dennis Miller."

"Does that bother you? Aren't you worried that sex could become the main activity around here, that people won't get the bigger message?"

"I don't have a message, Blue. Big or small."

"Then what were we just talking about?"

"I don't know," he shrugged. "What?"

"The dangers of sex."

"Sex is always dangerous."

"Are we talking medically or emotionally? Are you advocating celibacy?"

"I don't 'advocate' anything. Promiscuity works for some. Celibacy works for others."

I smiled. "Celibacy doesn't work. I've tried it."

"Really?" he said. "It works just fine for me."

"You? You telling me you're celibate? I don't believe it."

He pulled out his wallet and opened it. "See? No condoms. Is that proof enough?"

Suddenly, all I could think about was sex. Everything I looked at reminded me of sex.

We were in his bungalow watching TV. I forklifted half a dozen cheese puffs into my mouth. I had not anticipated spending my Christmas Eve bingeing on junk food and watching TV with a celibate cult leader. I guess I could have done worse.

"You don't believe me, am I right? About the celibacy thing?" He spoke around a mouthful of Cracker Jacks. "You think it's bullshit."

I slumped down in my chair and watched the final minutes of the news. Right after this, the "Dennis Miller Christmas Special" would be on. "Ssshh. I'm watching TV."

"You think I'm hustling you. This is some kind of pickup line."

"I didn't say that."

Thomas Q was stretched out on the sofa next to my chair. He reached the bowl of popcorn over our armrests and offered it to me.

"No thanks. Pass me the chocolate-covered cherries."

He sat up and snagged the bowl of chocolates from the table and handed them to me. I took three and dropped them in the bowl of cheese puffs in my lap. The table was covered with a dozen bowls of the best selection of junk snack food I've ever seen. Aside from the popcorn, there were Cracker Jacks, potato chips, Cheez Whiz on Ritz crackers, Nutter-Butters, pretzels, corn chips, mixed nuts, assorted candies, malt balls, those marshmallow cookie things, and more. Every time we finished a bowl, he'd jump up, run into the kitchen, and bring back a fresh bowl of something new and disgusting. Something delicious.

"I read that this is how the Moonies brainwashed their followers," I said, holding up a cheese puff. "They fed them junk food, keeping them on a sugar high and lowering their resistance to manipulation."

"Hey, if you're going to insult my cooking, give the cheese puffs back. I'll eat them."

I hugged the bowl to my chest. "Over my hardened arteries, pal."

"Seriously, you hungry? I can whip up an omelet or something nonbrainwashable."

"Forget it."

He tossed a Cracker Jack at me. It bounced off my cheek and dropped into my cheese puff bowl.

"Tell me, Blue, is the only reason you came back to my room with me because I said I was celibate?"

"Yes," I said.

"Then you do believe me?"

"I don't know. I want to believe you because you're a nice guy and I want to believe nice guys exist. You seem honest, sincere, sensitive, smart. That's how I know it's got to be an act."

He threw another Cracker Jack at me. It snagged in my hair. I plucked it out and ate it.

"Nobody's that good," I said. "I mean, you're not a priest or anything, not a monk. You haven't taken any vows, right?"

"I haven't taken any vows."

"And you weren't dumped by some conniving sex-goddess woman who took all your money and pride and left you crying so that you crawled into a bottle and lived in an alcoholic haze until you found God or paddleball or whatever and swore off women as devils? Nothing like that?"

"Well, in sixth grade, Hillary Toomis tore up my valentine and flushed it down the toilet. Does that count?"

"See, that's what I'm saying. A guy like you, what we used to call in preliberated days 'a good catch.' What does that say about all us women that you find us so resistible? Are you gay?"

"No. Not that I know of."

"Why would a guy like you become celibate?"

"I didn't 'become' celibate, Blue. I just haven't had sex for three years. Since starting this place."

"Why not? Don't tell me that the women around here don't throw themselves at you."

"Some do. Look, I'm not saying I plan to abstain from sex for the rest of my life. I've had other things on my mind."

"We're not talking about your mind."

"Sure we are. The way I am right now, it wouldn't be fair to a woman to get involved with me. They'd be disappointed."

"Physically?"

"Everything works, if that's what you mean. But people have expectations, even if they think they don't. They want love and affection, which I can give. But they want something more, something I can't give."

"Please don't say commitment. That would be too clichéd for you."

"Not commitment." He exchanged the Cracker Jack bowl for the malted ball bowl, popping three balls into his mouth and crunching. "Remember, we talked about the two paths of happiness. Love everyone or love no one. I've chosen to love everyone equally."

"That's a very Christian attitude."

"In theory. The theology suggests we're all one big family and should love one another equally. But we don't. We select some to love more than others. Mostly, we select our immediate blood families. Survival often depends on doing that."

"Survival is overrated. Especially if it depends on families."

I could feel him looking at me, studying me. I kept my eyes on the TV weather forecast while I continued to shovel cheese puffs into my mouth.

"Finally, this unusual story of Christmas spirit," the news anchorman said.

"That's right, Paul," his female coanchor said, smiling. "Seems those Robin Hood bandits are at it again. Harold and Naomi Henderson, the husband-and-wife bank robbers recently released from prison, have hit three banks in one day. All three in downtown Houston. Houston police say the ex-hippies were in and out of each bank in less than two minutes. The total haul for the day? Guess, Paul."

Paul shrugged. "A hundred thousand?"

She laughed. "Try zero. Actually, they made off with over two hundred thousand dollars, but by the end of the day anonymous donations began arriving at various Houston charities. In each case, the money was tied with a red ribbon and bow. The cash donations totaled exactly one hundred thousand dollars, although FBI investigators said the actual bills are not from any of the robberies."

Cut to filmed report. There was my old pal Agent Bigelow. He wore a grim expression. "The suspects must have laundered the money before sending it out. Therefore, we can't confiscate it, since it is a legal donation."

"Are you any closer to catching them?" a reporter asked.

Bigelow blinked slowly. "We have now launched the largest fugitive manhunt in five years. The FBI, various state police agencies, and local law-enforcement officials will be cooperating in an effort to catch the Hendersons. Hundreds of officers will be involved. Rewards have been offered for information leading to their arrest and conviction. Roadblocks and inspection points have been established on all roads leading out of our dragnet area."

Footage showed state troopers whooshing down highways, lights flashing. Cut to cops stopping cars, checking driver's licenses. Cut to a shot of a dozen or so floppy-eared bloodhounds sniffing the ground, one another, and the shoes of the cops.

"Mr. and Mrs. Henderson will be caught. They were caught before and will be again. It is inevitable." Bigelow's face tightened in moral indignation. "I just want to remind people that, while these cash donations may seem worthy, this is money that comes from you, the taxpayer. Also, these people are armed with loaded shotguns. This is not a joke. They are not Robin Hood. They are dangerous bank robbers. Potential murderers."

Cut back to the anchor desk.

"Sobering words from the FBI, Wendy," the anchorman said.

"Indeed, Paul. But local people seem to take it all in stride."

Cut to minister in front of church. Reverend James Farrow. "Stealing is definitely wrong. But I can't help but thinking they're basically good people."

Cut to middle-aged woman on the street. "It's terrible. Too much violence today. Somebody should tell them the sixties are dead and good riddance."

Cut to young couple, early twenties. He: "They shouldn't rob banks, I guess. But they're doing good with the money. It's not like

they're keeping it to buy BMWs or anything. That's what I'd do."
She: "I think it's the new social consciousness. The world is so
corrupt, the only way you can make an impact is through a dramatic
act like this."

Cut back to anchors.

"That's it for us tonight," Paul, the anchorman said. "See you
tomorrow."

"And Merry Christmas," Wendy said, waving.

"You bet. Merry Christmas, all."

Commercials.

"You okay?" Thomas Q asked.

"Sure. Why not? Weren't we just talking about family and how
important they are for survival? Whew. I'm pretty damned relieved
knowing my folks are out there in case I ever need them."

Thomas Q put down his bowl of malted balls and sat on the floor
at my feet. He didn't touch me, but I could feel his body being that
near. It had a soothing effect.

"If you want to talk, talk," he said. "But you don't have to."

"Talk about what?"

He shrugged. He turned his back on me and leaned against my
chair. His shoulder was touching my leg. He watched TV.

I tried watching TV, too, but I couldn't concentrate on the tiny
images. Dennis Miller made jokes. Thomas Q chuckled, munched
pretzels. I imagined there was a red button on the armrest of my
chair. If I pressed that button, then Dennis Miller and his entire
studio audience would die. I pressed the button.

I turned away from the TV, looked around Thomas Q's room. It
wasn't exactly a monk's cell, but it wasn't lavish. There was a bed,
a desk, bookshelves, lots of magazines all over the place. No artwork
on the walls. It looked like a college student's dorm room, except
for the twenty-five-inch Sony TV.

I stared at the back of Thomas Q's head. In a lot of ways, he
reminded me of Rush—a more sophisticated, handsomer, wealth-
ier, less greedy, less horny Rush. A polished Rush. Rush if he were
perfect.

"Let me ask you a question," I said.

"Can it wait until the commercial?"

"Sure."

He turned around. "I'm kidding. Go ahead."

"Okay. Hypothetical situation. If some maniac burst in here right now with an ax and said he was going to kill us unless you killed him first, would you kill him?"

"There's a typical Christmas question."

"I'm serious. I want to know if you consider him part of the bigger family."

"You want to know if I'd let him kill us rather than take his life." He nodded. "The answer is yes."

"Yes? Just like that?"

He turned back toward the TV. "You asked. I answered."

"I don't believe you."

"Okay."

"You'd let him kill me, too?"

"I'd let him kill me. You're on your own to do what you think is right. Look, we're all going to die, anyway. I chose to live a certain way and not have some maniac with an ax dictate my actions. It's values that survive, not individuals. And they survive only if we act on them." He sighed. "Is this really more important than Dennis Miller?"

"Pass the M&M's," I said.

He handed me the bowl.

I started crying.

My crying caught me by surprise, the way it sort of burst out of me. A huge sob like thunder, then the rain. I struggled to stop, clamping my mouth shut, squeezing my eyes closed. I forced myself to stop breathing. I didn't want to cry, damn it, and I wouldn't. If Thomas Q could be celibate for three years, certainly I could not cry.

But I failed. Tears seeped out from under my eyelids. Sobs bubbled out of my nostrils. I struck my fist against my thigh. Again. Harder. Again.

"Sorry," I said, opening my eyes.

Thomas Q was kneeling in front of me but not touching me. His face was calm and pleasant. He didn't have that panicked look guys get when they see a woman cry. He didn't look like he wanted to solve anything, fix anything, advise me. He just knelt there, waiting.

And I started talking. I told him everything. About my parents. The twenty-dollar bill I'd spent that got them caught. My split with them ten years ago. Our recent meeting above the bookstore. About my attempt to steal Kyra. My relationship with Lewis. About Rush.

Dennis Miller was over by the time I finished. An old Columbo movie was on. Robert Culp was the killer.

Thomas Q didn't speak. He just sat there looking sympathetic, but not patronizing.

My eyes hurt from crying and I was embarrassed. "I hardly ever cry," I said. "Once a leap year, tops."

"It's okay to cry—"

"I'm not asking for permission," I interrupted. "I'm just apologizing for unloading on you. I don't even know you."

"What I was going to say is that it's okay to cry, but next time put the cheese puffs down first."

I looked down at the bowl in my lap. The yellow-orange cheese dust was matted from my tears.

"Sorrow comes and goes," he said, taking the bowl from me, "but cheese puffs are forever. At least that's how long these have been in my cupboard."

I laughed, tasting the bitter mucus in my mouth. I leaned over the table and snagged a peanut butter–filled pretzel. As I chewed, I stared into his eyes. "How come you have so much time to spend with me? Aren't you the lord and master of this place? Don't you have other guests to enlighten?"

"I don't have to do anything. That's why I pay a staff." He grabbed a couple peanut butter–filled pretzels and began munching. "I'm a little like Joe Louis after he retired. You remember Joe Louis?"

"A boxer, right?"

"More like a god. The real thing. He was the heavyweight champion of the world. Some think the greatest fighter ever, except maybe for Ali in his prime. Anyway, here was Joe Louis, old, punch-drunk, greeting guests at some Las Vegas hotel. Paid to stand around and have his photo taken with tourists. That's me."

I stood up. "I'm going back to my room. Can we continue this interview later, as soon as I figure out which of us just got interviewed?"

"Sure. Call me."

I walked to the door. He followed me.

"What if there's an ax murder on the other side of this door?" I said.

"Then I'm glad you'll be the first one he sees." He reached out, grabbed my hand, and pulled it up until the palm was showing. He dropped some corn chips into my hand. "For the road."

I realized right at that moment that everything he'd told me was probably the truth. He did indeed love everyone equally, no one more than the other. He made you feel special in his presence, but the minute I was gone, he wouldn't be pining over me, wondering what I looked like naked. I had the feeling that if I asked him for money right then, he'd give it to me without question. But he'd do the same thing to a stranger on the street. That took a lot of pressure off me. I didn't have to be good, didn't have to perform, somehow be better than others. I didn't have to win him; he was already won. I understood what all those people who came here found so seductive. I felt as if I belonged to something larger than myself.

I closed my hands around the corn chips. "Thanks," I said.

Suddenly, I was kissing him. I had launched myself into his arms and locked my mouth onto his and we were kissing hard and deep and passionately. I pressed my body against his, my pubic mound riding his thigh. I expected him to push me off or something because of that whole celibacy thing. But he didn't. He kissed me right back and it was unlike any kiss I'd ever experienced. It was perfect.

He took me by the hand and walked me toward the bed.

"Wait a minute," I said. "Won't this ruin your record or something? Three years of celibacy."

"Records are meant to be broken. Don't you watch the Olympics?"

I hesitated. "Doesn't this seem a little weird. There must have been plenty of other women who wanted you in the past three years. Why me, why now?"

He shook his head. "I don't know. It's time, I guess."

I tugged my hand out of his. "Look, I know talking in code is part of this whole cult shtick, but this is my life. I need straight answers."

"I don't have an answer, Blue. Maybe three years is long enough. I want you. That's how I feel." He looked at me with a questioning expression. "What do you feel like doing?"

He was the perfect man. Masculine and feminine. Yin and yang. Everything in one. No ego. Nothing I could do would affect his life. He was like superman—invulnerable. There could be no chain reaction, no responsibility with him. I was free with him. I felt I could will myself to rise off the ground and float over to the bed.

That must have been what happened, because next thing I knew, we were naked between the sheets.

·24·

Perfect sex.

That's what I was thinking about.

Thomas Q was lying next to me, arms wrapping me tightly like I was a half-drowned body he was pulling up out of the surf. His face was buried in my hair. I could hear the sissing of his breath, feel it warm on my ear and neck. It felt vaguely tropical, warm breeze sweeping across a hot beach. His hands cupped over my hands. Our eyes were closed, but we weren't sleeping. We were recovering. Convalescing.

Doesn't every woman dream of this moment, the boneless time after sex when she can replay each frenzied movement and know that everything went absolutely right? When every gesture seemed spontaneously invented yet cosmically inevitable. So unconsciously choreographed that some primal memory of invertebrate mud lust must have been unleashed.

I smiled and opened my eyes. The room was dark. No light. No music. No sounds. For a moment, I imagined myself a vampire resting in my coffin after a heady blood feast. Sated.

"What are you thinking?" he asked softly.

"I'm trying not to think."

"How do you do that?"

"Become a Republican."

He laughed, his breath tickling my neck. He didn't say anything else. I knew he wouldn't. Somehow he knew I didn't want to talk right then, and he didn't push me. He let me drift.

Perfect . . .

Perfect . . .

Perfect . . .

I kept going over it in my mind. I had never experienced *perfect sex* before. I hadn't even known it existed. I thought it was some mythical beast, a unicorn or the Loch Ness monster. UFOs and drugged alien sex. You don't know it's possible until you are actually having it. I felt like a scientist who'd just discovered a new species of animal in the rain forest, a wondrous creature that would change forever how we view life on earth.

Thomas Q was right about one thing: Describing the experience would be like translating something for which there is no English word. Still, the teacher in me felt compelled to try. I'd need to do that now, while I could remember each feeling and sensation. However, part of the exhilaration during our sex was that the feeling kept changing, shifting from under me. As soon as it was one thing, a sensation I'd adjusted to, my body would shiver with a sudden thrilling hunger and everything instantly became something else, something a little scary at first, then compelling, then addictive.

Thomas Q hadn't moved in a couple minutes. His breathing was shallow and even. Perhaps he'd fallen asleep. "Are you asleep?" I whispered.

"Do you want me to be?"

"No," I said. "No."

He tightened his grip on my hand and moved his body even closer, although we were already touching.

Why had it been so impossibly perfect? There was nothing special about the actual mechanics. This went here, that went there. Just like it is with everyone else. We weren't all that athletic. No contortions, acrobatics, or muscle spasms. We didn't even do it that long; I'd gone longer with Lewis and with Rush. It was something else that made it so not of this earth. The intensity, I think. Rush had also been intense, focused, and that was good. But with Thomas Q, I sensed that what we were doing was somehow outside the realm of time and space and physics. Dust mites did not gather. Neutrinos did not pass through our bodies. Viruses did not breed inside us. Aging ceased. No cause and effect. Perhaps within a couple of minutes, even the memory of it would evaporate from my brain like the perfect crime.

"Is it still Christmas Eve?" he asked.

I twisted around to look at his alarm clock, an old-fashioned model with two bells at the top. "Yes. For another twenty minutes."

"Mmmmm," he said, and fell silent again.

Perfect sex. How would I explain that to my thesis committee?

Okay, if it wasn't the mechanics, then what was it? I remembered him moving on top of me. I was moving, too, rocking beneath him. My feet were flat on the mattress, my toes flexed as I pushed my hips upward. We were moving in rhythm with each other but somehow not in sync. His body had extra movement; it vibrated like a tuning fork. I could hear a single bass note echoing through his chest, but it was distant, as if someone had left a radio on down the street. Suddenly, I felt that vibration penetrate me, travel up each internal organ until my bones and skin were vibrating to that same rumbling note. It was as if he was a champion swimmer and I were the English Channel. He didn't want to conquer me or dominate me; he just wanted to be within me, show respect for my power, yet still make his mark. What we were doing wasn't fucking; it was collaboration.

The intimacy was almost too personal. As if he'd known me all my life, had witnessed every regrettable act, every embarrassing moment, knew me for everything I was and wasn't. There was no need to try to hide anything, to pretend I was sexier, smarter, prettier. It didn't matter what I lacked. Whatever I was was enough.

"Tonight's the anniversary," he said. "We should celebrate."

I jumped at his voice, startled. "Oh, right. Christmas. The anniversary of Christ's birth."

"No, not that," he said sleepily, yawning. "The anniversary of the first person cannibalized by the Donner Party. They ate their first human this day in 1846."

"And they say men aren't good at remembering anniversaries. What did you get me?"

He kissed my shoulder. "The survivors were down to boiling their blankets to make a gluelike soup. A group of fifteen—five women and ten men—left the main bunch of freezing and starving settlers behind and set out for help across the snowy mountains. After nine days of traveling, with no provisions and certain they would starve to death, they began discussing cannibalism."

"Is this your usual postcoital love talk? No wonder you've been celibate for three years."

"Does it bother you?"

"Hell yes."

"I'll stop." He stopped talking and snuggled closer to me.

But now I was curious. Why had he brought the unfortunate Donner Party up? Was this part of the Thomas Q spiritual experience that everyone raved about? "Go on," I said. "What about them?"

He lightly bit my shoulder, then continued. "At first, they thought they should draw lots to see who should be eaten. Then they debated having two men duel so they could eat the loser. In the end, they decided to wait for someone to die naturally."

"Jesus, wouldn't you kill for a recording of their dinner conversation? A lot of people saying, 'Quit staring at me like that!' "

"On Christmas Eve, a twenty-three-year-old man named Antoine fell asleep next to the fire. He was so weak and stupefied from hunger and cold that when his arm flopped into the fire next to him, he was too dazed to pull it out. One of the group pulled it out for him. But when it flopped into the fire a second time, they let it burn."

"They let it burn?"

"Uh-huh. Then they ate him."

My stomach clenched.

Thomas Q stirred, then sat up, his voice growing louder. "Others died and the survivors ate them. Their only rule was you couldn't eat your own relatives."

"Ha. Mine have been gnawing on me for years."

"Two Indians arrived to help guide them but got caught in the storm with them. One of the men shot the two Indians and they ate them. Before the final rescue party—there were four such parties— reached the last survivors, forty of the original eighty-seven had died. The survivors became adept at preparing their friends for dinner. Brains and lungs and livers made a tasty soup. One man named Keseberg passed up a leg of ox in favor of this human-organ soup. He claimed the ox leg was too dry."

"Is there a point, or is this like telling ghost stories at camp?"

"No point. But there is a curiosity. Why did those particular forty survive while the others died? Is there a correlation? A common thread that separates survivors from victims? The diners from the dined-upon?"

I didn't say anything. My stomach growled loudly as if to answer. Thomas Q laughed. "Hungry?"

I put a pillow over my stomach to muffle the sound.

"This is where it gets interesting," he said. "I read this article by Donald Grayson in the *Journal of Anthropological Research*. His research shows that men died at a higher rate than women, at twice the rate, actually. Isn't that odd? You'd think the men would be hardier than the women."

"Maybe the guys were generous with their food. Women and children first and all that."

"Nope. Almost all the children under five died, as did all the adults over fifty. One reason women did better is because some of the men murdered one another. But the main defense in surviving was one common denominator: family. Those with families had a higher survival rate than those who didn't. The Breen family of nine all survived, even their two small children. They didn't share their supplies with anyone outside the family. Plus the families provided emotional support, a reason to live." He adjusted the pillow behind him. "Anyway, that's what the article said. Interesting."

"What is it about sex with me that brought on this lecture about cannibalism?" I'd wanted my voice to sound light and joking, but I could hear the defensiveness in it.

"It wasn't the cannibalism I was thinking about. It's survival. The family thing. You know, after seeing the news piece on your parents tonight. Just got me thinking."

"Well, don't. Think about your own family. Do you have a family?"

He looked thoughtful, as if trying to remember. His hand moved across my stomach and down to my pubic hairs. It rested lightly there like a napping bird in a nest.

"It's not a brainteaser, TQ," I said. "Either you've got one or you don't."

"Not necessarily. Families are like ice sculptures. Right from the moment they are created, they start melting. As they melt, they change shape, become something else. Parents try to stop the process, keep their kids from maturing, but it can't be done, not without killing the family. Kids are the same way, though. They want to stop the process, too. Keep the parents frozen in time as their childish vision of perfection. You've got to let it melt; melting is part of what it is."

"Believe me, I never had a vision of my parents as perfect."

"Sure you did. You may not remember it, but you did. Now you're pissed at them because they went their own way."

"Their own way? We're not talking about some eccentricity here, passing out lunatic political fliers at the shopping mall, joining a nudist colony. They're robbing banks with loaded guns. People could get killed." I pushed his hand away from my body. "Not to mention the public microscope they've lowered over my life."

"You remember in high school there were always the kids everyone else made fun of. Maybe they were fat or ugly or gay or stupid or smart? And it always seemed as if those kids, despite being outcasts, were model citizens. They followed the rules to the letter. Then there were the hoods, the guys who broke every rule, most of whom dropped out or were thrown out of high school. My point is, moral laws have to benefit everyone. When they don't, when any group is systematically excluded from benefiting, has little hope of ever benefiting, then they are under no obligation to follow that law. Why should they? They didn't make it up and it's not doing them any good. To follow it would go against natural laws of survival, right?"

I crossed my arms stubbornly. "I'm not playing this word game."

"Right or wrong, that's what your parents believe. They feel no obligation to those laws."

"Are your parents still alive?"

"No."

"Then it's easy for you to pontificate about families, Mr. Voice of Fucking Reason. At least you're judged for what you do, your own actions. You aren't carting around your parents' dirty laundry on your back."

"Everybody's carting someone else's dirty laundry. That's genetics, Blue. That's upbringing."

I flipped the covers off and got out of bed. "You know, everything was so nice, so perfect. Why is it a guy screws you and suddenly thinks he has insight into your life?" I picked up my panties, shoved them into my shorts pocket, then stepped into one leg of my shorts. "Besides, where does that put you in this whole survival thing? If it's the detached ones with no family who die first, like in the Donner Party, where does that leave you? You can't get much more detached than a single letter for your last name."

"I'm not here to survive, Blue. Since no one survives, that would be a pretty stupid goal to obsess over, wouldn't it?" He gestured around to include the entire campus. "Everything ends. Even The Bend has its cycle, its time to end."

I stepped into the other leg of my shorts and hiked them over my hips. "Who the hell are you, the Ghost of Christmas Future? You sure can end a good mood. Damn."

"Don't go," he said flatly. There was no way to read any inflection. Did he want me to stay because he was nuts about me or because he was just nuts and they'd find my dead, partially clad body tied to a cactus in the morning?

"You miss Rush, don't you?" He said it so suddenly, I was stunned. There was no jealousy in his voice. Just curiosity, like we were girlfriends sitting around confessing.

I fished my bra out from under the bed. "You amaze me. You just pop out with whatever's in your head, no matter how stupid. You're like a child."

"It's understandable, Blue. You treated him badly. If he was a dog, he'd have run away. You were a bitch."

"Well, if I was a bitch, then treating him like a dog was appropriate, don't you think?"

He laughed. "Touché."

I shook my head as I strapped on my bra. "You don't know anything about it."

"Just what you told me."

"I talk too much."

"He sounds like a great guy. I doubt that he was permanently put off by your bad behavior. Love everyone or love no one. That's the way to end suffering. You're caught in the middle, Blue. You want to love somewhat. Risk-free."

"I'm a consumer advocate when it comes to love."

"Life doesn't have assigned seating, Blue."

"Is that supposed to make any sense? Are you just remembering an old fortune cookie you had as a kid?"

"I'm just saying that life's messy. You can't drive yourself nuts because it's messy. You're like the guy who always stops at the same market on the way home. He always wants bananas and they never have any. He gets so angry every day. He's got to quit expecting them to have what they've never had."

I snorted. "God, you're insufferable. You're just like every other guy, one hump and right away I've got a concert ticket to listen to your bullshit." I snagged my T-shirt from the chair. "Wrong."

He got out of bed, went to the kitchenette, and brought back a bag of orange peanut candy. "You're not responsible for everyone's fate. God may move in mysterious ways, but not *that* mysterious." He tossed an orange peanut to me.

I let it fall to the floor without reaching for it. "Hey, God to you is a paddle with a rubber ball attached. Made in Taiwan."

"Sometimes." He chewed and swallowed his candy. He made a swooning expression. "Right now, God is an orange peanut candy." He tossed me another one. "Eucharist, anyone?"

I caught it and put it in my mouth. I hadn't had one of those in twenty years. It tasted like Styrofoam made from sugar. "It's stale," I said.

"No, that's the way it tastes. You just don't remember."

I sat on the edge of the bed, my T-shirt in my hands. I was exhausted, drained of the will to move or think or care about anything. "I'm tired," I said, mostly to myself. "Tired of thinking about life. Worrying about how things will turn out. Why can't it happen the way it's supposed to, without any effort from me? I meet a man, instantly fall in love, have two painless births, raise perfect children who ask for my advice and never date anyone without my approval. My man can't keep his hands off of me our whole lives, never looks at another woman, and we have close lifelong friends we share a cabin with every summer at the lake. Our children have strong teeth and our pets strong bladders. Every morning, I would wake and feel bad that the rest of the world can't be as happy as I am. Is that too much to ask for?"

Thomas Q's hands rested lightly on my shoulders. Slowly, he tipped me backward until I was lying flat on the bed. I released my body from any obligation to me. Do what you want, I told it. It lay on the bed wearing khaki shorts and a bra. Then no shorts, no bra. Gentle hands and lips and tongue enveloped it like a silky cocoon. Then it was making love.

And it was . . .

. . . damn it all . . .

. . . perfect.

· 25 ·

When I first awoke in Thomas Q's bed in the morning, I realized he was not next to me and I panicked. Perhaps I'd dreamed him and The Bend up. Like in *The Wizard of Oz*. If I opened my eyes, would I see the lemon yellow walls and purple lamp shade of my motel room? Would my new clothes still be arranged in outfits around my bed? The TV smeared with my lipstick? My shoplifted watch on the nightstand beside my bottle of Extra Strength Tylenol? Worse, I would still be only forty minutes from home with no place to go.

I clicked my bare heels together under the covers, squinting my eyes tightly together. *No place like The Bend. No place like not home.*

I took a deep breath. The strong scent of sex in the sheets reassured me that it had all been real.

I smiled and pulled a pillow over my head. I did remember a real dream from last night, one about that wild dog I'd killed in the desert. It was not a surreal dream. Everything happened just as it had that day in the desert. It was like a black-and-white documentary: the car crash, the cracked windshield, me staggering to the road, the dog biting me with its dying breath, me smashing his jaw into mushy slaw. One strange thing: The camera work was kind of grainy and shot from a high angle, like from those bank surveillance cameras.

That spooked me a bit, so I opened my eyes. "Thomas?" I said, looking around for him.

"At your service," he said, entering from the kitchen with a tray filled with hot tea, fresh orange juice, and a toasted English muffin with an assortment of little packets of marmalade.

"Perfect," I said, scooting up to be served. I was smiling so hard, my jaw ached.

"The marmalades are from United Airlines," he said. "They serve only the best."

I tore open a packet and scooped all the contents onto an English muffin. I offered him first bite. "Not too symbolic," I said, laughing.

"What is?"

"Me offering you a bite."

He shrugged.

"The Adam and Eve bit? Sexual corruption. Kicked out of Eden. Childbirth is gonna hurt like hell. Any of this ring a bell?"

He thought it over, then shook his head. "No snake," he said, gesturing around the room. "Got to have a snake. Whole thing falls apart without a snake."

"Yeah? So take a bite," I dared. "Go ahead." I wiggled my fingers like I was putting a hex on him. "One bite. Come on. Yum, yum."

"I already ate," he said.

"Chicken. Cluck, cluck."

He grabbed my marmalade-covered English muffin and licked a bare path across it. He handed it back to me.

"You scalped it. You're going to hell for that, buster."

"In that case." He snatched my muffin again, bit off half of it, and handed back the rest. "I'm just going to do my morning exercises. You mind?"

"Right here? Sure, go ahead. It is common for males in the animal world to feed, then preen for the females they have just mated with." I clapped my hands with a royal pose. "Let the exercising begin, knave." I loaded up my muffin again and began eating. I was starving, ravenous. I couldn't remember ever being this hungry. Yet otherwise, my body felt wonderfully lithe and toned, as if while I'd slept I'd received a full-body massage.

He rooted through his closet for something. He was wearing

running shorts and nothing else. I studied his body for some clue as to why he felt so exceptional during sex. His skin was unusually pale for living under the desert sun, but his muscles were firm and well defined. But it wasn't just the strength in his body—Rush and Lewis both had strength—it was some fluid quality, as if instead of bumping up against his body, I was becoming infused with him, his strength becoming mine. I'd never felt that physically powerful around a man before. "TQ," I called. "You don't feel bad, do you?"

"Bad?" He turned and poked his head out of the closet. "Why bad?"

"I mean, about not being celibate anymore. Having done the dirty deed. Isn't it like breaking a winning streak or some sports metaphor?"

He made a face that said, Don't be dumb. Then he completely disappeared inside the closet. "Where is that damn thing? I had it yesterday."

"Lose your Thighmaster?"

He laughed. When he came out of the closet, he was twirling an old-fashioned majorette baton. He had a big fake smile as he recited, "And if you make me Miss America, I promise to end world hunger."

"Boy, when you come out of the closet, you really come out of the closet."

"Ever use one of these?" He stopped twirling and offered it to me.

"Me? I'm prohibited by public safety laws to twirl, bounce, or throw any objects." Actually, as a little girl I'd tried to learn how to twirl my friend's baton, but I ended up clunking myself in the eye. I had a shiner for a week.

"It's easy." Thomas Q twirled the silver baton, at first slowly, hypnotically. Like someone telling a story. Then faster and faster, until the baton disappeared into a fluid propeller blur. All that was visible were the white rubber ends orbiting his hand. He sent the baton spinning behind his back, under his legs, around his neck. He tossed it up a couple feet, as high as the ceiling would allow, and closed his eyes. He held out his hand and caught it without missing one rotation. He looked at me and smiled. "It's very good for hand-eye coordination."

"Your coordination is plenty good already." It wasn't like me to chat so suggestively, but I was in a very good mood—the best I'd felt in a long time. I just sat in bed munching my muffin, sipping my tea, watching him twirl. The spinning baton picked up even more speed now, whooshing around his fingers and hands as he did increasingly complex feats. His body twisted and spun while he twirled the baton as if he was dancing with it. A samba, a tango, an Apache rain dance. It reminded me of our lovemaking—how he moved with me but not the same as me. Like two people reading the same book but one understanding so much more of it. His movements and gestures, whether making love or flinging a baton, were ritualized and tribal, like an incantation. A calling forth. When he finished, he dropped to one knee and flung his arms out. "Go Muskrats!"

I applauded. "Very good baton twirling. And I mean that in a manly way."

He was drenched in sweat. He grabbed his T-shirt and mopped his face and chest. He blew his nose into his T-shirt. "How is that for manly?"

I laughed. God, it was nice lying in his bed, eating his food, smelling his body. The sheets were clean, the pillows soft. Why would I ever want to leave? Actually, I didn't have to. I had plenty of money coming in from Rush's film deal. No one outside knew I was here, so there were no reporters. For the first time in my life, I was completely free. I could even get a staff job here, just to keep busy.

I looked at him as he downed a glass of tap water. Some spilled onto his chest and dripped down his flat stomach. I started to feel the gravitational tugging of sexual desire. My vagina was heavy with blood. I was sweating. He smiled at me and went to the sink to refill his glass. Was it him I liked or just being here? It always comes down to this, every woman's bottom-line question: Am I falling in love with this man or with the idea of loving a man? I wasn't in love at all, of course, but I felt something. More than attraction, almost a compulsion. I had to be careful.

I pictured my parents on the run now, trying to avoid the hundreds of state troopers, FBI agents, and local cops that had joined the manhunt. The pack of hound dogs we had seen on TV last night. Five states were mobilized. Meanwhile, Naomi and Harold were probably holed up somewhere in a filthy dive having the best sex of their lives. That thought killed my own sexual desire.

I pulled off the covers and looked around for my tape recorder. "Can we continue our interview now?"

"Now?" Thomas Q asked.

"Sure, why not? Just a few questions about God, the universe, and ethics. I've been at The Bend for three days and I still don't know exactly what this place stands for. I keep expecting to wake up in the middle of the night and look out my window and see you all in black robes worshiping Satan or something."

He raised his hands in mock offering and intoned, "O Lord of Darkness, I offer this female to you as a sacrifice. And all I ask, O Evil One, in return is you teach me the latest dance steps to 'Achy Breaky Heart.' "

"Don't," I said. "That's too spooky."

He laughed. "You don't believe in the devil, do you?"

"No, but I'm afraid of people who do." I held up my tape recorder. "As I was saying, why don't you put some of your dogma in writing?"

"You want us to issue a handbook, like the Boy Scouts?"

"I just want you to answer some questions and give me straight answers."

"I've got a better idea," he said, looking at the bedside clock. The hands showed 8:33. He picked it up and began twisting the knobs on its back. When he set it down again, the clock's hands were at ten o'clock. "Let's pretend it's still last night. It's late. We are arguing. You want to leave." He ran over to the bowl of orange peanut candy. He tossed one to me. "Eucharist, anyone?"

I took a bite, reenacting last night. I felt foolish and naughty, as if we were recreating a crime for one of those reality shows. "It's stale," I said.

"No, that's the way it tastes. You just don't remember."

"I remember," I said, throwing off the covers. He climbed into bed beside me. He placed an orange peanut candy on my pubic hair. It looked like a painted Easter egg in a nest. He bent over and started nibbling on it, tiny pecks. His forehead bumped my hipbone.

I grabbed a handful of his hair and lifted his head up. "TQ, tell me something," I said. "If it's true you were celibate for three years, why did you suddenly sacrifice that for me?"

"It wasn't that much of a sacrifice, believe me."

"You know what I mean. There was a reason you chose not to have sex for three years, especially with all the opportunity around here."

"An experiment," he said, sitting up.

"I'm serious, TQ."

"Me, too. I stopped having sex because I thought sex interfered with my ability to see all people as being equal. Ones you want to fuck are always a little more equal. I wanted to test my theory."

"And?"

"I don't know. I'll have to see what happens."

"Why did you choose me to emerge with? What is it about me?"

"I didn't choose you, Blue. You chose me. I let myself be chosen, that's all."

I made a face. "What the hell's that mean?"

"See, you're pissed. I knew that would happen."

"Wow, you also have the gift of prophecy." I covered my crotch with a pillow.

He laughed. "Don't get mad, Blue. I told you, I treat everyone the same. There's no reason to select you over anyone else. You wanted me at a time when I was ready to be wanted. There's nothing insulting in that."

I didn't say anything. I ate another orange peanut candy.

He pulled the pillow from my lap. I let him. He was right, of course. It was the very fact that he hadn't seen me as special that had freed me so much last night. Now I was being a morning-after bitch in search of phony romance.

He kissed my navel. "I think you should run this place, Blue."

"Yeah, right."

He looked up and smiled. "You should definitely run this place." He returned to my navel and worked his way back to the half-eaten orange peanut candy, which he gobbled up and swallowed.

I looked at him. He was serious. If I said, Sure, TQ, I'll take over for a while, I knew he'd say okay and maybe disappear for six months. That's who he really was, the living embodiment of good-will, charity, and love. No wonder I couldn't trust him. Thomas Q truly loved everyone the same. I wasn't special, an overpowering femme fatale who had shattered his strict morality. He'd decided to be celibate for whatever reasons, then he decided not to be. I happened to be in front of him with my legs apart at the time. He didn't fall in love with that funny way I crinkle my nose when I smile, or the cute mole on my cheek, or my incisive analysis of movies, or my dry wit. My sensual body didn't drive him to distraction. I was just a human being, interchangeable with all other humans. When he made love to me, he wasn't expressing personal need, merely being a good neighbor.

"I mean it, Blue," he said. "Take over around here. You'd have a blast."

"I'm not fluent in doublespeak like you are. Besides, I don't really like people all that much. Their problems scare me. This place would go broke in a month."

"Let me worry about that. You just walk around, mingle with the guests. Be evasive. That's the secret of my success."

"If I ran this place, what would *you* do?" I said, playing along because I liked the attention.

"Learn the piano. I've always wanted to play Gershwin." He hummed, badly, from "Rhapsody in Blue."

I laughed. "For some reason, I assumed you could play piano. Could play all instruments. Wrote operas in the shower."

"Afraid not. I always wanted to play keyboard with a rock band, ever since I saw the Dave Clark Five on 'Shindig.' Unfortunately, I've got a tin ear." He laid his cheek on my pubic hair and looked up at me. "What do you say? Want to be the Big Enchilada around here? The Dalai Lama of psychodrama. The Ayatollah of rock 'n' rolla. Good food and no heavy lifting."

I shook my head. "I'd rather rob banks."

He leaned over and kissed me on the mouth. I wasn't sure how to respond. Was this for me because I was Blue, or was he merely feeling some surge of love for humanity? His mouth tasted of orange peanut candy, toothpaste, and my own genital scent. His arms slid around me. I felt myself getting lighter as his kiss grew stronger and more insistent. His fingers scooped under my buttocks and pulled me toward him. I felt dizzy. I pushed away before I lapsed into a coma.

"I think you're sucking up all my oxygen," I said.

"All your blood's rushing to your vagina in anticipation."

"You're looking a little anemic yourself."

We looked down at his engorged penis.

I pulled him on top of me.

He snagged my bra from the chair and fired a hook shot at me. It landed in a ball on my naked lap. "Hurry up and get dressed. We'll be late."

I looked at the clock. It said 2:40. "What time is it? In the real world."

"Ten after one. In the afternoon. Hurry." He ran around the bed, picking up my clothes and laying them beside me.

"What's the rush?" I shouldn't have said *rush*. The word caused my skin to flush with embarrassment.

"You wanted answers. I've got the perfect source. Everything you wanted to know about The Bend. Are you still interested?"

Actually, my enthusiasm for the subject was a little dampened by the soreness of my genitalia. We'd been in bed for four and a half hours, napping and having sex and talking and having sex. Had I ever done this before? I couldn't remember.

Somehow he got me dressed and dragged me over to one of the bungalows in time for a meeting of the Outreach Board. These were the ones responsible for the Show Up, Keep Low, Play Fair, and so on bumper stickers and T-shirts that had popularized The Bend. Whatever the outside world knew about this place and about Thomas Q came from their collective minds.

"Blue," Thomas Q said, "I give you the Outreach Board."

Two women and two men sat at a conference table, looking up at me. They were drinking iced tea with mint sprigs in the glass. A plate of doughnuts sat in the middle of the table. I wanted one of those doughnuts very badly.

"Hi," I said.

They returned my greeting, each introducing him- or herself.

Louise: a pretty young woman in hiking boots and shorts who looked like she'd gone through college on scholarships and fellowships. She had a long scar down one knee.

Edna: an attractive black woman, thirtyish, with very short hair and huge hoop earrings.

Easton: a fidgety young man who avoided eye contact.

Stan: an enormous older man in a Panama hat who looked so much like Marlon Brando, I couldn't be sure it wasn't.

"This is my cue to take off," Thomas Q said, rising. "I'm leaving Blue here to take my place. For the purposes of this meeting, she speaks for me. Anything she says is the same as if I said it."

"You mean totally worthless," Louise said.

"Exactly." He waved and walked out the door.

A long silence while they looked me over.

"Okay," Edna said to me. "Let's save the fucking world."

I took a seat and grabbed a doughnut. Edna poured me some iced tea. "Thanks," I said, spitting powdered sugar across the table.

Louise handed me a napkin.

"Here's my idea," Easton said, fidgeting with his watch. He unstrapped it and slid it across the table toward me. "We make a deal with the company that manufactures these. I already talked to them about costs and delivery and all that. Very reasonable."

Louise looked annoyed. "We talked about this last time, Easton."

"Without enthusiasm," the older man added, his voice nasal and raspy, exactly like Brando's. He'd been introduced as Stan Fletcher. I stared at him, still uncertain. The crooked nose, the bedroom eyes, the pursed lips. He caught me staring and winked. I looked away, embarrassed.

Easton gestured manically. "Last time you didn't let me explain. Just listen, okay? I've got it all worked out. We design some kind of logo for The Bend and put it on the watch. Or a picture of Thomas Q."

"No pictures," Edna, the black woman, said. "You know how he feels about that."

"Okay, then we do a cool Q logo, like with Malcolm X. That was big."

I picked up the watch and studied the face. It wasn't like any watch I'd ever seen. There were five tiny windows lined up across the equator of the watch. Digital numbers appeared in each window: 44, 134, 5, 5, 33. The last number kept changing, counting down. "What is this?" I asked.

"Mortality watch," Easton explained enthusiastically. "You program in certain information about yourself, like weight, height, blood pressure, cholesterol level, calories consumed per day, hours of exercise per week, number of cigarettes smoked, childhood diseases, stuff like that. Barring catastrophic events like a car crash or earthquake, the display then tells you how much longer you have to live. Years, days, hours, minutes, seconds."

"Easton, this says that you have forty-four years and loose change to live?"

"Right. However, you can reprogram it when things change in your life. You increase exercise, reduce fat intake, that sort of thing. It recalculates your life expectancy upward."

"Or downward," Brando said.

"In some cases. If you gain weight, stop exercising, have major surgery. Stuff like that."

"Like I said last time, Easton," Edna said, "I don't think it's healthy walking around with your life expectancy ticking away on your wrist. It's morbid, like carrying a fucking bomb."

"That's the point!" Easton said. He stood up and began pacing. "We're all ticking bombs waiting to explode. Like Thomas Q says, everything has its cycle. Even if we can't totally disarm the explosive, there are methods to slow the clock."

"Nice phrasing," Brando said, chuckling. "I still hate it."

I looked at my watch, which I'd shoplifted. I had the strange feeling they could all tell it was stolen. I covered it with my hand.

"My point is that we need to be reminded that our time is finite. This watch encourages people to make healthy choices, both physically and morally. Do you really want to eat that fried corn dog? you ask yourself when you look at your seconds draining like blood. Eat that fruit salad and add minutes to the clock. Same with a moral choice. Say you believe in God's judgment. Do you really want to cheat that person when your clock shows the time narrowing between your cheating and the day God judges that choice? See what

I mean? This thing encompasses all religions and all philosophies because it concentrates on what we have in common, impending death."

Brando clucked his tongue. "This preoccupation with death is unhealthy. Just wearing the damn thing will take years off everyone's lives. Every decision shouldn't be put on a life-or-death or afterlife basis. There's only so much angst we can each endure."

The discussion continued for several hours. At one point, Easton had Edna on his side, but only if they agreed to print commandments on the watch face. This led Louise to suggest they come up with some new commandments because the old ones were getting stale.

"I thought commandments were supposed to be timeless," I said. "That's what makes them commandments."

"We just use the term *commandments* to add moral urgency," Brando said. "They're more like guidelines."

"I jotted a few possible ones," Easton said, ignoring my point. He opened his Day-Timer notebook. "Uh, Dream Big . . ."

"Sappy," Louise said.

". . . Play Hard . . ."

"That's Reebok, Easton. Jesus."

Easton crossed it out. "Oh yeah."

Edna started laughing. "My mom wanted us to include Safe Sex. I told her the AIDS people already had that one. And the condom people."

"I have one I'm rather proud of," Brando said. "Eat Shit."

"Stan," Louise said, shaking her head. "We'd like to get done here sometime today."

"I'm perfectly serious," Brando said. "It's very Taoist. Like Keep Low. We're saying that eating shit is part of life. There's a certain amount of feces dining necessary to survive, to get by. Whether it's government shit or corporate shit or family shit, shit is there and it must be eaten. The thing that gets people in trouble is pride. They think they're too good, too special to eat shit. Once they get past that whole ego trip—"

Louise pretended to choke. "Ego trip, Stan? Are you having a sixties flashback?"

"Okay, self-actualization or empowerment or whatever the current pop jargon is. My point is that people need to set aside their egotistical selves. Eat Shit says it all."

Edna guffawed. "Hell, Stan, we might as well use Eat Me. It's got that whole 'accept me for who I am' attitude. Eat Me says that you should consume me, make me a part of you so that you can see that we are the same."

"Plus," Louise added, playing along, "it's already written on most of the bathroom walls in the country. If we adopt it as one of our commandments, every time people see it in a stall, they'll think of us. Using public rest rooms would become a spiritual experience."

"That opens a whole new area for us: Wipe Thoroughly, Flush Twice, Wash Hands." Edna and Louise grinned at Brando.

Brando smiled and tipped his Panama hat to them. "Point well taken."

Easton tapped his pencil on the table. "Can we get back to some serious work, please?"

"Can I ask a question here?" I said, raising my hand.

"Sure," Edna said. "What?"

"I came here to do a report on Thomas Q and The Bend because its popularity has grown so much so rapidly. People come out of here feeling rejuvenated, changed, somehow better. I don't get it. I've been here for days, I've interviewed Thomas Q . . ."

Except for Brando, they averted eyes, indicating they knew the extent of my interviewing technique with Thomas Q. I felt my face heating up, but I ignored my embarrassment and pushed on. ". . . and I still don't have a clear sense of what the dominant philosophy here is. What exactly are you advocating?"

"What do you mean?" Edna asked.

"Everything you say or talk about, it's like out of a fortune cookie. Where's the foundation, the substance?"

No one said anything. They stared at me.

"For example," I said, "do you believe in God?"

"God isn't an issue," Brando said. "We never discuss God. That's individual preference, like a favorite color."

"Then what is it you guys profess? What is it you believe? Progay?

Antiabortion? Pro–capital punishment? Antivivisection? Give me specifics."

They looked at one another, mentally handing off the hot potato. Finally, Edna cleared her throat and spoke. "None of us can claim to understand fully what Thomas Q is thinking. We get bits and pieces. Jesus didn't tell the people everything at once. He traveled around, gave a bunch of sermons. Over a period of time, when all the sermons were collected, the larger picture of Christ's philosophy emerged."

"Are you equating Thomas Q with Jesus?"

She laughed. "Not as the son of some God, no. But as an enlightened teacher, yes. Same as Moses, Muhammad, the Bab, the Buddha, Quaker George Fox, and a thousand others."

"But these commandments and watches and bumper stickers aren't even his idea."

"We know. He kids us all the time about what we're doing. Sometimes we find notes from him on our doors. 'Possible commandments. Shag Balls. Drain Puss. Pick Toes. Signed, Thomas Q.' But he doesn't try to stop us. All he'd have to do is come in here and ask us to disband and we would. That's part of what we admire—he's not afraid of having us make him look foolish."

"He doesn't tell anyone how to do anything," Louise said. "He creates situations. He puts people together. He discusses a TV show, screens a certain movie. I don't know, somehow it all comes together to form a pattern. It's all indescribably revealing. All so . . ."

"Deep?" I said, trying to keep the sarcasm from my voice.

"Ms. Erhart," Brando said. "Don't you think we know how foolish this must all seem? Grown adults sitting around discussing two-word clichés that we pass off as wisdom. But if there is any part of Thomas Q's so-called philosophy that we are able to articulate, it is that wisdom is found in the everyday objects and words. He doesn't believe that philosophy, especially moral philosophy, should be so complex that the average person cannot fathom it. What good is it then? If a priest has to explain the Bible or a professor has to dissect Hegel, then the point is lost. We've all gotten lazy, delegated our power to politicians, our parenting to the school system, our morality to ministers. That leaves us plenty of time to play Nintendo." He took a deep breath and stared at me the way he (if he truly was Brando) had stared at Lee J. Cobb at the end of *On the Waterfront.* "The Bend gets its name from what every road, whether well traveled or less traveled, has in common. Each has a place where you can no longer see what comes next. Even a straight road bends away at the horizon. No matter what road you choose, it takes you places you cannot foresee. It bends into the unknown."

Edna picked up. "We just help people anticipate those bends and get through them a little easier."

"Lessons in survival," Louise said. "That's what we offer."

Brando opened his chubby palms as if he was about to scoop up water. "For example, Show Up is taken from whatever wit said that ninety percent of success in life is just showing up. We tell people not to be afraid to try new things. But also we want to remind them of the benefits of discipline. Show Up because the harder you work, the luckier you get. And we want people not only to accept their responsibilities but to dedicate themselves to those responsibilities. If you have a job, show up every day and do your best. If you have a family, show up and be there for them." He turned his palms down and pressed them against the table. "We want people to see there's more meaning in things than first appears, whether it's a two-word cliché or life itself."

Edna nodded a silent amen. "Unlike most other religions or philosophies, we aren't in the business of telling people how to see the world; we just put glasses on their eyes so they can see better for themselves."

Easton fidgeted impatiently with his mortality watch. "What about my watch idea? Can we get back to that?"

They all looked at me as if I was a lone holdout juror. "Thanks, that helps me out a lot," I said, scribbling furiously in my notebook to avoid their stares.

Finally they returned to their discussions and arguments. They went on and on.

And on.

For hours. Voices were raised, compromises made. Lunch was ordered, delivered, and devoured.

I contributed very little to the discussion, preferring just to take notes. Occasionally, my opinion was sought, but I was so noncommittal that soon they ignored me. That's how I wanted it. I'd gotten too caught up in all this, anyway. I'd come here to write my thesis and ended up screwing my subject. I can't imagine my thesis committee would compliment me on my research methods.

I kept glancing at the door, expecting Thomas Q to pop back in and rescue me. We had been here almost six hours and he still hadn't returned. And the meeting didn't show any signs of coming to a close. When the discussion got around to what to order for dinner, I decided it was time for me to excuse myself.

I stood up, ready to make my announcement, when someone flung open the door and shouted, "Fire! The whole fucking place is on fire!"

Everyone ran.

· 26 ·

The fire lit up the night sky in a festive way. Everyone was running gleefully toward the flames like we were South American villagers celebrating some saint's holiday. Even I found myself suddenly jogging away from the boorish Outreach Board, who followed solemnly behind me, slouching en masse toward the fire. I was exhilarated. After all that sophomoric yakking around the conference table, I was relieved to see something as uncomplicated as fire. Fire did not require interpretation or explanation or bumper stickers. Fire knew what it wanted to do and it did so with awesome efficiency.

A sudden wave of hot air sucked at my face. I staggered back a couple of steps and blinked some moisture back onto my eyes. I removed my glasses and let the fire blur into a clump of shimmering light. Finally, the heat was too much and I retreated to a neighboring bungalow where the air was cooler. From there, I watched the fire rant and rage and pace frustratedly through the crumbling bungalow. Thick torsos of flames winged with smoke flew out of windows. Just as suddenly, they were yanked back inside. Fire was imprisoned by its need for fuel; it could never leave the carcass it fed from. Hunger kept it from being a god. Like the rest of us.

I plopped down on the grass, hidden in the dark shadows of the bungalow and shrubbery. I could see but not be seen. I wanted to be alone while I watched. A guilty pleasure.

Other guests gathered in small groups to watch the blaze. Some offered to help fight the fire.

Thomas Q waved off any guest involvement. "And steal my moment of glory? No way!" he joked, and everyone relaxed. He and a man and a woman in staff polo shirts seemed to have the fire under control. They had formed a triangle around the small burning bungalow, each training a fire hose on the blaze. The staffers concentrated intensely, stiff with responsibility; Thomas Q looked as casual as if he was watering the lawn. The flames, which moments ago had been flailing and thrashing, calmed under the rush of cold water. Rush.

"Hey, Estelle, tell me something," Thomas Q shouted, pointing to a pudgy elderly woman in a white terry-cloth robe. She was in her seventies and her hands and head trembled like Katharine Hepburn. Her glasses were thicker than mine, ballooning her eyes comically. The way she fretted, it was obvious that this was her bungalow being destroyed. "Estelle, did you start this fire?"

Estelle turned to the tall elderly man by her side who wore an identical robe. She was horrified. She raised a shaky finger and pointed it at the building. "No, Thomas Q, I certainly did not. I swear."

"That's not what I heard," Thomas Q said sternly.

"Heard? What did you hear?"

"Luther there told me you left your vibrator running when you two went to dinner. Damn thing must have overheated."

Estelle looked shocked a moment, then she laughed heartily, throwing her head back and pulling her robe tighter across her bosom. "Thomas Q, you are such a brat." She playfully swatted Luther on the arm. Luther shook his head to proclaim his innocence. Everyone standing around laughed. It was like a town picnic in Mayberry.

This place was like a lot of things. A South American festival. Mayberry. A Yuppified commune. A sit-com Utopia. The thing that it wasn't was *real*. Not a natural habitat for the human organism. Could Thomas Q survive outside this rarefied environment any more than Goofy could survive outside the Main Street Parade or Batman outside the safety of a comic book? Was this kind of humanity and goodness and love able to exist only in a vacation spot, in a walled-in community, away from the struggle of daily existence, freeway traffic, GNP, bad haircuts, fast-food calories? The flames finally died, their passion for burning drowned. Sprinklers in the ceiling still sprayed out water. Overhead, amidst the rising smoke, black cinders circled like locusts. One wall had collapsed and we could see into the room where Estelle and Luther had been staying. Their bed was black rubble. Everything else was charred or melted. I wondered if they'd had sex on the bed. Seventy-year-old sex, slow and brittle and patient. Were their sheets stained with their ancient fluids? Did the fire touch those stains and suddenly flare like a sunspot?

The crowd seemed edgy, waiting for something more to happen. When nothing did, they started to wander off.

Thomas Q shut off his hose and dropped it on the ground. He went over to the other two staffers and conferred. They continued watering the house while he chatted with them. He pointed at the rubble, gestured, and they nodded.

I sat on the grass, invisible in the shadows, and watched everyone drift away. Brando led Louise, Edna, and Easton back to the conference room. I scooted farther into the darkness so they couldn't see me. No way was I returning to that room with them. I'd rather throw myself in the fire.

Two white golf carts pulled up and more staff members in identical polo shirts climbed out and gathered around Thomas Q for instructions. He led two of them back to Luther and Estelle. He held Estelle's hand while he spoke. "Anything irreplaceable in there, folks?"

Estelle and Luther exchanged glances, then Estelle answered. "Not really. Just clothes, some books—"

"My wallet and cash and credit cards," Luther added. "My girdle, you know, the back-brace thing the doctor makes me wear."

Thomas Q smiled and waved his hands. "No problem. First, Tim and Barbara here will drive you to your new bungalow so you can get some rest. Call room service and order something extraspecial. On the house. Meantime, you give Tim your sizes and by the morning he will have an outfit of clothing delivered for each of you.

Don't worry about his taste, because tomorrow afternoon Tim and Barbara are driving you into Scottsdale for a visit to the mall. We have accounts at all the stores there. Buy whatever you need to replace what you've lost. As for cash, Barbara will hand you a thousand dollars in currency tomorrow, as well. Is that enough?"

"Too much," Luther said. "I only had about three hundred in my wallet."

"Two hundred," Estelle said.

"The rest is with our compliments. As is the remainder of your stay here. For the inconvenience." He patted Luther's back. "Anything else you need?"

"My back brace."

"Give Tim the details, he'll pick one up for you. Anything else?"

Estelle raised her hand. "Toothbrushes. And toothpaste."

"Barbara will get those right to you."

"Sensodyne toothpaste," Estelle said. "That's the only kind we can use. Luther has very sensitive gums. They bleed."

"I'll go by the sundries shop and bring some right over," Tim said.

"Thank you, Thomas Q," Estelle said, kissing him on the cheek. "You are a wonderful man."

"Aren't I?" he said, smiling. He kissed her forehead.

Tim and Barbara ushered Luther and Estelle to the golf cart and drove them away.

Thomas Q walked over to where two of his staffers were roping off the charcoaled building remains and helped them for a while. Then he climbed into the smoking debris and poked around. I studied his movements, which were as focused and efficient as the fire had been. The fire had been powerful, but Thomas Q had been the one to put out the fire, to restore order, to place Luther and Estelle in a new bungalow, and not just replace what they had lost but make them better off than before. To magically transform tragedy into comedy.

A siren wailed in the distance. I turned to look and saw a vague flashing of red.

Thomas Q came out of the building, clapping soot off of his hands.

"What did you find?" one of the staffers asked.

"Arson," he said simply. "I'm going to want reports. Who was around here when the fire broke out, that sort of thing. By morning."

"Of course," the staffer said.

"Who do we have on the computer tonight doing application background checks?"

"Denhey."

Thomas Q thought, made a face. "Get Jacobson. Freeze new applications and have her start doing deep background checks on current guests. I especially want to know if there are any criminal records and if anyone was ever affiliated with any cults."

"Jesus, Thomas Q, you think this is some kind of payback?"

Thomas Q shrugged. "Could be anything. Payback. Some insurance scam a guest is working out. Some cult nut who's infiltrated as a guest or even as staff."

"One of us?"

Thomas Q laughed. "Don't be so shocked, Sam. We can all be fooled by people, even me. Just make sure Jacobson includes the staff in her computer checks. We'd better dig up something before more fires break out and someone gets hurt."

A fire engine screeched to the curb and four men in heavy gear jumped out. A police sedan also pulled up and a short man in a rumpled suit jumped out of the passenger side before the car had even stopped. He looked angry.

"Fire's out, Chief Roberts," Thomas Q said to the angry man. Thomas Q offered his hand, but the man ignored it.

"You don't mind if we check, do you, swami?" Chief Roberts sneered.

"Help yourself."

Chief Roberts dispatched the fire fighters. They picked around for a few minutes, then returned.

"It's dead, Chief," one of the men said.

"Looks like arson," another said. "Some alligatoring over by the door. Flash burns. Signs of an accelerant."

"Great," Chief Roberts said. "Fucking great." He walked back to his car and held out his hand. The driver reached through the open window and slapped the radio microphone into it. Chief Roberts muttered angrily into the mike, then tossed it back through the open window. His mood was even worse when he returned. "This is now officially a crime scene, swami. I've got a fire marshal from Phoenix on the way to investigate, so make sure none of your loony guests mucks around with the evidence. Understand?"

"I understand." Thomas Q touched his forehead as if making a mental note. "Don't muck. Keep loons away."

Chief Roberts looked around the place with disgust. He stared straight at me for a moment, but I was too hidden in the shadows for him to see me. "Listen to me, swami, it's just bad luck that your land technically falls within the boundaries of our little town. Because that makes you and your Q-balls my fucking headache." He sighed and stuck his hands in his pockets as if to keep himself from strangling someone. "We're just a tiny town. Fire department and police department in one building, sharing office space. We got one fire truck and two police cars."

"I believe this establishment pays an enormous amount of the tax money that goes toward buying that equipment. Am I right?"

"Big fucking deal. You bozos blow in here three years ago and the folks who've been paying their nickels and dimes every day all their lives are suddenly supposed to suck hind tit? My point is this, we don't have the manpower to drive all the fuck the way out here because your people are smoking dope or freebasing or something and get careless. Am I clear, swami?"

"Drugs are not allowed at The Bend, Chief Roberts. You know that."

"Sure. Whatever. My point is this, keep control of your people out here, okay? You guys want to romp around bare-naked and stick flowers up your assholes, that's okay with me. As long as I don't read about it in the newspapers. We don't want no Jonestown or Waco in Arizona. You people want to kill yourselves with Kool-Aid or AIDS, move to California. Got me?"

Thomas Q nodded. "Cut down on the flowers in our assholes."

Chief Roberts took a step toward Thomas Q. "Do I look like a man with a sense of humor?"

"You ran for sheriff, didn't you?"

One of the fire fighters laughed and Chief Roberts gave them all a withering glare. "Secure the area, okay? You want to get out of here tonight or stay on and bitch about your lousy childhoods to the swami?"

Thomas Q laughed, not meanly, but as if genuinely appreciating Chief Robert's sarcasm. Chief Roberts looked up as if pleased, then caught himself and scowled at his men. "Let's go, girls. You make nice with these folks and the swami might bring you some special brownies."

Two of the fire fighters returned to the burned bungalow and began wrapping the building in yellow tape.

Chief Roberts motioned to his driver in the police sedan. A tall man in an ill-fitting suit got out and walked over to the chief. His suit hung on him as if he'd recently lost a lot of weight. Also, he walked with an odd bounce, as if not used to moving so lightly. His shoes were freshly polished, but they were so worn and scuffed that they were long past the point where polish did them any good. "Yes, Chief?" he said.

"Steve, I want you to stay here, question everybody who saw anything. Question the occupants of the bungalow. Question whoever you want. Especially the swami here. Stay all night if you have to. I'll send someone by later to pick you up."

"Sure thing, Chief," Steve said.

Chief Roberts turned back to Thomas Q. "What's your situation here?"

"Situation?"

"Insurance situation. I imagine you're adequately covered."

"My policy is available for inspection, Chief. I will provide a copy for you by morning."

The chief began gnawing at a stubborn cuticle on his thumb. "How's business? Business good?"

"Steady."

"You make a tidy little profit, though, right?"

"My books are open to you and your department, Chief."

"So this fire wouldn't be some kind of wacko publicity stunt to drum up more business?"

"In my experience, Chief, people rarely find arson an incentive to visit a resort."

Chief Roberts finally managed to bite off the offending cuticle and spit it out. It took a couple spits, though, to get it off his tongue. "Look, swami, right now me and my men are involved in a five-state manhunt for those hippie bank robbers. I've got roadblocks to set up. Communications networks to establish. All kinds of technical stuff. I don't have time for this bullshit." He snapped his fingers at Steve and held his palm out. Steve dropped the car keys into his hand. "Sergeant Meyers will take care of the investigation. Maybe we'll catch your arsonist in the same dragnet we're setting up for those bank robbers. Within the hour, I'll have a roadblock half a mile down the road from here." He grinned as if he'd just had a brainstorm. "I'll tell my men to be especially thorough searching your guests coming or going. Extremely thorough. I hope my men aren't too rough, but when it comes to arson, better safe than sorry, right?" He climbed into the car and drove off.

Sergeant Meyers pulled out his small notebook and began asking Thomas Q questions. Who was staying in the bungalow? What time did the fire start? Who reported it? Who stayed to watch the place burn? I leaned forward, listening for my name, not even sure if Thomas Q had noticed me earlier. If he mentioned my name, the cops would immediately link me up with my parents and somehow I would become a suspect. My whole life, I was always one of the usual suspects. Ever since my parents' arrest, I'd been branded a bad seed. Even in school, if something was missing, eventually someone always said, "Go ask Bonnie and Clyde's daughter." Despite my lifelong role as Goody Two-Shoes Hall Monitor Extra-Credit Slave, I was always pictured in people's minds as the ten-year-old girl being driven away from that Texas motel in the back of a police car.

I listened hard, but Thomas Q and Sergeant Meyers had lowered their voices. I got on my hands and knees and crawled a few feet closer, stopping at the edge of the shrubbery. Would he tell them about me?

A shadow passed out of the corner of my eye. I looked over at the parking lot that stretched out behind the bungalows. Someone ducked down between two cars. I stared at the cars for a long minute. Nothing. Maybe I'd imagined it.

"Have you ever had any trouble like this before?" Sergeant Meyers asked Thomas Q.

"You mean fires? No, never. I was relieved to see the hoses worked okay. And the sprinklers."

"Yes, you handled the situation very well. This fire could have been much worse. I've seen them level these kinds of bungalows in a matter of minutes. The Ascot Resort down the road had an accidental fire about eight years ago. Burned down half the place." Sergeant Meyers studied the rubble. "It's a miracle no one was killed. Somebody must have been saying their prayers." Sergeant Meyers's face reddened. "No offense."

Thomas Q laughed. "That's okay, Sergeant, we aren't a religious order. We don't believe in miracles. We place our faith in preparedness. My staff and I have monthly fire drills. Smoke alarms and sprinklers are checked every two weeks."

I saw the movement again. The same man popped up from between the two cars, looked at Thomas Q and Sergeant Meyers, whose backs were to him, and sneaked away. With the lights from the parking lot glowing behind him, he was only a dark silhouette. I couldn't distinguish any specific features—except his right hand. It was larger than the left, somehow bulkier, like a fiddler crab claw. Suddenly, he hunched down behind the cars and ran off. The bungalow next door blocked my view of where he went. I debated about yelling out to Thomas Q and Sergeant Meyers. Perhaps this was their arsonist. Why else would he sneak around like that?

I tiptoed toward the back of the bungalow, stooping as I walked, keeping in the shadows. Maybe I would see this mysterious figure getting into a car. I could memorize the license number or something. There was no evidence against him and I didn't want to falsely accuse anyone. Nor did I want to reveal myself to Sergeant Meyers. I'd pass on the license number to Thomas Q and he could tell the cops.

I rounded the corner, taking very small steps, being as quiet as possible. I pictured David Carradine dancing across the rice paper in the beginning of *Kung Fu*, never leaving a mark. That's how I moved now, with great stealth, my arms winged out as if I was balancing on a tightrope.

"Hey," a voice behind me whispered. Startled, I jumped forward, scratching my forehead on the shrubbery. I spun around as he stepped out of the shadows. His right hand was wrapped in a gauze bandage. "What's the game? Can anyone play?"

Rush grinned.

· 27 ·

"What are you doing here?" I asked.

"Ssshhh." He put his finger to my lips and backed me farther into the shadows in an awkward fox-trot.

"Rush . . ."

"What happened here?" he whispered, nodding at the stitches in my forehead.

"Liposuction," I said.

He laughed.

"What are you doing here?" I repeated.

"I came to see you. We're business partners, remember?"

Even though he was whispering, there was something odd in his voice. Or maybe I was just suspicious after seeing him skulking around the parking lot. "How did you find me?" I asked.

"Followed the three wise men bearing gifts. By the way, Merry Christmas." He grinned and held out his bandaged hand in a fist. "I didn't have time to wrap it, so . . ." He opened his hand. Sitting on the white gauze that encased his palm was a folded square of paper the size of a postage stamp.

"What happened to your hand?" I asked, touching the gauze.

"Paper cut. I gotta stop buying that bargain toilet paper."

I shook my head. "Why are you in such a good mood?"

"Open your present," he said. "Like that fly you told me about."

"I'd better not find your old chewing gum in here." I unfolded the paper and smoothed it against my thigh. It was a check. I tilted it in the darkness, trying to snag enough diffused light to read the print. I made out the big bold logo of the movie studio, the same logo I'd seen on a hundred big-budget movies. I had to admit, seeing that logo gave me a little thrill. But reading the amount on the check gave me an even bigger thrill: fifty thousand dollars. It was the largest amount I'd ever seen on a check. I couldn't help but delight in the fact that it was a hell of a lot more than Harold and Naomi ever got in a single heist.

"Is madame pleased?" Rush asked in a phony English accent.

"Depends. What's this for?"

"Good-faith advance. The studio hotshots love this project and look forward to meeting you. They want to wash your feet, bear your children."

"Good faith," I repeated. I liked the sound of that. I looked up at him, but his face was too hooded by shadows to read any expression. "How did you find me, Poundcake? I'm supposed to be lost."

"I called Mitzi. She blew your cover, Bugsy. Want I should rub her out?"

"She couldn't have. I haven't told her I was here."

He shrugged. "She wouldn't tell me anything over the phone; she said the FBI had your place bugged. Is that true?"

"Possibly. I don't know."

"It doesn't matter, we'll use it in the movie, anyway. Give it that creepy *Three Days of the Condor* feel. You remember that movie? Robert Redford, Faye Dunaway? A paranoid's wet dream." He rubbed his hands together cheerfully. "I love talking like a producer. It's so crass." He pointed at three imaginary people. "Fuck you and you and you. Now get out!" He rubbed his hands together and smiled. "See? It's fun. Now you try."

I poked his bandaged hand and he winced. "What did Mitzi say to you?"

"Like I said, she refused to say anything on the phone. But an hour after she hangs up, she faxes me that you are staying at The Bend. Apparently, your insurance company called her about your car crashing near here. Sweet little genius Kyra figured the rest out. She knew you had the hots for this Thomas Q guy."

"Don't be a dope," I said, but I felt my face flush. I was glad it was dark.

"I was speaking metaphysical hots, of course. Academic lust." He gave me a questioning look. "Right? Purely academic? You're not becoming one of his disciples, are you? You're not going to shave your head or start burning incense or play the sitar?"

"Is that what you came down here to talk to me about? My salvation?"

"Maybe." He reached out to touch my face. Behind him, a flashlight beam slid across the grass toward us. He saw me tense and looked over at the disk of light just seconds before it would have crawled up his leg. He grabbed me around the waist and lifted me against the bungalow, his body flattening me to the wall. We slid down behind the bushes. The beam wandered on until it grew weak. Then it disappeared.

"Nothing," Sergeant Meyers said. "Wind, I guess." His shoes scuffed the sidewalk as he walked away.

"Why are you hiding?" I whispered in our mutual crouch.

"I'm not hiding," he said. "I thought you were hiding."

"Bullshit. I saw you out in the parking lot. You were sneaking around like you'd just humped the farmer's goat."

His face stiffened. He stood up and brushed imaginary dirt from his pants. I knew he was about to lie before he said anything. "I wasn't in the parking lot, Blue. That must have been someone else."

"It was you. I saw your bandaged hand. You were bobbing up and down, ducking behind cars. What are you up to?"

He shook his head. "What did these Q-balls do to you out here, hook you up to a Quija board? You're seeing ghosts."

"Really? Then let's go over and I'll introduce you to Sergeant Meyers. He's investigating the arson next door." I took Rush's arm and pulled him away from the building. "Come along, Casper."

"Fine, I'll go if you want. But do you think that's the kind of publicity we need right now, Blue? I just made a deal for a lot of money. More than *half a million dollars*. You want the money? All you have to do to get the money is go back to L.A. with me and meet the studio people and then sign the contracts." He plucked the check from my fingers and dangled it above my head. "Something that you may not be free to do if we get mixed up with this stupid arson business out here in Granolaville."

From this angle, a thin shaft of light seeping in from the parking lot allowed me to look Rush in the eyes. He returned my stare without flinching. That flicker of deceit I'd seen earlier was gone. Cable-ready honesty was radiating from his eyes with such intensity, I was getting third-degree sincerity burns.

I snatched the check from his hand and tore it in half. "Rush, tell me why you are really here or the deal is off. Nobody gets anything."

Rush threw the photograph on the coffee table. "That's why I'm here. Right there. I drove all the way out here to Bumfuck, Arizona, because of that."

I leaned over and looked at it. I'd expected some grainy photo of me shoplifting my watch or smashing that poor dog's head, something scandalous he was afraid might screw up his movie deal. But I wasn't even in this photo. As I leaned closer, I could see that it had been clumsily scissored out of a book. Actually, the photo was two separate time-lapse photographs side by side. In the first, a dusty brown lizard was being sniffed by a curious dog. In the second, a thin stream of bright red liquid squirted from the eye of the lizard into the face of the dog. The dog's blood-spattered face recoiled in terror.

"So?" I said, handing back the photo. "You defaced a book. Probably a library book."

"You asked why I'm here." He tossed the photo back on the table and pinned it under his finger. "This is your answer."

"A lizard?" I said.

"A Texas horn lizard."

"I don't get it. What's the joke?"

"No joke, Blue." He pulled a chair around and sat down so that he was facing me. Our knees almost touched. "I've been doing some research, trying to figure out why you and I have such trouble communicating. Did you know there are over six thousand active languages on the planet? Six thousand. Did you know that?" "I didn't know that, no." "But that's important. See, that's my point here. Six thousand languages and people suck at communicating. Humans pride themselves on their superior language skills, but they don't seem to be able to say the simplest, most natural things to one another. And communication between you and me hasn't worked from the start. My mistake was thinking we spoke the same language, you and me."

"We don't?"

"Not at all. We make familiar noises, sounds the other recognizes but doesn't fully understand."

"Like now, for instance."

He ignored me. "So I decided that to talk to you man-to-woman, I'd need a whole new language. Normal man-to-woman language won't do. Your eyes glaze over, your lips press together, and you tune out. *No habla* sweet talk, baby. To you, intimacy is a foreign language."

"I'll bet you rehearsed that speech," I said.

He smiled. "All the way here. And it's not a short drive."

"Can't you just speak to me, Poundcake? No clever patter, no snappy dialogue. No show biz."

"I've tried that. Usually all that happens is you disappear. You climb in your car and find another cubbyhole to hide out in. It's like chasing a groundhog. So I'm trying something different." He pulled a dog-eared paperback book out of his pocket and slapped it against his palm. "Ta da! A *Field Guide to Animal Behavior*. See, this is your language, Blue. This is what you speak. Mating rituals, courtship habits, hunting patterns. You can't talk about any human emotion unless you defang it by putting it in the context of all animal behavior. You can't see one star, only constellations."

"I hope you didn't drive all this way to lecture me on my faults. I don't need any help with that."

"It's not a fault, Blue. It's an obstacle. Between you and me."

My bladder started to contract. I had to go to the bathroom. But if I got up now, Rush would think I was just hiding out again. I crossed my legs. "You take things too personally, Rush," I said. "And that is a fault. Nothing people do is personal, nothing special. Everything everyone does is just biology. Universally hard-wired responses. The only difference between humans and other animals is that we get better press."

"We can think; we have reason. Free choices."

"Reason is a liar; it has a hidden agenda. Biology can't lie. That's the beauty of it, the purity. No choices, no guilt."

"See, that's what I mean. That's why it's so hard to talk to you. Everything I say gets reduced to pithy statements suitable for the classroom lecture hall. You see everyone as a specimen. We make love and I have the feeling you're thinking, Hmmm, Subject A seems to be responding to penile stimulation. I figure the only way I can climb off the petri dish and become real to you is to learn your language. Study the rituals, the lingo, the buzzwords of biologists. If I knew how you expressed yourself, maybe I'd figure out what you were trying to say to me."

"I say what I mean, Rush. No bullshit. You know that."

"No one says what they mean, Blue. No one knows for sure what they mean. I've been talking for fifteen minutes and I haven't even come close to saying anything. At least not what I'd come down here to say."

I started to respond and abruptly stopped. I didn't know what to say and, for once, I didn't want to let just anything blurt out. When he'd started his whole monologue about the lizard photograph, I'd thought maybe he was just kidding around, one of his droll jokes. But I could see now he was serious. And not just serious—he seemed sad and angry. I didn't want him sad, I realized, or angry. In fact, I was happy he was here. That surprised and confused me, especially considering what was going on with Thomas Q. Who needs an old boyfriend showing up when you're busy having perfect sex? Seeing Rush was like being in a foreign country and spotting someone you know walking down the street. We were both foreigners here at The Bend. We didn't speak the language of self-actualization and selfless love for humanity. Like me, Rush was corrupt, cynical, flawed. Having him here made me feel less a fraud.

He held up the photograph of the lizard. "You know what this thing does when he's scared by a dog?"

"What does he do?"

Rush held the photo directly in front of me, his finger tracing the stream of fluid from the lizard's eye to the dog. "The muscles contract around the veins leading from his eyes. The blood starts damming up around his eyes like a water balloon, which causes the eyelids to swell shut. Eventually, the pressure ruptures a capillary and the eyelid peeks open just enough to squirt out a blast of blood six feet or more. That stream of blood is one-fifth of the lizard's entire blood supply. Usually, all that blood is frightening enough to repel any nosy dog."

I pulled the photograph closer. I found the lizard fascinating. How could such a defense mechanism have evolved? Why spurt blood instead of the odoriferous yellow liquid skunks spray? Why from the eye? The blood was harmless, so its power was in persuading the sniffing dog that the blood might be its own. The lizard was an illusionist really, an artist. In a way, Rush had indeed learned my language, had tapped into the mysteries of life that truly interested me. I took the photo and studied it. "Can he do this only once in a lifetime or does he regenerate?"

"She can do it every day if she wants to. One-fifth of her blood every day just to frighten away the curious. The poor thing jettisons her own blood just to escape anyone interested in her."

I looked into Rush's eyes as he stared at me. That sliver of brown floated in his right eye like the needle of a compass. I tried to gauge what I felt right then. Something surged inside of me when I looked at him; something in my chest lurched forward as if to nudge me into his arms. But I had to consider the bigger picture, the long run. Where would we be a year from now? Chasing after some mass murderer's mother to sign her life story away?

Rush leaned back in his chair and sighed, exhausted and beaten. "Sorry. I think I overprepared for this. This isn't working out the way I rehearsed it driving out here. It went much better in my car. Somewhere outside Barstow, we were supposed to be having passionate sex by now."

"Autoeroticism," I said. "Common freeway phenomenon."

He chuckled wearily and leaned his head back on the cushion. He stared up at the ceiling. He looked tired and hopeless. "How do you like it here? Is it weird?"

"No weirder than being compared to a blood-squirting lizard." I shrugged. "Okay, it's a little weird. Conversations tend toward the strange. But everybody's nice and they all seem very sincere."

"As my boss at the agency used to say, 'Once you learn to fake sincerity, you can own the world. But don't fake it so well you convince yourself.' "

"Quite the philosopher. And humanitarian."

"She was a hell of an agent. She used to—"

A sudden boom like thunder sounded outside. We looked at each other. A louder boom rattled the windows. Car alarms chorused in the parking lot.

"Earthquake?" I asked.

"Bomb!" he said, jumping to his feet.

"Sounds like it came from the parking lot."

Rush hurtled the coffee table and knocked over a lamp on his dash toward the door.

"Where are you going?" I asked, running after him.

"My dog! Russell's in the fucking car!" And he was gone.

· 28 ·

I dashed out the door almost as fast as Rush had, but somehow by the time I was outside, he had disappeared. I kept running, looking for him. Other people also hurried in the same direction, many in bare feet or slippers. Some carried their frightened pets under their arms. One Asian woman ran with a cockatoo perched on her shoulder. A young couple in matching silk pajamas ran with their luggage knocking against their knees. A few people had cameras around their necks; one ran while squinting through a video camera. I searched for Rush among them. Nothing.

I'd lost him again.

I stampeded with the others toward the parking lot. Running felt good. I remembered running all the time as a child, sudden unmotivated bursts down the sidewalk, just to feel the ache in my side. The way we were all running now seemed somehow fake, not inspired by anything real, but as if we were all poorly rehearsed extras in a disaster film, pretending Godzilla was looming behind us.

I couldn't see any flames, but arcing high over the bungalow roofs I could see the halo of light cast upward by the new fire. And the gray smoke corkscrewing into the black sky. I zigged across lawns and zagged around bushes, dodging dawdlers and children. Still with an eye out for Rush.

A siren suddenly wailed to life. Probably the fire truck that had been parked outside the torched bungalow. It didn't have far to go, only down the block, make a right, and into the parking lot. Still, the siren blared for the full fifteen seconds of travel. The noise added urgency and we all seemed to run even faster.

Even as I leapt over a cat that suddenly skittered out from under a bush, I wondered if Rush had been here at all or if I had just imagined him. Most of my previous visions had been confined to seeing the microscopic in the universe. Lurking threats invisible to the naked eye. Perhaps now I was conjuring up larger creatures. No one else had seen Rush with me. I could have been napping in my room this whole time, dreaming he'd been sitting there with me. Maybe I'd needed to hear him say what he'd said. I'd needed someone to pour his heart out to me, if for no other reason than to remind myself what was wrong with pouring hearts. Sweet Rush, waving that silly book and lizard photograph. Writing that bizarre but touching script. Perhaps I'd imagined that, too. Who would ever do such things today? Romance is an illusion, Blue, without biological necessity. It creates false expectations; it is destructive to a relationship. Besides, we'd already copulated, so there was no need to continue a courtship ritual. He'd gotten the best of what I had to offer a man. Any clearheaded assessment of my qualities should have led him to conclude I was not a prime candidate for life everlasting together. He was better off with someone who didn't see black holes in her bathroom, didn't wince at the sound of atoms moving about, didn't chase dust mites across the carpet. A scalpel-wielding nutcase whose fingertips were stained with the internal organs of a thousand sacrificed grasshoppers.

Plus, I never put the toothpaste cap back on the tube. And I've been known to wear my underpants inside out to get another's day wear out of them and avoid doing the laundry. Also—I had to admit this—I was not that good at sex. I enjoyed it thoroughly, but I don't think there was ever a time I didn't feel that I had somehow not performed up to the man's expectations. Had done something too fast, too slow, too hard, too soft, been too quiet, too loud, left something out. Except with Thomas Q. With him, it was perfect because I never felt he had any expectations. His sexual movements were so patient, as ritualized as a samurai committing suicide, that he would have had the same experience whether it had been me lying there or a high-priced call girl or a hunk of soft wood. I could never disappoint him. He had made me feel like a great lover.

I was better off with someone who had no expectations.

And yet. As I ran, inhaling fresh smoke, I thought of Rush not really being here tonight and a cold knot of loss twisted through my stomach.

The crowd of rumpled bathrobed guests had bunched up along the parking lot. When an occasional flame rose above their heads, they all looked up and said, "Aaahhh." I pushed and elbowed my way to the front line where I could watch the burning car being surrounded by fire fighters. They waded close to the flames, their clear face masks down, and sprayed the fire with foam from their red extinguishers. The rest of us stood at the edge of the parking lot like shipwrecked survivors lined up on the shore watching our boat sink. At the earlier fire, there had been an atmosphere of jubilation, as if the burning bungalow had been a special-effect treat presented for our vacation amusement. People had laughed and cracked jokes at that fire. Now people were afraid. No one joked; no one laughed. Fire had gone from a court jester to a vengeful god. A few took pictures, but most stood around hugging themselves and shaking their heads. Some speculated that this was the work of cult terrorists or maybe an assassin out to get Thomas Q the way Mark Chapman had gotten John Lennon.

"That's Thomas Q's car," I heard a woman say. "They got his car."

"The names Lennon and Thomas both have six letters," someone responded.

"They want to crucify him," a man said. "Like Michael Valentine Smith in *Stranger in a Strange Land*. Anyone read that?"

Someone said he'd read it in college and the man smiled and said, "Remember 'grokking'?"

"Marilyn, James Dean, Jack Kennedy," a woman said. "They always cut them down. The good ones."

Only one of those people had been murdered, I wanted to tell her.

"Judy Garland, Janis Joplin . . ." the woman continued, listing the "good ones."

I saw Thomas Q standing by the fire truck. He stared into the flames of his burning car with no expression. He could have been watching fish pacing in an aquarium. His hands were thrust into the pockets of his khaki shorts and he was lazily chewing gum. He even yawned.

Sergeant Meyers arrived in a golf cart chauffeured by a staff member. He ran up to Thomas Q and started asking questions. I couldn't hear what they were saying. Thomas Q shrugged a lot.

I looked all around me, but still no Rush.

When the firefighters stepped back from the car, the fire was dead. Thick gray smoke rolled off the car and swept over the crowd. Some coughed and backed away. The blackened hulk of Thomas Q's car smoldered between two other cars parked beside it. The other cars were singed, their paint blistered on the sides bookending the burned car. An exploded door from Thomas Q's car was sticking through the windshield of one of the other cars.

I couldn't recognize the make of the destroyed car, but it looked a lot like my Honda, especially after mine had burned up out in the desert. Just an inexpensive compact car like most people drove. Then I realized something: This was the same area of the parking lot where I had seen Rush earlier, where he'd been skulking around. An icy jolt blew through my brain like an ice cream headache.

I closed my eyes and massaged my temples. Why would Rush set fires? Was he jealous of Thomas Q and myself? Maybe he'd seen us together, seen me coming out of Thomas Q's bungalow, became enraged. Or maybe he was afraid I wouldn't want to leave and go back to Los Angeles to sign movie contracts. He thought fire would drive me from the barn as if I were a horse. Or maybe he just thought the fires would add more melodrama to my story, make it more cinematic, jack up the price in Hollywood. He could just see Michelle Pfeiffer or Demi Moore running from a burning building, wearing something sheer and short, something titillating but PG-13. When Rush looked at me, did he see me at all, or did he imagine the actress who would play me?

I slid my fingertips under my glasses and pressed them against my eyelids. That seemed to relieve some of the pressure. It was difficult for me to imagine Rush doing anything so violent, so destructive as setting fires. Then I remembered his script to me. The burly guy Tito crushing that kid's hand to make a point. And hadn't Rush let the air out of Lewis's tires? And hadn't he pissed on that reporter? But I had held him between my legs, felt the gentle urgency of his thrusting, I had experienced him in the depths of his biological imperatives and seen no hostility.

I opened my eyes. Nothing had changed. The fire fighters were packing up their gear. Thomas Q was walking around the wreckage of his car. He kicked at a burned clump now and then. After kicking at one steaming clump, he squatted down and plucked a plastic cassette case out and held it up to the crowd. "My Van Morrison tape is untouched!" he shouted happily. The crowd broke into spontaneous applause. Thomas Q danced around with the tape over his head singing "Moondance" and everyone laughed.

And as they laughed and applauded, I could feel the mood of the crowd lighten, as if the dank smoke that had been choking them into fear now lifted toward the sky. Amazing. I was laughing and applauding with them, my own mood brightened. I smiled at my former suspicions and broodings.

Then I saw Rush.

Farther down the parking lot, deliberately moving in the shadows, he kept far from the rest of us who watched Thomas Q clowning and dancing. I couldn't make out his face from here, but I saw the bandaged hand. And, trotting faithfully by his side, Russell.

"Dog bite," Rush said, indicating his bandaged hand. "Vicious dog bite from a remorseless killer dog." He leaned over and growled in Russell's face while vigorously scratching the dog's fur. "Pure evil. Look in those eyes. Teeth like daggers and the soul of an ax murderer. Beelzebub with paws. Satan's golden retriever."

Russell's huge jaw hung open so that he looked like he was grinning at the compliments. He sniffed at the gauze bandage on Rush's hand, then gave it a lick. Rush pulled his hand away. "Hey, keep your infectious drool to yourself."

The dog barked twice.

"That means 'fuck you' in dog talk," Rush said to me. He gave me a concerned look. "You okay, Blue? You look a little pale."

I sat stiffly in my chair, both hands tightly gripping the leather arms. I had the whirlies again. Rush's brisk scratching of the dog was sending a disturbance into the universe, upsetting the delicate balance in the room. Molecules randomly slammed into one another like billiard balls. Neutrinos passing through our bodies screeched out discordant notes like a violin bow brushing across frayed strings. Rotted skin flakes dropped from our bodies and clattered onto the carpet like broken dishes. Dust mites munched on those skin flakes as loudly as if they were chomping potato chips. Blood bubbled through the dog's veins toward the spot where Rush was scratching. Loose dog hair buzz-sawed through the air. I could even hear myself hearing, the individual notes of each sound bouncing off my eardrum like baseballs off a trampoline. I closed my eyes and took a deep breath.

"Are you going to puke?" Rush asked. "You look like you're going to puke. You want a pot or something?"

"I'm not going to puke. I think the smoke from the fire got to me, that's all. My lungs itch a little."

"I'm sorry I spooked you earlier, Blue. I didn't know at first you were hiding."

"I wasn't hiding. And you didn't spook me." I was lying, of course. Rush's appearance had hit me like a stray bullet from a drive-by shooting. So had his sneaking around in the shadows. I was no longer certain about him, whether he had indeed set the fires, had blown up Thomas Q's car. Whatever structure I had managed to put in my life the past few days here at The Bend was now destroyed. Just as I was reorganizing my life, creating order and a fresh start for myself, Rush had swept in and devoured order as quickly as that fire had swallowed Estelle and Luther's bungalow and Thomas Q's compact car. With Thomas Q, I knew where I stood in the universe, just another piece of flotsam in constant motion—passionless matter that didn't matter. With Rush, all order was demolished. I didn't know what I felt, what I should do, what mattered.

I took off my glasses and the room settled down. Sound returned to normal. Perhaps I was being irrational. I hadn't actually seen Rush do anything; he just acted suspicious. Hell, so did I. I put my glasses back on and petted the dog. "Why did Russell bite you? You try to get his paw print on one of your contracts?"

"First of all, he didn't bite me. Russell doesn't bite. It was more of a dental mishap."

"Dental mishap?" I snorted.

"Exactly. I was brushing his back teeth, way, way back where the red ferns grow. My whole hand was practically down his throat. The phone rings, he jerks his head, and his front canine rips a four-inch gash across the back of my hand. Eighteen stitches and a couple hypodermic needles later, here I am. That's my story of pain and sacrifice."

"Tylenol," I said, pointing at my purse.

"No thanks. It doesn't really hurt."

"For me."

"Oh. Sure." Rush stepped over the dog and strode quickly to my purse, dug out the Tylenol, filled a glass with water, and brought it to me. I swallowed both capsules at the same time, a real pro.

"So," he said, "what the hell's going on around here with all the fires?"

I looked up at him. "Did you set them?"

His face paled, so white that I thought he might drop over. Then color seeped back in. "Why would you say that?" he snapped angrily. "That's a fucked thing to say."

"Come on, Rush. I saw you sneaking around in the parking lot after the first fire. Then a bomb goes off in Thomas Q's car, right in the same area of the parking lot where I saw you. That was you, right?"

"Yeah, I was there. But I didn't set any fires."

"Why were you sneaking around?"

"I don't like fires, that's all."

"You don't like fires? That's the best you can come up with?"

He pulled up his sweater and turned around to show me his naked back. The white cables of scar tissue paralleled his spine. "Remember my last fire experience?"

"I remember," I said, feeling stupid and insensitive. "It's just that first you sneaked into The Bend, then you sneaked around the fires—"

"I didn't sneak into The Bend. I came in the front gate. Okay, I was going to bullshit my way in, but all I said was that I was your partner, showed them the *Hollywood Reporter* with our names linked. They made a call to Thomas Q and they let me in. No bullshit required. What you saw in the parking lot wasn't sneaking; it was avoiding. Fire makes me physically ill. I get nauseous." He held up his hands as if under arrest. "Am I free to go, Officer? Have I answered your questions?"

"Shut up," I said. "You should have just told me all this up front."

"Telling you that fire makes me sick isn't the kind of sweet talk I came down here to share."

"Beats your lizard story." I went over to the TV and turned on the news. I wanted to see what was up with my parents. Most children would just pick up the phone and call to catch up with their folks; I had to tune in "America's Most Wanted." I flipped around until I caught the local newscast. The anchor was a woman wearing gold earrings the size of quarters and a silk scarf wrapped around her neck that made her look like she'd just had neck surgery. She introduced a reporter who delivered a live report from a traffic accident in Phoenix.

"Food?" Rush said.

I waved at the courtesy refrigerator, which was fully stocked by the staff. He came back with a Coke and a Baby Ruth candy bar and plopped on the sofa beside me.

"There's real food in the cupboard," I said. "You can heat up some soup or chili, something healthy."

"I didn't think you'd want me near the stove. You know, open flames." He made the demented face of a pyromaniac and cackled, "Burn, baby, burn!"

Annoyed, I pointed at his candy bar and Coke. "Did you check off that card they have? You're supposed to check off the items you take."

He stuck the still-wrapped candy bar into his mouth to free his hand, reached into his pants pocket, and pulled out a couple dollar bills, some change, and his car keys. He smacked the money and keys on the coffee table. "The car keys are in case I go back for the salted peanuts."

We watched in silence as local sports and weather were reported. Christmas carolers were shown wandering a neighborhood, but with an armed police officer hidden among them who only lip-synched the songs. Apparently, last year they'd been mugged by a group of marauding teens. The viewer was left to guess which of the robust singers dressed like Dickens's characters was the gun-toting cop.

This was followed by a few upbeat Christmas stories—charities in hospitals, volunteers at a homeless shelter, a high school class who decorated an animal pound so the dogs and cats could have a festive holiday.

Then a picture of my parents armed and toting cash out of a bank flashed up in the corner of the screen beside the anchorwoman's face, which was still smiling from those upbeat stories.

"Finally," she said, her face suddenly serious, "local authorities, in cooperation with state and federal law-enforcement agencies, have begun instituting one of the largest dragnets in recent Arizona history. Harold and Naomi Henderson, the so-called Hippie Bandits, have robbed over a dozen banks since their recent release from prison. Authorities estimate their total cash haul to be more than half a million dollars. The FBI has issued a statement that expresses confidence that the bank-robbing husband-and-wife team will be behind bars within two days. Once they are arrested, one agent told us, they will probably never get out of prison for the rest of their lives. Meanwhile . . ."

The screen filled with footage of the exterior of Mitzi's house.

". . . the Hendersons' daughter, Blue Erhart, has disappeared from her Orange County, California, home. Apparently, she drove away four days ago and has not returned since."

Cut back to the anchorwoman.

"Some police authorities we talked to speculated that she was probably on her way to join up with her notorious parents, either in an effort to talk them into surrendering"—she smiled and tugged her scarf up over her nose, Jesse James–style—"or to assist them in their crime spree."

The TV crew's laughter echoed in the background. She yanked her scarf back down, revealing a big happy smile. "And that's the news on this Christmas Day. From all of us here at the station, Merry Christmas. And remember to drive safely. We want you to *watch* the news, not *become* the news." She waved at the camera as it pulled back. Credits rolled. The crew's laughter could be heard behind the theme music. She chuckled at her own whimsy.

I got up and shut off the TV. I turned to Rush, who was feeding some of his candy bar to Russell. "The couch pulls out into a bed. There are some extra blankets in the closet."

"Oh, it's going to be like that, huh?"

"Like what?"

"*It Happened One Night.* Clark Gable and Claudette Colbert in that motel room. They hang a blanket between them. The Walls of Jericho. Don't you remember?"

"I don't speak filmese, remember? I speak biology, animal behavior. Were there any blood-squirting lizards in the movie?"

Rush pulled open the sofa bed, gathered the blankets from the closet, and neatly made his bed with military corners. "I'm getting undressed now," he said. "You might want to turn your head." He kicked off his shoes. Then he pulled off his sweater and laid it neatly on the chair. Ditto his pants. He sat on the edge of the bed, his bare back facing me, and pulled off his socks. The burn scars down his back looked like icing in the dim light. When he was stripped down to only his white underpants, he slipped under the covers. He patted the mattress beside him and I thought he was doing that to beckon me, but then Russell lumbered up onto the bed and flopped down beside Rush. I laughed.

"Don't laugh," he said. "At least in *my* bed there's some affection."

"Not too much, I hope."

"You're disgusting, Amelia."

"I know, Poundcake." I walked over and sat beside him. I leaned over and kissed him, not a kiss to start anything up, just enough to show I cared. "My not sleeping with you isn't to punish you or anything, you know. I just need to think."

"Thinking's good," he said.

"What about feeling? Intuition?" I said sarcastically. "Living in the experience?"

"I don't trust all that crap. Unless it's in a movie, of course. I want all that stuff in my movie because that's what makes the audience feel good. And when they feel good, I make money. But that's why movies mostly end when the couple gets together. Nobody wants to know what they go through afterward. Thinking gets a bad rap in movies."

"Thinking can make you crazy."

"No, trying to make sense of things makes you crazy."

I leaned over and kissed him again. He kissed back. We clacked front teeth. We tried it again. His hand slid around my waist and up my back, leaving a trail of vibrating cells wherever he'd touched. When I'd kissed Thomas Q, I'd felt as if we were on a raft floating down raging Colorado white-water rapids. Millions of tons of water churned and boiled beneath us, kept from us only by a thin layer of rubber. The danger of being sucked under was always there, but I wasn't afraid because Thomas Q knelt in the raft, paddling serenely, controlling our movements as we cut through the treacherous waters. Somehow I knew we'd never capsize. Kissing Rush was like being plunged into the ruthless water, both of us swept through the currents, both of us somersaulting out of control as we clawed and kicked and slapped at the water, trying to grab hold of each other. But even as we expended all of our energy to do so, at the back of our heads was the nagging question, What then? What happens after we link up? Do we both get swept under the water, our bones twisted into abnormal postures like that guy in *Deliverance?*

I pulled away from Rush's lips. "This isn't the kind of thinking I had in mind."

He didn't say anything. He didn't try to talk me into anything. He just waited.

I got up. "I'm not being a tease, okay? I don't do that." I backed up toward my own bed. "I'm sorry. I just need to sleep, let things settle. Okay?"

"Good night, Blue," he said quietly.

"Night," I said.

✽ ✽ ✽

I wanted to masturbate so badly.

I couldn't seem to help myself. I'd tried thinking about my life, but I couldn't stay focused. I'd tried sleeping, but my mind wouldn't settle down enough. The only full night's sleep I'd gotten since leaving my home was that night with Thomas Q. I needed to relax. I let my fingers slip down my stomach and ease under the elastic of my underwear. I slid over the flattened hairs and let my fingers rest right on the spot. Slowly, I rubbed in a circular motion. The bones in my wrist cracked like a broom being broken over a knee.

Damn!

I pulled my hand out, lifted my head, and looked over in Rush's direction. He didn't move, still seemed to be asleep. Well, even if he had heard, he wouldn't know what that sound meant. I could have rolled over in bed, a bone cracked, not uncommon. He didn't know.

Frightened by my near discovery, I turned onto my side and tried to go to sleep again. An hour later, still wide awake, I rolled onto my back and eased my fingers back between my legs. Strictly therapeutic, I thought. Like taking an aspirin or getting a massage.

The muscles in my legs started to flex. Heat was radiating from my vagina. I could smell myself, the damp richness. My fingers were cramping, but I was so close . . . sooo close . . . soclosesoclose . . .

"Can't sleep?" Rush asked from across the room.

I nearly sprained my wrist yanking it from under the covers. "Huh?"

"I guess different people have different methods of thinking."

"What are you talking about?" I said breathlessly. I could hardly breathe.

He didn't say anything for a minute. "Did you really like my script? The one I wrote for you?"

"Yes, I liked it. I told you."

"Wasn't too goofy?"

"No, just goofy enough."

"Were you deeply touched yet completely amazed at the hidden qualities you never suspected I harbored within?"

I laughed. "I was until you said 'harbored within.' That cost you points and disqualified you from the bonus round."

He chuckled. We didn't say anything for a couple minutes. I didn't care anymore whether or not he knew that I was masturbating.

"Rush?" I asked. "Why do you like me?"

"Is this a trick question, like 'Do you think I need to lose weight?' "

"No. I just can't figure out what you see. And you can't say 'smart, pretty, and funny.' That's every guy's litany to any woman who asks."

"Maybe that's what every guy sees in the woman he cares about."

"Okay, let's concede smart, pretty, and funny. What else? Why me rather than, say, Geena Davis, who is also fairly smart, pretty, and funny."

"Geena won't return my calls." He took a deep breath. "Okay, I'm going to be serious, but then you have to answer one of my questions. Deal?"

"All right."

"This is what I see in you: I see a woman who looks at the world in a way that makes the world seem a much more interesting and vital and exciting place than I had ever seen it through my own eyes. To be near a mind capable of that is . . . thrilling."

I waited, expecting some kind of punch line. When none came, I realized he meant it. That's how he saw me. He was crazy, of course. But then, how different was it seeing me as that kind of person from me seeing microscopic creatures screaming through my life?

"Now my question," he said.

"What?"

"What's Tofu Thomas Q really like?"

I could tell from his tone that he suspected something might have happened between us. "He's perfect," I said.

"Smart, pretty, and funny?"

"Yes, but not in a studied way. He's so relaxed. He's the most comfortable person I've ever met. Like he knows nothing can hurt him. He's fearless."

Rush didn't say anything. I could hear his fingers scratching Russell's fur. Russell snorted.

"Good night," I said. Rush didn't answer. I turned over and tried to sleep. Impossible. I thought about walking over and crawling in bed with Rush, how nice it would be to lie there, even with Russell snorting beside us. Being with Thomas Q would be like living with a plastic surgeon; I'd always wonder when he looked at me if he was thinking of ways to improve me.

A couple hours passed with me drifting in and out of sleep. In one hazy half-awake spell, I hit my elbow against the headboard and sat up swearing. And that's when I suddenly realized that Thomas Q had lied to me.

He had *lied*.

He was not perfect.

I jumped out of bed, threw on some clothes, and ran out of the bungalow.

·29·

Technically, I suppose, I was breaking the law.

If you wanted to get real picky, you could call it burglary. Or breaking and entering. Certainly tresspassing. Maybe one or two other little minor felonies. If I got caught, things could get sticky. That didn't stop me. I broke and entered.

Really, they'd left me no choice. I'd tried to do this right, tried going through proper channels, tried talking to the right people. But that got me nowhere. They'd stonewalled me.

"Where is Thomas Q?" I had asked the administrator behind the counter. I was still breathless from running. My chest heaved and he watched it heave with interest. When I caught my breath, I asked again. "Thomas Q. I need to see him."

He gave me a terse judgmental look that said he knew I'd screwed his boss but that didn't cut any slack with him. "He's not here, Ms. Erhart."

"Where is he?"

"I can't say."

"Who can say?"

He'd shrugged, drank from his Pepsi can. "I really can't say."

"You can't say, nor can you say who can say? Is that right?"

He'd sighed and stroked his little blond goatee. "I'm kinda busy right now, Ms. Erhart."

That was true. Since Thomas Q's car exploded, more cops had shown up. On the walk over here to the office, I'd spotted three or four uniformed police wandering around, checking the grounds, stopping people and interviewing them. I'd avoided them by sticking to the shadows. But even in here, three more uniformed officers traipsed back and forth behind the counter, poking through file folders and in file cabinets, checking guest registers and credit-card receipts. The person in charge was a black woman. She wore a dark brown lipstick that made her look like she had a chocolate smear on her mouth. Apparently, she was the fire marshal from Phoenix they'd all been waiting for. "This isn't enough," she told the gray-haired woman in a Bend staff shirt.

"That's what you asked for," the gray-haired woman said.

"I asked for all guest information."

"That's what you have right there in front of you."

"What I've got is a list of names. What I want is to see the applications. It's well known that your guests don't just make reservations—they have to apply. I need to see those applications."

"Those applications are classified. Privileged information."

"Look, lady, you are not a goddamned government, so *classified* don't mean shit. And you aren't a lawyer, so there's no privileged information. Are we clear?"

"Give her the files, Geri," my goateed guy said. "Thomas Q said to give them whatever they ask for. We're here to help."

The fire marshall from Phoenix smiled. She was very pretty for a fire marshal. "Also, I need the current insurance policies on this whole place. All of them."

"I'll get them," the goateed guy said. He put his Pepsi can on the counter and turned to walk away.

"Where is Thomas Q?" I asked before he could slip away. "Just point me in the right direction."

"I'm sorry, but I'm very busy here. You can see that, can't you?"

"I don't want any of your time. Just point."

He sighed wearily. "Perhaps if you left a message . . ."

"A message? Sure, here's my message." I reached across the counter, picked up his half-full can of Pepsi, and poured the fizzing brown liquid across his desk behind the counter. The soft drink splashed across his papers, calendar blotter, telephone, and computer keyboard. Loose notes floated. Ink on phone messages ran. I dropped the empty can on his desk. "That's my message."

He nodded with a deadpan expression. "I'll see he gets it. Good night."

The window was open, so it was a simple matter to nudge out the flimsy screen and climb through. I couldn't remember ever climbing through a window like this, not since I was a kid and Grandma had lost her keys. She'd given me five dollars for being so brave (and not to tell Grandpa).

Thomas Q's office was dark. The only light came from the crack under the closed door, on the other side of which was the pretty fire marshal, her crew, a couple cops, the blonde goateed boy, and the gray-haired lady. I slid my feet silently along the wooden floor like an old woman in slippers on her way back from the bathroom. I could see general shapes, a few edges, but nothing clearly. I needed more light.

My hands groped back and forth in front of me until they brushed the desk. I felt around for a lamp. I bent the adjustable gooseneck until it was less than an inch from the desktop. I clicked on the lamp. A bright white light the size of a softball shone on the desk blotter. I looked over at the door, expecting someone to come bursting in. But no one did.

"Ed, go on over to that diner place and get us all some burgers or something," the fire marshal said.

"Okay, May Ellen," Ed said. "Burgers okay, guys?"

Affirmative grunts.

"You folks want anything?" Ed asked.

"Coffee, please," the gray-haired woman said.

"Nothing," my goateed guy said.

I was safe. So far. I had perpetuated a successful burglary. Now what?

What was I looking for? All I knew for sure was that Thomas Q had to have been the one to tell Mitzi where I was. He was the only one who knew about my car crash, knew where I was, and knew who Mitzi was. I had told him everything, spilled my guts that first night. But I hadn't told him that I hadn't yet called the insurance company. I had wanted to avoid the inevitable publicity that would have immediately come crashing down around me if I'd reported the crash.

Thomas Q had phoned Mitzi. He had deceived me. Deception was the tool of the flawed, the needy, not of the perfect.

I moved the lamp across the desk, still keeping it less than an inch above the top. Maybe somewhere here among his papers was a reason for his underhandedness. But his desktop was clean. Nothing but copies of the *Utne Reader* and *Esquire's* Dubious Achievements issue. The desk blotter was also a monthly calendar planner, but all the dates were blank: no schedule, no appointments.

I rifled through a couple desk drawers but found nothing useful. Frustrated, I decided to sit down in his leather desk chair and rest a minute or two. But when I rolled out the chair, I saw a brown file folder lying on the seat.

A blue sticky note was stuck to the front of the file folder. The printing said. *From the desk of Dianne Jacobson.* Handwritten beneath that: "TQ, is this what you wanted?"

Hand-printed on the folder's tab in black felt pen: "Rush Poundstone."

I opened the folder and began reading the top sheet: "Record of Arrests."

I climbed out of the window, lowering my feet to the ground. My toes stretched out to feel solid earth. They touched down like a ballet dancer.

Two hands grabbed me by the waist.

"Hey!" I gasped, so frightened, I tasted bile rising in my throat.

The hands pulled me away from the window and set me down gently. I knew whose hands they were by the touch.

"Rush, damn it," I said as I turned.

He saw the file folder in my hand, his name prominent on the tab. He looked at my face and his expression suddenly changed, almost melted. His lips shrink-wrapped around his mouth; his eyes retreated into some dark cave.

"Why didn't you tell me?" I asked.

"Not here," he said, nodding at the empty window. "Scene of the crime."

I took his hand and pulled him away from the building. I knew exactly where to go next. I marched with big military strides.

Neither of us spoke. We kept to the shadows of the building, avoiding all the uniformed cops and fire fighters wandering around. Odd, but the whole place seemed different now, magically transformed. Before tonight, any excursion outside the bungalow seemed soothing, a mellow stroll through a friendly park. Now everything seemed dangerous and sinister. Everything lurked.

"Arson, Rush. Jesus." I didn't look at him. I just kept leading us across the lawns.

"Let me see."

I handed him the file folder. He read as we walked. When he finished, he closed the folder. He handed it back to me. "Dry reading. I'll wait for the movie."

"It's true, then?"

"Yup, it's all there. Plot, conflict, characterization. A big finish."

"You're being a jerk."

He yanked on my hand, bringing me to a stop.

"What?" I said.

"Let me explain, okay? It's not what you think."

"You don't know what I think."

"True. I never have. But I know what I'd think if I read this file." He nodded at the file folder. "Yes, I was arrested for arson. I burned down a producer's house. I was fifteen." He pulled his hand from mine and started pacing in circles. With both hands, he vigorously scratched his scalp as if jump-starting his brain. His hair stood up in mussed tufts. "My dad was an arsonist, a professional torch. He'd learned his craft doing special effects for the movies. But, being an ambitious family man, he'd branched out, torching warehouses, apartment buildings, whatever. We didn't know, my mom or me. We just thought it was neat that he worked on movies. Sometimes we'd go watch them film some big explosion or something he'd helped rig. I met Paul Newman once when I was thirteen. He shook my hand and said, 'Study hard or you'll end up a bum like me.' I thought that was so cool."

A couple cops came around a corner and headed toward us. I grabbed Rush's sweater and yanked him against the bungalow behind the bushes. We crouched there in silence until they passed by. "Come on," I said. I grabbed another handful of sweater and pulled him to his feet. "Come on."

He followed. "Don't you want to hear my sad story?"

"I'm listening. Can't you talk and walk?"

"Sure. If you can sympathize and walk."

"Skip to the arrest. What happened, Daddy want you in the family business?"

He paused, staring at the ground as we walked. "He took me for a drive one day when I was fourteen. I thought he was scouting locations for a movie. Sometimes they had him do that. Dad wasn't very high up in the special-effects world—he was just a technician, a grunt. Low man in the f/x food chain. Maybe that's why he became a torch—he felt unappreciated. I don't know. It doesn't really matter, I guess."

"He took you on a drive . . ." I prompted. We were almost there and I wanted to hear the whole story before we arrived.

"Right. We drive through downtown L.A. and suddenly we're parked in front of this burned-down warehouse. I mean, total destruction. Just charred rubble around a black hole in the ground. 'Son,' he says, 'what would you say to a person who could create something like that?' I remember being startled by him saying 'create' like that. Like it was a sculpture or something." He paused, lost in his memory. "Anyway, to cut to the chase, Dad tried to teach me the business of arson. He made it sound exciting, like cops and robbers. Like a movie. Only we weren't doing anything wrong, just helping some people around some bad laws, helping them collect insurance money so they could start over and be happy. Hell, to hear him tell it, we were doing God's work."

I stopped, looked him in the eyes. "And the fire?"

His jaw clenched. "Yeah, the fire. It was my second time out with him. We never told Mom. She was pleased to see her two men out doing father-son stuff once a month. My first fire had been simple, a small yacht in San Pedro. The thing went up, burned for a few minutes, than sank like a stone. Almost disappointing." He waited for some reaction from me. I didn't have one. "Anyway. The second fire was actually at some producer's mansion up in the Hollywood Hills. Most of Dad's work came from movie people. There was always some sleazy producer who needed to cash in on his insurance policy so he could finish financing his low-budget Hell's Angels movie or something." He took a deep breath. "So, we torch the place, I get careless, get caught inside. Some burning banister hand-carved from imported Italian wood falls on my back. That's how I got my scars. Dad rushes me to the hospital emergency room, drops me off, and that's the last I ever see him or hear from him. I get arrested, but they let me go. Not enough evidence. My mom is in shock, of course. She's horrified at what we'd done, embarrassed because she'd never suspected. She's also angry at me for fucking up and causing Dad to take off, and pissed at herself for having loved him in the first place. I guess that's why I went into law, to prove to her that I was good, that she hadn't spawned some kind of monster, even if she'd married one. Of course, the supreme irony was that I was a lousy lawyer. A terrific law student but a lousy lawyer. I guess that's what attracted me to your story in the first place. We're alike."

"Look, having just committed burglary and theft, I'm in no position to take the moral high ground here. But, I've got to know, are you setting the fires around here? Did you blow up Thomas Q's car?"

"No. Why would I? I've just made the deal I've been waiting my whole life to make. I have no reason."

"I shoplifted an eighty-buck watch with ten thousand in cash in my pocket. Screw reason."

"You shoplifted?"

"What, you think you know me and that's something I'd never do?"

He shook his head. "No, I don't know you. But I want to."

We arrived. The bungalow was across the lawn. There was a dim light inside.

"Here's the thing, Rush. I believe you. So if it's not you setting the fires, it has to be somebody else. What bothers me is the coincidence of having someone once arrested for arson on the premises while these fires are popping up." I told him why I believed Thomas Q had been the one to tell Mitzi where I was. "I think he did some computer checking after I spilled my guts to him that night. I think he found out about you, your past, and told Mitzi, knowing you'd eventually find out. He wanted you here."

He laughed. "You mean to frame me? Like on TV or something?"

"All I know is that something's not right. I've had the feeling of being manipulated ever since I arrived here."

"How so?" He looked into my eyes. "Did you do something you didn't want to do?"

"Not really. I haven't been brainwashed or anything. I'm not going to hang around airports collecting donations. I just . . . I don't know how to put it. It's a feeling of too much influence, like when you've lived at home too long." I took his hand and started off across the lawn. "Did he ever kill anybody in his fires? Your father?"

"I don't know. That's the hard part, not knowing just how bad he was."

I laughed.

"What?" he said.

"I'm the daughter of bank robbers and you're the son of an arsonist. I was just trying to imagine what kind of offspring we would produce. The Antichrist."

Once across the lawn, we stopped talking. I crept up to Thomas Q's window. The blinds were closed, so I couldn't see inside, but the window was open just the tiniest crack. I heard voices, muffled voices—a man and a woman.

"He's in there," I whispered, my lips right next to Rush's ear for maximum security. My lips brushed his skin and I tasted him. It made me want to lick his ear.

He pressed his lips to my ear. "Why don't we just knock?" His warm breath on my ear caused me to shiver and I bumped my head against his mouth. "Ooww!" He jerked his head away and touched his lips. He pulled his fingers away and there was a drop of blood. "Love hurts."

I pressed my mouth to his ear. "We can't just knock. I don't want to confront him without evidence." I stooped down and began searching the ground.

Rush stooped beside me. "What are we looking for?"

I found a twig and held it up. "This."

With the same surgical precision I used to dissect grasshoppers, I worked the twig under the crack of the window, angled it upward, and pried apart the slats of the miniblinds. Rush bent over so his head was next to mind. We squinted into the room.

They were naked. On the bed.

The only light came from the open bathroom door. Not enough to make out the faces, just body movements. There was no mistaking what those movements were.

I watched. The woman was on top. I saw only the outline of her back as she lifted and lowered herself slowly. He moaned in a way that he had never moaned with me.

I felt Rush looking at me, trying to read my reaction. I didn't have one. I didn't feel jealous really or used or anything I thought I should feel. None of the usual emotional repertoire. I felt like a biology student again, watching a film on the curious reproductive habits of human beings. *Notice how, in the throes of passion, the female of the species begins to shake her head side to side, even though she is rocking her hips front to back. This unusual feat of dexterity can be attributed . . .*

The woman stopped for a moment, leaned forward, and started kissing him. As she leaned forward, the light from the bathroom outlined her buttocks. Familiar boxy buttocks.

"Mother!" I gasped.

"What?" Rush whispered. "Holy shit."

I pulled my twig from the window, fell against the wall, and slid to the ground.

"Oh, man," Rush said. "Your *mother's* in there?"

I sat there for a moment, clutching the file folder to my chest. I tried to think things through, figure events out, trace the chain of events. But it was like trying to map DNA using a magnifying glass. I couldn't see the whole picture, and the bits that I could see frightened me by their randomness. The back of my head hurt. I must have scraped it sliding down the adobe wall.

Rush sat on the ground beside me. He didn't say anything. He didn't try to comfort me. He just sat beside me and waited.

"Here you are," a familiar voice said.

I looked up. Thomas Q stood smiling, fully dressed. It couldn't have been him inside with my mother.

"I got a call from my staff that you were looking for me, Blue. I hear you left a rather messy message." He chuckled. "I figured you'd try here next. I guess I should have told you, I have more than one residence at The Bend. A small concession to security. Not an effective one, I'm afraid." He looked at Rush. "Hi, Rush. Thomas Q."

They shook hands. Rush didn't get up.

Thomas Q looked down at me. "I suppose you want to finish that interview now. You probably have a few more questions now." He offered his hand to help me up.

I looked at his hand floating there in front of me. The palm open, waiting for me to take it. Suspended in air like the wing of an angel. For the first time since the prison announced my parents' release, maybe for the first time since I was ten, I knew exactly what I wanted to do. So I did it.

I reached up, grabbed hold of his little finger, and quickly snapped it backward until I heard two loud cracks like cricket calls.

Thomas Q choked out a small gasp but otherwise didn't make a sound. Tears welled up in his eyes and his lips paled. He held his wounded hand against his chest. "I must admit, Blue, that really hurt. Very painful."

"Pain's an illusion," I said.

The miniblinds flashed open and Harold and Naomi stood framed in the window, naked. "Blue?" my mother said. "What the hell are you doing here?"

· 30 ·

Thomas Q wrapped the white gauze around his broken finger. No one offered to help him. No one spoke. The four of us sat on the sofa like jaded theater critics while he paced back and forth in front of us, delivering his soliloquy.

"Okay, you have questions. I know. And I'll answer them." Thomas Q pulled the gauze tighter. He no longer showed any pain or discomfort. It was as if the finger weren't even his.

"I gotta tell you, Blue, this hurt. I'm not talking spiritual pain. I'm talking burning, physical, eye-gouging pain. You took me completely by surprise. I'm okay now, of course. I'm getting my mind around it slowly. You get your mind around the pain like a hand and slowly close into a fist. The way a blanket can smother a fire. Poof! Pain is gone. But in the meantime, big yeow."

He put the gauze down, picked up a pair of fingernail clippers, and started chopping through the gauze.

"I lost my scissors somewhere," he explained. He picked up the white adhesive tape and started wrapping the gauze with the tape, spiraling down his finger like a barber pole. "This is kind of neat, isn't it? Like at the end of those English mysteries where the inspector from Scotland Yard gathers all the suspects in a room and uncovers the murderer. Well, you certainly are all suspects, aren't you? If I open that door and yell 'Police!' you'd probably all get arrested for one crime or another.

"But that's not what this is all about. Okay, you all want to know what is going on. I know each of you thinks you've somehow been betrayed by me. Somehow manipulated. Set up." He shrugged. "Well, actually, that's true. You have."

He sat on the coffee table, facing the four of us.

"For my part, I have set into motion a certain series of events, did certain things, brought people together. All part of a plan. First, yes, Blue, I did contact Mitzi. I didn't speak to her personally, of course, since, in case your phone really is tapped, I didn't want the FBI knowing you were here. So I called a friend who, by the way, really is an insurance adjuster, and he went over and played his role. Why? Because I wanted Rush here."

He looked at Rush as if expecting Rush to jump up and start yelling or take a swing at him. Rush just sat there staring back, like a producer listening to some writer pitch a script idea. Finally, his dream come true.

Thomas Q picked up the folder that contained Rush's criminal record. "I left it on my desk for Blue to find. Well, not on my desk—I didn't want to be too obvious. But close enough that you'd find it. I'll get back to that in a minute. Now, Naomi and Harold."

My parents looked at each other, then back at Thomas Q. They were dressed in K Mart sweats, Dad's stomach stretching the cloth as if it was some fabric-durability test. Dad crossed his leg, his bare toe brushing Mom's shin. Absently, he reached over and touched the spot on her leg he'd kicked. Just a fleeting touch, as brief as a hello kiss. Also absently, she reached out and touched his hand as he was pulling it back. I watched out of the corner of my eye. They didn't look at each other, never said a word, probably had no memory of even having made these simple gestures. The unconscious sign language of love, the fidgeting of affection. I felt a sudden swelling of envy. I wanted my body to work like that, hands and arms and legs to flutter off by themselves to speak love to another body. To let our skins do the talking.

". . . was the hard part," Thomas Q was saying, "finding you both and getting the word out to you that you had a safe haven here. I still know people; I have nefarious connections. My years as a deprogrammer gave me a healthy knowledge of the underground, even the old leftist politicos from before. You were both right in coming here. There's no way you could have escaped the dragnet they have out for you. Best to hide out here and wait. Among friends and family.

"Of course, the fires have changed the mood around here somewhat. Now the place is crawling with police, fire marshals, insurance investigators. We're bound to get media attention. And when the next fire breaks out in"—he looked at his watch—"thirty-six hours and twenty-seven minutes, I suspect the police will have no alternative but to launch a house-to-house search of the entire Bend. Roust everybody. Naturally, they'll find you."

He hesitated, waiting. We just sat and watched him.

"Really? No response? I expected someone to leap for my throat." He looked over at Rush. Rush crossed his arms and smiled.

"Blue." Thomas Q smiled at me. "I once told you that everything runs its course, that everything must end. Even The Bend. When the T-shirts and bumper stickers start making sense, that's the time to give it up. Don't you agree?" His face got serious, and he looked sad for the first time since I'd known him. "The fire next time, right?"

He stared down at his hands for a while and I think we all disappeared to him. Whatever pain and sadness he was feeling now was psychic. Maybe he was trying to get his mind around it to snuff it out. He didn't seem to be succeeding.

The file folder slipped from his hand. He caught it before it hit the ground. When he looked up, his face was serene again. Composed. "Now, what does all this yakking mean to all of you? What is it Lear said, 'My love's more richer than my tongue?' Well, Naomi and Harold can't leave here without being caught by the cops. And thirty-six hours from now, they won't be able to stay, either. Rush can't be seen here, not with his arson record, even though he was never charged. No way would they ever make a case against you stick, but the publicity is bound to make your movie friends nervous about doing business with you. I've arranged it so that the police won't know you've been anywhere near this place. Computer glitch, clerical error. Your name is gone. But in thirty-six hours, one of the guards at the gate will suddenly remember letting you in to visit a guest. That puts everyone here in a bit of a bind." He pointed his bandaged finger at me. "The only one who has any real freedom around here is you, Blue."

He picked up the adhesive tape and wrapped his finger in another layer. He bit the tape loose.

"I know you all think I did all this just to fuck you up. That's not true. We all want something here. Each one of us. The question is, How do we get it?

"Naomi and Harold want to escape to safety and avoid doing another twenty years in prison. Rush wants to avoid being investigated for arson. Blue wants to see her loved ones free and happy. And I want . . ." He went to the window, looked out through the blinds, surveying his realm. He was silent for several minutes.

Suddenly he spun around and smiled. "I want what Blue wants. I hadn't known that until meeting her." He looked at me with some grateful expression. I didn't even know what it was he thought I wanted. I didn't know what I wanted.

"I'm impressed at how relaxed you all are," he said. "Amazed, really. That's good, because I think everything can be worked out if we all make the right choices now. Any suggestions?"

I looked over at my mother. It was not like her to remain quiet for so long. She had a wisecrack for every occasion. But as I looked into her face, for the first time since her arrest twenty years ago, I saw helplessness. I saw the woman who had screamed at the state troopers as they'd driven me away, her face twisted with anguish and loss. My father had his stoic face on, but he was never very good at stoic. His eyes were rimmed in red; he bit his lower lip.

I read an interview once with John Lennon. He said that every song he ever wrote was pure torture. Except maybe ten. Those came to him full-blown, words and music. All he had to do was transcribe. I guess that's inspiration. Since I'd never felt it before, I could only guess at what it must feel like. Until that moment. Right there in Thomas Q's bungalow, for the first time in my life, I was inspired.

I stood up. "I have a plan," I said.

Thomas Q bowed and held his arms out, giving me the stage. " 'The wheel is come full cycle.' " He smiled at me in a fatherly way. As if he knew what I was going to say, what my plan was. As if, indeed, he had inspired it.

I stepped toward him, grabbed his thumb just four digits from his bandaged finger, and pulled it hard like the handle of a slot machine. Bones popped like champagne corks.

Thomas Q yowled with pain.

Lesson #6

Failure to wear protective glasses may result in permanent vision loss.

· 31 ·

We circled the block for the fifth time. My hands were shaking so badly, my mother's wedding ring clacked like chattering teeth against the steering wheel. My teeth would have chattered, too, but I was busy biting my tongue. Rush kept nervously clearing his throat and tugging on his pants. Neither of us had spoken for twenty minutes.

"Are you scared?" Rush asked.

"What? Yes."

"Good. I didn't want to be the only one." He cleared his throat. Tugged his pants.

I turned the corner and circled the block again. Drove past the pizza shop, the Brooks Brothers clothing store, a travel agency with a poster of a luxury liner with a logo above it: PUT LIFE ON CRUISE CONTROL. The rest of the stores were a blur, the usual potpourri of Los Angeles shops. When we arrived back at where we'd started, I went around again. We didn't speak during the next few circles, either.

I was too scared to do what we'd come here to do.

I was starting to recognize people. I was getting a warm sensation in my chest. I was starting to feel sentimental about this neighborhood. I thought of it as mine now, my new neighborhood, a place where I could get to know people. Be on a first-name basis with the guy in the wool cap at the newsstand. Ask the old lady walking her dachshund how Oscar likes the chew toy I bought him last week. Get parking-meter change from the pizza boy, who would leer at me as I walked out of the shop, his high school textbook open on the counter. I felt like waving to my new friends.

"We're going to run out of gas," Rush said.

"Give me a minute. I'm almost ready."

"Yeah?"

"Almost."

"I hope so," he said. "These rubber gloves are making my hands pucker."

I nodded. My fingers were starting to bloat, too. "Soon," I said. "How do I look?"

"Older. But sexy for your age. Like Lauren Hutton." He patted his bulging foam gut. "How about me? Ho, ho, ho."

I glanced over at him. He was bald, with just a fringe of gray hair. The rubber waddle hung from his neck, giving him the appropriate triple chin. Tinted contact lens altered his eye color. Three hours of makeup gave him realistic wrinkles and moles. He looked sixty and on the verge of a coronary. "Daddy," I said.

He reached over and tugged my wig straight. "Mitzi's a genius," he said. "You look just like your mother. Actually, it's kinda scary."

"Is my butt boxy enough?"

"For what?" He smiled.

I tried to smile back, but my face was frozen into a grim expression of impending doom. My fingers were numb from choking the steering wheel. The reason I kept circling the block was because I couldn't uncurl them. Numb as they were, they continued to tremble a tap dance on the wheel.

"You think we're making a mistake?" I asked.

"Absolutely. You just figured that out?"

"You want to back out?"

"Do you?"

I said, "No."

He was silent for another tour of the block. Then said, "I have to ask you, Blue, in case I don't get the chance later. Why did you take it?"

"What? Take what?"

"My file folder back at The Bend. The one with my juvenile record in it. Why'd you take it from Thomas Q's office? Why didn't you leave it for the cops?"

"I didn't want the police to accuse you falsely of anything."

"But you didn't know it was false. For all you knew, I was in fact the arsonist. I could have easily bombed that car, burned that bungalow. My hand was bandaged. I had motive and opportunity. Speaking as a lawyer, albeit a bad lawyer, there was no reason for you to doubt the empirical evidence."

I thought about that. He was right, I had no way of knowing. In fact, as a scientist weighing the evidence, I should have turned his butt in. Why, then, had I taken the stupid file? And I don't want to hear about love. Love, love, love. Love is no excuse for stupidity. What if I had been wrong and Rush had been guilty? I had been wrong about Thomas Q. I had been wrong about a lot of people and a lot of things. But how can one ever know what's right? There's way too much information available and yet it's never enough, it's never *all* the information. How can we make life choices about people without all the information? You can't. Yet, when we're wrong, we bear all the guilt. Choosing mates is like me buying my parents those ice cream cones that hot Texas afternoon. I was filled with hope and love and self-sacrifice, only to sell them down the river because I didn't know about marked bills. Give up the illusion of informed choice, people. The best that you can hope for is maybe. Maybe this is the right thing; maybe this is a good thing. Maybe.

I thought about Mitzi and her wacko Maybe Factor. She had said it all that night over leftover moo shu. Hope that maybe you're right and act accordingly. But at least act. Do. I had studied the smartest scientists in the world, had read the writings of the wisest religious and ethical philosophers in history. And it all came down to Mitzi, the perennial second banana who never gets to sing the love songs.

"Blue?"

"Hmmm?"

"Why did you steal the file?"

"I don't know, Rush," I said. "Good faith, I guess."

His hand patted my thigh. "I'd kiss you, but my lips might fall off."

"You can't kiss me anyway, not looking like that. It would be too gross." I made a face and shivered.

"Just a fatherly kiss, my dear." He flicked his tongue disgustingly.

"Don't do that! Yeech. You're making me sick." I turned the corner and slowed down. The back of my neck tingled. "I think I'm going to park this time, Rush. I really do."

He cleared his throat, tugged his pants. "Okay. I'm ready."

"You're ready?"

He nodded. He reached down under the seat and pulled out the shotguns, keeping them on his lap and out of sight. I could hear him breathing faster.

"Are you sure you want to do this? You don't have to. I can do it alone."

"Yes, I want to do this. This way, I can sell my own life story to the movies."

"I'm serious, Rush. I can do this alone."

"No, you can't."

I sighed. "No, I can't." I patted his thigh. "Are you really, really sure?"

"Yes, I'm sure. Now please stop asking me that. It's getting harder to lie."

I laughed, but it came out weak and pinched. Then I saw the bank ahead. A woman with a briefcase went in. An old man with a cane came out. An Asian man and woman went in. My mouth and eyes went dry. My hair hurt. I felt like a first-time sky diver being nudged toward the open airplane door.

I gripped the steering wheel harder. This is where I've always been heading, ever since that day the FBI drove me away from the Texas motel. This is where I had to end up. It was as inevitable as gravity. It's what everyone wanted, the press, the people out there who followed our lives. Everyone. They wanted drama. They wanted tragedy. Like those gunfighter movies—*Shane, Destry Rides Again, Heaven With a Gun, Kung Fu*—the audience always waits for the peace-lover to be pushed into strapping on his guns again. We admire Jesus' restraint, but we'd pay a lot more at the box office if He'd have grabbed the cross, used it as a battle-ax, and kicked some Roman ass.

The bank sat there. It hadn't moved an inch. This is what I had been destined for.

I looked over at Rush; he looked at me.

"This is it," I said.

He blinked rapidly under the heavy makeup and plastic gunk.

"Quiet on the set," he said. "Action!"

We jumped out of the car, our shotguns stashed in our coats, and ran toward the bank.

Yesterday, at The Bend, we had discussed my plan. We were not in agreement.

"Blue, I forbid it!" my mother said. "I will not go along with it."

"Shut up, Mom," I said.

Dad jumped in with, "Your mother is right, Blue. It's too dangerous."

"Shut up, Dad," I said.

"Don't talk to me that way, Blue. I'm still your father."

"You haven't been my father for nineteen years and I haven't been your daughter. So it's a wash."

Rush and Thomas Q sat on the sofa. Rush was wrapping Thomas Q's crooked thumb with gauze and adhesive tape. The barber-pole stripes were perfectly aligned.

"You don't know what you're doing, Blue," Mom said. "It's not as easy as they make it seem in the movies. You don't just waltz in and waltz out. You could get hurt. You could get killed."

"Besides, it's totally unnecessary," Dad said to me. "Your mother and I are not afraid of being caught, or of going to jail."

I said, "Is it really that hard to live with each other? Do you really need the threat of separation?"

He turned to Naomi for help. Usually, she would have jumped in by now with a sharp retort. Instead, she looked at Dad with uncharacteristic sadness. She lowered her head. "Let her do it, Harold."

"But—"

"We need her, Harold. We need her if we're going to have a life outside this room."

"She doesn't know what she's getting into."

Mom looked me in the eyes. "She knows."

Thomas Q gently laid his bandaged hand in his lap. "There really is no alternative, Mr. Henderson. Not if everyone in this room is to get what they want."

"You're about one opinion away from tasting buckshot, asshole," Mom snapped.

"Knock it off, Mom." I turned to Thomas Q. "What is it you want, TQ? I mean, you've gone through a lot of trouble to arrange all this. You've burned property. Risked my parents' freedom. And Rush's. What is it you get out of it all?"

He held up his bandaged hand. "Mittens."

"I wouldn't goad her," Rush warned. "You've still got eight fingers to go."

Thomas Q thwacked his damaged hand hard against the coffee table. The table jumped. An empty glass fell onto the carpet. The pain must have been excruciating, but Thomas Q's expression didn't alter. He smiled at me. " 'I am a man more sinned against than sinning.' "

"You're a fucking moron," Dad said.

Mom turned to me. "I can't believe you slept with this guy."

"Mother!" I yelled. "Jesus." I looked over at Rush.

He shrugged. "It's kinda obvious," he said.

"We don't have time for this," I said. "We have to make plans. Figure our moves." I was fidgeting, pacing, hyped up on embarrassment.

Thomas Q closed his eyes for a minute. The rest of us were so on edge, we couldn't help but watch him. Slowly, he opened his eyes. They glistened slightly. His lips moved, but he did not speak, as if he were tasting the words first for ripeness. He looked up at each of us, going from face to face and smiling. But I could tell he wasn't looking at us as individuals, but, rather, as if we were parts of a larger whole. Appendages of a larger creature: family. I saw Thomas Q now as I had never seen him before, as I'd not permitted myself to see him. He was alone in his own universe. Love all or love none, that was his credo. He was right, of course. His logic was perfect. But marooned here among the rest of us who couldn't measure up, he had chosen to create The Bend, a place where people would gather and pretend to be a family. His family. "What do I want?" he asked. He stood and walked to the TV set. He picked up the TV *Guide* and began leafing through the pages. "I want what everyone wants. To disappear."

Dad groaned. "I know a couple guys in the joint who might be able to help you out there."

I couldn't conjure the right words to explain what Thomas Q was saying, but somehow I knew what he meant. As if the words had seeped through my skin and were sticking to my heart, thickening around it. I just knew. I looked over at Mom; she looked at me. She knew, too.

"All right," I said to everyone. My voice was loud and commanding. "We've got to get moving. Time to shake our butts. TQ, you get your insurance guy to go over and get Mitzi to a secure phone. We'll call her and have her meet us at a motel in L.A. She's a makeup whiz. She'll have Rush and me looking like you two in no time."

"You'll need some padding," Mom said, slapping her butt but looking at my chest.

"So will he," Dad said, grabbing his belly.

"I'll tell her to bring extra."

"Here, you'll need this, too." Mom twisted off her wedding ring. The skin underneath looked pale and soft. "Don't lose it. I want it back."

"What? This symbol of shallow bourgeois values?"

She laughed. "Don't make me kill you."

I screwed the ring on my finger and turned to Rush. I waggled my hand in front of him. "Presto. We're married."

He nodded and walked across the room to the refrigerator. He pulled out a Coke. "Want one?"

I shook my head. I walked over to him and lowered my voice so the others couldn't hear. "I know I'm kind of an idiot about these things, but I do care for you, you know."

He smiled, licked a drop of Coke from his lip. "Naturally."

I wanted to touch him, a small brush of the fingers the way my dad had touched my mom. But thinking about it already ruined the idea of the gesture. I turned back to the others. "Okay, then. Here's the plan: Rush and I drive to L.A.. Nobody's looking for us, so there's no reason to detain us at the roadblocks. You two sit tight. After we rob the bank tomorrow and they show the videotape to the FBI, everyone will think it's you."

"Make sure you drop one of the shotguns with their fingerprints on it," Thomas Q said.

"Right. Once they think you guys are in L.A., they'll drop the dragnet here and you can escape. Drive to Canada or Florida. Write your memoirs."

"Which I hope you'll give me an opportunity to represent in Hollywood," Rush added.

Mom laughed. She liked him.

I continued, "Meantime, don't rob banks, don't even jaywalk."

"Keep Low," Thomas Q said.

"After a while, they'll lose interest in you. You'll be relatively safe." I stood in front of them, looking back and forth between them. "Okay?"

"We don't want them to lose interest," Dad said.

"Robbing banks is what we do," Mom agreed. "It's what we believe in."

Rush said, "If you want to change things, you should run for office. With your notoriety, you'd probably get elected to Congress."

"The system doesn't work," Dad said. "From the day a U.S. senator takes office, he has to raise fourteen thousand dollars a week, every week he's there, just to stay in office. There's no time to help people. That's our point. The system doesn't work."

"No shit, Dad," I said. "No system has 'worked' in the history of human beings. There's always injustice and corruption and all that crap. You want a perfect system, become a bee or an ant. Termites have it down pretty well. We can't all hide out until the world is perfect. We'll never come out."

"That doesn't mean we shouldn't try to make things better," Dad said.

"Play Fair," Thomas Q said.

"Dad, we can't have all the dinner conversations we never had over the last twenty years all at once right here. There's no time. My point is that I want you guys around to argue with me, discuss with me, and teach me. Okay?"

Harold and Naomi exchanged looks. Dad nodded. "Okay."

"Good. Now, Mom and Dad, teach me how to rob a bank."

We walked into the bank and split up.

Rush walked over to the table and started scribbling on a deposit slip. I waited in line for a teller. I turned this way and that to make sure the various surveillance cameras got clear shots of my face. My hands were shaking in my pockets. My fingers and the tip of my nose were icy. My wig felt too tight.

When it was my turn, I walked up to the woman teller with short black hair. She was about fifty, with no eyebrows except the ones she'd drawn on. They looked like the lines on graphs that show business is sharply falling off.

"Yes?" she said. "May I help you?"

I slid the note to her with the usual demands and warnings about alarms, written in my mother's handwriting, and waited for her to give me the cash. Simple transaction and we'd be out of there in another minute. Tellers were trained to give the cash with no resistance, to hand it over and wait for the police. Dad and Mom had filled us in on the details: Banks found it was cheaper to be robbed than install and maintain effective security. Mom had groused, "Only when the robbed tellers began collecting workman's compensation for stress-related illnesses did banks begin beefing up security." She'd launched into her union versus management speech until Dad finally cut her off. The only security this bank had was the young black guard standing over by the customer service counter. He had a gun on his hip, but that shouldn't be a problem. Even he had strict instructions about risking customers' lives. Everyone in the bank attended seminars instucting them just to hand over the money. Comply, they were told.

The teller in front of the me finished reading the note, looked up with a sneer, and leaned forward. "Fuck you," she said. "I'm not giving you a fucking dime."

· 32 ·

THE HEIST

INTERIOR—BANK—DAY

BANK PATRONS and BANK PERSONNEL going about their business.

RUSH scribbling at courtesy table. Trying to look inconspicuous, despite the ton of rubber makeup glued to his face, the bald cap, the contact lens, and the thick girdle of belly padding around his middle.

SECURITY GUARD, early 20s, African-American, rocking back and forth heel-toe, heel-toe, still humming Christmas songs because that's all the bank played for the past two months. Friendly kid, smiles and says hello to the patrons. Has a nervous habit of playing drum solos on his gun holster.

ANGLE ON ME AND TELLER

I'm waiting for the TELLER to finish reading Mom's holdup note. She reads with her mouth pursed into a tight O, a put-upon expression that reminds me of my fifth-grade teacher. I expect her to grab a pen and start grading the note.

She finishes reading the holdup note, looks up at me with a sneer. She tosses the note back at me.

> TELLER
> (snorts)
> Fuck you. I'm not giving you a fucking dime.

> ME
> (stunned for a beat)
> What?

> TELLER
> Next!

FREEZE THE ACTION

while we listen to my voice-over narration.

> ME
> This wasn't the plan. I was supposed to slip her the note, take whatever cash she gave me—no matter how small, it didn't matter. Then Rush and I would walk out, making sure to leave a shotgun behind, perhaps on the sidewalk outside. Now things were going to get tricky.

RESUME ACTION—ANGLE ON ME AND TELLER

as I pull my shotgun out from under my coat, rack it loudly for effect, and aim it at the teller's Etch-a-Sketch eyebrows.

> ME
> Give me the goddamn money and shut up!

WIDE ANGLE ON ENTIRE BANK

as Rush jumps into action. He whips out his shotgun and pumps
in a shell right next to the ear of the security guard.

> RUSH
> No moving, no shooting.

He takes the guard's gun and jams it into his own huge waistband.
He motions at the floor with his shotgun. Everyone drops to the
ground in unison like a synchronized swimming team.

Rush smiles at me proudly. I can see the yellow stain Mitzi painted
on his teeth to simulate my dad's teeth.

> ME
> (to teller)
> Cash. Now!

> TELLER
> (unimpressed)
> Fine. You want money, I'll give you money. Heaven
> forbid you should have to work for it like I do. Have
> to change three buses to get here.

Grudgingly, she begins to stuff the bag with cash.

> ME
> (to crowd)
> Maybe you heard that we don't load our guns.
> (clear my throat because no one can hear my
> unexpected whisper)
> Maybe you heard we don't load our guns. That was
> true, once. But before any of you get a heroic twitch,
> ask yourself, Are you feeling lucky?

> TELLER
> (snorts)
> That's from *Dirty Harry*, you moron.

CLOSE-UP OF MY FACE

as I realize that I've just used a line from a movie while robbing a bank. I'd forgotten the dialogue Mom had written for me and substituted my own vague memory.

ANGLE—ME AND TELLER

as I grab the bag of money from the surly teller.

> TELLER
> (sarcastically)
> Thank you for your patronage.

> ME
> What the hell's wrong with you? You trying to get shot?

> TELLER
> This is the fifth time in eight years that I've been robbed. Me personally, my window. It makes me mad. What have you people got against me?

> ME
> I'm sorry. You just happened to be next when I was in line. It's not your fault. An accident of chance.

> TELLER
> (raising one thin eyebrow)
> Freud said there are no accidents.

WIDE ANGLE ON BANK

Rush joins me as we hurry out of the bank. On our way to the door, a teenage boy wearing a backpack comes in, looks at everybody on the floor, looks at us coming at him, and immediately drops to the floor.

We turn and head for the door. We hear the loud CLICK of a gun being cocked. We look behind us.

The teenage boy, maybe seventeen, is sitting on the floor pointing a gun at us.

> BOY
> Hold it! Stop!

It's instinct, I guess, but without a word, both Rush and I swing our shotguns up and point them at the boy. The boy looks as terrified as we do.

> ME
> Please don't make us use these. Please.

I beg shamelessly. When we first agreed to hold up the bank with guns, Rush and I agreed that under no circumstances would we use these guns. We would give ourselves up first. No one would be hurt. But that was then, in the security of Thomas Q's bungalow. Now we are facing prison. And I know that if I fail here today, my parents will also go to prison.

> ME
> Put the gun down, kid. Just put it down.

The boy's eyes are darting around nervously.

He's caught somewhere between self-preservation and living the heroic fantasy he'd always dreamed of. He can see himself being slapped on the back by friends, admired by that girl at school he's been afraid to ask out. Some free dinners, a medal from the mayor. Cops are his buddies. But he can also picture himself lying on the ground with half of his guts spread across the linoleum.

He's paralyzed between those two visions of himself. Never before has he had such power over his own future.

> RUSH
> What are you doing with a gun, kid?

> BOY
> Huh?

> RUSH
> You in some kind of gang?

> BOY
> No, I, uh, just, you know. I was carrying it. My dad's.

> RUSH
> He know you've got it?

> BOY
> No. He's going to be pissed.
> (beat)
> Unless I use it to bag me a couple bank robbers.

This was bad. Now using the gun was his only way out of punishment from his father.

I look over at Rush. Even beneath the layers of Mitzi's makeup I can see the terror in his eyes. We are faced with capture, with going to jail. The only thing that stands between us and freedom is this kid with his father's gun. Neither of us wants to go to jail for twenty years. Neither of us wants to hurt this kid.

                    ME
What is that, a .32?

                    BOY
Uh-huh.

                    ME
A .32 at best might wound one of us, but probably
won't kill us. That means we'll both have the chance
to fire at you. What kind of damage will two shotgun
blasts do to your body, do you think?

Long pause while teenage boy decides which fate is worse, body
ripped to shreds by shotgun blasts or what people might say about
him backing down.

                SECURITY GUARD
                (from the floor)
Shit, man, put the fucking gun down and let these
people get on out of here. You're risking everybody's
life.

The teenage boy looks over his shoulder at the other patrons sitting
on their hands. He immediately lowers the gun to the floor and
pushes it away. He tucks his hands under his butt.

We immediately dash through the doors.

Rush, as rehearsed, trips on the way out the door. He lets shotgun
with Dad's fingerprints slide out of his hand. We leave it behind as
we hurry out of the bank. Rush is so shaken, he fumbles with the
door.

                    RUSH
Would you have shot him?

                    ME
    No.

Rush looks at me hard, trying to decide whether I'm telling the
truth. I show him no expression, push him through the door.

                    RUSH
    Next time, I say let's go somewhere like Bolivia,
    Sundance, let's go somewhere like Bolivia.

We burst through the door into the sunlight. The CAMERA
FREEZES US in midstride. The image drains under the harsh
sunlight, brightens until the screen is nothing but brilliant white.
Bleached-bone white.

· 33 ·

I drove.

Rush stared out the windshield.

We didn't even try to talk for the first twenty minutes. Adrenaline overdose had short-circuited our nervous system. Most of our attention was spent on maintaining breathing, forcing the air in and out. I couldn't even remember what it was like to breathe without conscious effort. To anybody glancing into our car, we must have looked like a couple of crash dummies heading for a wall.

"Blue," Rush said, his voice quiet and solemn. "I know what you said before, back in the bank. But would you have? Would you have shot that kid?"

"No."

He nodded. "Okay."

I sighed. "I don't think so. I hope not."

"But you're not sure?"

I shook my head. "I'm not sure."

"Me, neither. I keep saying to myself, No way. But I was afraid, Blue. I was afraid of going to jail for twenty years. If he hadn't dropped his gun . . ." He shrugged and let out a long sigh. "I don't know."

We didn't talk again for a while. We had scared ourselves more than the bank robbery had scared us.

I kept my eyes on the rearview mirror, checking for cops. After a while, I became more interested in the wrinkled face looking back at me. I squinted at the mirror. "You think this is how I'm going to look someday? Like this? I look like Gertrude Stein."

"I look like Frankenstein." Rush scratched his double chin. "No offense to your dad."

"We should take a photograph so we have something to check ourselves against in twenty years."

Rush scratched again, harder. "When can we take this goop off? It's starting to smell. Can you smell it?"

"Hang on until we get back to the motel. Don't pick."

He scratched again and a hunk of his chin came off in his hand. He held up a flap of waddle. "Oops."

I turned on the all-news radio station. The announcer rattled off a string of sports scores. I turned down the volume.

"Hey, I wanted to hear how the Lakers did."

"Are you kidding me?"

He smiled. "Duh."

We were on the San Diego Freeway heading south to our motel room in Seal Beach. We had a rented car waiting for us there. This car belonged to a staff member at The Bend who would report it stolen later tonight. We were to ditch the car at the Long Beach airport and hop a bus to our motel, which was a few miles farther down the coast. Everything had been planned by my folks. We would hide out in the motel for a couple days, just to be sure. Meantime, with the dragnet lifted in Arizona, my parents would drive east; they wouldn't tell us where.

"What was that teller's problem?" I said. "Doesn't she pay attention at staff meetings? Give robbers the money and shut up. That's the drill."

"I'd have shot her," Rush said. "Pow. Taken her whole head off."

"You'd have signed her up for a sitcom."

"Next time, it'll go smoother."

I snapped around and pointed a finger at him. "Don't even joke."

Rush held up his hands like a surgeon. "If we don't get these rubber gloves off soon, my hands are going to look like Mickey Mouse's."

"We don't want to leave any fingerprints in the car. We want them to find just the ones my parents left."

"How about I just take them off, let my hands breathe a few minutes, maybe dry them off before a fungus grows. I promise not to touch anything."

"All right. Just be careful."

"Yes, dear." He peeled off the gloves. Some of the rubber makeup Mitzi painted on to make them look like real skin flaked off onto Rush's trousers. "Yeech. I feel like a leper."

"Don't make fun of lepers."

"Sorry. I mean, the dermatologically challenged."

I laughed.

"Top story," the radio announcer said. *"The downtown Wells Fargo bank was just held up twenty-five minutes ago by a man and woman tentatively identified by witnesses as suspected bank robbers Harold and Naomi Henderson. No shots were fired. No one injured. The suspects have escaped."*

"Hear that?" Rush said. "We've escaped." He reached for the radio knob to turn up the volume. I slapped his naked hand away and did it with my gloved fingers.

"However," the announcer continued, *"one fast-thinking lad managed to memorize the license plate of the getaway car."*

"Damn!" I said.

"Police have released the license number: 2MGR340. The car was a white Toyota Camry. If you see this car, please phone the police immediately. Do not attempt to apprehend yourself."

"Apprehend yourself?" Rush said. "How do you apprehend yourself?"

The announcer repeated the license number twice and gave a phone number to call. I looked out the window at the other drivers all around us. I expected all of them to suddenly look over at us in unison and reach for their car phones. But nobody looked at us; nobody craned to read our license number. We were still invisible.

"We need to ditch the car," Rush said.

"No we don't. Just change license plates before we get to the airport. That's what Dad said to do. Unless you know something about hot wiring."

Rush shook his head. "Father knows best. Where do you want to do the switch, a mall or a supermarket?"

"Listen . . ." I said, shushing him.

"Agent Bigelow, aren't you surprised about the Henderson's pulling this heist in Los Angeles? You were so sure you had them boxed in around the Texas-Arizona area."

"Not entirely," Agent Bigelow responded. "True, we concentrated our efforts in the Southwest. But we've been expecting them to make their way to Los Angeles for quite some time."

"Bullshit," I said.

"And now that they've shown up, we have mobilized the state police and all local law enforcement agencies. The freeways are being patroled even as we speak. There are about twelve bank robberies a day in Los Angeles and we catch eighty percent of the perpetrators. I like our odds."

"But aren't eighty percent of robbers also drug users, making them easier to catch?"

Bigelow was silent a few seconds. Then said, "I still like our odds."

"I'm starting to like their odds, too," Rush said.

"We're okay."

"Maybe we should make the switch now. And get out of this makeup. We are still another forty minutes from the motel. Forty minutes of police cars cruising."

I looked in my rearview mirror, expecting to see a fleet of police cars gaining on us. Nothing yet. But I didn't like the jailhouse ache in my gut. "Yeah, I think that's a good idea."

He slipped his surgical gloves back on and climbed over the seat into the back. "I'll lie back here and change."

I started crossing lanes, moving toward the right to exit. "We're getting off at Manhattan Beach. We can switch plates here."

"Fine." I heard the tearing of tape, the rattling of a belt, trousers, sliding down legs. "I'm nearly naked back here. Does that excite you?"

"I don't need any more excitement in my life for another ten years."

"You know what we should have done? We should have driven over to those guys at the studio and let them see us in these outfits.

They'd have creamed. They'd have hidden us out in their Malibu homes. Ah, hell, they're probably all in Aspen skiing the New Year in."

As I drove down the off ramp, I spotted a city police cruiser across the street, stopped at the light. I opened my mouth to warn Rush, but nothing came out, just a kind of strangled gargle.

"What?" he asked.

I couldn't answer. I couldn't stop the car, either. There was traffic behind me and I had no light or stop sign to keep me. And there was nowhere to turn. I was going to have to drive past them, separated by one foot of asphalt.

I had a terrible premonition: I saw Rush and myself being thrown to the ground, the FBI slapping cuffs on our wrists, dragging us off to their cars. And then we spend the next twenty years in prison, apart, writing letters. My parents have their child, a little girl, who comes to visit Aunt Blue for twenty years, maybe writes a report or two in school about me.

I gripped the steering wheel in the proper ten-till-two position I'd been taught in driver's ed. I didn't want to look too stiff, but I didn't want to appear too casual. I wanted to look distracted, like I had a lot on my mind, too much to care about cops.

I rolled toward them, my speedometer needle quivering at thirty-five, the speed limit.

"Keep low," I whispered, as if the two officers in the cruiser could hear me.

"What's going on? What's the matter?"

"Keep low," I said again. Then I realized that was one of The Bend's Ten Commandments. That made me laugh. I laughed hard. I drove past the police car laughing heartily to myself, probably looking crazy, all alone in a car and laughing my ass off.

"What?" Rush whispered. "What's so funny?"

I didn't look at the cops. I just kept driving. Driving and laughing.

"What the hell's so funny?" Rush asked.

I checked the mirror. No sirens, no flashing lights. The signal changed and they drove straight ahead.

"Are you going to tell me what's going on?" Rush demanded.

"Sure," I said. "I just peed my pants."

* * *

Rush kept watch outside the car, pretending to check our oil, while I squirmed around on the floor in the back of the car, changing my clothes. The odor of urine was pungent. It smelled like fear, like what you'd find trickling down the hind legs of a gazelle being chased across the African savanna by a toothy lion. I couldn't even remember when I'd actually wet myself, the exact moment. Before I'd passed them, during, after? I suppose I should have been embarrassed, but I wasn't. After what Rush and I had just been through, I was surprised every orifice on my body didn't open wide and start pitching out whatever fluids, solids, and organs were in there. After what I'd put it through, my whole system should have abandoned ship.

I climbed out of the car, wearing black jeans and a blue sweater. I rolled open the window to let the car air out.

Rush walked over. "You look good."

"Did I get all the makeup off?"

He licked his thumb and rubbed a spot on my chin. "There. Still a little gunk, but you look like you're peeling from a sunburn or something."

I looked around. We were on a residential street of modest homes. Very quiet. No traffic, no pedestrians. Lots of dense bushes and pet fences bordering tiny lawns. Many of the front windows displayed some kind of small Christmas decoration. One had a cardboard Hanukkah menorah taped to the door. Most of the houses needed painting, but with the ocean only a couple blocks away, the salt air was brutal.

Rush leaned against the car and gestured at the houses. "I look around at this quiet little neighborhood and I'm filled with profound gratitude. Makes me want to drop to my knees and kiss the pavement. You know what I mean? I'm still free. Makes me want to move into one of these houses, have kids, join the PTA and Neighborhood Watch, wear a barbecue apron with a goofy saying on the front. That's after only twenty-five minutes on the run. I can't imagine how your folks must feel."

"Or why they'd risk it," I said.

"Why did we?"

I turned away and pretended to scout the street. "We'd better start looking for fresh plates."

"Maybe we should just cover up a couple numbers with mud or something. I'm not anxious to tempt fate again. We might have already used up our luck."

"Let's stick to my parents' instructions. This is one area where I trust their judgment."

"Yeah, you're right."

"We'll just look around here," I said. "See if there's a plate we can steal, make the switch, and get the hell out of here."

Rush nodded. "We should check the alleys. These beach towns never have enough curb parking, so lots of the locals park their second cars in the alleys. That'll give us some cover."

"We've got to do this fast, Rush. I mean fast."

"Hey, that's why I'm called Rush. Other than that sexual problem."

He started to walk around me toward the trunk. I grabbed his hand as he passed. He stopped, looked down at our clasped hands as if unsure what he'd snagged his hand on. He looked at me.

I shrugged. "Don't make a big thing of it."

"What?"

"I just wanted to touch you. I, uh . . ." I shook my head. "I can't think of any analogy in nature, okay?"

He smiled. "You're pretty mushy sometimes."

"This is as mushy as I get. I've always had trouble with sentiment. I know we women are supposed to breathe that stuff into the air the way plants turn carbon dioxide into oxygen, but I just never got the hang of it. It doesn't mean I don't feel something."

"What do you feel?"

I started to pull away, but he tightened his grip on my hand. "This probably isn't the best time for this."

He leaned over and kissed me. I touched his face with my hand. Gummy residue from his makeup stuck to my fingers. I pressed into his body. His arms wrapped around me.

When we broke apart, we didn't say anything. Yet my body felt transformed. My skin, my hair, my limbs, they all seemed to fit me for the first time. When we spoke from now on, the rest of the world would need subtitles to understand us.

He pressed his face against my neck and inhaled. He grinned and kissed my cheek. "Maybe we should continue this conversation in safer quarters," he said.

"Right." I popped the trunk and pulled out the screwdriver. "Let's go."

We jumped back in the car and cruised a few alleys. There were plenty of cars to choose from. But we wanted to make sure we picked a place where there was the least chance of getting caught.

"There," I said, pointing at a Jeep Cherokee spattered with mud.

"Why that one?"

"The gate next to it. A bunch of fliers are stuck in the handle. Three newspapers on the ground. Doesn't look like anybody's been home for a few days. The Jeep still has a lot of mud on it, but it hasn't rained in a week. Some of that would have come off with just local driving. I figure that car's been sitting there for a couple days. Owners are probably out of town, visiting relatives for the holidays."

"Amazing, Holmes!"

"Yeah, yeah. Just hand me the screwdriver."

"I'll do it," Rush offered.

"Better if I do it. In case someone from one of these other houses comes along. I'm a woman—they'll probably give me the benefit of the doubt if I make up a story. You, on the other hand, look like a criminal and would probably be lynched on the spot."

He handed me the screwdriver.

I unscrewed the front license plate in about a minute. I had three screws off of the back and was cranking on the fourth when the wooden fence door jerked open. I twisted around, startled. The first thing I saw were those rolled fliers blowing out of the rusty metal handle. They hung in the air like colored kites.

A skinny woman of about twenty-two wearing a full-length apron stood there holding a tiny handgun. It looked like a toy. She didn't look angry. She wiped her nose with the back of her free hand.

I smiled at her and stood up. "Hi, I know this looks weird, but we're just—"

She shot me.

· 34 ·

The sound of the gun was funny, not a loud boom as I'd expected. Just a sharp crack. Like stepping on an eggshell or biting down on an ice cube.

I'd also expected to be thrown up against the Jeep, a massive hole in my chest. Then I'd slide to the ground and lie there listening to the wet sucking around the hole as I breathed my last few breaths.

But all I felt was a sharp tugging at my jeans and a stabbing in my left hip as if I'd brushed up against a loose nail. I touched my hip and felt the oily blood.

"Shit," I said, looking up at the woman. "You shot me."

She didn't say anything. Her expression remained one of profound detachment. She wiped her nose with the back of her hand again. There was dried dough and flour on her apron where she'd wiped her hands. She'd interrupted her baking to come out here and kill me. She raised her gun and pointed it at me again.

"Don't shoot me. Jesus. They're just license plates. I'm sorry."

"Too late," she said. She fired again.

My attention had been focused on the barrel of her little gun, so I didn't notice how or when Rush had managed to get out of the car and jump her. But he'd grabbed her wrist just as she was firing the second time. The bullet pinged into the grill of the Jeep. He twisted her wrist until she shrieked and dropped the gun from her hand. He picked it up before releasing her wrist. She stepped backward and rubbed her wrist, glaring at him.

"You okay?" he asked me, helping me up. "You okay?"

"Pain is an illusion." I winced.

"Don't," he said, his face stony with fear and rage. "Don't joke, okay?"

"Sorry. I'm fine, just nicked me. I could use some Tylenol."

"You crazy?" he shouted at the woman. "They're just license plates. You don't shoot someone over that."

She glared at him angrily. "They're mine."

He walked over to her and peered into her eyes. "Christ, she's stoned. She's higher than the *Hindenburg* and she's walking around with a loaded gun."

I nodded at my would-be assassin. "Well then, kill her and let's get going."

"Don't kill me!" The girl started sobbing. Big sobs and actual tears, from zero to sixty in two seconds. She dropped to the ground and hugged her knees to her face. Her skirt fell away and we could see she wasn't wearing panties. I looked over at Rush. He made a face at me. I laughed.

The woman continued crying so hard that some of the dried dough on her cheek became moist again. She wiped her face with her hand and the dough stuck to her hand. "Please don't kill me," she begged. "I didn't mean anything. I was just, you know, protecting my property. My boyfriend's skiing. He left me in charge."

Rush shook his head. He helped me into the car. My hip hurt more now than it had before, as if someone had rubbed Ben-Gay in the wound. Rush went back to the girl's Jeep, removed the final screw, and took her plates. He screwed them onto our car.

"What are you gonna do?" she asked.

"Go back inside," Rush told her. He held up her little gun by the trigger guard, like a cop with evidence. "If we get arrested, I'll give the cops this. It has your prints on it. I doubt it's registered. Also, I'll tell them you shot her in a dispute over a drug deal. You figure out if it's worth it to wait until tomorrow to report your plates are mysteriously missing."

Rush climbed back into the car and we drove down the alley.

"She won't say anything," he said. "We'll be okay. How're you doing?"

"Feels like someone's twisting a corkscrew into my hip."

"I should have done something to her. Punished her."

"How? Let the air out of her tires? Piss on her car?"

"I would have pantsed her, but someone beat me to it."

I laughed. Laughing jiggled my hip and sent a serrated edge of pain through me. "Thanks for saving my life."

"You owe me big for this, Amelia."

"Just drive, Poundcake."

I adjusted in my seat, looking for some position that wouldn't hurt. Rush was right. The little sniper wouldn't call the police, probably wouldn't even be able to identify us, anyway. But then, she wasn't our biggest problem. Our biggest problem was the police car speeding down the alley behind us with its sirens blaring and lights flashing.

"Fuck!" Rush said, and floored the gas pedal. The car jumped out of the alley and he spun it around the corner and we screeched down the quiet street, smoke curling from our tires. The police car followed close behind.

I turned and looked behind us. "Two cars."

"Fuck," he said again. "Fuck fuck fuck."

"I told you not to do this with me," I snapped at him, suddenly angrier at him than I was scared of the cops. "I warned you back at The Bend that it was dangerous. Why didn't you believe me and go home to your damned dog? You had to play shining knight, didn't you? Don't you have any instincts for survival?"

"Do you mind! I'm in the middle of a fucking car chase!"

He spun the car around the corner. The car tipped a little and slammed down, clacking my teeth together. Instantly, he took another corner. The cops fell behind but were still within sight. He reached over and touched my hand. "You're getting mushy on me again, Amelia."

I squeezed his hand hard. "Just remember to get my cell number right when you write."

Rush pulled his hand away so he could wheel the car around

another sharp curve. I could still hear the sirens, but I couldn't see the cruisers. "Someone must have heard her shots," he said. "You believe this? We rob a goddamn bank in the middle of the day and get away. We try to steal a couple license plates and suddenly they're all over us."

"Whoever called the cops must have described our car. They know who we are. Who they think we are."

"We're going to have to abandon the car," he said. "I can't outrun them in this heap. They'll have a couple dozen cars here soon and a helicopter. We'll be the lead story on the eleven o'clock news. Freeway chase ends in tragedy."

"You want to surrender?"

"Hell yes! I sure don't want to feel a dozen slugs tearing through my back."

I didn't say anything. He spun around another corner and then another. We had a little more space between us and the sirens.

He looked at me. "Can you run?"

"Yes."

"I'm serious. I mean *run*."

"I can run."

"Good." He slid the car around another curb and zoomed down a narrow alley. "Grab the bag."

I reached over the seat and snatched the black garbage bag where we'd stashed my parents' clothes and the hunks of rubber we'd peeled off our faces. Also the money from the bank. The bag smelled like urine, since I'd used Mom's clothes to mop up the front seat.

"Okay," Rush said, "when I stop this car, don't hesitate. Throw open the door and run with me. Got it?"

"Yes." My hip was burning like an iron, but the bleeding had already stopped. I grabbed the door handle and waited for Rush's signal.

The car jerked to a sudden stop in the middle of the alley. We flung open our doors and ran off without closing them. As I ran, fists and legs churning, gasping for air, lungs burning, that's what I thought about—those open car doors. It seemed so untidy.

* * *

"Dogs," Rush said. "They've got fucking dogs."

"One dog," I said. "One dog. How much ground can one dog cover?"

The cops were poking around our abandoned car. One of them poked; the other four watched the dog. The dog sniffed around the driver's seat. He climbed in the car and I couldn't see him. Suddenly, he jumped out and started pulling at his leash. He was trying to come straight in our direction. The cop holding his leash looked over toward us. We ducked out of sight.

"Damn," I said. "He's good."

Rush snorted. "Russell could do the same thing. Piss is no challenge."

"It's not a contest, for Christ's sake. Anyway, Mitzi and Kyra are taking good care of Russell now. And if we don't think of something, they'll be taking care of him for the rest of his life."

Another cop lifted our shotgun from the car and carried it back to his cruiser. The cops chatted among themselves. They pointed in a lot of different directions. Finally, two cops and the dog started down the alley we had traveled a few minutes earlier. The dog sniffed the ground, looked around, then kept coming. He looked very confident.

"We're outta here," Rush said. We ducked back down behind the trash bin. Both of us crawled on hands and knees away from the alley's opening. When we were out of sight, we scrambled to our feet and ran as hard as we could.

A couple blocks later, we were in another alley. We had crossed over from the residential section to the business section. Downtown Manhattan Beach. The doors back here opened onto small businesses. All the windows were barred and the glass lined with cardboard or painted black. Radio Shack had a lot of empty cardboard boxes stacked up. There was also a small hardware store and an Italian restaurant. The smell of fried food and garbage wormed through my stomach.

"Maybe we should try to blend in with the crowd," I suggested. "Act like shoppers. They didn't get a clear look at us. They're looking for my parents, remember?"

"They've got a dog, Blue. We hang around acting nonchalant,

they're going to sniff us out. We've got to outrun them or throw the dog off."

"I'm being tracked by a pee-sniffing mutt. Jesus." I thought about that for a moment. "Come on," I said. I lifted the lid of a trash bin. "Help me find a plastic bag. A usable one."

Rush didn't ask questions. He dug into the trash bin and rooted through the slimy garbage with me.

"This do?" he asked, holding a plastic bag up. It had half a head of rancid lettuce in it.

I grabbed it and turned it inside out, dumping the lettuce. "Keep lookout." I went behind the bin, dropped my jeans and underpants, and squatted over the bag. I'd already emptied my bladder earlier, but I managed to squeeze out another half a cup of urine. I twisted the top of the bag and tied it in a knot. I pulled my pants up.

Rush stood there holding a garbage bag containing my parents' clothes. I stood there holding a plastic bag full of warm amber piss.

"Now what, 007?" he asked.

"Decoy." I took his hand and pulled him out of the alley and onto the main street. Like most downtowns of beach cities during winter, this one hardly had any pedestrians. Even street traffic was sparse.

"Hey." I waved to a man on a bicycle who was stopped at the light. He wore those tight padded biking pants and a helmet. His sunglasses were tinted yellow. Behind my back, I handed Rush the bag of urine. "Excuse me, sir, can you give me directions? We're kinda lost."

He looked at the red light, which turned green. He shrugged and lifted his bike onto the sidewalk. "Sure, where you heading?"

I limped a little as I approached him. My hip was hurting again. I tugged my sweater down over my hip so he couldn't see my wound. Rush walked behind me.

"You know where Apple Street is?" I asked.

"Apple Street?" He thought, looked around in several different directions. "I know Maple Street and Walnut Street. Is it residential?"

"Uh-huh. Near a schoolyard, I think. Or a fire station. My aunt's directions weren't very clear. She said everybody knew the street."

He seemed to take this as a challenge and began reciting streets named after fruits and vegetables. I kept talking to him. Actually, he was kind of charming, a divorce lawyer. Out of the corner of my eye, I saw Rush wedge the knot of the urine bag under a piece of metal on the bike's rear fender. He stabbed the bag with a toothpick he'd found in the alley. Urine dripped like an IV down the fender, onto the tire, shimmied down the spoke, and splashed onto the sidewalk.

"Well, I'll just call my aunt back and get better directions," I said. "Thanks, anyway."

"No problem," he said. He climbed onto his bike and pedaled off.

Fifteen minutes later, from the McDonald's across the street, Rush and I shared fries and a shake and watched the police dog sniff the sidewalk and gleefully run off in the direction of the cyclist.

The five-state dragnet moved on in search of my urine.

Lesson #7

Exact change required.

· 35 ·

The universe is in a constant state of flux. Yet nothing changes.

Two years ago, dressed as my mother, I robbed a Los Angeles bank and then anointed Manhattan Beach with a trail of my urine. Today, I am driving home from school next to a stack of eleventh-grade essays on "Those Remarkable Intestines." I pop the glove compartment and dig out a Baby Ruth, tearing it open with my teeth and chomping into it with great anticipation of that exquisite first tang of chocolate on my tongue.

I am no longer a celebrity. My fifteen minutes ended when the movie came out.

I turn the corner onto my street, a pleasant cul-de-sac of detached homes in the moderate price range. Realtors call them "starter homes," because they're the only thing a lot of young couples starting out can afford. Most of the couples who live in this neighborhood are younger than I. Their yards are weighted down with tricycles and dog shit. In the summer, Peter from next door and Justin from down the street, both ten this year, set up a lemonade stand and charge a dollar a glass. They sell very few glasses. Justin wants to lower the price and do more volume. But Peter always convinces him that it is classier to sell fewer glasses for more money. It makes me happy to know that this debate of economic philosophy will probably continue for at least another two summers. And each summer, I will buy my usual glass once a week on my Sunday jog. I park at the curb because there's not enough room in the garage. I'll get to the reason why in a minute. First, I check the mail. The mailbox is a custom job, looks like a lizard with his mouth open. A gift from Rush. He painted the eyes bloodshot.

Bills, ads, magazines. Nothing from my parents. I haven't seen them since our clandestine rendezvous three months ago in Montana. They were working at a dude ranch there, calling themselves Nadine and Dwayne. Mom had black hair and looked like Joan Jett. She barbecued for the guests. Dad had lost some weight and stopped smoking. He still knew how to handle a horse, though, and he did some showing off for us that I knew would cost him a long night with a heating pad. Still, we applauded from atop the corral and he waved his cowboy hat at us as he rode another lap.

Mom and I went for a walk along the creek and argued about the upcoming presidential elections. I had never heard of the candidate she was supporting.

"How do you like my hair, Mom?" I asked.

"What? It's nice."

"Not too long?"

She shook her head. "It's fine."

I laughed. Some of my friends complained that their mothers constantly picked on them for being too fat or thin or dowdy or showy. Hairstyle seemed the favorite battleground. Mom had never been like that. She worried over my mind, but she never had a need to criticize me. I only recently realized the difference.

She stooped by the river and plucked a flower.

I laughed. "You're picking flowers, Mom. This is starting to look like a douche commercial. For those days when you don't feel . . . fresh."

"TV commercials destroy any confidence a woman has in herself. They convince her that without exterior products she is incapable of being attractive or sustaining a relationship." She waved a disgusted hand. "Don't get me started."

I plucked a flower just like Mom's.

"You know what this is?" she asked. "What kind?"

"No," I said.

"Me, neither." She laughed and stuck it in her hair. She took mine and stuck it in my hair. "The douche twins," she said, laughing so hard, her flower fell out of her hair. At that moment, she was the most perfect mom in the world and I wished we'd never stop walking along this river.

Mom and Dad left Montana six weeks ago and I have no idea where they are. They haven't written or called. They can't. The FBI is still after them. But they manage to get messages to me on occasion through friends. Plus, I get to read their words every couple months in *Rolling Stone*. My parents are writers now, penning articles about "Underground America." A counterculture travelogue describing places they've been, their observations about the people in those places. At the beginning of each article is a boxed disclaimer from *Rolling Stone* management informing the reader that Harold and Naomi Henderson are fugitives and that the magazine does not pay them for these articles, printing them only as a matter of public record and information. However, Dad told me once that someone at the magazine managed to get a few bucks to them now and then through third parties.

I take my key out and unlock the front door. I have to jiggle the key a bit to get it out of the lock again. Another thing to add to the list of what needs fixing around here. It would have to wait until next month's paycheck. Things are a little tight now. That's not the way it was supposed to be, I know, what with the movie deal and all.

The movie deal. That didn't work out quite as we thought it would. The studio wined and dined me like crazy. I met lots of stars: Michelle Pfeiffer, Demi Moore, Geena Davis. But between the time I signed the contract and the script was finished, a young girl in Iowa was arrested for killing two of her high school teachers. The teachers were married to each other and each, unknown to the other, was having an affair with the young girl. And each tried to talk her into killing the other so each could collect the insurance and run away with the girl. Confused (and pregnant), she killed both of them and ran away with the couple's teenage son. My movie went on the back burner.

It was made, though, as an HBO movie. The reviews were very good. Brian Dennehy played my father, which gave Dad a big kick. He was a big fan. Mom was less enthusiastic about Piper Laurie playing her. She still wanted Jane Fonda, even though she thought Jane had "lost a lot of her political credibility" since marrying Ted Turner.

Demi Moore played me. I thought she was pretty good. She made me seem much more interesting than I am. *TV Guide* said it was the most electrifying performance of her career. She got nominated for an Ace but lost to Glenn Close. *People* was kind of cruel, titling their review "Sometimes Moore Is Less" and claiming she was too subdued. It got good ratings, though, and came out on video. There's a nude scene showing Demi's naked breast. I'm told my students rent the video and freeze-frame it on that moment. Some of them look embarrassed when they see me, as if it had been my breast they'd seen.

I open my front door and, as always, take a deep breath. I love the smell of my house. It smells like the inside of a bread box. I bought it from a couple who had to leave the state, so I got it a little cheaper than the market price. That was fortunate because I never got $600,000 for the movie rights. Because it was made as a cable movie, I got $200,000, which almost covered the house. (By the way, the money from the bank robbery Rush and I pulled went to the Native American Education Foundation. Rush's choice. He claims to be part Navajo.)

I drop my briefcase off at the bottom of the stairs. My study is back behind the kitchen, a converted bedroom. I'll take it in there later. Right now, I have urgent business upstairs.

I make it to the bathroom in the nick of time. I pee and feel my bladder relax. "Bliss," I say with a sigh.

The bathroom door bursts open. The video camera zooms toward my lap. "Extreme close-up!" he shouts.

I tug my skirt over my knees and hold my hand up in front of his lens. "Jesus, Rush. I'm peeing."

"That's the point," he says. "Everybody has home movies of playing croquet or barbecues. I want ours to have the grit of real life. Guerrilla home videos. Cool idea, huh?"

"Cut," I say, and he comes out from behind the lens to kiss me. I stand up and lower the lid, conserving precious California water.

"How is she?" I ask.

He pulls me down the hall, filming me again. He walks backward. He points the camera at my feet. Later he'll probably add the sound effects of ducks quacking.

For a while in Hollywood, Rush had been the flavor of the month. Every day, he went to meetings at the major studios. They talked deals, he pitched ideas, and aspiring writers who'd read about him in *Variety* sent their scripts. But when my movie started to lose some of its heat, so did Rush. None of the meetings came to anything; no deals were actually made. He got fifty thousand dollars for putting my deal together, nothing more. He spent it on buying this house with me and renovating the garage as his office, where he runs his independent production company. Mostly, that consists of making phone calls to people until they finally return one. He remains optimistic.

He works at the agency again. They promoted him, which gave him a fancy title and a company cellular phone but no more money. He still kisses a lot of ass.

Sometimes he stands in front of the mirror and kisses the glass. When I ask him what he's doing, he says, "Homework."

"Here she is," Rush says, pointing his camera down at the crib and circling slowly. "Here's Mommy."

I pick up my daughter and kiss her cheeks and forehead. "Hello, Amelia. Is Amelia getting as tired of Daddy's Alfred Hitchcock impression as Mommy? Hmmm?"

"Hold that look!" Rush says, zooming in on my face. He lowers the camera, kisses Amelia, then kisses me, then brings the camera back up.

People think of happiness, I think, as a place you visit. Like a vacation in Hawaii or Disney World. Two weeks in Happiness, then back to real life. That's wrong.

I'm guessing now, because I'm a little short on scientific evidence. But I say happiness is the state of not expecting, not anticipating, not waiting for things to happen. Not waiting for your life to start.

Thomas Q was right. It's all been said before. We are destined to be born just as ignorant of ourselves as the cavepeople were of themselves. And every word we utter, every thought we have, every feeling we experience, every insight we relish from birth to death will have been thought, felt, experienced, and relished before us. And none of it will make any difference. Is anything lonelier than knowing that?

The thing is, so what? People spend a lot of time worrying about their flaws. They diet, exercise, dress up, pray. We're afraid of the imperfections in one another; they threaten us. They could be contagious. People want to be perfect. I don't think people are flawed. Calling them flaws is a moralist's language, not a biologist's. Biology sees no flaws—every living organism is perfect, flawless. Existence is the proof of perfection. Because once a species becomes anything less than perfect, it fails to survive. Love is part of our survival technique. We need it to survive. If we don't accept that, we become extinct.

I never finished my thesis on Thomas Q. I never finished my religion degree. Three weeks after the robbery, when The Bend had been evacuated of all guests and staff, the whole place burned to the ground. Thomas Q was never found, though his personal effects— watch, wallet, keys—were found in the rubble. Since there was no one to claim the insurance money, it went to a secondary beneficiary, a small Methodist college in Pennsylvania. They built a football stadium with it, which made me laugh for a few days.

Once Rush got mad thinking about Thomas Q. "The bastard manipulated all of us like puppets. I'm not complaining about the results; I'm satisfied about that. But I just hate the idea of how he did it. We all ended up doing exactly what he wanted us to do. What right did he have to play God?"

"Because we let him," I said.

A month after Amelia was born, a package arrived from Singapore. It was a wooden paddle with a rubber ball attached by an elastic string. No note.

"Who do you love more, Amelia, Mommy or Daddy?" Rush says, filming.

"Rush, don't ask her that. She's barely six months old. You'll traumatize her."

"Afraid of the answer, huh?"

"I smell a bet."

"Three changes," he suggests.

"Deal."

We shake hands. This is an old game with us. We each say our name (to Amelia, Daddy and Mommy are our names), and whichever one she makes a significant noise after is the winner. All our bets consist of the same thing, the number of diaper changes the other has to do solo. Rush owes six changes already, which is why he's so anxious to bet.

We lean over the crib.

"Mommy," I sing.

Amelia looks over at the window.

"Daddy," Rush says, making a goofy face.

Amelia pulls my hair.

Back and forth we go, getting no reaction.

Mitzi is still acting. After a two-month campaign for the role of Dulcinea, she's playing Don Quixote's sister in *Man of La Mancha*. Rush showed her how to let the air out of the theater director's car tires, which she did twice already. Apparently, her terrorist attacks are working, because the director promised her the role of Maria in *The Sound of Music*.

Kyra is attending the local university and baby-sitting for us on occasion. She still dresses in bib overalls and Keds. Also, she has a boyfriend who Mitzi and I are convinced will break her heart.

"There," Rush says. "I win."

"That's drooling, which doesn't count as an affirmative sound. Mommmmyyyy."

Amelia's eyes droop, open wide, then close. She is asleep. I kiss her on the forehead and smell her skin. I can never get too much of her smell.

Rush lifts his camera again and starts filming.

"You forfeit," I say.

"She's asleep, for God's sake."

"She fell asleep after hearing my name and before hearing yours. In anticipation of hearing yours, she nodded off. I rest my case."

"You're a worse lawyer than I was."

"Okay, it's a tie." I press my cheek against Amelia and close my eyes. Having a baby did not make me happy. Nor did marrying Rush. Not being afraid to do either made me happy.

When I open my eyes, Rush is circling Amelia and me, filming again. He gets in these filming moods every so often. I suppose I should be annoyed, but he is such an enthusiastic father that I don't mind.

"I'm going for that mother-daughter bonding thing here, Blue," he says. "Act happy."

"What?" Act happy? The words strike me as funny.

"Act happy," he repeats.

I start to laugh. I can't stop. I don't want to stop.

"I said act happy, not insane," Rush says. But he is laughing, too.

Amelia wakes up and starts crying. I bounce her in my arms, but I am still laughing. Amelia stops crying and stares at me blankly. "Mommy," I say to her, and she giggles and waves her arms and legs. "Mommy," I say again, and she rocks her head side to side, squealing and giggling and drooling onto my sweater. "I win," I tell Rush.

Rush lays the camera on the changing table. He comes over and wraps his arms around Amelia and me. We kind of sway there. He looks at Amelia and says, "Mommy's a cheater. Did you know that about her?"

"So what?" I say.

And we sway in a cradle of arms and drop food for the dust mites who celebrate below.